Romantic Suspense

Danger. Passion. Drama.

Hostage Security
Lisa Childs

Breaking The Code
Maria Lokken

MILLS & BOON

HOSTAGE SECURITY
© 2025 by Lisa Childs
Philippine Copyright 2025
Australian Copyright 2025
New Zealand Copyright 2025

First Published 2025
First Australian Paperback Edition 2025
ISBN 978 1 038 94057 5

BREAKING THE CODE
© 2025 by Maria Lokken
Philippine Copyright 2025
Australian Copyright 2025
New Zealand Copyright 2025

First Published 2025
First Australian Paperback Edition 2025
ISBN 978 1 038 94057 5

MIX
Paper | Supporting
responsible forestry
FSC® C001695
www.fsc.org

Published by
Harlequin Mills & Boon
An imprint of Harlequin Enterprises (Australia) Pty Limited
(ABN 47 001 180 918), a subsidiary of HarperCollins
Publishers Australia Pty Limited
(ABN 36 009 913 517)
Level 19, 201 Elizabeth Street
SYDNEY NSW 2000 AUSTRALIA

Printed and bound in Australia by McPherson's Printing Group

Hostage Security

Lisa Childs

MILLS & BOON

Books by Lisa Childs

Harlequin Romantic Suspense

Bachelor Bodyguards

Hostage Security

Hotshot Heroes

Hotshot Hero Under Fire
Hotshot Hero on the Edge
Hotshot Heroes Under Threat
Hotshot Hero in Disguise
Hotshot Hero for the Holiday
Hunted Hotshot Hero
Hotshot's Dangerous Liaison
Last Mission

The Coltons of Owl Creek

Colton's Dangerous Cover

Visit the Author Profile page
at millsandboon.com.au for more titles.

Dear Reader,

I've been missing River City, Michigan, and the Payne Protection Agency, and I hope that you have been as well. I felt like it was time for another franchise to open up with more bachelor bodyguards. After having former military and police officers as bodyguards, it felt like time for a change—for some bad boys. So reformed outlaws and Logan Payne's brothers-in-law, Garek and Milek Kozminski, open up their franchise with security guards who share their kind of background. These are men and one woman who've had to overcome hard times and mistakes and make new lives for themselves. After five years in prison for a crime he didn't commit, Josh Stafford is looking for a fresh start. But his first assignment with the Payne Protection Agency plunges him back into the past and into danger. He's not the only one whose life is at risk, though. Natalie Croft hoped to never see Josh Stafford again after he broke their engagement and her heart, but if she wants to save what matters most to her, she has to work with the bachelor bodyguard. Josh and Natalie get a lot of support from characters we've met before in River City, like matriarch Penny Payne-Lynch.

I hope you enjoy this return to River City with the continuation of my Bachelor Bodyguards.

Happy reading!

Lisa Childs

With great appreciation for my wonderful readers and a special shout-out to the ones who post the most wonderful reviews that make writing so rewarding: Vicki Watts, Elaine Sapp, Bea Followill and Tammy Morse. I'm very sorry if I missed your name and you've been posting reviews. I very much appreciate all my readers!

Prologue

"Have you changed your mind?" Garek Kozminski asked his brother-in-law Logan Payne during the opening celebration of the most recent franchise of the Payne Protection Agency in River City, Michigan.

Logan was also Garek's boss and one of his best friends. It hadn't always been that way; they'd once been enemies. Logan had believed Garek's dad had killed his dad, while Garek and his siblings had believed their father had been framed for the police officer's murder. Eventually they'd been proven right, but by then it had been too late for their dad—he'd been murdered, too, in prison.

"Changed my mind?" Logan asked, raising his voice so that Garek could hear him above all the other people at the party. "About what?"

Garek gestured around the warehouse space that had been sectioned off into rooms with glass walls and high-tech equipment. On the exterior brick walls hung vivid artwork; most of the partygoers were looking at that more than anything else. "Have you reconsidered agreeing to this franchise of the Payne Protection Agency, the Kozminski branch?" Garek was opening it with his wife and his brother Milek.

Logan snorted. "It's a little late now. While I regret losing some of my best bodyguards, I don't dare back out of our agreement. My wife and yours would kill me."

Stacy and Candace were standing together, their arms around each other as they watched nieces and nephews putting a puzzle together in the middle of the concrete floor. Stacy was petite with long wavy titian hair while Candace was tall with short black hair.

His heart swelling with love, Garek chuckled. "Yeah, I don't know which one I'm more afraid of. My sister would come up with some clever, creative way to kill you."

Stacy was a world-renowned jewelry designer.

"While Candace will just make it hurt. Badly," Logan said with a chuckle.

Candace, Garek's beautiful wife, was one of the toughest Payne Protection bodyguards. And after Logan's younger brother, Cooper, and Logan's twin brother, Parker, started their own branches, there were a lot of bodyguards. Except for the ones who were off on assignment, all of those bodyguards had showed up to celebrate the opening of this branch.

Logan sighed and began, "I'm going to regret losing you and Candace and—"

"No mention of me?" Milek Kozminski interrupted as he joined them. While Logan with his black hair and blue eyes looked exactly like his twin, Parker, and their younger brother, Cooper, and half brother, Nick, Milek and Garek could have been twins, too. They both had blond hair that they probably wore too long, and their eyes were the same weird silvery gray color.

"He's happy to get rid of you," Garek teased his younger brother. "You're always slacking off on the job. So easily distracted. I'm not sure how Amber puts up with you."

Milek was as renowned as their sister for all the vivid art that hung from the walls in the new agency. It also hung in galleries, museums and personal collections around the world.

Totally unoffended, Milek grinned. "I'm not sure how my lovely wife puts up with me, either. She could do so much better. She's brilliant and beautiful." And as devoted to Milek as he was to her.

Garek, Milek and Stacy hadn't had an easy start to life with a father who was a thief who had spent so many years in prison, not for theft but for a murder he hadn't committed. They'd had to rely on each other after he went away, doing whatever they'd had to in order to support and protect themselves. But their lives eventually changed for the better.

And that was mostly because of the Paynes.

Penny Payne-Lynch rushed up and hugged first Milek and then Garek. "I'm so proud of you two," she said, tears sparkling in her coppery brown eyes. Her hair was the same coppery brown with only a few fine silver strands wound through it. She was the most amazing woman. Even when everyone else had thought the Kozminskis' father had killed her husband, she had tried to help them, tried to take care of them just like she took care of not only the four kids she'd raised on her own after her husband's death, but everyone else.

"Thank you, Mrs. P," Garek said. "Couldn't have done it without you." And he really couldn't have.

"None of us could have," Logan agreed, and when his mom stepped back from the Kozminskis, he hugged her, too.

"You all give me too much credit," she said. "It's your hard work that has reaped all the rewards you so richly deserve."

"The work is just starting here," Garek said.

Someone called out to Penny and Milek, and the two walked off arm in arm to greet whoever had called out. Probably the chief of police, who was also Penny's second husband, Woodrow Lynch. Not that he would be the chief much longer, if he had his way. He'd expressed his desire to retire soon, no doubt to spend more time with his beautiful wife.

Milek's wife, Amber, walked up seconds after her spouse left with Penny.

"You just missed him," Garek said, pointing after his brother.

"You're the one I wanted to talk to," the River City district attorney said. "We both know my darling husband isn't going to be doing the administrative work. You and Candace are."

Garek chuckled at how well his sister-in-law knew her husband and him and his spouse. The woman was brilliant.

"And they both have my support," Logan said.

"They're going to need it," Amber said. "I'm working to get

some of the gun rights restored to your new bodyguards, but it's not going to be easy."

Garek shrugged. "I didn't hire them to shoot people," he said. "I hired them to protect them but mostly to protect their things. Our branch is focusing on special security."

Logan chuckled. "That whole *it takes a thief to catch a thief*?"

"We're more focused on stopping the thieves," Garek said. "We're hired to prevent thefts."

And he'd just taken on a big client that morning: an insurance company that was concerned about the recent spate of theft claims they'd paid out, because all their clients were getting robbed around the same time, and the new CEO wasn't comfortable with coincidences.

Neither was Garek.

"How are they going to do that without weapons?" Logan asked.

"Speak softly and carry a big stick."

Garek wasn't the one who'd repeated the old quote. It was the chief of police who'd walked up with Penny and Milek. The tall man with the iron gray hair reminded Garek of the character Tom Selleck played on one of his favorite TV shows. Looks weren't the only thing Chief Woodrow Lynch shared with the character; he also had the same idol. President Teddy Roosevelt was who had said the quote first.

Speak softly and carry a big stick...

"A stick isn't much protection when the other people are armed," Logan pointed out.

"Hopefully nobody will need a gun or a stick," Garek said. "Just our high-tech security systems." While he was happy to emulate his brother-in-law and start up his own branch of the security business, he didn't want to suffer the losses that Logan had. In addition to losing his dad when he was a kid, Logan had also lost some of the bodyguards who'd worked for him. While some of them had left to start or work at the other two franchises, a couple of them had died.

Garek looked around the warehouse, his gaze resting on each of the new guards he'd hired.

Ivan Chekov and Viktor Lagransky had the same Oliver Twist

upbringing that Garek and his siblings had, and they'd even had the same Fagin, a greedy crime boss who'd forced his own nephew and the kids of his former employees to commit crimes.

Blade Sparks was even bigger than Ivan and Viktor and had had to use his size to support himself. Dark-haired, dark-eyed Josh Stafford wasn't as big as the other new employees, but he was tough. He'd had to be in order to survive his five-year prison sentence.

Milek had hired him based on Amber's recommendation. Or maybe her insistence. She'd once accepted Josh's plea deal for a crime she didn't think he committed. But she didn't know why he would take the blame for something he hadn't done.

Garek did. He'd done the same to protect someone he loved.

So he understood all of his new employees very well. They had already suffered enough in their lives. Some of them had lost people they'd cared about, and some had lost their freedom for a while.

He had to make sure that he kept them all safe now, so that they didn't lose their lives, too.

Chapter One

Five years behind bars for something he hadn't done could have made Josh Stafford incredibly bitter. But he was the one who'd turned the proverbial key in his own cell door and thrown it away, along with everything else from his old life. Everything that had mattered to him.

But he was out now, for the past few months, with a second chance and a new career in security with the Payne Protection Agency. The picture on his security badge, which was clipped to his pocket, didn't look that different than his prison ID. Same dark hair worn a little too long, same scruff on his face, same dark eyes that had seen too much over the past five years but hadn't seen enough before that. While the Kozminski brothers, who ran the branch of the agency Josh worked for, had given him a second chance to prove that he was trustworthy and honorable, he didn't expect anyone else to give him one.

And so he'd opted to keep his distance from the new client the agency had just taken on.

The work he did to protect Croft Custom Jewelry, he did at night when nobody would see him guarding the perimeter, but he would see if anyone tried to break into the building to steal anything. While at first he'd been apprehensive to be anywhere around *her* again, he was glad he'd been assigned to her family business because all he'd ever wanted to do was keep her safe.

All he'd ever wanted to do was keep everyone he cared about safe. That was why he'd taken the blame all those years ago even though he hadn't committed the crime.

But that was all in the past, and there was no sense looking back. He could only look forward. At the moment, though, he was looking down as he climbed the stairs to his apartment on the fourth floor. The building, which had once been a school in downtown River City, Michigan, had no elevator. Ordinarily Josh didn't mind having to walk up all those flights. The stairwell was wide with terrazzo flooring and steps and concrete block walls. Because he was so damned tired, he had to watch where he was going to make sure he didn't trip and fall.

But as tired as he was, he wasn't eager to go to sleep because he always saw her then…in his dreams. That was the only way he'd seen her for the past five years. And it was the only way he intended to see her now because he couldn't meet up with her in person, not after how badly he'd hurt her. The nicest thing he could probably do for her was to never see her again.

Which was not going to be a problem since she had tried only once over the past five years to visit him. And that had been at the very beginning of his sentence.

He released a ragged sigh that echoed off the concrete walls of the empty stairwell. Since it was daytime, most of the other tenants were probably at work or school. Finally, he reached his floor and opened the steel door to the hall, and that silence stretched like a cocoon around him. Until he stepped into the hall, and the door slammed shut behind him, the sound jarring and unexpected, like a gunshot.

Nobody had been in the stairwell besides him, so there must have been some kind of air flow issue that made it slam, like a door opening on another floor or maybe one on this floor.

Definitely this floor.

As he approached his door, he noticed that it was open and swinging slightly in the splintered frame, the dead bolt banging against the damaged wood trim. Someone had broken into his place.

A laugh bubbled up the back of his throat. Why the hell would someone break into his apartment? He had nothing to steal.

The only piece of furniture he owned so far was a bed. Actually, it was just the king-size mattress and box springs sitting on the floor of the one bedroom. And if the thieves had managed to carry that thing down four flights of stairs, they'd just about earned it.

But what if they weren't after something to steal?

What if they were after him?

He reached for his weapon. It wasn't a gun. Not yet. But a lawyer, actually the River City district attorney, was working on getting his gun rights restored. In the meantime, he carried a can of pepper spray, which had also required special approval for an exemption.

Maybe if he'd considered some of the consequences of taking the blame...but there would have been more consequences if he hadn't. So he wouldn't have done anything differently.

But he might not be able to say the same this time as he edged closer to his damaged door. Because his can of mace wouldn't be much protection against a gun.

He pushed open the door, and a piece of the splintered frame dropped onto the floor in front of him. Had someone kicked it open or pried it with a crowbar? And why had none of his neighbors reported the break-in?

He glanced around the hall, checking to see if any of the other doors along it were in the same condition as his. But they were all tightly closed and probably locked as well. Nobody else's place had been broken into but his.

Why his?

And had none of his neighbors heard anything? Or were they like the neighbors he'd had the past five years, and they ignored what they heard and saw because they didn't want to get involved?

He could hardly blame them for that, though, since he'd done the same thing himself. Even before prison, he'd ignored a situation until it was too late.

He should probably ignore this broken door, too, and call the police to deal with it instead. But...

He passed through the broken doorjamb into the hallway of his apartment. The foyer closet was partially open, clothes jammed in the crack. With the pepper spray canister in one hand, he used the other to open the door. He glanced inside, but there was nothing in it but empty hangers and the coats lying on the floor.

He continued down the hall to the galley kitchen on one side with the bathroom on the other. The cabinets in both were open, drawers upended on the floor. Someone had been looking for something.

The living room was untouched, probably because it was empty of anything to search. But his bedroom was a mess, clothes tossed out of the dresser and the closet, pockets turned out of his jeans. And the mattress hadn't been stolen, but it had been slashed, and so were the pillows. The breeze blowing through the open window sent the stuffing tumbling across the hardwood floor.

What the hell had someone been looking for?

The only thing he'd had that cost any significant amount of money was the mattress. Hopefully it wasn't ruined because he was too damn tired to go out and buy another one. He was too tired to deal with the police right now, too. The burglar was gone, and nothing had been stolen. So what could they do?

Check for fingerprints while keeping him awake asking questions he couldn't answer?

He had no idea why someone would break into his place. Clearly they'd been looking for something, but he didn't have anything anybody would want.

Maybe the previous tenant had, and the burglar just hadn't realized they had moved.

But then Josh noticed a slip of paper sitting atop the old thrift-shop dresser. An ink pen held it in place even as the wind blowing through the open window lifted the corners of it. The pen was heavy, made of metal not plastic. And the logo on it and the company name had every muscle in Josh's body tensing.

Croft Custom Jewelry. That was the new client Josh hadn't wanted to go anywhere near and reluctantly had but only after business hours.

So he wouldn't see her.

Had she been *here*, in his apartment? Was she the one who'd been looking for something?

But why?

Five years ago, she'd taken back the only thing he'd ever had of value: her heart.

His hand trembled a bit as he reached for the note, unfolded it and read the words spelled out in block letters:

Hand over the diamonds, or you'll never see your son again.

"What the hell?" he muttered.

He didn't have any damn diamonds. He didn't have a son, either, at least as far as he knew.

Unless...

The last time he'd seen her, she'd wanted to tell him something, but he hadn't given her the chance. He hadn't wanted to put her through anything more than he already had, and so he'd insisted on a clean break.

But she hadn't protested. She hadn't tried again to see him. And wouldn't she have if she'd been pregnant with his child?

No. It wasn't possible. This whole thing was a mistake. But he needed to find out for certain, and he needed to make sure that there wasn't some child out there in trouble.

Along with her sister, Dena, Natalie Croft had grown up in the family business, sleeping in a crib in the backroom during the day while her mom and dad worked. Her dad was in sales, out front, running things while her mom had been the talent behind the scenes, making the jewelry until rheumatoid arthritis ended her career. They'd found other designers to work with, other people to create the engagement rings, necklaces and heirloom pieces for which the store was known. Croft Custom Jewelry was a well-respected establishment in River City, Michigan.

Natalie sat in the backroom of the store now, but she wasn't designing jewelry like her mother had. Despite all the years she'd watched her mother make the custom pieces, she hadn't learned or inherited that talent from her. She wasn't artistic like her mother; instead her talent was numbers. As a child, she'd been able to figure out the taxes and add up the invoices for her dad's sales.

Unlike her sister who hadn't wanted to spend any more time in the store after she grew up, Natalie was now the accountant for the family business, responsible for the payroll and taxes as well as all day-to-day expenses and receivables. Usually her job was pretty easy, and it didn't take much time, so she could spend the majority of her days where she really wanted.

But lately...

Inventory had been disappearing, leading to an issue with their insurance company which had threatened cancellation of their policy or denial of their next claim if they didn't upgrade their security. So right now, Natalie was staring at the monitors that played back the security footage from the night before.

At the insurance company's recommendation, they had hired the Payne Protection Agency to install a new security system for them. It was so much better and more high-tech than their old one that the images were vivid on the screen now, not blurred. So there was no doubt in her mind who stood outside the store night after night, staring at it.

The sharp nose, the granite jaw, the dark, deep-set eyes were all unmistakably his. And the way her heart pounded so fast and frantically at the sight of him confirmed it.

He was out. When had he been released? And why was he hanging around her family business night after night?

"It's him, isn't it?"

She jumped at the sound of her brother-in-law Timothy Hutchinson's voice. She'd forgotten he was standing behind her in the backroom because she'd been so fixated on that screen, on *him*, just like she'd been in college. She'd had no idea then who and what he really was. She'd found out too late...too late to save her heart from breaking.

"What was his name?" Timothy persisted. "You brought him over to my and Dena's house a few times for dinner and games, but that was years ago. I'm not even sure why you stopped seeing him."

Dena knew, but Natalie, horrified and embarrassed, had sworn her older sister to secrecy. Because of their sometimes-tumultuous sibling relationship, Natalie was a bit surprised that Dena had kept the secret. But then her older and more socially conscious sister had been horrified and embarrassed, too. That was about the only thing Natalie had in common with her sibling.

They didn't even look that much alike.

With her weekly trips to the salon, Dena kept her hair a pale blond with nary a split end while Natalie kept her hair its natural dark blond in a clip on the back of her head. She wore glasses instead of the contacts that Dena wore—a shade paler than her dark blue—while Natalie's eyes were a mossy green instead. She also dressed for comfort whereas Dena dressed in the latest fashion whatever it was and however much it cost. Dena had always cared more about appearances and status than Natalie ever had. Growing up, Dena hadn't had time for the family business because she'd been too busy with cheerleading and student council, with anything that made her popular.

While growing up, Natalie had been focused on the jewelry store, school and then later college. And when she'd met a certain young man in college, on him.

But all Natalie cared about now was…

"Who is he?" Timothy prodded her.

Her throat thick with emotion, Natalie could only whisper the name, "Josh Stafford."

Timothy released a sudden gasp and pointed to one of the monitors, the one with the live feed from the camera that covered the front of the store. Josh's handsome face filled that screen now as he pulled open the door.

Natalie gasped at the sight of him and at the realization that he was so close to her. All she had to do to see him in person, to talk to him, to touch him, was just step out of the backroom and walk through the showroom. It wasn't at all like the last time she'd seen him, when he had been behind security glass like the expensive pieces they kept locked in the cases in the store.

He hadn't always been untouchable to her, though. She remembered all too well and all too often how much she'd touched him and he had touched her. How they'd kissed with such passion and intensity, how they'd…

What was he doing here?

What did he want? Or maybe more importantly, what did he *know*?

Milek Kozminski was well-aware that there had been a lot of truth behind Logan and Garek's teasing at the party for the launch of the newest franchise of the Payne Protection Agency. Logan probably wouldn't miss having Milek on his team, and Garek and Candace probably weren't super thrilled about including him in their new branch.

Milek was always more focused on his art than the bodyguard business. But painting was such a solitary and sometimes all-consuming experience that he felt isolated while working on his latest project. So he enjoyed taking breaks from his art to work with his extended family when he wasn't with his wife and his son and their toddler daughter.

This franchise that he, Garek and Candace had started was also near and dear to his heart because it focused on protecting beautiful things, like art. But he knew that Garek and Candace did the majority of the work, so he'd urged them to get away for a few days for a romantic retreat. With them gone, he was in charge. But maybe that was fate since he, more than anyone else, could understand what Josh Stafford was feeling.

He followed the man into Croft Custom Jewelry, catching the door just as it was about to swing shut on him. Unlike the door at Josh's apartment that wasn't going to shut tightly anymore, not until the entire jamb was replaced. The police were there now, processing the scene, but the break-in had Josh too unnerved to stay and wait for someone else to find the answers he needed. The police had taken the original of the note left for him and had promised to assign a detective to investigate as soon as possible.

But Josh had been too impatient to wait for answers and had decided to seek them out himself. Milek hadn't wanted the younger man to be alone. Most of their new staff were loners, though. They didn't have the family and relationships that Milek had always been so lucky to have. Josh seemed even more alone than the others, but maybe that was due to his choosing as much as circumstances.

After the break-in at his place and that mysterious note, circumstances had changed. And Milek knew all too well how that felt, to have that inkling, that suspicion.

Of course Josh had to find out what the truth was, he had to know what was going on.

If there was any truth to the note...

They would find out here.

At least that was what Josh believed, but he'd seemed almost reluctant to admit it, as if he didn't want to even consider the possibility that he had a child. Maybe that was why he called Milek about the break-in, why he waited for him and the police to arrive at his apartment before he charged off here. He'd wanted to believe what he kept insisting to Milek, that it was all a big mistake.

Someone had picked the wrong apartment.

He didn't have any diamonds, and he definitely didn't have a kid.

But despite how often Josh had repeated that to Milek, to the police and to himself, he must have had a niggling doubt, something that compelled him to come here. Croft Custom Jewelry wasn't the only one of their new clients who had diamonds, so there had to be another reason that Josh wanted to check them out first.

Because the note had mentioned his son? A son Josh claimed he didn't have.

A dark-haired young woman stood behind one of the jewelry counters and looked up with a smile when they entered. But there was no sign of recognition on her face at the sight of Josh. An older man stood behind another counter, and he looked past Josh to focus on Milek instead. His gaze was a bit blurry, like he might have cataracts, but then he blinked and tried to focus or maybe tried to place him.

"I'm Milek Kozminski with the Payne Protection Agency," he introduced himself to the man. "You met with my brother, Garek, over security." Garek and Candace met with all their clients. But the guy probably thought Milek was Garek.

The older man's head bobbed. "Yes, of course. The insurance company and my daughter insisted on having the new system installed. I hate it. No matter what I do, I keep setting off the damn alarm."

The younger woman laughed and then smiled at Milek and Josh. "Mr. C is not great with technology."

That was something that he and Garek heard often. Garek more than Milek since his older brother handled most of the complaints. Garek was the charmer, or so Candace claimed, but she hadn't fallen for him because of that but despite it. She was too no-nonsense to tolerate charmers or complainers. And Milek was usually just too distracted.

"Is that why you're here?" Mr. Croft asked. "Did my daughter, Natalie, ask you to come by to show me how it works again?"

"I didn't ask them here," a female voice said, and it was so cold that Milek nearly shivered while Josh's long body stiffened and his jaw clenched.

"Why are you here?" another male asked. This one was younger than Mr. Croft, probably in his late thirties to early forties since his hair was thinning and fine wrinkles fanned out from the corners of his eyes.

"We have a concern that the security might have been breached," Milek admitted even though he shared Josh's hope that the note left for him was a mistake. Verifying if the diamonds were still here would prove that it was. "We want you to check to make sure that nothing is missing."

"And nobody…" Josh muttered beneath his breath.

The others probably didn't hear him, but Milek did. If a child had been taken, his safety was their main concern, more so than any material possession.

"We've been checking the security footage," the younger man said. "And he's been here every night." He pointed at Josh. "Casing the place."

Milek tensed now. He'd been judged because of who and what his father had been, because of who and what he had been. That was why he and Garek had wanted to hire staff who needed someone to give them another chance. And Amber had insisted that no one deserved that second chance more than Josh Stafford.

"He hasn't been casing the place. He's been protecting it," Milek corrected. "Josh is one of our security specialists. And please, we need you to check your inventory. Now."

Because he had a feeling…

He wasn't like Penny Payne-Lynch, with her infamous sixth sense for knowing when someone she cared about was in danger, but maybe he'd spent enough time around her that he was picking up on the same cues she probably did.

The undercurrents.

They were in this room, in the looks between Josh and Mr. Croft's daughter. And Milek got swept up in those undercurrents as did Mr. Croft and the other man. While the dark-haired woman remained where she was standing, the five of them headed toward the backroom, where some monitors played back the footage of Josh standing outside in the dark.

Milek felt like he was the one in the dark now, unaware of the history between Josh and their client's daughter. "We need to know if any diamonds are missing," he said. "If I remember right…" from his brother's notes "…loose ones are kept in a safe."

But the safe was more like a bank vault, the door to it nearly as big as a regular door.

"In there," Mr. Croft confirmed as he pointed at the door. Then he gestured at his daughter. "Please, you open it, Natalie. I can't remember how with this new system."

She touched his forearm briefly, as if comforting him. Then she approached the door and punched in a long series of numbers. Obviously she'd had no problem remembering it. Who else had memorized it?

And why? The code was supposed to change frequently. The Crofts had chosen this system over the one that required fingerprint access, probably because this system was cheaper. But in the end, would it wind up costing them more?

Once the lock clicked, she pulled open the door and stepped back. "I need to find the inventory list."

Her father shook his head. "I remember what should be here…" And when he stepped inside, he gasped. "They're missing!"

"What, Daddy?" she asked with alarm making her voice sharp. "What's missing?"

"The diamonds," Mr. Croft said. "The ones we just bought to be used for the custom engagement rings. They're gone!"

Milek probably should have been concerned about how his and his brother's new business had apparently failed one of their first clients. Garek and Candace would be upset about that, especially since they'd set up the security system themselves. But Milek wasn't worried about the missing diamonds.

He was worried about the other part of the note that had been left in Josh's apartment. Because that note had been right about the diamonds, it could be right about the other part.

About Josh's son…

Chapter Two

The diamonds were gone.

Natalie's brother-in-law stepped inside the vault and confirmed it while she stood next to her father who'd gone pale and shaky.

In the five years that Josh had been in prison, Claus Croft had aged, but Natalie hadn't. She looked exactly the same as she had when Josh first met her in college, naturally beautiful with her golden hair and deep green eyes. There were no lines on her smooth skin, no hardness in her face or her curvy body. Until she looked at him, then she tensed, and her gaze hardened.

"You were outside here," she said. "Night after night. If you were really guarding the place, you would have seen someone get in and steal them."

"I would have," he confirmed. "If someone from outside had come in and taken them."

She gasped. "You're saying this is an inside job?"

"I couldn't care less about the diamonds right now..." Josh began.

"What the hell!" the brother-in-law exclaimed. Timothy something.

Josh had met him a couple of times, but the guy was so average that nothing much stuck out about him or was at all memorable.

"They're worth hundreds of thousands," Timothy continued.

Then he turned toward Milek. "We hired your agency to protect them, not to steal them."

"I didn't steal them," Josh said. But clearly the note writer wasn't the only one who suspected that he had. "What I really want to know is about the kid."

Natalie's face grew as pale as her father's, and the older man had to steady her now with a hand on her elbow. "What?" she asked so softly that her voice was just a raspy whisper.

"Someone broke into my place," Josh said. "And left me a note. 'Hand over the diamonds, or you'll never see your son again.'"

She shook her head so vehemently that her glasses slipped down her nose, and her hair spilled out of the clip, which dropped to the floor. "No…"

Despite her denial, panic and something else, something warm, gripped Josh's heart, and he knew it was true. Not just about the diamonds but about his son. He had a son. But unlike the note writer had implied, Josh had never seen him before. He needed to see him now, to make sure that he was safe.

"Where is he, Natalie?" he asked. "We have to make sure he's all right."

Josh wasn't. He hadn't been this scared since those prison bars had closed, locking him up for something he hadn't done. But now he wasn't scared for himself. He was scared for someone he hadn't even met: his son.

Natalie felt how her father, with his early onset Alzheimer's, must sometimes feel, like she didn't know what was going on.

Seeing Josh on that security footage had been shocking enough, but now he was here, crammed into the backroom with her and her father and Timothy and one of the Kozminski brothers. She wasn't sure which one because the two of them looked so much alike.

She wasn't even sure what the men were saying now because the only thing she could hear was a sudden buzzing in her ears.

Then Josh touched her, his fingers sliding under her chin like he used to do just before he tipped her face up to his. So he could kiss her like he had so many times before. But when he lowered his head, it wasn't to kiss her, because there was no passion or desire on his handsome face. There was only impatience and fear.

"Natalie!" he nearly shouted at her now. "You need to tell me. Do we have a son?"

"We? Natalie, who is this?" her father asked, sounding as befuddled as he usually did lately. But this time he had reason to be since she was, too.

Josh pulled something from his pocket and unfolded it. "This isn't the original note. The police have that—"

"The police?" she squeaked.

This was real. This was happening. It wasn't all some strange dream she'd had after having two too many glasses of wine at book club.

"Read the note," he told her.

She could barely focus, but she pushed her glasses up her nose and read the words, in crude block letters, that he'd already recited:

Hand over the diamonds, or you'll never see your son again.

Then she shook her head, like she had just moments ago. "This makes no sense." So few people knew the truth...

"You don't have a son?" Josh asked.

She couldn't deny him, not her sweet little boy. "Yes, *I* have a son." But Henry was all hers, nobody else's, even though she could remember, and often did in pulse-tingling detail, the night that they had probably made him. The night Josh had asked her to marry him and make him the happiest man alive. And she'd been so happy, too, so foolishly happy.

"Where is he?" Josh asked with such urgency that her heart started pounding even faster and harder than it had since the instant she'd seen him on that video surveillance.

"He's probably still in school," she said. But then she noticed the time. The morning had already slipped away from her while she'd been studying the footage on the security cameras, while she'd been studying Josh. "No. He'd be done already."

"So where is he now?" he asked.

"He...he's with my mom," she said.

"You need to make sure that he's actually there. Now!" he demanded.

Even before the words were out of his mouth, she reached for her cell and pressed the contact for her mother. One ring pealed out of the speaker and then the voicemail began to play.

"This is Marilyn, please leave a message. I prefer that to texts so I don't have to put on my glasses and let everyone know that I'm old."

Usually that voicemail brought a smile to Natalie's face but not now, not this time. After the beep, she said, "Mom, call me right back." But she didn't wait for a response before dialing again. And again...

Each time it went to voicemail after that lone first ring.

"Where could they be?" Josh asked.

"I... I don't know," she said. "He would have just gotten off the bus, so they should be home."

Josh said, "Let's go—"

"We need to call the police first," Mr. Kozminski interjected, and he was pulling out his cell phone. "A detective is being assigned to handle the case. They're going to need to talk to you and they'll look for the boy."

But Natalie grabbed her purse from the desk. She didn't care about the diamonds. She didn't care about anything but making sure that Henry was safe, that he and her mother were all right. Digging in her bag for her key fob, she rushed out the back door to the alley where there were a few employee parking spots.

Before the door could swing shut behind her, someone caught it. Then a big hand closed over hers, taking the keys from her. He clicked the button, flashing the lights of her little SUV.

"I'll drive," he said as he slid beneath the steering wheel on the driver side.

Sparing them both an argument, she took the passenger seat. She was shaking so badly now that she wasn't sure she could drive herself safely to her parents' house. And with Josh in the vehicle as well, she probably would have crashed for certain.

"Do you remember where my parents' house is?" she asked him.

"They haven't moved?" he asked.

"No." Neither had she. She lived there, too. The old Tudor house was big, in a safe neighborhood, and she and her mom helped each other—her mother with Henry, and lately Natalie had to help her mom with her dad. Fortunately, he was just in the early stages, and on a medication that seemed to be helping him remember more.

Josh turned the SUV to head just east of downtown. He glanced across the console at her and said, "You should keep trying to call your mom."

The cell phone was still in her hand, but every call kept going directly to voicemail. "She could have just put it down and forgotten about it," Natalie said, which was what she hoped. "She does that a lot, especially when Henry gets home from pre-kindergart—"

"Henry?" Josh interrupted, his voice gruff. He cleared his throat and asked, "That's his name?"

"Yes." She'd named him after her maternal grandfather, who'd been such a sweet man.

"Is he my son, Natalie?" Josh asked, his voice cracking now with emotion.

She could only whisper, "He's mine."

"Natalie—"

"You chose," she reminded him. "You chose when you committed those crimes. That was what you told me when I went to see you that last time…" Tears rushed up to clog her throat and sting her eyes, but she blinked them away. "You said you chose that life over me. And you wanted me to leave and never look back. You didn't want to ever see me again."

After that day, she hadn't wanted to ever see him again, either. But she had, and she did, every time she looked at their son. Henry had his dark hair and his dark eyes and his impish little grin. She needed to see her sweet son now, needed to hold him and make sure he was okay.

"Hurry," she urged as yet another call went to her mother's voicemail.

Marilyn Croft hated her cell phone, but with her husband's recent diagnosis, she never went too long before she checked it for messages. So why hadn't she called back yet? Or at least picked up?

"None of this makes sense," Josh muttered beneath his breath. "How could someone know what I didn't even know myself? Who did you tell?"

"Not many people know," she admitted. "Just my sister and my mom." They hadn't even told her father. He just knew that it was some boy from college who hadn't wanted anything to do with being a father.

And it had been. She'd met Josh in college, his senior year, her junior. He'd been going for criminal justice, which was incredibly ironic now, while she'd been going for accounting and business management. Then after graduating, he'd stayed on for his master's degree while she finished up her senior year. Once she graduated, they'd planned to get married. Although he hadn't been able to afford a ring yet, he'd proposed. And she, who'd been raised in a jewelry store, hadn't cared about the ring, just him.

She'd been so excited to spend her life with him. And the night they'd celebrated their engagement had been so full of passion and excitement. Every kiss, every caress had been like a surge of electricity going through her body, making her feel more alive than she'd ever felt. More hopeful. More loved. More in love.

Then everything had gone so wrong.

Just like today.

"This has to be a mistake," she said. Henry and her mother had to be safe.

But that note had been right about the diamonds. They were gone.

Was Henry gone as well?

When Josh turned onto the tree-lined street where she lived, she started reaching for the handle. And once he steered her SUV into the brick-cobbled driveway, she threw open the door and jumped out before he'd even fully braked.

"Natalie!" he called out.

She ignored him and ran for the side door of the two-story Tudor house, but before she could reach for the handle, the door blew open. It hadn't been closed. Henry wasn't always good with closing doors. That had to be what happened.

And that meant he was here, surely. Or maybe...

"Henry!" she called out as she stepped into the mudroom. "Mom?"

His backpack wasn't hanging from the hook in the little cubby where he usually hung it once he got off the bus from morning kindergarten. It should have been there. But the hook was empty.

She glanced at her watch, the one her mother had personally designed, with the diamonds around the mother-of-pearl face, for Natalie's graduation. Henry should have been home nearly an hour ago.

"Mom!" she yelled, and she stepped onto the first stair of the three leading up to the kitchen. Before she could go up another, a strong hand caught her elbow.

"Wait," Josh whispered, his voice low and deep.

His breath was warm against her ear, but instead of heating her, it made her shiver.

"Stay here," he said as he brushed past her. His hand was in one of his pockets. Was he carrying a gun?

Was he armed?

He was a security guard or something, so maybe he was. But instead of making her feel safer, a chill rushed over her. She didn't want weapons around her son or her mom. She didn't want them to see that ugliness, to be any part of what Josh Stafford had been part of.

Maybe that was why she'd taken the easy way out the only day she'd visited him in prison. When he'd told her that their life, their love, hadn't been real and that he didn't want to see her again, he'd given her an out. An excuse.

To not tell him that she was pregnant.

That life they'd lived together might not have been real, but the life they'd created was. And her baby, even in those early stages of her pregnancy, meant everything to her. She'd chosen to put her child first, and she'd never wanted Henry to be part of Josh Stafford's sordid world of stealing and prison sentences.

But Josh was here now, probably out on probation. And the diamonds were stolen.

And where was their son?

She had to know, so she ignored what Josh said and started up the steps after him. He tensed, but he didn't turn back. He just kept walking, through the kitchen, which was empty.

The coffeemaker was still on, though the coffee had burned down to sludge in the bottom of the pot. Usually, her mother tossed it out shortly after Natalie and her dad left for the store. The breakfast dishes also sat in the sink, the toast crumbs and bits of egg still stuck to them. And there was a bowl on the table that was more than half full of oatmeal. Henry's barely touched breakfast.

She opened her mouth to call out again, but the way Josh was moving, so stealthily, kept her silent, too. Was someone else here with her mom and son, keeping them quiet like Josh's presence was keeping her silent?

But she wasn't scared of him; she was just scared, scared of what they might find…if anything. Or maybe that was what scared her most, that they wouldn't find anything or anyone.

As they went from room to room, they found each empty of all but personal possessions. There were no people in the house but the two of them. They even checked the backyard but found that empty as well. The swing was swaying gently in the breeze as if an invisible hand was pushing it.

"Where are they?" she asked herself aloud, her heart beating so hard that she barely heard her own voice.

"Does your mother have a vehicle?" Josh asked.

She nodded.

"Is it here?" He was already walking toward the detached garage that sat farther down the driveway than the house, near the swing set in the backyard.

Natalie hurried after him. The side door was unlocked, as always, and he opened it and stepped inside. "There's a car here," he said.

"That's my dad's," Natalie said of the late model Cadillac. They'd talked him out of driving although he sometimes forgot that he wasn't supposed to, so they also hid his keys. "My mom has a small SUV like mine." But it was gone like her mother, like her son.

That had to be a good thing, though.

"This means they have to be somewhere together," she said, and she started to back out of the open door. "That they're fine."

"Then why isn't she answering her phone?" he asked. He remained inside the garage, staring at the concrete floor.

"If she's driving, she won't answer it," she said. Her mother had to be driving, which meant she was okay, that they were okay.

"Wouldn't she have told you if she was taking him somewhere?" Josh asked.

The hope she'd momentarily felt dropped to the bottom of her stomach. "Yes, she would have." She mostly definitely would have.

Her mother didn't take Henry anywhere without running it past Natalie first. Even though she often spent more time with Henry than Natalie was able to because of work, Marilyn was very respectful that Natalie was Henry's mother and should always have the final say on where he went and what he did.

"Unless it was just a quick trip somewhere," she said. Natalie had told her mom that she didn't need her approval if they were sticking close to home.

"Would they have gone to your sister's?" Josh asked. "Should you call her?"

Natalie tensed. "No. My sister doesn't like kids. She says they're too loud and sticky even though Henry is neither of those things." Well, maybe sticky sometimes, but that was just if his grandpa made his PB&J sandwich instead of her or her mom.

But maybe she should check with Dena. Not wanting to talk to her, though, especially if Timothy already had, she sent a text:

Have you seen Mom and Henry?

An automatic message came back:

In an appointment until four pm.

What was Dena doing now? Haircut? Manicure? Or maybe some type of exercise class? Or she could be volunteering somewhere. She did occasionally do that, but Natalie wasn't sure where and how often. And sometimes she wondered if she really did or if she just used the volunteerism as an excuse to stay away from the store and away from Dad now.

"Dena's phone is on do-not-disturb," Natalie said, which probably meant that Timothy hadn't talked to her yet, either. That was good, though. The last thing she needed to hear was Dena gloat about the poor choices Natalie had made. "She wouldn't have it on that if she was with Mom and Henry." Dena would probably welcome a distraction if she was with them. She and Mom had never had much in common, and Dena barely paid attention to Henry.

Josh was curiously quiet.

"Maybe they just went to the store or to grab some fast food," she said. It was lunchtime, and despite having breakfast and a snack at school, Henry was usually ravenous when he got off the bus. "Or maybe she took him to the park to play." Natalie took another step toward the side door of the garage. "We should go look for them."

But Josh was squatting down now. He continued to stare at the concrete floor as if he was intently studying the cracks in it or the finish of it. "No," he said. "We need to call the police and make sure that they're on their way here."

"But why?" she asked, her heart beating fast and hard again at the gruffness and seriousness of his voice. "My mom and Henry are gone somewhere together. It's not just Henry who's missing, so that note was a hoax. I'm sure that they're fine."

But the diamonds were gone. Why lie about one thing but not the other?

"We need to call the police and make sure they're on their way," Josh said again, his voice even gruffer as if he was struggling to get out the words. "There's blood here, Natalie. This is blood." And he pointed to a small puddle on the concrete that, if she'd noticed earlier, she would have thought was oil. But it was red; she could see that now when he stepped away from it.

The brightness and wetness of it indicated that it was fresh. Someone was hurt so badly that they were bleeding. Her mother or her son or both?

Fear overwhelmed her, making her knees weak and her head light. Her legs shook so much that she started to crumple to the concrete, but Josh caught her, pulling her against his chest into his strong arms. But he was shaking, too.

She wasn't sure if it was with fear or with rage. He was entitled to both. A kidnapper had told him he had a son before she had.

"We'll find them," he said. "We will find them."

But she couldn't believe him. She couldn't believe anything he told her. He'd lied to her before. He'd broken promises to her before. He'd broken her heart.

And if he didn't keep this promise, if they couldn't find them...

She couldn't let her mind or her heart go down that dark route. She couldn't consider any possibility other than finding them.

And when they found them, they had to be all right. They *had* to be.

"Mimi," Henry whispered.

It was dark, wherever they were, and Henry hated the dark, especially this kind of dark where he couldn't see anything at all.

Or anyone.

But Mimi was here somewhere, too.

She was sleeping. At least that was what the person in the mask had said.

Why were they wearing a mask? It wasn't Halloween for a long time yet.

And this wasn't a fun game of hide-and-seek like that person said they were playing.

Just playing...

Who was that person?

They talked so funny that Henry couldn't tell if it was girl or a boy. With the hood of their big puffy coat up over their head and the mask on their face, Henry hadn't been able to see if they had long hair or short or anything else about them.

Then they'd put something over his head, too, so he couldn't see where they were going for this dumb game.

Tears burned in his eyes. He hated this game.

"Mimi," he called out again.

"Ummm." The sound, more like a moan, came out of the darkness.

"Mimi!" On his hands and knees, Henry crawled around on what felt like a concrete floor. It was cold and hard, like the floor in the garage where Mimi had fallen. She'd been so sleepy even before she fell. But he hadn't seen her fall. He wasn't even sure that she had...on accident.

"Mimi?" He reached out, trying to find his grandmother in the darkness, and his hand touched something warm and soft. "Mimi..."

She didn't answer him, though; she just moaned again. Sometimes Mommy groaned when he hopped into bed with her in the morning and tried to wake her up to play with him. But this was different than that.

"Mimi?" He patted her soft hair. It was so white that he could see some of it in the darkness. But it wasn't all white, like it usually was, there was something in her hair, something sticky.

Not like the gum that he accidentally spat out in Chelsea Oliver's hair or like the peanut butter and jelly that oozed out of the sandwiches that Grandpa made. He put a lot of both on the bread. Too much, Mimi said. But Henry liked them like that, and Grandpa knew that. He remembered that. He remembered a lot of stuff. He wasn't losing his memory like everybody kept saying, usually when they thought Henry was asleep or not around.

Thinking about those sandwiches had Henry's stomach growling. It felt hollow and empty. He was hungry. All he'd had to eat today was breakfast because he hadn't gone to school. So he hadn't had his snack.

Or lunch.

They'd missed the bus this morning. He wasn't sure why, but something had been wrong with Mimi. She'd been acting like Grandpa, a little confused and really tired, too. And when the bus passed the house, she'd promised to drive him to school. But when they got to the garage...

That person had been in it, waiting for them in the mask. And somehow Mimi fell down.

Henry wasn't sure if the person pushed her or if she just

slipped. But before Henry could scream or do anything, the person had put their gloved hand over his mouth.

"There is no school today," they told him. But that was a lie. Henry knew it. He'd seen the bus go by.

"Today we're playing a game of hide-and-seek. I'm going to hide you and see if someone can find you." The person took their hand away then.

And all Henry had been able to say was, "Mimi..."

"She's going to be okay. She's just sleepy today."

That was true. She had seemed sleepy all morning even though she'd had a lot of coffee. She hadn't even noticed that Henry didn't finish all of his oatmeal. He wished he had now because his stomach growled again.

But he wasn't just hungry. He was scared. And not the fun kind of Halloween scared or watching-a-scary-movie scared. He was really scared.

"Mimi," he whispered this time. Because it just occurred to him that he didn't know where that person with the mask had gone. Where were they?

It had been a while since they brought him and Mimi here, to this hiding place. But someone was supposed to be looking for him.

Just before the person had closed the door and locked them into this place, they'd told Henry who was supposed to find him.

"Your daddy."

Henry didn't even know that he had a daddy. Mommy said it was just them, like that was all it ever was. Just him and Mommy and Mimi and Grandpa and Aunt Dena and Uncle Timothy.

If Henry had a daddy, he must have been hiding this whole time. So he had to be good at this game. Hopefully he would find them.

Soon.

Chapter Three

In that moment when he first pointed out the blood and Natalie nearly collapsed, Josh had caught her and closed his arms around her. But touching her evoked so many overwhelming emotions, it had nearly been his undoing, like seeing that blood had been hers.

Whose was it?

Her mother's? Or their child's?

Their son. The son Josh hadn't even known he had. And his name was Henry.

Now, as Josh and Natalie stood on the cobblestone driveway outside the garage where crime-scene techs were collecting evidence, he was torn between wanting to comfort her and wanting to confront her with his anger over keeping his son's existence from him. But could he really be angry with her after what he'd done?

After how he'd lied to her?

And he hadn't lied to her just about the thefts he hadn't really committed. He'd also lied to her when he'd told her their relationship wasn't real. Because it had been all too real to him.

The first time he met her, in the campus bookstore, he'd been attracted to her realness. As well as being naturally beautiful, Natalie was straightforward and honest. When he asked her out, she told her upfront that she was an old-fashioned girl. She didn't sleep around and was looking for the kind of commitment and devotion that her parents had.

She'd told him about the jewelry store they had started and how they worked hard to make it a success, spending so much of their time there. And even though they spent all that time together, they never got irritated with or sick of each other. How they enjoyed every minute they were together, laughing and joking and loving. Then she'd laughed and said that she'd probably scared him off.

He hadn't been scared; he'd been impressed.

Almost immediately his attraction to her grew from interest to love as he got to know her better, her kindness, her cleverness and her sense of humor and her passion.

When she first told him about her parents, he wasn't able to understand how they could spend every moment together and never get sick of each other. His parents hadn't been like that and had divorced shortly after he was born. But after spending time with Natalie, he understood because that was the way he'd loved her—completely, passionately. Even now, all these years later, he could feel the silkiness of her lips against his; he could taste the sweetness of her.

No, despite what he'd told her that day she'd visited him in prison, his love and their relationship had been very real. And he'd imagined their love lasting a lifetime.

But he'd been sentenced to eight years in prison—though he'd served only five with good behavior—Josh hadn't wanted her to make the sacrifices he'd chosen to make. And so he'd done what he'd thought was magnanimous and selfless in the moment—he drove her away from him for her safety and for her happiness.

He'd driven her away too well. She'd only visited the prison that one time to see him, and she never returned. After that, she hadn't even sent him a letter or a card during his incarceration. Definitely not a birth announcement for their child.

She wasn't the only one who'd never visited him, though. His father had disowned him, and his sister...

He couldn't think about Sylvie right now. He couldn't think about anything but his son. And he had to put aside his anger at Natalie for not telling him about Henry, especially since that was definitely more his fault than hers.

He had to focus on what mattered most: finding Henry and the little boy's grandmother as well.

After Josh called the police about finding the blood, it hadn't taken them long to show up at the scene. Some of the techs had even been pulled away from the jewelry store, but a missing child took priority over all else.

The head detective and heir apparent to the current chief's throne, Spencer Dubridge, was leading the investigation. But the chief was here, too, along with his wife who also volunteered with victim services. At least, that was what she'd told him and Natalie when she'd introduced herself.

But Josh wasn't the victim. An innocent child and his grand-mother potentially were. God, he wanted to believe what Natalie kept muttering to herself.

"This is all a mistake. They're fine," she whispered. "They have to be fine."

But her face was still as pale as it had gone when she'd seen the blood, and her body was trembling slightly. He ached to hold her again, to comfort her.

But he'd already made her a promise that he might not be able to keep. That, depending on who was wounded and how badly, he might have already broken. He might not be able to get her mother and their son safely back home.

But he intended to do everything within his power to try.

Natalie had never felt as helpless as she did now. Not even the day that she'd gone to see Josh in prison had she felt as out of control of her own life as she did now.

Crime-scene technicians, officers and detectives walked in and out of her family home and the garage and the yard. They even canvassed the neighborhood, going from door to door, in-terviewing the neighbors to find out what they'd seen and heard that morning.

"You didn't know that Henry didn't go to school?" the dark-haired detective asked Natalie.

She shook her head. "No. I thought he went." Henry hated

missing school. He liked learning as much as he liked socializing with other kids.

"The school didn't call you to question his absence?" the detective asked. "They claim they talked to someone."

She held out the cell phone she'd been grasping in one hand because she really believed, or at least hoped, that her mother was going to call and tell her that this was all a misunderstanding. That they were both fine.

She unlocked the phone before the detective took it from her hand. He scrolled through her call log and then moved onto her texts and then her settings.

"I don't have any missed calls," she said. "They probably called my mother." Because the school knew that Marilyn was the one responsible for getting him on and off the bus. She also volunteered at the school, sometimes with Natalie and sometimes in Natalie's place as a room parent.

"They claim they spoke to someone—"

"My mother then. So they must be fine." Or maybe Henry was the one who'd been hurt. But if her mother had talked to the school, she would have called Natalie, too. Why hadn't she called? Or was she not who'd spoken to the school?

The detective handed back her cell. "I sent a link from your phone to one of the crime-scene techs. We'll put a trace on this and on your mother's phone, too."

"Can't you ping it now and find her location?" Josh asked. He stood next to Natalie, but he wasn't touching her like he had earlier, like how he'd held her when she initially fell apart.

Maybe that was why she could think clearly now, because he wasn't touching her. He wasn't reminding her of the past, so she could focus on the present.

"Oh, my god!" Natalie exclaimed. "I can do that. We put that app on all of our phones so we can track each other." That was because of her father, though. Natalie had never used it to find out where her mother was. Usually, she knew; Natalie had never had to look for her until now. She fumbled with her cell, trying to find the app.

"I checked it," the detective interjected. "Her phone is not showing up, and according to our techs, it's because it's turned off. That's why we can't ping it."

"Maybe it's broken. Maybe that's what happened in the garage," Natalie mused, her mind flitting from scenario to scenario. "Maybe Mom fell onto the floor or something, and her phone broke. And she's bleeding and she drove herself to the ER with Henry." Natalie reached out and grasped Josh's arm, which tensed beneath her fingertips. "We should go to the ER."

She wasn't sure why she was including him now when she hadn't for all these years. Despite how they ended things, she could have sent him pictures of their son or some of his artwork from school. She could have made both Josh and Henry aware of each other. She could have told them about the other. But it had been easier, for her, to pretend that Joshua Stafford had never existed. Then she didn't have to remember how badly he'd disappointed and hurt her.

But he had also given her the most precious part of her life: Henry.

"We've already checked the hospitals," Detective Dubridge assured her.

Which meant that her mom and Henry weren't there, or Dubridge would have told her already. She wished not finding them at the hospital meant nobody was hurt. But it could also mean they were hurt but hadn't been able to seek medical treatment.

"What else are you doing to find them?" Josh asked the question that was burning the back of her throat.

Because it seemed to Natalie that they were all just standing around.

She knew that wasn't true. She was the only one who was just standing around, helpless to help her son. Josh had been walking around, talking to his boss and the techs and to the detective. He'd even gone to a few of the neighbors' houses, too, before coming back to her.

"Using those photos you gave me, we have an Amber alert out on Henry with his description, as well as a description of Marilyn Croft and her vehicle, too," the detective said.

Josh just grunted like he wasn't impressed or maybe he just

didn't think it was enough. She definitely didn't. But she had no idea what else to do, how else to find them.

"I know how you must feel," the detective said.

Josh snorted now, as if he didn't believe him.

"Nine months ago, shortly before we got married, my wife was abducted," the detective said. "A dangerous criminal, Luther Mills, took her hostage as he escaped from the courthouse during his trial."

Josh gasped then, and Natalie turned to find that the color had drained from his face. "Luther Mills," he murmured beneath his breath.

"I remember hearing about that," she said. "It had a positive outcome." But then she remembered why. "She was a Payne Protection bodyguard and former police officer, so of course *she* was able to protect herself."

Not like Henry or her mother who, thankfully, had no experience with violence or even with violent people. Despite how confused Natalie's father sometimes got, he was always kind and gentle. Everyone in Natalie's world was kind and gentle and law-abiding, except for Henry's father. Josh was the only person close to Henry who'd actually committed a crime.

"When Keeli was taken hostage, she'd just discovered she was pregnant with our baby, a little girl who's now eight weeks old," the detective said. "And the hell I went through thinking about them…" His voice, gruff with emotion, trailed off.

"Hell," Josh muttered, his voice gruff as well with emotion. Hell.

That was exactly what this was.

Natalie could only hope that she was able to navigate her way through it to find her son and her mother safe and well.

Penny wasn't sure what to do. She'd only just recently volunteered to work for the River City Police Department's victim services. She needed something to do since her full-service wedding planning and venue business hadn't been very busy lately, not since her son Parker's bodyguards had all gotten married. The last couple wedded six months ago. Every member of Parker's team had found love while protecting the people associated with the high-profile murder trial of a dangerous drug-dealing gang leader. For a while, it had seemed like some of the bodyguards and the people they'd been assigned to protect might not survive, but it was the perpetrator who'd died.

Luther Mills.

And the man who'd killed him walked up to her now. "I just blew it," Spencer Dubridge said with a heavy sigh, and he shoved one of his hands through his dark hair.

"What?" she asked with alarm. Was it already too late? "Did you find the little boy? Is he not all right?"

"I don't know," he said. "I was trying to comfort and relate to the parents, and I blew it. It's a good thing the chief brought you here, Mrs. Lynch."

"Penny," she reminded him. "And there is no way to comfort parents whose child is missing." It didn't matter how old that child was, either. But to have one as young as this little boy, who wasn't quite five yet, missing had to be an absolute nightmare.

He nodded. "True. It was bad enough when Keeli was missing, and finding out she was pregnant with Barbie at the time. And now that Barbie's here, I can't imagine ever not knowing where she is."

At Woodrow's request and with his wife's urging, Spencer had agreed to come back early from his family leave to help find the missing boy.

"So I really can't relate to what they're going through," he said.

But Penny figured he could, and so did Woodrow; which was why he'd asked Spencer to cut his leave short to lead the case. They both remembered all too well how upset he'd been when Luther Mills had been holding Keeli Abbott hostage.

"Since my wife agreed that I needed to do whatever I could to help out if there's a little boy hostage, I was happy to come back early for this case, but the chief can't really believe that I'm the person who should take over for him," Spencer said. He gestured back to where Woodrow was talking to the parents now.

Penny followed his gaze, and her heart skipped a beat as it always did when she looked at Woodrow Lynch. With his silver hair and blue eyes, he was so good-looking, but it was more than his appearance that had attracted her. It was his very soul. Hers had recognized a kindred spirit in his.

They were meant to be together, and they just *fit*.

While the couple with whom her husband was talking didn't look very comfortable with each other at all. When the man reached for her, the woman stepped back and walked away from him.

Not that people had to be in love with each other to have a child.

Penny wasn't naive enough to think that, not when her own late husband had surprised her with a son she hadn't known he had with another woman. She hadn't learned of Nicholas's existence until several years after her husband Nick Payne's death.

Apparently, from what Milek had shared with her, Josh Stafford hadn't known about his child's existence, either, until whoever had broken into his apartment had left a note claiming they'd abducted his son.

She couldn't imagine the fear that they were all feeling, Josh and Natalie and most of all that little boy. But somehow, it was almost as if she could *feel* it.

Some people thought she had psychic powers because she had an uncanny ability to sense when people were in danger. But she didn't think she was psychic as much as she was empathetic, and sometimes she could just feel what other people were feeling no matter where they were.

Like now, as she studied the couple who stood so far apart, she could feel the fear both parents were feeling for their little boy. She was also feeling something else, the tension between them, the betrayal, the pain...

They had left a lot unsaid and unfinished between them.

But she wasn't feeling just the parents' fear now; she was also feeling a child's fear. The little boy was alive, she believed that. She just prayed that he stayed that way until he could be found.

Chapter Four

"That's the detective you have leading this investigation?" Josh asked, gesturing toward where Dubridge stood next to the chief's wife. He wasn't just skeptical of the detective's abilities, he was furious with him.

For the first time since this whole nightmare began, Natalie hadn't been able to stop her tears from falling. And this time, unlike the times before when she'd been scared and upset, she hadn't allowed him to comfort her. She'd stepped back before he could even reach for her, and now she stood alone by the swing set, her back toward them, but her shoulders were shaking as she obviously sobbed alone.

Her loneliness echoed hollowly inside Josh. He'd felt alone like that for five long years.

Would it have made a difference if he'd known about his son? Would he have told the truth all those years ago? Amber Talsma, now Kozminski, would have believed him. She'd always thought he was taking the blame for something he hadn't done.

But he had his reasons for doing that, life and death reasons for other people. Even for Natalie. Because if he'd told her the truth, her life would have been in danger.

There had been so many threats. Amber had suspected as much and had promised to protect him if he told the truth. But he hadn't been able to trust her with other people's lives, too. And in the end, she'd had no choice but to accept his plea.

That was also why she'd recommended Josh to her husband for this job.

But Josh wasn't the only employee of the new branch of the Payne Protection Agency who had a criminal record. Could it be one of them? They would have known how to disarm the security system. But if they'd stolen the diamonds, why would they take his son, too? They already had what they really wanted.

His head pounded with confusion and exhaustion. And he felt unsteady now, so unsteady that Milek gripped his shoulder as if he'd noticed it, too. "Spencer is one of the best," Josh's boss assured him.

"Since so many of River City PD's finest went into private security, he's definitely the best we have left," the chief said. "And I hope he agrees to become chief soon, once his family leave is over."

So he came back early for this case, for Henry. Josh couldn't summon any gratitude, not with his skepticism and his exhaustion weighing so heavily on him.

"You look like you're ready to drop," Milek said as he tightened his grip on his shoulder. "You were awake and working all night. You need to get some rest, Josh."

Josh shook his head. There was no way he could sleep, not until he knew where his son was, which was ironic since until just a few hours ago he hadn't even known he had a son. He had to make sure that the little boy and Marilyn Croft were both okay. "I have to find Henry."

But he had no idea where to look. He had no idea why anyone would have taken the little boy, let alone where they might have taken him. Josh didn't have the damn diamonds. So did that mean there were two separate situations going on? Someone had stolen the diamonds, and someone else had taken Henry and his grandmother?

"You need to let Dubridge do his job," Chief Lynch said. "He'll find him."

Josh's stomach knotted with dread. He couldn't leave it to him.

And it wasn't just Dubridge he didn't trust. He really didn't trust any police officer, not after what happened to him.

Amber had figured out he hadn't done what he'd taken the blame for, so shouldn't some of the police have figured it out, too? Maybe some of them had been paid to not look into it any further, or maybe they'd just been more eager to close a case than to find out the truth.

Not that he'd really wanted them to find out the truth back then. He'd felt guilty and protective of the real perpetrator and had been convinced he was doing the right thing, that it was the only way to keep the people he cared about safe.

And it had been.

But he'd hurt Natalie. And he'd hurt himself. And he'd lost out on years with his son. Yet if he hadn't done what he had, he might not have a son at all because Natalie might have been hurt physically as well as emotionally.

But Luther Mills was dead now. He wasn't the threat he'd once been to Josh, to Natalie and to the person for whom Josh had taken the blame five years ago. But after he'd taken the blame, that person hadn't come to visit him any more than Natalie had.

Even though he'd urged her to go somewhere else and start her life over, he had still expected her to send him cards. Or call...

He'd made a huge sacrifice for someone who hadn't really seemed to appreciate it. Hurt and a bit resentful, he hadn't reached out to her, either, during his time in prison or since his release. He'd made even more sacrifices than he'd realized, like fatherhood.

And the person for whom he'd taken the blame...

Had she turned her life around? Or was she still stealing? Could she have been the one who'd taken either the diamonds or his son?

Because Natalie couldn't listen to the men any longer, she stood far enough away in the yard that their voices were just low rumbles, like thunder way off in the distance. They had no idea how she felt, no matter what they claimed. She was Henry's mother. She was the one who was supposed to protect him and keep him safe and always know where he was.

And she had no idea.

And she was so damn scared. Not just for him but for her mother, too. Because if someone had truly kidnapped her son, they wouldn't have gotten Henry away from his grandmother without one hell of a fight. She remembered the blood on the garage floor.

Maybe it wasn't Henry's or her mother's, though. Maybe Henry's *Mimi*, as he'd always called her, had hurt whoever tried to grab him, and they were hiding somewhere. Maybe they were safe and unharmed.

That was why they hadn't turned up at the hospital ER or anywhere else. They weren't hurt. They were hiding until it was safe to come out. That had to be the case. So maybe Natalie should try to call her again. Or send a text that the police were here, and that it was safe to come home.

Natalie had been clasping the phone so hard in one hand that she had to unlock her fingers from around it to touch the screen. But just as she reached out to start a text, her mother's specific ringtone rang out: "Mama Said" by The Shirelles.

Mama couldn't have known that there would be days like this, though. That on the very same day an old love would come back into Natalie's life, she might have also lost her most important love: her son.

Her finger shook as she swiped to accept the call. "Mom!" she exclaimed. Either her excitement or the ringing of her cell had Josh and the detective both rushing toward her.

"Give the phone to Josh Stafford," a voice rasped out of the speaker of her cell.

That was not her mother's voice. She'd never heard a voice like this before. It didn't even sound human.

"What? Who is this?" she asked, her voice cracking with fear. "Why do you have my mother's phone? Where is she? Where is Henry?"

"Give the phone to Josh Stafford," the person repeated.

How did they know Josh, and how did they know that they were together? That he was here?

She glanced around the area, checking to see who was watching her. Everyone in the nearby vicinity was staring at her, but she was the only one on a call. But the detective was furiously texting on his, hopefully trying to find her mother's location.

Josh plucked her cell from her hand. "This is Stafford," he said.

"You know what you have to do—"

"I don't have the damn diamonds," he interjected. "And you have to know that."

"I don't care," that weird raspy voice replied. "If you don't have them, you need to find them if you want to see your son again."

"I haven't *ever* seen my son, and you've given me no proof that you actually have him," Josh said.

Natalie's breath caught. What was Josh doing? Was he trying to make the person angry?

Despite what she'd hoped just moments ago, Natalie knew she was wrong. Her mom and Henry weren't hiding somewhere until it was safe to come out. This person calling from her mother's phone was proof enough that they'd taken them hostage. Her mom and Henry were gone, the only thing left behind a small pool of blood. Despite her earlier doubts, or maybe hopes, that was proof enough for Natalie.

Her hand shaking, she reached to grab her cell back from Josh, but he held it away from her.

"Call back on FaceTime," Josh demanded. "Show me my son, prove that he and his grandmother are both unharmed, or you won't get anything out of me." Then he swiped to disconnect the call.

"That wasn't enough time," the detective said.

Fury bubbled up inside Natalie. Fury at the person who'd taken her son, but mostly fury at Josh. She swung out, slapping his shoulder so hard that he staggered back a step. "No! No! How dare you! How dare you hang up! How dare you!"

Josh reached out and grasped her shoulders. "We have to have proof, Natalie. We have to know…"

That he was still alive.

He didn't finish saying it, but she knew what he meant. "This is all your fault!" she yelled at him. "This is all your fault!"

"I don't have the diamonds," he said.

"Then how the hell are you going to get him back?" she asked. "How the hell are you going to save Henry and my mother?"

"I don't know," he said softly. "But first we need to know if they're alive."

The horror of that struck her so hard that her knees nearly gave way. But he was already holding onto her. Then his arms closed around her.

She wanted to hit him again. To slap him away, but she found herself hanging onto him as her world spun out of control. Just a short while ago she'd been hopeful that her son and her mom were all right, that they were safe.

But now she knew the nightmare was really happening. Someone had taken her mother and her son. What if it was too late to save them?

Henry must have fallen asleep because a noise jerked him awake. But when he opened his eyes, it was still dark. Like night.

But he didn't think he'd been asleep for very long. He and Mimi were still wherever that person had taken them, and they were lying on the cold hard floor. Mimi was next to him, her body soft and warm against his back.

She wasn't moving, though. She was still asleep.

"Mimi?" he whispered.

Then he heard the rumble of an engine, and a little while later, there was an echo of footsteps on something metal or hard. He must have woken up because of that vehicle. And it was still outside running.

Mimi's car? That was what the person had driven here, with Henry in the booster seat in the back and Mimi lying on the seat next to him. But the person had put that hood over his head then, so Henry wasn't sure where and how that person had been driving.

With their mask on?

"Mimi," he whispered, as those footsteps got louder. "Somebody's coming!" Maybe it was his daddy. Maybe he'd found them.

He had to be really good at hide-and-seek since Henry hadn't seen him his whole life.

Metal rattled, and then a garage door slid up. The person who ducked under it was still wearing that weird mask. It wasn't his daddy who'd found them. It was the person who brought them here coming back. Why?

This game wasn't fun. Henry didn't want to play it anymore. He wanted to leave. And he knew he should get up and run, try to get to that car and get help for Mimi.

But he was just a little boy. He didn't know how to drive. And Mimi...

She couldn't run.

She couldn't even wake up.

"Mimi?" He shook her shoulder, trying harder to get her to answer him.

With the light streaming in through that big open door, he could see that she wasn't just sleeping. She was hurt. Blood was sticky in her hair. It had matted it down and turned the white to a dark red. There was a cut and a bump on her forehead, but it looked like the blood had dried on it. She wasn't bleeding anymore.

But why wouldn't she wake up?

"Mimi?"

"Ummm..." she muttered.

"Mimi needs help," Henry said, his voice so squeaky it hurt his ears. He was scared, but he was getting mad, too.

"She's just tired," the person said.

But that person was lying. Henry could see the blood now. He knew she was hurt. "She's got a cut," he said. "She needs to go to the doctor."

He hated going to the doctor because of the shots they kept giving him. But maybe the doctor wouldn't give Mimi any shots. Maybe he would just do something to make her wake up.

"I'm tired, too," the person said in that weird, whispering voice. "Your daddy isn't playing the game like he's supposed to."

That was why Daddy wasn't here yet. He wasn't playing. Henry didn't blame him; he didn't want to play this dumb game, either.

"I need you to make him play," the person said.

But Henry didn't know how he was supposed to do that when he didn't even know who his daddy was.

Chapter Five

Oh my God.

Josh's stomach churned with nerves and fear. "What if I just screwed up?" he whispered to Milek. He didn't dare say it any louder. He didn't want Natalie to hear him.

She was with Penny now, but they were just a short distance from where he and Milek stood by the swings. Natalie and Penny were on the cobblestone driveway, sitting in some folding chairs that Penny had taken out of the back of her vehicle. They weren't allowed inside because the house and garage were still being processed as crime scenes.

"What if I pushed the kidnapper too far when I hung up?" Josh asked. "I know I'm supposed to try to keep them on the phone so it can be traced."

"I doubt they would have stayed on the line long enough for us to trace the call," Dubridge said as he and the chief joined them. "They already knew to turn off the Find My Phone app because we weren't able to pull up the location, either."

"You handled that exactly right," Chief Lynch assured him. "You need to have proof of life."

Especially after seeing that blood. Josh had to find out if his son and the boy's grandmother were okay or if one of them had been hurt. Josh wanted so badly to see his son in person, too. For the first time.

He'd seen the pictures Natalie had shared with Dubridge, of the little boy with brown hair and heavily lashed eyes. His smile had a gap where his two front baby teeth had fallen out and his adult ones had yet to come in.

"And getting to see the boy might give us clues as to where he's being held," the detective added. "It was definitely the right move."

"Guess my criminal justice degree didn't entirely go to waste," Josh muttered.

The chief and the detective exchanged a look. "You have a background in criminal justice?"

He sighed over their obvious surprise. "You thought I was just a criminal?"

"Amber doesn't and didn't ever believe that he was guilty of the charges," Milek spoke up in his defense.

"But yet she and a judge accepted his guilty plea," Dubridge pointed out. "And that judge sentenced him to eight years in prison."

"So instead of trying to find my son, you've been wasting time checking me out," Josh surmised.

Dubridge narrowed his dark eyes and stared hard at Josh. "You have a criminal justice background. You don't think I should have checked you out? Your place was broken into and tossed because someone was looking for diamonds they think you stole."

"I didn't take them," Josh insisted. "Until today I hadn't stepped foot into Croft Custom Jewelry in more than five years." And then he'd only been there once, when Natalie had showed him the place after hours. They'd made love in that backroom where earlier today they'd discovered the diamonds were missing from the safe.

"But obviously, since you share a son, you have a history with the owner's daughter," Dubridge said.

"I didn't know I had a son," Josh said. "I had no idea she was pregnant when I pled guilty..." To something he hadn't done. "I had no idea."

Dubridge flinched as if he could commiserate. From what he'd told them earlier about his wife and his baby, he probably could.

"Natalie said that only her mom and her sister knew," Josh told them. He didn't believe Marilyn Croft had left him that note and abducted his son. Natalie and her mother had always been so close, and from what Natalie had shared, they seemed even closer now that Marilyn was helping raise Natalie's son, *their* son.

"And her mom is gone," he murmured. With Henry. Or so he hoped. He hoped the little boy wasn't alone with a kidnapper, and he hoped that nothing had happened to Natalie's mother. But he'd found that blood in the garage, and Marilyn hadn't been offered in exchange for those diamonds. Only the little boy.

Did that mean the boy's grandmother was already dead?

And what about Henry?

Impatience and fear churning inside Josh, he snapped, "Why the hell aren't they calling back?"

"Maybe they weren't with your son when they made the call," Milek suggested. "Maybe they called from somewhere else."

"And where is her sister? The officer cordoning off this area said that nobody has tried coming to this house," Dubridge said. "Why isn't her sister here with her?"

"Dena Hutchinson's phone is on do-not-disturb," Josh said. "Natalie thinks she's getting a spa treatment or something."

"It's the *or something* we need to check," Dubridge muttered. "We'll track her down and confirm what her involvement might be in this situation."

Natalie didn't have the relationship with her sister that she had with her mom. She and Dena didn't even have one as good as the one he had with his sister. Dena had always made it clear to Natalie that she would have preferred to be an only child. They weren't close. While his sister...

Josh couldn't think about her now. He hadn't even talked about her much to Natalie when they'd been dating, and the two women had never met. It hadn't been that he was ashamed of her, but maybe he'd been ashamed of himself. And then...

None of that mattered now. All that mattered was finding Henry and his grandmother.

"From what Natalie said about her sister, Dena doesn't like kids," Josh told the detective. "She says that they're sticky and loud." So why would she kidnap one? And her father owned the jewelry store, so it wasn't as if she'd had to steal to get her hands on some diamonds.

Dubridge chuckled. "I can confirm the loud part already. Barbie is tiny but has one hell of a set of lungs."

Josh felt a pang of envy that he'd missed that, that he'd missed seeing Henry born, seeing him as a baby. Hell, with every minute that passed without the kidnapper calling him back, Josh was getting more and more afraid that he might have missed seeing his little boy ever.

But he couldn't let himself consider that as an option. He had to focus on finding him instead.

"Well, given how Dena feels about kids, I hardly think she would kidnap one," Josh pointed out.

If only he could be as certain that his sister wasn't involved in this…

But he hadn't seen or talked to her in so long. Maybe she'd done what he'd told her to, maybe she'd made a new, better, *safer* life for herself. But…he hadn't wanted to know if she hadn't.

That was why he hadn't tried to find her while he'd been in prison or even since his release. He considered asking Dubridge to track down his sister now, too, but Josh wanted to talk to Sylvie himself first. He wasn't sure he would be able to trust what she told him, though.

He wasn't sure that he could trust anyone anymore. Sylvie hadn't been honest with him all those years ago until it was too late.

And then his dad had turned his back on him.

And Natalie…

Even Natalie, whom he'd loved for being so straightforward and honest, hadn't told him about his son.

But before Josh talked to Sylvie, he wanted to talk to his son, wanted to make sure that he was still alive. "Why aren't they calling back?" he asked again.

Nobody answered him. Probably because everyone else was scared to say out loud what they were thinking. What he was beginning to think…

That it was too late for proof of life.

* * *

Natalie couldn't stop shaking, and it wasn't just with anger now. She was so damn scared. For Henry and for her mom.

Where were they?

What were they going through?

Which one of them was hurt? Were they both hurt now? Or worse?

Why hadn't the person called back yet?

She stared at the phone lying in the palm of her right hand. The detective had a trace on her cell, but he'd said the last call hadn't been long enough to ping more than the main tower in River City.

River City was the biggest city on the west side of Michigan. It was even bigger than Detroit. So that didn't narrow down the location of her mother's phone or of her mother and Henry.

She'd cursed Josh for hanging up that call too soon, for not giving them enough time to trace it and for not giving them a chance to get Henry on the line before he hung up. But the detective had assured her that Josh did the right thing.

Mrs. Lynch sat next to her, holding her left hand while in her right, Natalie held her cell, willing it to ring. "They will call back," the older woman said as if she could read Natalie's mind.

But then she was a mother, too. She had to know that Henry was all that was on Natalie's mind, making sure that he was all right, that she got him back. She was worried about her mother, too, and having Mrs. Lynch here holding her hand did give her some comfort. But it was bittersweet because it made her think even more of her mother.

Marilyn Croft wasn't just her mother, though. She was Natalie's best friend. They were so close. Marilyn was always there for her and for Henry and for everyone else that she loved.

Where was she now?

Was she all right?

"Ms. Croft," Detective Dubridge said as he returned to where she and Mrs. Lynch were sitting. "We should get in contact with your sister."

"I think she's at a salon or maybe a doctor's appointment." Guilt jabbed Natalie. She'd forgotten all about Dena and her father and Timothy. They had a right to know what was going on. She should have called them already. "I better tell her and my dad."

"What salon?" the detective asked. "And do you know what doctor she sees? We'll check them both."

She furrowed her brow, trying to recall the names. "I don't know…"

"You've never gone with her?"

She shook her head. "No." She nearly smiled as she reached up to touch her messy hair. "I haven't been to any salon in a while." Let alone one with her sister. Dena was six years older than Natalie and had never wanted to do anything with her. Natalie was probably the first child that Dena thought was sticky and messy and loud.

"You're beautiful," a deep voice murmured.

It wasn't the detective, but Josh who'd walked up beside him. And the way he looked at her made her feel beautiful. But then his face flushed as if the admission had embarrassed him. She flushed, too.

Then she focused on the detective again. "I don't know where she goes. Did you ask her husband?" Hadn't the detective been at the jewelry store investigating the missing diamonds before she and Josh discovered that Henry and her mother were missing, too?

"Or I can…" She should have already called Timothy. Her dad and Timothy and Dena all had a right to know what was going on with the people they cared about. They were going to be so upset that Mom and Henry were missing.

The detective glanced around the area. "Where is your brother-in-law?"

She hoped he was still with her father, but before she could reply, Josh answered for her, "Dena's husband, Timothy, was at the store earlier when we discovered that the diamonds were stolen, like the note claimed."

"The note claimed you took them," Natalie reminded him and herself.

Had he taken them? She wanted to believe that he hadn't, but after what had happened in their past, how he'd lied to her...she couldn't trust him. She would never make that mistake again.

"I didn't," he insisted.

"That's not what the person who took our son believes," she said as the anger and frustration bubbled up inside her again. She wasn't as mad at him as she was at whoever had taken their son, but she was still angry that Josh was part of this, that he might even be the cause. "And if you don't produce the diamonds, how are we going to get our son back?"

That was the real question. While the others didn't think Josh had blown it, she was worried that he had. Why would the person call back if they believed Josh didn't have what they wanted?

And what would the kidnapper do with her mother and her son then if they couldn't use them to get what they wanted? Or what might they have already done to them?

Was that why they hadn't called back yet?

Milek's cell rang, startling him and everyone else standing around outside the Crofts' home. The crime scene. There had definitely been a crime here. And at least one person was injured, two missing.

He pulled out his phone and glanced at the screen. "It's Garek calling," he said aloud and apologetically to the tense people staring at him.

They were all waiting for a call but not this one. Someone in the office had probably told Garek or Candace what was going on since Milek had already called in all the bodyguards for backup. He'd put out an all-hands-on-deck request for everyone to work on finding Josh's son. But despite his efforts to lead the search from the Payne Protection side, he wouldn't have put it past someone to call his brother or sister-in-law because they didn't think he could handle this situation.

Despite issuing orders on what everyone should do, like searching through video surveillance in the area of the Crofts' house and the store for anyone suspicious, he wasn't sure what other steps to take that the River City PD wasn't already taking.

But he wasn't handling it all alone. Logan, Parker and Cooper were pulling in their crews to help, too, and their sister, Nikki

Payne-Ecklund, was coordinating with the police, too. They all had more experience than he did or even Garek and Candace.

Milek hadn't called his brother and sister-in-law because he suspected that after all the stress of getting the business up and running, they really needed to get away and have some alone time. Also, he didn't know what more they could do other than what he, Logan, Parker and Cooper already had their crews doing.

He wasn't sure what more anyone could do until they knew for certain that the little boy was alive. The difference between a rescue and a recovery was huge. He knew that.

So maybe he could use Garek and Candace's help. But he hesitated before swiping to accept his brother's call. Detective Dubridge was damn good at his job as well as every other Payne Protection bodyguard in town already doing everything they could to help.

"Call him back later," Josh said. "We don't need any distractions right now."

But he was clearly distracted and distraught, alternating between cursing himself and cursing the kidnapper. And the way he kept looking at Natalie Croft...

It reminded Milek of all his conflicted feelings when he'd found out Amber had had his son. Like Josh, Milek hadn't learned about his little boy until he'd thought it was already too late. He thought then that he'd lost them both.

He hadn't, though. They had found their way back to each other. And they had made a life together, a home. They were happy.

Milek hadn't known Josh for very long, but he wanted that for him, too. From what Amber told him about the younger man, Josh deserved happiness for the sacrifice he'd made.

Why was the kidnapper taking so long to call back?

Milek declined his brother's call. Like Josh said, he could call him back later. If he needed his help.

Otherwise, he intended to leave Garek and Candace out of the loop, at least for now. They'd probably just arrived at their romantic destination, so they wouldn't be able to return quickly anyhow.

Penny stood up from where she'd been sitting next to Natalie. "You got this, Milek," she assured him as she squeezed his forearm. "We're all working together."

He wasn't worried about how he was going to handle this, though. He was worried about Josh. And that little boy, who was out there somewhere, possibly bleeding, probably totally afraid...if he was even still alive.

But the more time that passed since Josh's demand for proof of life, the more Milek feared that they weren't going to get it.

Chapter Six

Josh felt just like he had five years ago when he'd had to make some tough decisions and choices. He felt like he was being torn apart between guilt and love and fear.

"I can't do this anymore," he muttered to Milek. He couldn't just stand around and wait for the kidnapper to call back. "I can't just do nothing like the police are doing."

"The police are doing something," Dubridge said defensively. Yet all he seemed to be doing was eavesdropping on conversations.

Josh threw up his hands. "What? Have you found my son?" *My son*. The words would have felt foreign to him just hours ago, but now they came from his heart. He hadn't seen the little boy before, but he'd claimed him.

Dubridge just stared at him.

"What about the diamonds?" Josh asked. They would need to find them in order to negotiate for Henry and hopefully his grandmother's return as well.

"With Nikki Payne-Ecklund's assistance, we're going over all the security footage from the jewelry store," Dubridge said. "We'll figure out who took them."

"Nikki is good," Milek assured Josh. "And she isn't looking just at that security footage from the store but all the doorbell camera coverage in the area of the Crofts' home. She's a com-

puter genius. She'll be able to blow up the footage and see things
that other people might have missed."

Had Josh missed it? Had those diamonds been stolen during his night surveillance? Taken right out from under his nose,
just like other things had happened that he'd had no idea about
until it was too late?

"And we also know that Mrs. Croft might have been drugged,"
Dubridge added, his voice pitched low. "The techs discovered a
high dose of sleeping pills dissolved in the pot of coffee."

"My mother was drugged?" Natalie asked. She was standing
now, pacing like Josh while she stared at the cell she clutched.

"We don't know that she actually drank the coffee, or if she
did and had enough of it to affect her," Dubridge clarified.

"But how?" Natalie asked. "My dad and I were here this
morning. We both had the coffee, and we're fine."

"It must have been put in the pot after you left then," Dubridge said.

"Did anyone show up to the house as you were leaving?" Josh
asked. The detective had already taken a timeline from her, but
Josh had been so distracted and tired that he couldn't remember exactly what she'd said. He needed to focus now for his son.

Natalie shook her head. "No."

"We're checking with the neighbors and have requested all the
video footage off their video doorbells or other surveillance cameras," Dubridge said. "So far, we haven't seen another vehicle
pull into the driveway after yours left with you and your father
inside. But someone could have come through the alley that runs
behind all the houses on this street and the ones to the east of
it. We haven't found any cameras that point into that alley yet."

"So whoever it was must have walked through the alley and
the backyard and then driven off with them in Mrs. Croft's vehicle," Josh said. "Wouldn't they have to know her for her to let
them into the house so they could slip pills in the coffeepot?"

"Someone could have gotten inside when she was upstairs
with Henry, helping him get ready for school," Natalie said.

"Would she have left the door unlocked?" Josh asked. Because then anyone could have slipped inside.

Natalie shook her head. "No. Dad always locks it behind us when we leave. It's something he never forgets to do."

"Then if she didn't let them in, whoever got those pills in the coffee had a key," Josh said.

It had to be someone she knew. Or maybe Natalie was wrong about her dad. Maybe he had forgotten. Josh's paternal grandmother had had Alzheimer's. It was an insidious disease. It didn't make people forget just things, but people, too. Some even forgot who they were. So it wouldn't surprise him if her dad had forgotten to lock it.

But Natalie bristled with defensiveness. "You're blaming my family. While Dena isn't a fan of kids, she would never hurt Henry, and she would definitely never hurt our mother."

"What about your dad? Your brother-in-law?" Josh asked.

"My dad… He has early onset Alzheimer's," she said.

"So you don't know what he would do," Josh pointed out. He knew all too well. Grandma had done some wildly out of character things.

"My dad was with me," Natalie said. "The entire time. There's no way he had anything to do with this. And his medication is helping. He really remembers better now than he has for some time."

"What about your brother-in-law?" Josh asked. "Was he at the store when you got there?"

Natalie tensed now, her brow furrowed. "I don't know. I don't remember…"

Josh wasn't sure that he believed her. "Don't remember, or you don't want to consider it?" he challenged. "It's easier to blame me."

"I wasn't the one who blamed you," Natalie said. "Whoever wrote that note blamed you."

He didn't understand that, either. Why him? Just because he was the ex-con? The easy scapegoat? But why take his son if they didn't really believe he'd taken the diamonds? For some reason they must think that he had.

"None of this makes sense," he said with a groan of frustration.

"We were hired to improve the security in the store because

you were already having an issue with theft," Milek reminded Natalie. "Your insurance company was going to cancel your policy over it."

Natalie's face flushed.

"This sounds more and more like an inside job," Josh said. And he hoped like hell that it was. If it was someone from her family, they were less likely to hurt her mother and her son than a stranger would.

"Those could have been customer theft. They went missing from the showroom, not the vault, and nothing was as valuable as those diamonds," Natalie said. "And those were not taken until after we hired the Payne Protection Agency at the request of the insurance company."

The theft of the diamonds could still have been an inside job, but inside the Payne Protection Agency or the insurance company as well as Croft Custom Jewelry. Everyone inside the agency knew about the system and could probably get access to the codes. And the insurance company had insisted on knowing the security system and the measures taken to protect the inventory they insured. Someone from either one of those companies could have figured out how to bypass the system and steal those diamonds.

But why take his son?

His cell rang. It was probably Garek calling him since Milek hadn't picked up moments ago. But when Josh pulled his phone from his pocket, the screen was lit up with a blocked number requesting a video call. And a sudden chill gripped him.

Telemarketers didn't make video calls. This wasn't spam.

"I'm going to take this," he said.

Milek began, "If it's Garek..."

Josh swiped the screen to accept and immediately hit the record button. The screen of his phone went dark. Had they hung up on him? Had they realized he was recording the call?

"Hello?" he said into the speaker. "Is anyone there?"

His screen got a little lighter, light enough for him to see the pale face of a child. The boy blinked long, dark lashes and focused on the phone. "Daddy? Is that you?"

Josh froze, like his vocal cords were paralyzed. He didn't

know what to say, what to think… He could only feel the emotions that overwhelmed him.

Relief. The boy was alive.

Fear that he was being held somewhere and for something that Josh didn't have.

And love…

"Daddy?"

That was a word Natalie had never heard her son say before. She always told him that it was just the two of them, that some kids didn't have daddies and that was okay. They had Grandpa and Mimi and Auntie Dena and Uncle Timothy instead. And they made up for it.

Henry never argued with her, but she suspected he never totally accepted what she said and that he wanted a father like his friends had. And she could hear that in his voice, the hopefulness in that one word.

And the fear…

Josh just stood there, staring at the screen he held, while he was struck mute for some reason. From shock? Or the same fear that was coursing through her?

"Hey, honey," Natalie said. "Mommy's here." She pressed up against Josh's side so that she could see her little boy. His face took up the entire screen, but it was like shining a flashlight on it in the dark. He looked ghostly and pale. "Are you all right?"

He nodded. "Just hungry."

She would have been alarmed if he wasn't always hungry. But she still hated the fact that he was, that he was wanting for anything, and she wasn't able to give it to him.

"Mommy, I want to come home," Henry said, and there was a slight whine in his voice now, "but Daddy has to find me. Is that man my daddy?"

Josh cleared his throat as if he was trying to find the words. But they didn't come out.

So Natalie answered, "Yes, honey. This is your daddy. He's been gone for a long time. That's why you didn't meet him before this."

"He was hiding," Henry said. "So he knows how to play this game."

"I... I do know how to play," Josh said, his voice gruff.

"This person has different rules, though," Henry said.

"What are the rules, honey?" Natalie asked. She didn't know if the detective had put a tracker on Josh's phone, but she wanted to keep her son talking no matter what.

"Daddy needs to get something first to the person in the mask. And then they'll give Daddy a clue to where me and Mimi are, so he can find us."

"Is Mimi okay?" Natalie asked, her heart aching with fear for her mother and her son.

Henry's head bobbed. "She's sleeping."

Was that because of the drugs in the coffee? Her mother usually drank a couple cups in the morning. How high had the dosage been?

Or was she not sleeping at all?

"She's not hurt?" Natalie asked him.

"She fell and hit her head," Henry said, his voice shaking as a tear streaked down his cheek.

A moan coming out of the darkness reached the speaker on the phone that someone held in front of Natalie's little boy. And then she heard her mother's voice calling to him, "Henry? Henry?"

"I'm here, Mimi," he said. "We're going to be okay. Daddy will find us."

"Daddy has to find something else first," that weird raspy voice spoke from the darkness. "And when he has the diamonds that I want, we will make sure he finds you."

Then the screen went entirely black, the call ended.

She reached for the cell, to grab it out of Josh's hand, to somehow call Henry back, to keep him on the line, to keep watch over him to make sure he was safe.

But Josh held it out of her reach as he turned around and handed it to the detective. "I recorded it," he said. "But I want Nikki to go over the video."

The detective didn't argue. "She's already working with our crime-scene techs. She's had clearance for years. I'll get this to her."

"Can you use the video to find him?" Natalie asked hopefully.

The detective didn't quite meet her gaze. "We'll try. But the video was really dark. Hard to see anything but your son. And I didn't hear any background noise, either."

"So you don't think you'll find him from it," she concluded.

And again, the detective didn't argue with her.

"Then *you* have to find him," she told Josh. "You have to give back those damn diamonds!"

"I didn't take those damn diamonds," Josh said. "I didn't take anything now or…" He shook his head. "That doesn't matter. All that matters is getting Henry and your mother safely back home."

She waited for him to promise that he would do that, like he had earlier. But he didn't make that promise again.

And she suspected that he was telling the truth. He didn't have those diamonds. She actually wished that he did. Because if he didn't have the diamonds and couldn't find them, they might never get their son back. She should have been happy that she'd seen Henry, that he was alive and her mother was alive.

But for some reason she was even more afraid. Maybe because now it was all so real. Before she'd been able to hang onto her hope that this was just a mistake and that her mother and son were somewhere safe.

But they weren't safe. And her mother was hurt.

Natalie was hurting now, so much so that she couldn't stop the tears from coming. But just as he hadn't made her any promises, Josh didn't try to comfort her, either.

He was gone.

Penny's heart ached for Natalie, for her pain and fear. She closed her arms around the young woman and hugged her tightly. "Your son and your mother will be all right," she said. At least she hoped that was the case. "With River City PD and the Payne Protection Agency working on this together, they will find them." She'd personally witnessed the miracles they'd managed to pull off so many times, all the lives they'd saved.

But lives had also been lost.

Natalie drew in a deep breath and pulled back, her face tearstained and flushed. "I just don't understand."

Penny shrugged. "People do a lot of horrible things to each other for a lot of senseless reasons."

"Greed," Natalie said, her voice sharp. "This is about money, about diamonds."

"They'll find those, too," Penny said.

"You don't think Josh has them?" Natalie asked.

Penny shook her head. "I don't know Josh very well. But Amber Talsma, Milek's wife, is a dear friend and like a daughter-in-law to me just as Milek and Garek and Stacy are like children to me."

"What does Amber have to do with anything?" Natalie asked, and she pushed up her glasses to peer through her lenses at Penny, probably wondering if she'd lost her mind.

"She's the district attorney," Penny explained, and she felt a surge of pride in the young woman who truly was like another one of her children. "She met Josh when she was the assistant district attorney who reluctantly accepted his guilty plea."

"Reluctantly?" Natalie asked. "Why?"

"Because she didn't believe he did it," Penny said. "She always thought he was taking the blame for someone else, that he was sacrificing himself for whoever was really guilty. And a man who would do that, he will do anything to get his son back safe and well."

Anything.

Like sacrificing himself again...

Chapter Seven

Josh had the confirmation he'd been waiting for, that he'd needed so he could figure out his next move. His son was alive. Mrs. Croft was alive, too, but injured. He didn't have much time to find them, especially if he used any of that time to find the diamonds first. As exhausted as he was, he couldn't work out which was the right avenue to pursue.

The diamonds or his son.

The police and the Payne Protection Agencies were working both angles as well. They were already going over all the security footage from the jewelry store to try to find out when the diamonds disappeared. Dubridge had sent himself the recording of the video call from Josh's phone. Nikki and the crime-scene techs would work together to discover what they could from the video of his son.

But Josh had something else he needed to find out about that cell phone, the one that the Payne Protection Agency had issued to him.

Nobody else had that phone number. He had no friends left from before he'd gone to prison. His own father had stopped talking to him once he'd taken that plea bargain. Josh hadn't reached out to him or his only other remaining family since his release.

So how the hell had the kidnapper gotten the number?

Josh damn well intended to find out. He slipped away from

the Croft house in the long black SUV that Milek had left the keys in and drove straight to the old warehouse that had been converted into offices for the newest branch of the Payne Protection Agency.

There weren't people milling around the place like there had been at the opening celebration several weeks ago.

Josh believed Milek when he said that he'd rallied all of the Payne Protection Agencies to help find his son. So they must have been working out of the other branches. Nikki and her husband worked for Cooper Payne's franchise, so maybe they'd all gathered there.

Because it didn't look like anyone was here.

The main offices for Garek and Candace were empty and dark behind their glass walls. Milek had a desk, but it was out in the open area, like Josh's and the desks belonging to the other security agents. That was what Garek and Candace called them. They weren't bodyguards like the other Payne Protection Agencies. They were security specialists.

Josh snorted, and the sound echoed off the concrete floor and metal ceiling. Some security. One of their first jobs, and a bag of diamonds had been stolen and two people abducted.

What a freakin' mess...

A chair creaked, and then a blond head appeared above one of the cubicle walls. "Hey, Josh."

"Ivan."

The man wasn't an ex-con like Josh and some of the others, but that might have just been because he'd never been caught. His uncle, Viktor Chekov, had nearly gotten away with all his crimes until Garek and Candace finally got him where he belonged, behind bars for the rest of his miserable life. Or maybe Ivan's crimes had been committed in his youth, like the Kozminski brothers, and so his juvenile records had been sealed or expunged.

"Did they get ahold of you?" Ivan asked.

Josh tensed. "Who?"

"The person who called for you," he said. "I couldn't tell if it was a man or a woman. And the number was blocked, but they said it was urgent and that you would want the call."

"So you gave them my number?" Josh asked.

Ivan nodded. "What? Shouldn't I have done that?"

In his mind, Josh could see his little boy's pale face, tears trailing down his cheeks. His long lashes blinking furiously as he fought the tears, as he tried so hard to be brave. And he could hear the echo of that little voice calling him Daddy.

"No, I'm glad you did," Josh said, his own voice gruff with the emotion rushing up to choke him.

Ivan came around the low glass walls of the cubicle. He was a big man, bigger than Josh, with broad shoulders and the arms of a boxer. He had the slightly crooked nose of one, too, but not as crooked as one of the other specialists, Blade Sparks, who had actually been a boxer.

"I also contacted Nikki Payne, so she'd be ready to do her magic with your phone to hopefully track down the caller," Ivan assured him. "Milek gave us all the heads-up, so I know about the break-in at your place and about the diamonds and the kid. I had a feeling that was *the* call."

"It was," Josh said, emotion choking him. It might have been the most important call he'd ever taken, especially if Nikki was able to track down the caller. And if she wasn't, maybe she and the River City PD could get something off his recording of the call to lead them to where the little boy and his grandmother were being held.

"Are *you* all right?" Ivan asked. He was a giant of man, but until this moment of kindness, Josh hadn't considered that he might be a gentle giant.

Josh had come to the office to question his coworkers because he wanted someone to blame, someone to have stolen those diamonds or taken his son, so that he could get the little boy back. "Are you the only one here?" he asked.

Ivan nodded. "A few of the others have been in and out. We're all working."

While the agency was new, it was already busy with new clients. Many of which were due to that insurance company that had urged its clients to increase security given the recent spate of losses.

"We're working with the other branches of Payne Protection, doing everything we can to try to find the kid and the diamonds," Ivan assured him. "I have the shift at this office in case something comes through here again, like that call, or something else."

Like what? Another note? More ransom demands? Or something worse… Like a finger or an ear? Wasn't that what kidnappers sometimes sent to whoever they were trying to get ransom from?

"We got this, so you don't have to worry," Ivan said. "You can get some rest. You had the night shift. If you need someplace to stay because yours is a crime scene, you're welcome to crash at my house." He reached into his pocket as if reaching for his keys.

"No," Josh said. "I'm not going to be able to sleep until…" Until he found his son.

"You want to find who broke into your place and left that weird note," Ivan finished for him. "I get that. But it sounds like it was a mistake. You didn't take the diamonds."

"No, I didn't," Josh said. But why was Ivan so certain of that? "How do you know that?" Had Ivan taken them? Josh didn't know his coworkers very well yet, mostly because he wasn't sure he wanted to get to know them. He'd spent the last five years trying to stay uninvolved and away from the fray.

The taller man shrugged those broad shoulders. "I grew up around good men and bad men. I got pretty good at being able to tell the difference."

If only Natalie could tell the difference…

If only she believed that Josh was a good man.

But she still suspected he might have taken those damn diamonds, that he was to blame for their son being abducted.

"You think I'm a good man. What do you think about the others?" Josh asked. "Because all of this feels like an inside job…"

"The diamonds?"

"And my son," Josh said. "Someone took my son."

Ivan reached out then and grasped his shoulder like Milek had earlier today. "I'm sorry, man. I heard there was mention of him in the note, but I didn't even know you had a son."

"I didn't, either," Josh admitted. "I had no idea my fiancée was pregnant when I went to prison. So I don't understand how someone else did."

"The mother," Ivan said.

Natalie might have told someone besides her mom and sister. But she hadn't taken their son. She clearly loved the little boy too much to put him through the fear he was feeling now. And the boy was hungry.

Josh's own empty stomach clenched at the thought. He should have taken over that call, he should have made more demands when he had the chance. But he'd been so struck over seeing his son for the first time that it was like he'd been paralyzed.

"She didn't have anything to do with taking him," Josh said with certainty.

"What about the diamonds?" Ivan asked.

Josh tensed. He would have automatically said no if not for Sylvie. Since his judgment of his sister had been so off, maybe it was off about Natalie, too, because he certainly had never suspected that Sylvie was a thief.

But he hadn't really known his younger half sister at all or what was going on in her life. He was only four years older than her, but his father had been granted full custody of him, so he hadn't often seen Sylvie while they were growing up. They hadn't talked much while he'd been in college, and they hadn't talked at all when he'd been in prison.

He had no idea what she was doing now. Despite her promise to him to get away and start a new life, she could have been lying to him. She could still be stealing.

The office door opened, and Milek walked in, but he wasn't alone. The other security experts from this franchise were with him. Blade Sparks and Viktor Lagransky. Like Ivan, they were big and burly with scars and tattoos. They looked more like henchmen than employees.

Were they also suspects?

"We're here," Milek said. He must have called one of them to pick him up from the Croft house where Josh had left him. But he didn't sound angry with Josh at all. He sounded supportive when he added, "And we're going to do everything we can to get your son back."

But would it be enough?

And were they all working to help him? Or had one of them taken the diamonds? Blade, Viktor and Ivan were all like Josh; they had a past they were trying to leave behind them. But what if that wasn't possible?

What if one of them wasn't able to escape from their former life? What if that was what happened with Sylvie, too?

Josh needed to find his younger sister.

But the person he wanted more than anything to find was his son.

Josh was gone. Natalie wasn't even sure how he'd left her house since her SUV was still there. Currently, she was riding with Chief Lynch in a River City PD SUV back to Croft Custom Jewelry.

"The techs processing the jewelry store said your father is very upset," the chief said, as if warning her as he pulled his vehicle into the alley behind the place.

Guilt weighed heavily on her. Concern for Henry had taken over earlier, and she hadn't thought about how her father would feel about all of this, how confused and perhaps terrified he would be.

And Timothy didn't handle him as well as she did. Even before her dad had gotten Alzheimer's, he hadn't had the best relationship with his only son-in-law. She wasn't sure why because she thought they were quite a bit alike. They handled their clients with charm and their wives the same way. Maybe that was the problem, though; they were too much alike.

While Dena had found a man to marry who was like their dad, Natalie had gone in the opposite direction. Even before she learned Josh was a liar and a thief, she'd known he was different from her dad. Back then, she'd thought he was straightforward and honest, like she was. She'd believed he would always tell her the truth, no matter what it was. Like if she overcooked the chicken or if he hated a movie she loved or if an outfit was unflattering...

But those things were so petty and unimportant compared to the big things, the things that had sent him to prison.

But was Mrs. Payne-Lynch right? Was Josh really innocent? But why plead guilty? Why go to prison for something he hadn't done? Who could he have been trying to protect?

Certainly not Natalie. He'd nearly destroyed her. If not for Henry, she wasn't sure how she would have ever found happiness again.

"What do you know about Josh Stafford?" she asked the chief.

"I know he's determined to find your son," he said.

"What about the diamonds?" she asked. "Do you think he took them?"

The chief sighed. "I don't know, Ms. Croft. I don't know him personally. I haven't even lived in River City all that long. I was a bureau chief in Chicago."

With the FBI.

She knew Woodrow Lynch's history. And that should have made her feel better, confident that he would find her child, but she'd learned to trust no one after Josh broke her heart. So she really couldn't trust Josh, especially now that he'd disappeared.

Apparently, he wasn't the only one. When she glanced around the alley, she noticed that Timothy's car was gone, too. "My brother-in-law isn't here?" she asked.

"We had to close down the store to check the inventory and process the scene," the chief said. "He may have left because of that. He could be on the way to your house or at his. I know Detective Dubridge spoke to him before he left."

Their salesperson, Hannah, was gone as well. Her moped wasn't here. But that made sense. If the store wasn't open to the public, she had no reason to stay. No sales to make.

But Timothy would have had to help with the inventory. Despite her father realizing that the diamonds were missing earlier today, he wouldn't have been able to remember everything else that they had and didn't have since so many things had disappeared before those diamonds.

"I think Dubridge let him leave because he was trying to find your sister," the chief remarked.

"That's good," Natalie said.

While Dena wasn't as close to them as Natalie and her mother would like, she did love them and Henry. So she would want to know what was going on. Even though they weren't much alike, they were still sisters, so Natalie should have tried harder to find her before now, to tell her what was going on.

If only she knew herself what that was... Why the diamonds, her son and her mother were all gone. And now Josh, too.

Milek had brought in the others to help, but at the moment, Josh was just interrogating all of them, asking them where they'd been, what they knew about the jewelry store and the diamonds and about him.

"We're here to find your kid," Viktor Lagransky said. "Not be interrogated, Stafford."

"Yeah, man," Blade Sparks said.

He was big, like Ivan Chekov, and had once been a professional boxer. While Ivan had a juvenile record for things he'd had to do as a kid in order to survive, much like Milek, the crime Blade had committed and been imprisoned for had been more of an accident. The guy hadn't realized his own strength until it was too late.

"This isn't an interrogation," Milek assured them all.

Blade snorted. "Yeah, right."

"Why shouldn't it be?" Josh asked. "Who else knew that security system well enough to get into the vault and steal those diamonds?"

"Everybody who works at Croft Custom Jewelry," Ivan replied.

The others nodded.

"The CEO of the insurance company figures that recent spate of thefts were inside jobs," Milek said. "But he isn't sure if it's the inside of his company or of the ones he insures. That's what we're supposed to find out—who's responsible, while also protecting the assets."

But the diamonds had been stolen along with a child and his grandmother. So Josh was justified in questioning his coworkers. Milek needed to question them, too.

He also needed to call Garek and Candace since they'd handled the initial interactions with the insurance company CEO and the owners of the businesses they were protecting. Garek and Candace would have to return early from their trip. But until they were back, he was in charge.

"We all need to provide our whereabouts for today," Milek said.

"Today?" Ivan asked. "But how do you know when the diamonds were stolen?"

"I don't," Milek said. "But we know when the boy was taken, and he is our priority."

"We need to find the diamonds, too," Josh said.

Milek sucked in a breath, surprised that the boy's father didn't agree with him.

"The kidnapper wants them," Josh said. "Exchanging them for my son might be my only way to get him and his grandmother away from whoever is holding them hostage."

Hostage security was their top priority then.

"We'll figure this out," Milek said. They had to. Lives were at stake. He bypassed his desk and headed toward Garek's office. He had to call his brother, and he didn't want everyone else to hear him. He already suspected they didn't respect him like they did Garek and Candace.

But Josh followed him through the door. "Thank you."

"For what?" Milek hadn't done nearly enough, not yet, because the boy was still missing.

"For making them provide their alibis and for helping me," Josh said.

"I will personally check all those alibis, too," Milek assured him. "You can get some rest."

With dark circles rimming his eyes, Josh looked like he was about to drop. But he shook his head. "I won't be able to sleep or eat or do anything until Henry is found."

Milek sighed. "I know what you're feeling. I missed years of my son's life. I didn't learn about him until I thought he and Amber were dead."

Josh sucked in a breath. "Oh my God."

"It worked out for me," Milek reminded him. "Their deaths were faked, and they were put into witness protection. Eventually we found out who was after her, and she was able to come back to life with our child."

Josh just stared at him.

"It all worked out," Milek said. "And it will all work out for you, too." It had to. He couldn't consider anything else. It was bad enough they'd lost those damn diamonds. They couldn't lose the child and his grandmother, too.

"This isn't a cover or a ruse," Josh said. "That little boy and his grandmother are in danger. Because of me."

"You didn't take the diamonds," Milek said. Unless Josh had been lying. Unless Amber was wrong about him. But she was rarely, if ever, wrong. "So this isn't your fault."

As if refusing to be absolved, Josh shook his head. "I made a big mistake."

"Everybody makes mistakes," Milek said. He'd made more than his own share. "It's never too late to fix them or at least make up for them."

"It will be too late if something happens to my son."

Milek couldn't argue with him about that. All he could do was try to help him rescue the boy. No matter what he had to do, just as little Henry's father was no doubt prepared to do anything to protect him and get him safely back.

Chapter Eight

Five years ago, Josh had accepted the blame for a crime he hadn't committed in order to protect the people he loved. His sister. Natalie. Even his mother...

Even though he would do the same thing all over again, he also realized there were consequences because of what he'd done. Everyone believed now that he was a criminal. That was why the person who'd taken his son believed that he had those damn diamonds. That was why they'd kidnapped his son and Marilyn Croft.

Was one of Josh's coworkers responsible for the kidnapping or for the theft?

They had all provided alibis for around the time his son must have been abducted, but Josh didn't know if they were actually telling the truth about where they'd been. Milek promised he would verify all of them. While Josh didn't trust his coworkers, he did trust his boss. Well, not all of his bosses, since the timing of Garek and Candace's getaway seemed suspicious to him.

But Josh trusted Milek. Milek really could relate to the hell that he was going through, that Natalie was going through right now, not knowing where their son was.

Natalie...

Josh needed to see her again, to make sure that she was all right. With Milek's permission this time, he borrowed another vehicle, one of the long black SUVs the Payne Protection Agency leased, and drove toward Croft Custom Jewelry. Milek had told Josh that Chief Lynch had dropped her off at the jewelry store where her father had been left alone with the crime-scene techs processing the place. Lynch had been about to have one of his officers drop her SUV at the store, but Josh had said he would take care of her and her father.

He'd thought he was taking care of her five years ago when he'd accepted the plea bargain, when he'd lied to her. He'd been trying to keep her safe. But he hadn't known then that she was pregnant with their son. Knowing that wouldn't have made any difference, though. He probably would have been even more determined to protect her. She'd had her family and her friends and her career and her strength.

While Sylvie…

She hadn't had anyone. She'd never had anyone but him. But protecting her and Natalie had cost him so much. It had cost him Natalie. And his son. And his freedom.

And now…

All of this.

Like Josh told Milek, it was his fault. If only he'd known what was going on with Sylvie, if only he'd been less self-involved, he might have been able to help her before it got too bad. Before it put her and him and Natalie all in danger. Now Natalie and their son had once again become collateral damage of their relationship with him. He wouldn't blame her for hating him.

He hated himself for putting his son in danger. The only way he could make it up to Natalie for everything he'd put her through was to find their son. He needed her help to do that, though, because he needed to figure out when the damn diamonds went missing. Even if none of his coworkers had taken Henry and Marilyn Croft, that didn't mean they hadn't taken the diamonds. In fact, he would sooner believe one of them had committed theft than a kidnapping.

But was he being as unfair to them as whoever had taken Henry was being to him? Was he assuming just because someone had once been a thief that they still were?

Thinking of thieves made him think of Sylvie.

What if it was true of her? What if she was still a thief? He had to find her. He had to know.

But first he had to make sure that Natalie was okay. And her dad. And he had to try to pinpoint when the diamonds were stolen.

He drove into the alley where there were no vehicles. With only one light burning dimly in the shadows between the buildings that lined it, the alley was dark and empty. Josh wasn't sure anyone was still at the store. Maybe she'd called a cab for her and her dad.

He could totally understand her not wanting to stay here, for wanting to get out and look for their son like Josh wanted to look for him. But first he had to figure out where to look.

He parked near the back door. He'd walked this alley so many times over the past few weeks, just like he'd walked around out front. His presence was meant to deter late-night robbers, and it must have worked because he had never seen anyone lingering anywhere around the building after hours.

He doubted the theft had happened then, that he'd missed the thief. But if the theft had happened in broad daylight and while the store was open, then this thief was bold.

Daylight was beginning to slip away now as the afternoon turned into evening, and that came early here in spring in western Michigan.

He jumped out of the SUV and headed toward the back door. Before he could even knock, it opened to Natalie's anxious face. She must have seen him on the surveillance camera.

"Did you find him?" she asked, her voice a low whisper. "Did you find Henry and my mother?"

God, he wished he could say yes. But guilt and regret choked him, and he could only shake his head.

"The diamonds?" she asked.

A short while ago, she accused him of taking them. Did she have her doubts now? Did she believe him?

"Who is that, Natalie?" a voice called out. "Is that your mother?"

"No, Dad, it's not Mom."

Josh lowered his voice now. "Did you tell him that they've been taken?"

Tears shimmered in her green eyes. "I don't know how to…"

He could relate to that. He hadn't been sure how or even what to tell Natalie all those years ago. If he'd told her the truth, he knew there was no way she would have let him go to prison for something he hadn't done. She would have gone to the assistant district attorney, the judge, even the press. But he'd already been threatened into pleading guilty or people would be hurt. And if anyone had messed up that plea deal, they would be hurt, too.

He couldn't have handled being responsible for Natalie getting hurt. But then he'd hurt her himself. It was the only way he'd known how to keep her safe, though. Because she would have done whatever necessary to protect him. She'd loved him back then. He had no doubt about that.

Natalie loved loyally and completely and fiercely.

He'd never had anyone love him the way she had…except his sister.

Sylvie.

And having to choose between them had nearly destroyed him. But in the end, he'd done what he'd had to in order to protect them both. If doing what he had cost him his son, he would be destroyed for certain.

The look on Josh's handsome face drew Natlie toward him. He looked so…shattered. She stepped closer to him and started reaching out her hand toward his face, to touch it, to comfort him. Because he clearly needed it as much as she did.

"Natalie!"

Her father's shout startled her, making her jump. She was torn between wanting to comfort Josh and wanting to comfort her dad.

He'd been so upset since the chief had dropped her off earlier, and she'd found him alone except for one of the crime-scene techs that had remained. The red-haired woman, named Wendy, had been concerned that Claus might hurt himself.

He would never do that. Natalie had no doubts about that.

Sometimes he got frustrated when he couldn't remember something, but he never got violent.

The doctor had warned them that it could happen, though. That he'd seen the sweetest, most loving grandmothers become physically combative. And maybe that would happen one day with her father, too.

But it hadn't happened yet.

He'd been doing so well until today, until all of the upheaval. She rushed back inside, though, just to make certain that he was all right.

"Natalie, what is this mess?" her father asked, pointing at the fingerprint dust that was all over the backroom. "Your mother is going to be so angry when she sees this in her workroom." It hadn't been her workroom for years, though. "We have to clean it up. Who made this mess? Your sister? She doesn't love the store like we do."

Natalie suspected her sister was jealous of the store or at least the time and attention their parents had given it, just like she seemed to be jealous of the time and attention they gave Natalie and Henry. Natalie had been trying to call Dena and Timothy both since she'd returned to the store, but neither of them was picking up.

Hopefully Timothy had found his wife by now, and Dena knew that their mother and Henry were missing. Maybe that was why she wasn't accepting Natalie's calls because she blamed her for this, because Natalie was the one who'd brought Josh into their lives. However briefly and however long ago, he still had an effect on them.

"We'll clean it up tomorrow, Daddy," Natalie assured him. "Mom will understand. She won't want us to stay late."

He nodded. "Yes. Yes. Marilyn is an angel. My angel. But my angel has a temper," he said with a chuckle. And he glanced at the Rolex watch on his wrist. "It's getting close to dinnertime. We better hurry home, or she might throw our supper out."

Tears burned Natalie's eyes, and she closed them to hold them in. She couldn't cry in front of him, she couldn't let him see how upset she was.

She couldn't tell him about Mom.

Not now.

Wasn't it getting close to what the doctor called *sundowners*? When the sun went down, Dad was the most confused. It was when he struggled to remember things and people. He hadn't forgotten any of them yet, though. He knew his family, and he knew how much he loved and appreciated them all.

Especially her mother.

"Daddy, I don't know how to tell you..." She had no idea how to broach this horror with him.

"Who is this?" he asked, staring over her shoulder.

She'd nearly forgotten Josh. But he was here, in the backroom with them now.

"Did you make this mess?" Claus asked him sternly.

"I didn't do this, sir," Josh replied, gesturing at that dust all over, at all the markings the techs had left behind. "But I do feel responsible."

Her heart jerked. Had he taken the diamonds? She'd been so hopeful that he hadn't, that he was innocent. Not just now but all those years ago like Penny Payne-Lynch had tried to convince her. But would anyone willingly go to prison for something they hadn't done? And if he'd done it to protect someone, who was it?

"How do you mean you're responsible, son?" Claus asked, and his brow furrowed. "You look so familiar to me. Henry?"

Their son all grown up would look exactly like his father. "Henry is still a little boy, Daddy," Natalie said. "But this is his father."

Her father's brow creased more, and he rubbed his temples. "I... I'm sorry. Sometimes I get so confused..." He gazed around the backroom. "Like now... I just want to go home. Natalie, please take me home."

Her heart lurched. God, she wanted so badly to take him home. But like the store, it was a crime scene, too. Unlike the store, she wasn't sure it had been cleared yet. Only a theft had happened at the store, while no one was certain what had happened at the house. An abduction but there had been blood, too. "Daddy, I don't know how to tell you..."

"Your wife and Henry are on that overnight trip with the school," Josh said.

Natalie turned toward him, shocked that he'd come up with a lie so quickly. Because of how easily he had, she wondered if she would ever be able to trust him. But then she remembered that he'd once lived with a grandmother who'd had dementia. Maybe he'd had reason to lie like this before. Maybe it was how he'd dealt with her. Regardless, she asked, "Wh-what are you doing?"

"Just reminding your dad that Mrs. Croft isn't home tonight, and the house is being fumigated," Josh continued his string of lies. "So we need to bring you to your daughter Dena's house, Mr. Croft."

Her father focused on Natalie, as if he wasn't sure he should believe Josh, either. But she realized that this was probably for the best. That, in fact, it was kinder to lie to her father than to tell him the truth, which would undoubtedly devastate him.

Was that what Josh had thought he'd been doing all those years ago? Being kind when he actually broke her heart?

She drew a breath, forcing down that old pain and resentment. Then she smiled and nodded at her father. "Remember, Daddy?"

Probably because he was too proud to admit he didn't have any idea what they were talking about, her father nodded, but his forehead was still all deep furrows. "What about you, honey? Where are you staying?"

She smiled with amusement and appreciation that he was sharp enough to remember that she wouldn't feel comfortable in Dena's house, that she would rather stay with one of her friends instead of feeling like the inconvenience Dena had made her feel since they were kids.

"She's staying with me," Josh said, "until Henry comes back."

Natalie's pulse quickened. Did he mean that? Not that she would actually agree to stay with him. She wasn't sure where she was going to go. Maybe she would just hang out at the police department until they found her son. Maybe her constant presence would compel them to work around the clock until her little boy and her mother were rescued.

"And who are you?" her father asked again.

"Josh Stafford." He held out his hand. "Henry's father."

Her dad extended his hand to shake, then he saw the fingerprint dust on his skin. "Oh my. I'm sorry. I need to clean up." Still fastidious about his appearance, he rushed off toward the bathroom.

She stared after him, concerned but also grateful for the reprieve. The tears that had been stinging her eyes slipped free now, sliding down her face beneath her glasses.

"Oh, Natalie," Josh said, and he reached for her.

She stepped back, though, knowing that if he touched her, she would lose it. She would dissolve into helpless sobs. And she didn't want to feel any more helpless than she already felt right now. "I'm okay."

"Bullshit."

"Yes," she admitted. "But you would know. You spew lies like they're easier to tell than the truth."

"To a person with dementia, it's sometimes better to lie than to upset them, especially in a situation like this," Josh said, confirming that he'd lied to her father out of kindness. "My dad and I always met my grandmother where she was instead of trying to correct her or make her remember because that just upset her more. As Dad said…" there was a strange wistfulness to his voice "…we had to meet her in her world wherever it was at the time. Her childhood, her adolescence or some dream she'd had that seemed so real to her."

Natalie remembered him telling her that in the past, too, and his patience with his grandmother was another reason she'd fallen for him. She'd thought he was such a good man then. And part of her, her heart, was beginning to believe that he still was.

"My dad is usually better than this," she said. "It's just been a confusing day for him."

Josh sighed and touched his own head, mussing up his thick brown hair. "Not just for him."

She couldn't imagine how shocked he'd been when he found that note in his apartment. But she couldn't bring herself to apologize to him, not after what he'd put her through. No matter what his reason was or his guilt, he'd hurt her more than anyone else ever had. Until now…until someone had taken her son and her mother.

"We should get your dad out of here," Josh said. "And we can't bring him back to your house."

She nodded. "I know."

"Call your sister and let her know we're bringing him to her," he said.

"She wasn't picking up earlier when I tried calling." But she pulled out her cell phone and gasped when she saw that the screen was dark. The battery had completely run down. "I—I can't..."

"Call her from the store phone," he suggested.

"I tried that earlier, too. I called Dena and Timothy both from my cell and from this phone."

"And neither of them picked up?" he asked, his dark eyes narrowing slightly.

She nodded. "I don't know what's going on with her and Timothy," she said in a whisper. "When the chief dropped me off, Dad was alone with a crime tech. Timothy just left him here. Even Hannah was gone."

Josh flinched. "I'm sorry. That must have been so hard for him to have no one here that he recognized."

Again Natalie's heart reacted to his kindness and understanding, warming. Josh had only been around her father a short while, but he understood more than her brother-in-law did about how leaving her father alone would affect him. But then Josh had experience dealing with a loved one with dementia.

She would rather deal with that, though, than the suspicions plaguing her now. Not about Josh this time, but about her own family.

"I don't know where they are or what they're really capable of," she whispered. "My sister or Timothy..." Or even Hannah.

But the saleswoman was inconsequential. She didn't have access to the vault. She couldn't have taken the diamonds. But Timothy...

"I'm afraid to find out what's really going on around here," Natalie admitted. "More than those diamonds have gone missing."

"That was why your insurance company wanted you to hire us," Josh said.

Of course he knew about that. And he probably knew that those thefts had been happening for a while.

"When were you released?" she asked.

"Eight weeks ago," he said.

The thefts and losses had happened before then. So he couldn't have taken those things and really hadn't taken the diamonds.

Instead of being relieved that he wasn't the thief she'd thought he was, she was scared. Since he didn't have the diamonds, how the hell were they going to get their son back?

After that phone call with his daddy, the person in the mask had given Henry and Mimi food. So Henry wasn't hungry anymore. He'd eaten a bunch of the pizza. It was all meat and no veggie, just like he liked. Whoever was wearing that mask knew what he liked.

It had to be someone he knew who was playing a game with him and his daddy and mommy.

They'd brought pop, too. His favorite flavor, grape soda. And a lamp so it wasn't so dark anymore.

And they had an air mattress and blankets now, too. So they had somewhere to lie down that wasn't so cold and hard anymore. Mimi was lying on the bed, but she wasn't sleeping. She looked a little confused, though, like Grandpa looked when it got dark out.

Henry scooted closer to her and snuggled up against her. She was shaking a little. But she shouldn't have been cold. He wasn't cold anymore. And he wasn't even as scared as he'd been before. He'd seen his daddy and talked to Mommy.

"We'll be okay, Mimi," he told her, petting her hair that was still a little sticky. "My daddy is going to find us. He just has to find something else first for the person in the mask."

"What?" she asked in a whisper, like she was afraid that person was out there listening to them.

But Henry knew they were gone. He'd heard the footsteps walking away and then that engine had faded away again. "They're not here anymore," he assured her. "They drove off. I heard the car."

"What do they want?" Mimi asked.

"Diamonds," he reminded her of what the person said, like

sometimes he had to remind Grandpa. And then he doubted himself for a second.

Diamonds was the word that the person had used, wasn't it? He'd heard it before when Mommy and Grandpa and Mimi talked about work. They talked about diamonds and rubies and emeralds and different colors of gold. He knew it was all worth a lot of money, but diamonds were worth the most.

He and Mimi must be worth the most, too, if somebody wanted diamonds for them. And if they were worth the most, that person wouldn't hurt them. Not if they wanted the diamonds...

"Henry, we have to figure out how to get out of here," Mimi said, but she sounded a little sleepy again. And she didn't move.

"Don't worry, Mimi," he said. "Daddy will find us."

He'd seen him. For the first time in his life. And he could see how much he looked like him. They had the same brown eyes and hair.

But Daddy had looked worried.

And Mommy...

She had sounded scared, like Mimi did. And now that pizza and pop flipped around a little bit inside his tummy as Henry felt scared again, too.

Wasn't this just all a game? It was a stupid game, though. Because even the air mattress and the lamp didn't make this place anywhere near as nice as his bedroom.

And Mommy and Daddy weren't here, either. He wanted Mommy, but now he wanted Daddy, too. He wanted him to play the game and win.

Henry was really good at games. Mommy wasn't because she always lost. So maybe being good at games was something he got from his daddy, like his eyes and his hair.

Daddy had to be good at games because he had to win. He had to find them.

Chapter Nine

Josh glanced into the rearview mirror, checking on Natalie who sat in the back seat next to her father. She held his hand, but Josh didn't know if she was comforting her dad or seeking comfort. Or maybe both. Because they both needed to be comforted right now.

Josh did as well, but he'd learned five years ago to stop looking for it. All he could do now was focus on finding Henry and the diamonds.

Before her dad returned from the bathroom, Natalie had shared with Josh when the diamonds must have gone missing. She hadn't checked for them the day before, but she remembered them being in the vault the day before that, on Wednesday. So sometime between Wednesday afternoon and Friday morning, they'd gone missing.

And, albeit reluctantly, she'd admitted that she was beginning to share his suspicions about it being an inside job. But which job? Stealing the diamonds? Or abducting their son? Or both?

The kidnapper had to be someone close to Natalie in order for them to know that her son was Josh's, because he doubted anyone he knew was aware of Henry. Josh hadn't even been aware that he had a son. But for some reason the kidnapper must have believed he knew.

"Here," Natalie said, her voice a little sharp but it sounded more like nerves than irritation with him. "Turn right here. This is their street."

"Whose?" Claus asked. "Where are we, Natalie? And who is our driver?"

"Josh, Mr. Croft," Josh reminded the older man, and he glanced in the rearview to see Claus's gray-haired head bob in acknowledgment.

"Yes, yes, Henry's father," the older man said. "Where is Henry?"

"With Mom," Natalie said. "On that overnight trip for school, remember?" Despite rebuking Josh for lying, she must have decided that it was the better alternative to upsetting her father.

Claus nodded again, like he remembered, but there was clearly confusion in his blue eyes. Josh flashed back to his grandmother, to that cloudy look of confusion that had so often been in her dark eyes.

"Timothy and Dena's house is at the end of the street," Natalie said, pointing toward a modern house that was all windows and concrete.

Josh pulled into the wide driveway and studied the structure. He didn't like it, but given the neighborhood and the design, the thing must have cost a lot. "This wasn't where they lived before." He remembered them living in a modest house five years ago.

Natalie sighed. "No. Timothy's parents passed away, and they inherited some money."

"That's what they told you?" he asked. "I should have Milek check on that." Just before he'd left the Payne Protection Agency, Josh had asked his boss to check on something else for him besides those alibis.

Sylvie.

"I went to his parents' funerals," Natalie said.

"I meant the inheritance," Josh explained.

She shook her head as if trying to clear it of confusion. "Oh, I understand what you mean…" Had her brother-in-law really inherited money, or had they stolen it? "I just can't believe they would do that to our family," she murmured.

"Do what?" Claus asked. "What are the two of you talking about?"

"Nothing, Dad," she said. "We're at Dena and Timothy's."

"Why?"

"You're staying here tonight, remember?"

He glanced around. "Where's my bag? Your mother would have packed me an overnight bag."

Behind the lenses of her glasses, tears sparkled in Natalie's eyes, but she smiled. "I'm sure your things are already here."

Claus was the same size as his son-in-law, so he would be able to wear his clothes. But what he was going to wear was the least of Josh and Natalie's concerns about her father. Claus was clearly very dependent on his wife. If he learned she was missing...

And hurt...

Josh's stomach churned with concern for her. Mrs. Croft had to be okay. Because just as she clearly took care of her husband, she was hopefully taking care of her grandson right now. Comforting Henry like Natalie was comforting her father. Although during that video call, it had seemed the other way around, like Henry was comforting his Mimi.

He was a sweet little boy.

Josh had to close his eyes against a sudden rush of tears of his own as yearning overwhelmed him. He wanted his son to be safe and sound. He wanted to meet the little boy, to hold him...

"Are you okay?" Claus asked, and his hand settled on Josh's shoulder.

He smiled. "Yes."

"We better get you inside, Dad," Natalie said. "Dena will be cross if you're late for dinner."

The older man snorted. "Your sister doesn't cook." He chuckled. "But she will be mad if her takeout dinner got cold waiting for me." He opened the back door.

And Josh opened the front.

Natalie hopped out on his side and asked, "What are you doing?"

"I'm going inside with you," he said.

She shook her head. "No. That's a bad idea."

He shook his head now. "Nothing's a bad idea if it gets us closer to the truth."

She narrowed her eyes and stared at him. "What do you know about the truth?" she asked in a soft whisper.

He knew then that no matter what, she would never forgive him and never trust him again.

Part of him had already known that, which was why he'd never reached out to her during those years in prison. As well as keeping her safe, he had also wanted her to move on and be happy. And after he was out, he purposely hadn't looked her up. He really hadn't wanted to know what he'd lost.

But now that he knew...

He had that look again, the one he'd had in the alley behind the store. That shattered look that made Natalie want to reach out to him.

But just like then, her father called out, "Are you two coming?"

He hadn't rung the bell yet. Maybe he couldn't find it. The place was so stark and modern that it didn't have anything like a regular doorbell. It just had a camera style one, so Dena should have already opened the door.

If she was home...

Natalie had tried once again to call Dena and Timothy from the store, but nobody had accepted her calls. Her stomach pitched with the dread and doubts she'd already been feeling. They intensified now.

But the door finally opened behind her father, startling him. "Claus," Timothy greeted his father-in-law. He'd never called him Dad. "What are you doing here?"

"What do you mean?" Natalie asked. "Don't you know what's happened?" Surely the detective had tracked down her sister and brother-in-law by now and told them that Henry and her mother had been kidnapped.

"Of course I know about the theft at the store," Timothy said. He pointed over her father's shoulder to Josh. "The one he pulled off. Why would you bring him here, Nat?"

She hated when he called her Nat, just like he hated if anyone called him Tim. But she ignored it. "Where's my sister?"

He sighed. "I just got home and heard the shower running. I assume it was her since we're the only ones who live here."

"You haven't talked to her? She doesn't know?" Natalie asked. "And why the hell weren't either of you picking up your phones?"

He pulled his cell from his pocket, and his face flushed. "I must've turned it off."

"I tried calling Dena, too, and she wasn't picking up. Where was she?" Natalie asked. "And what does she know? What did you tell her?"

He shook his head. "I didn't tell her anything. I haven't talked to her. I don't know what she knows. Like I said, she must be in the shower, and I just got home."

"You just got home from where?" Josh asked the question. "You weren't at the store."

"There was no reason for me to stay after I gave the police the inventory of things that we're supposed to have," Timothy said, his tone condescending.

"You heard about that note that was left at my apartment," Josh said. "You knew that…" He glanced at her father, who was looking from one to another of them like he was watching a television show.

Josh had more consideration for her father than his son-in-law was currently showing, than Timothy had probably ever showed.

"I knew that was bullshit," Timothy finished for him. "Some sick game you're playing to cover up the theft."

"Theft?" her father said. "What's going on?"

"Nothing, Dad," Natalie said. Then she turned on Timothy. "Go get Dena. That note wasn't a lie. The diamonds aren't the only things that were taken."

Timothy stumbled back, inside the open door. Natalie followed him inside. She had to reach back to pull her father through the door, though. He might have resisted if not for Josh helping guide him into the foyer which was concrete and marble. The house looked more like a gallery than a home.

All the color had drained from Timothy's usually flushed face. "What…what do you mean?"

"She means that him getting out of prison is already destroying this family!" Dena said as she came down the stairs. She was dressed in some kind of silky jumpsuit that had deep wrinkles in it. Her pale blond hair was bone-dry and her makeup was a little smeared as if she'd been wearing it for a while. Had Timothy lied about the shower?

"You know then?" Natalie asked her sister.

Dena nodded, and her throat moved as if she was struggling to swallow. "A police car pulled me over, and I was taken in for questioning like a common criminal." She pointed at Josh. "Like him. You brought this on yourself, Natalie, getting involved with him. I knew you were still hung up on him."

Heat rushed to Natalie's face. Just because she hadn't dated after her broken engagement and her broken heart didn't mean that she'd never gotten over Josh. But she wasn't going to argue with her sister right now. "I brought Dad here because he can't go ho—"

"Of course he can't!" Dena interjected. "And that's your fault, just like you're the reason your son and our mother are in danger."

"What…what are you all talking about?" Claus asked, his voice gruff.

"Daddy—" Natalie began.

"Daddy," Dena said as she ran down the rest of the marble steps to hug him. "I'm here for you. Let's get you upstairs to the guest room now."

But Claus planted his feet and looked back at Natalie and Josh, as if they were the ones he trusted for answers. But they'd been lying to him.

"It's all right, sir," Josh told him. "You should go with Dena."

Natalie hugged him, though. "I'll be back in the morning," she said.

"Where are you going?" Dena asked as if surprised that Natalie wouldn't feel welcome staying. "You can't go back to the house, either."

The only place Natalie wanted to be was with her son and her mother. So maybe she would park herself at the police station until she knew where they were.

"Where were you all day?" Josh asked her sister.

Dena's nose wrinkled as she sniffed. "Who are you to ask me my whereabouts?"

"The police must have already asked you where you were when Henry and your mother went missing," he said. "What did you tell them?"

"Whatever I told them is none of your business," she replied.

"Henry is my son," Josh said.

"You've never been a father to him," Dena said. "You were just a horrible mistake my sister made that's come back to haunt us all. Now get the hell out of my house before I call the police to arrest you for trespassing."

Anger coursed through Natalie. But she wasn't sure why she was so angry with her sister. Because she was telling the truth, that this was Josh's fault? Or because Dena had threatened the man that Natalie had once loved, the man who, like her, had a son being held hostage? Or was Natalie mad because her sister didn't seem to care that Henry was missing, and their mother...

Or maybe Dena did care and that was why she was lashing out, because she was feeling as scared and helpless as Natalie was feeling?

Natalie had never been able to figure out her older sister. They'd never had any common ground where they could meet, not even their old childhood home or the store, since Natalie loved them both and Dena hated them.

"It's all going to come out," Josh said, his voice almost chilling in its intensity. "Whatever secrets you two have, they're all going to come out in this investigation."

"You're a criminal, not a cop," Dena said. "You're not investigating anything. You're just trying to cover up your crimes."

"I'm trying to find my son," he said. "And if you cared about anyone but yourself, you would do everything you could to help."

Dena gasped. "How dare you come in my home and talk to me that way!" She turned toward Natalie. "What are you doing here with him? You swore you were done with him when he went to prison, but I suspected it wasn't over." She glanced at her husband. "I even told you that she wasn't over—"

"I want answers, too," Natalie said. "No. I want my son. I

don't care about anything else. I want my son and our mother safely back."

"Marilyn?" Claus said. "Where's Marilyn?"

"With Henry," Josh said. "Remember? She's with Henry. They'll be home soon."

He was lying again so her father wouldn't get upset. Natalie had to remind herself of that because she wanted so badly to believe Josh. But they were no closer to finding Henry and her mother. And she doubted they were going to get any answers here.

"Get out of my house!" Dena said. "Now!"

"Why are you yelling at Henry's dad?" her father asked.

Dena shook her head. "You don't know, Daddy. You don't remember what he put her through, how he nearly destroyed her. How can *you* forget, Natalie?"

She hadn't forgotten. And she certainly hadn't forgiven, either. But right now, he seemed like the only other one as determined to find their child as she was. And if Penny Payne-Lynch was right, and Josh had taken the blame to protect someone else...

He might still be the man she'd thought he was. A good man.

"Let's go," Natalie said to him. And she turned and headed back out the door he'd left open behind him.

Still in the foyer, Dena screamed, "Don't be an idiot again, Natalie! Don't go anywhere with him!"

But Natalie ignored her sister, as she often had to, and kept walking toward that SUV.

Josh closed the door to the house and rushed back to the driver side while Natalie climbed into the passenger seat. He pulled his cell phone out of his pocket and sucked in a breath. Then he punched in an address.

"Where are we going?" she asked, not that she really cared. She just had to get away from here, from her sister's accusations and her father's confusion and Timothy's dumb denials. She couldn't handle anyone else betraying her. She'd already dealt with Josh's betrayal all those years ago.

But what if he hadn't betrayed her? What if he'd been protecting someone, like his lie to her father was to protect him from fear and upset?

But even if hadn't committed the crime for which he'd gone to prison, like Mrs. Lynch believed, that didn't mean Josh hadn't betrayed Natalie. In fact, if he'd gone to prison for something he hadn't done, he might have betrayed her even more than she'd thought he had. Because who had he been covering for?

Natalie knew about his grandmother and his dad. She knew that he had a sister, too, like her, and like her and Dena, they hadn't been close. They hadn't even grown up in the same households since they had different fathers and his had had full custody of Josh.

So would he have lied for his sister? Or for his mother, even though he'd talked less about her than he had his sister?

At the moment Natalie wasn't worried about the past, though. She was worried about the present and the future, if her son and her mother would have one...

Penny should have gone with Natalie to take care of her father. Or better yet, she should have taken care of him for Natalie. The last thing that young woman needed was more stress, but Penny had had to help out with a couple of her own grandchildren.

And so she'd left that poor girl alone.

But seeing her grandkids just reinforced her fear for the missing child.

For Henry...

By the time Penny had been able to get away again, the jewelry store was dark and empty. So now she was at the Payne Protection Agency office, where just a couple of months ago they'd had that party to celebrate its opening.

"Do you know where they are?" she asked Milek, who looked nearly as exhausted and overwhelmed as Henry's father had earlier today.

"Garek and Candace are on their way back," he said. He sat at his brother's desk now. "I should have called him right away."

"You're handling this," she said. "But I was asking about Josh and Natalie." Her heart ached for them as if it could feel their pain.

Milek sighed and nodded. "I have a pretty good idea where he's heading. I'm not sure that they're together, though. But he did text me an approximate time frame for when the diamonds got stolen."

"From Natalie?" Penny assumed.

Milek nodded, and a lock of pale blond hair fell over his forehead into his silvery eyes.

So Josh and Natalie were together. For some reason that made her feel a little bit better. "They need to be there for each other." Josh had lost too many years with the woman he'd clearly loved and with their son. "Nobody else can understand what they're going through..." Penny murmured.

"I can," Milek said. "That's why we need to pull out all the stops to find that little boy and his grandmother, especially since it sounds like she's already hurt. With Garek and Candace on their way back, everyone in all the Payne Protection offices will be working on this."

Like they had when Milek's child and the woman he loved had gone missing.

At least, if Josh and Natalie were still together, they didn't have to worry about each other. Not like Milek had had to worry about Amber.

"You know how it feels, too," Milek said. "There were all too many times that you didn't know where one of your children was."

Including the children Penny's heart had adopted. She had experienced that horror of not knowing where your child was and if they were alive or dead.

She wouldn't wish that horror on her worst enemy, let alone a young couple who'd already suffered too much.

Chapter Ten

"This is a mistake," Josh murmured as he pulled along the curb outside one of the old, downtown River City Queen Anne Victorians that had been converted to a multifamily property. It wasn't a mistake like the wrong address or that his sister wasn't living here—though she probably was. It had been a mistake to bring Natalie with him.

"This is the address you put in the directions for," she pointed out. "Whose is it? Why are we here?"

"You're not the only one having doubts about family," he admitted.

"Family? What are you talking about?"

He shook his head. "It doesn't matter. This shouldn't take long. Just wait for me here." But once he stepped out on the driver side and walked around the front of the SUV, Natalie was already waiting on the sidewalk.

"No. If you think this is a lead to our son, I'm going with you," she said. "Wherever you go."

That was why Josh had lied to her all those years ago. He knew his plea deal was sending him to hell, and he hadn't wanted to bring her with him. Just like he didn't want to bring her here to talk to Sylvie. But he didn't want to waste time arguing with her, either, especially if he was already wasting his time.

"This might lead nowhere," he warned her.

Natalie shrugged. "Where do you think this person or these people might lead us? To Henry or to the diamonds?"

"I don't know," he said.

And he really had no idea. He'd lost touch with his sister like he'd lost touch with Natalie. He hadn't even known that Sylvie still lived in River City. He'd wanted her to leave, to start over again somewhere else, somewhere safe. But Milek had found her here.

He headed toward the porch that wrapped around the side of the enormous house. Next to the door was an intercom panel with a list of names. He found the button for *S. Combs* and pressed it.

He half hoped that nobody answered. That Milek was wrong and Sylvie didn't live here.

That she wasn't in River City anymore.

That she hadn't lived here in years. That she'd kept her promise to start her life over somewhere else, somewhere safe.

The door buzzed and unlocked. And he wasn't sure why. Had she just buzzed him in, or had someone else heard the intercom and unlocked the door?

"Who is S. Combs?" Natalie asked, her face tense.

"Sylvie."

"Sylvie?" she repeated the name. "You already have a girl-friend?"

He snorted. "Sylvie is my sister."

While he'd mentioned his younger sister to her a time or two, he'd made it clear that they weren't close, and he had never introduced the two. And even now he wasn't sure why. Despite his denial, had he realized something was going on with his younger sister?

Or maybe he'd just been worried that Natalie would feel the same way Sylvie did, that he should have tried to spend more time with her growing up, or to get his dad to take her in instead of leaving her where he had, with their narcissistic mother. But he'd been just a kid himself then.

"Combs? Is she married?"

"We have different fathers," he reminded her. Though Sylvie wasn't sure who hers was. Their mother hadn't always been truthful.

"Oh," Natalie said. "I remember you saying that and that you hadn't grown up together…"

While he hadn't introduced them and he'd spared her a lot of the details, he had mentioned Sylvie to her before. That he had a kid sister he didn't get to see often because of his dad having full custody of him.

Because Josh hadn't wanted Natalie to know how messed up his mother was, he hadn't told her why his dad had it or that he and his mother didn't get along, just that his dad had gotten full custody of him after the divorce. And Josh had lived with him and his grandmother while Sylvie lived with their mom and who-ever Monica Combs had been involved with at the time. None of them had lasted even as long as Josh's father had.

"Her apartment number starts with a two, it must be upstairs," Natalie said, and she walked across the foyer, with its scarred hardwood floor, to the double staircase. She walked up one half of it, toward the landing that wrapped around the two-story foyer.

Josh sucked in a breath and rushed up to join her just as she reached out to knock on the door of unit 2C.

The door must not have been closed tightly because it creaked open. And his heart started pounding fast and hard as it re-minded him momentarily of his place that morning, of finding it broken into. But the doorjamb wasn't splintered. Nobody had forced their way inside this apartment.

Light spilled out along with the smell of cinnamon and nut-meg. "Come on in. I've got the coffee brewing, so we can study all night," a female voice said.

Studying.

She was in school. At twenty-four. Maybe she'd gone back and was working on a master's or something.

A laugh rang out. "Hopefully it won't take us that long to figure this out…"

And he had a strange feeling that maybe she was studying something else. Something unrelated to school and higher edu-cation.

As a teenager, she'd pulled off some major heists. She would have been able to figure out how to steal those diamonds, especially if she'd studied the security systems that the Payne Protection Agency used.

The floor creaked beneath his weight as he walked into her place. It was small. She was only a short distance away, sitting at a table next to a row of cabinets and appliances.

At the creak, she looked up and froze. Her mouth fell open, and her eyes widened.

She looked nothing like him. Her hair was blond with streaks of brown and red mixed in with it. And her eyes were a very pale gray or blue, it was hard to tell which.

She jumped up from her chair so quickly that it fell back against the cabinets. Then she ran for him, throwing her arms around his neck. "Oh my God! Josh! When did you get out?"

His hands automatically went to her back, to hold her to him for a moment. She was his baby sister, and he'd missed her so much. But part of him also resented her for the sacrifice he'd had to make. And if she'd had anything to do with Henry being taken…

He would never forgive her or himself. He put his hands on her shoulders and pushed her back. "I've been out about eight weeks," he admitted.

Her silver eyes widened. "Eight weeks? That's great. I thought you were going to be in there eight years, so you got out early."

"You would have known if you'd ever come to visit," he said, pain jabbing his heart.

"You told me not to," she reminded him. "And you weren't the only one who warned me to stay away…"

"Luther's dead now," Josh said. "He hasn't been a threat for nearly a year now." So why hadn't she started coming around again?

"Luther's organization and his reach didn't end with his death, and his organization included all kinds of criminals and people you wouldn't expect to be criminals. He had police officers and crime techs and people within the court system on his payroll, too," Sylvie said. "There is still a threat."

Could it have been someone within or associated with that organization who'd taken Henry?

"I need you to tell me the truth," he said. "I need to know if, even though Luther Mills is dead, you're still stealing for Mom, to pay off her debts?"

"Mom's dead, too," Sylvie said.

Pain jabbed his heart, though he shouldn't have been surprised, not with the way their mother had lived her life. But still, she was his mother. She'd given him life. And in giving his father full custody of him, she'd given him a better shot at life than she had his sister. "I'm sorry," he said. "Overdose?"

Sylvie nodded. "She died just a year after you went to prison."

"For something you did," Natalie said, speaking up from behind Josh. "Is that what happened? Is this who the DA thinks you were covering for?"

Sylvie's eyes widened even more as she stared at Natalie. "Who·is this? A cop? A lawyer? Why did you bring her here? Are you trying to send me to prison now?"

"We're here because *our son* and my mother are missing," Natalie said, her voice cracking with emotion. "And your brother thinks you might have something to do with it." And clearly Natalie now suspected the same thing.

Sylvie gasped and pressed a hand over her mouth. And Josh didn't know if she was shocked to find out he had a son or shocked because he thought she had something to do with his abduction.

Then tears welled in her eyes, and he felt like he had when she was a little girl. When she would cry every time he left to go back to his dad's, pleading with him to take her with him. Not that he'd gotten to see her that often. But when he had, it had been heart-wrenching, just like it was now.

But he couldn't let her tears distract him from what really mattered now. From whom. Sylvie wasn't a child anymore.

Henry was.

"I need to know, Sylvie," Josh said. "Would anyone from Luther's organization have come after my son? Or those diamonds?"

"What diamonds? And how would they have known about your son when I didn't even know you had one?" she asked.

He hadn't known, either. But he refrained from mentioning that now.

"And I stayed away from you," Sylvie said. "I kept you out of it."

"But not out of prison," Natalie muttered.

"I…" Sylvie swallowed hard. "I didn't know what to do. I still don't."

"What about you, Sylvie?" Josh asked. "Did you take those diamonds? Or my son?"

She shook her head, and the tears slipped free, sliding down her face. "No, I wouldn't have even if I knew. And I can't believe you would ask me that."

He felt a pang of guilt, but then he reminded himself yet again that she wasn't a little girl anymore. "Can't you understand why I would find it hard to trust you?"

If only Sylvie had told him what was going on with their mother and being forced to steal to cover Monica's debt to Luther Mills, maybe he would have been able to do something before it got so bad.

Before all their lives were in danger…

But clearly, Sylvie wasn't going to admit to anything even if she was involved. He turned to walk away and found that Natalie had already left. He could hear her footsteps on the stairs and rushed after her.

Natalie was in such a hurry to get away from that apartment, away from Josh and his sister and their lies, that she missed a step. She might have fallen if a strong arm hadn't slid around her waist and caught her. She fell against his body, which fell against the wall.

"Careful," Josh said.

"You weren't," she said. He wasn't careful with her heart all those years ago. "You lied to me."

He hadn't been the thief she'd thought he was, but he'd hurt her all the same. He hadn't deserved his punishment—he'd chosen it. He'd chosen to leave her. And then he'd pushed her away when he'd doubled down on his lies.

Unless maybe it hadn't been a lie when he said he'd never loved her. Because how could he have chosen prison over the life they would have had together if he actually loved her?

"I couldn't tell you the truth," he said. "I know you would have turned her in."

Natalie sucked in a breath. But she couldn't deny it.

"Everything was always so black and white for you," he said.

"It was for you, too," she said. "You were the one with the criminal justice degree. I was just focused on my numbers." And him. He'd been the entire focus of her world that had revolved around her love for him. She'd fallen so damn hard.

So hard that despite how much he'd hurt her, she'd never fully recovered. She'd never really gotten over him, especially when their son reminded her every day of his father.

"It was black and white for me," he said. "Until it came to my sister."

"And you chose her over us," she said. "You chose her over our son."

"I didn't know you were pregnant," he said.

She flinched. But then she reminded him, "You knew that I loved you. You knew that I'd accepted your proposal, your plan for us to get married, and you broke all your promises to me."

"I'm sorry, Natalie," Josh said, his voice gruff. "I'm so sorry. I just didn't know what to do."

"The right thing," she said. "How hard is that?"

"You heard about Luther Mills. He was a ruthless drug dealer with so many powerful people on his payroll that he literally got away with murder for years. You know there were threats. And because of those," he said, "I figured that the right thing to do was to lie and take the blame."

"Then you're not the man I fell in love with after all," she said. "Because he would have known what the right thing really was." She tried to tug away from him, but her foot slipped on another step.

And he pulled her even closer. "I loved you," he said. "I loved you so much, and I hated hurting you. But I couldn't let her go to prison or worse."

"Worse than prison?"

"That man that she was stealing for—"

"Luther Mills," she said. Now she knew why Josh had reacted the way he had when Detective Dubridge mentioned the name.

"Mills would have killed her if he thought she was going to turn on him," he said. "And if she'd been arrested, he might have thought that she would. Potential witnesses to his crimes always wound up dead. Anybody who threatened his operation wound up dead."

Until the Payne Protection Agency got involved. Everybody in River City was aware of what happened from all the news coverage of his arrest and his trial and then his death. River City had seemed like a war zone around that time as Luther tried to take out witnesses and prosecutors and even the judge's daughter.

Luther Mills had failed.

And that was partially why the insurance company had recommended the Payne Protection Agency. Because they'd earned a reputation in this city for getting the job done.

Until now…

Until those diamonds had been stolen.

And their son and her mother.

"I'm sorry, Natalie," Josh said. "I am sorry. And if there was anything else I could have done so I wouldn't hurt you that wouldn't also risk your life or my sister's…"

"It's too late now," Natalie said. "It's too late for us." She believed that he hadn't been a thief then or now. But even though Josh had his reasons for hurting her all those years ago, the past couldn't be undone. He couldn't take back all that pain he'd caused her and all the years they'd lost, not just with each other but with their son.

While she could understand his reasoning, if he'd really believed that lives were in danger, and even forgive him because of that, she couldn't forget. And because she couldn't forget, she couldn't trust him.

But she couldn't deal with all these feelings, old and new, pummeling her right now, not when she should be focused only on finding her son and her mom.

So while it was too late for them, they had to make sure that it wasn't too late for their son.

Henry jerked awake and called out, "Mommy!"

But when his sleepy eyes focused, he could see that he was

still in that weird room with the metal walls and the concrete floor. The lamp was burning yet, so it wasn't dark like it had been earlier.

But he was still scared.

And despite the blankets and the air mattress, he was cold and stiff. Even with Mimi's arm around him. She was holding him, but she was asleep again.

And the skin around that cut on her forehead was swollen and bruised, like the worst bruise he'd ever seen. She probably still needed a doctor.

And Henry needed his mommy. But it wasn't Mommy who was supposed to find him. "Daddy…"

He had to find them soon. Henry wanted to go home to Mommy. He wanted to make sure that Mimi was all right, too. Because even when she was awake, she seemed more like Grandpa than herself right now.

Confused.

But she wasn't too confused that she wasn't scared, which made Henry scared, too. She didn't think this was really a game like the person in the mask had told them.

And Henry was beginning to think it wasn't, either.

If it wasn't a game, then were there any rules for finding him? Even if his daddy found those diamonds, would the person let him know where they were and how to find them?

Or would they just leave him and Mimi here forever?

Chapter Eleven

Natalie was right. It was too late for them. Josh had hurt her so badly that he didn't blame her for not being able to forgive him or even to understand why he'd done what he had five years ago. But back then, and even now, he couldn't see another way to keep everyone he'd loved safe. His sister's and mother's lives had been threatened, and his own and even Natalie's, so he'd no choice but to plead guilty.

Now his son's life was at stake, and Josh still wasn't sure if it was because of him or because of Sylvie.

She stood in the open doorway to her apartment, staring down at them on the stairs.

"I'm sorry," she said. "I'm sorry that your son…my nephew is missing." She looked from Josh to Natalie. "And I'm sorry about…everything else."

Natalie stiffened. She was obviously and understandably not ready to forgive his sister any more than she was ready to forgive him.

"Sylvie, if you know anything, please, tell me," Josh urged her.

She held up her hands. "I didn't take the diamonds, I swear. I left that life behind just like I promised you I would. It just took me a little longer, but that's another story for another day."

He nodded because if she couldn't help him, he was just wasting his time here. "Yeah, we really have to get going." Maybe

Milek and the others from the Payne Protection Agencies had made more progress than Josh had. Or Detective Dubridge and the River City PD might have figured out something from that video phone call Josh had recorded. He wanted to see it again himself, to search for clues and to see his son again. "We need to go to the police—"

Sylvie gasped again, like she had earlier with a shock that sounded almost painful.

"Not about you," he said. "About Henry."

"Henry," she repeated the name with a sad smile. "That's cute. But if someone's got him, didn't they tell you not to involve the police?"

He shook his head. "There was nothing like that," he said. "No threat to not call the police. Just that I needed to hand over these damn diamonds that I didn't take—"

"Sucks to be accused of something you didn't do," she interjected. Then her face flushed. "I was talking about stealing the diamonds. But you know that better than anyone. I am sorry."

He shrugged off her apology. Just like Natalie had said moments ago, it was too late. Too late to undo what was done, to give him back those five years.

"So where did these diamonds go missing from?" Sylvie asked.

Natalie cleared her throat. "Croft Custom Jewelry."

Sylvie's brow furrowed beneath a lock of tawny hair. "That little family store? They had that much on hand?"

Natalie cleared her throat again. "Not usually, but there is often a rush of engagements around now."

"Wouldn't that be around Valentine's Day, not a month later?" Sylvie asked.

Natalie's lips curved slightly. "There are sometimes more engagements after, because someone was expecting a ring and was more than a little disappointed with a box of chocolates."

Sylvie chuckled. "Makes sense. So what are we talking about? Diamonds already in rings?"

"No. They were loose stones. Different cuts and carats, ready to be put into rings."

Sylvie whistled slightly. "So worth a lot of money?"

Natalie nodded.

"I might have some idea of how to help you find them," Sylvie admitted.

Josh felt sick. He'd started to believe that she was telling him the truth, that she'd left that old life behind. But obviously she still had connections to it. He wanted to be the protective big brother he should have been for her when they were younger, before everything had gotten so out of hand. But right now, he didn't care about the past or even about the future.

He just wanted to get that little boy and his grandmother back home. He started up the stairs toward his sister. "Okay, tell me how…"

And even if it led to his arrest, like it had the last time he'd listened to his sister and held *something* for her, it would be worth it if they got Henry and Marilyn Croft back.

Natalie was numb with shock and exhaustion. The coffee cup she held had gone cold while Josh's sister sent a flurry of texts and answered some calls, her voice pitched low. One of those texts had probably been to send away whoever was supposed to come over to study with her because nobody else showed up at her place.

Natalie took a sip or two of the nutmeg-and-cinnamon-spiced coffee Sylvie had handed her, but the caffeine churned in her empty stomach. She couldn't think about herself right now, though. She could think only of Henry.

Was he hungry still?

Was he cold?

Was he scared?

Or did he still think this was all some damn game?

Josh had chugged a couple cups of coffee already. But then she remembered that he'd been awake all night, watching her store. Protecting it.

If only someone had been protecting their son…

Mom had obviously tried. How badly was she hurt?

A little cry slipped from her lips as she thought of the blood on the garage floor. Of her mother being drugged and then hurt.

Josh settled next to her on the small sofa and slid his arm

around her. "You're exhausted," he said. "Let me get an Uber to drive you back to your sister's place."

She shuddered at the thought of going back there to judgmental Dena and oblivious Timothy. Her father was the least confused of the three of them because he always knew what mattered most. Family.

That was clearly what had mattered most to Josh five years ago when he'd chosen his sister's safety over the life he and Natalie had planned. But he hadn't known then about the life they'd started. What would he have done if he'd known she was pregnant?

Unfortunately, she hadn't found out until after he'd already pled guilty to something he hadn't done. Would he have been able to undo that? Or were he and Sylvie right that Luther Mills would have hurt them more, all of them, if Josh hadn't taken the blame for something he hadn't done?

Luther Mills had obviously wanted Sylvie to keep stealing for him. Or maybe he'd been worried that if she was arrested, she would have turned over evidence against him?

No matter his reason, Luther Mills had had no compunction against killing. He'd killed a young police informant in front of the teenager's sister to send a message to anyone coming after him. And that young man hadn't been his only victim. After Luther's death, countless other crimes of his and of the people on his payroll had been exposed.

But there was speculation that not everybody on Luther's payroll had been discovered. That there could be others. So that danger he'd posed might not have ended even with his death. The man had been that evil.

Knowing that, Natalie couldn't stay angry with Josh if he truly believed he'd been protecting her by pushing her away.

Instead of pulling away from his touch, as she had before, she leaned into him, drawing from his warmth and strength. Her numbness receded as she began to feel again. And it wasn't just the fear this time. She also felt that tingling awareness she'd had from the first moment she'd met Josh Stafford in the college bookstore.

He was so good-looking and strong and warm. Her first impression of him had been right, that he had been protective then. He'd been protective of his sister and mom and even of her.

He just hadn't protected her heart. So no matter how much she'd loved him once, she would be foolish to trust him with her heart again.

She sucked in a breath and eased away from him now. But there wasn't a lot of space that she could get away from him on that small sofa, so she still felt the heat of his body, still felt the awareness in hers.

Maybe she should go back to her sister's. But the thought of seeing Dena again made her stomach churn more than the coffee had.

Maybe Dena had lashed out because she was worried about their mother and Henry. But Josh's sister, who'd just learned of his existence, seemed more visibly concerned about Henry than Dena, who'd been part of his life since his birth. Albeit a small part.

"At least close your eyes for a bit," Josh suggested. "Try to get some rest."

"You were up all night last night, weren't you?" Natalie asked. She'd seen him on the security footage; she knew that he hadn't had any rest.

He nodded. "But I'm used to not getting much sleep."

Maybe that was just because he worked nights, or maybe that was because of being in prison. She couldn't imagine how hard the past five years of his life had been.

"There's no time to sleep now," Sylvie said as she held up her phone. "I have a possible lead. Someone I used to know was approached about a bag of diamonds—"

"Let's call Detective Dubridge!" Natalie exclaimed.

Sylvie shook her head. "You'll never see those diamonds again if you involve the police. And people would probably get hurt as well."

By people, Natalie suspected she meant herself. Or maybe she meant Henry. And if that was the case, then Natalie had to agree with her that it wasn't wise to call the detective no matter how dangerous this might be.

"I'm worried about you getting hurt," Josh said.

"He'll give *me* details about this person, in person, but only me." Sylvie dropped her cell phone into a bag she was draping over her shoulder. "I'll meet with him and let you know what I find out."

"No," Josh said. "If you're really out of this life, I don't want you getting involved in it again. Call him back. Tell him he's going to meet with your brother instead."

"It doesn't work like that," Sylvie said. "You can't just go in my place."

"So it's not like prison," Natalie muttered, her bitterness overwhelming her.

"Tell him I'm an ex-con," Josh said.

"You can go with me," Sylvie said, "since you obviously don't trust me, but you can't go alone."

"I won't be alone—"

"I said no cops."

"Milek Kozminski isn't a cop any more than I am."

"Kozminski?" Sylvie asked, her voice cracking slightly. "What do you know about the Kozminskis?"

"I work for two of them now," Josh said. "Milek and his older brother, Garek, and Garek's wife, too."

"The Kozminskis are thieves. You don't want me in that life, but you're in it?" she asked.

"I work for them at the Payne Protection Agency. They're good guys," he said. "But since you're not aware of that, your fence probably isn't, either."

"He's not *my* fence," Sylvie said, but her face was flushed. "Not anymore…"

"I don't care what he was or is," Josh said. "I just want to find those diamonds, so when the person holding Henry calls back, I can tell them I have what they want."

Sylvie sighed. "All right then. I'll set it up." She pulled her cell from her purse. "What's your number?" she asked him. "I'll forward you the location."

Natalie stood up. "I'll go with you."

Josh snorted. "Not a chance. You should go back to your sister's—"

"I'd rather stay here," she said. With his sister, not her own.

Hopefully her father was asleep now. But she wouldn't have been much comfort to him, not with how upset she was.

Then it occurred to her that Sylvie probably didn't want her here. She wasn't sure where else she would go, though, since her home was still a crime scene. "I can go somewhere else… if you have to study."

Sylvie held up her phone. "I sent a text canceling that. This is more important."

Natalie felt a sudden flash of warmth toward Sylvie Combs.

But Josh hesitated a moment, looking from one to the other of them. "I don't think this is a good idea," he said.

"It probably isn't," Natalie agreed. "But if we need those diamonds to get our son back, it's worth it." But he was the one taking the risk, and from the way his sister talked, it might be his life he was risking.

"I don't know if you should stay here with Sylvie," he said.

Which of them was he worried about? He probably thought Natalie was furious with his sister because she'd let him go to prison for something she'd done. And he also didn't trust his sister any more than Natalie did.

"This guy isn't going to wait around for you," Sylvie warned him. "And I'm not going to corrupt my nephew's mother during the short time she'll be here." She must have concluded he was worried about Natalie.

Josh's lips curved into a slight smile. "I'd like to think you wouldn't try, but even if you do, Natalie is incorruptible."

That was why he hadn't told Natalie the truth five years ago. He'd believed she wouldn't let him plead guilty for something he hadn't done, and she would have gone, maybe to the wrong people, to try to save him from prison. And in trying to save him, she would have put herself, him and his sister in danger.

But did he know that she would have done that out of love? Or had he thought she was too judgmental and self-righteous back then?

And maybe she had been. Because she couldn't understand why people would do anything against the law…

But now, loving her son like she did, she knew that she

would do anything to keep him safe, even steal some damn diamonds herself.

"Go!" she urged Josh. "We will be fine." She really did feel more comfortable with his sister than her own right now. She couldn't imagine how Sylvie would have gotten inside the store, past the security system and stolen the bag of diamonds. It made much more sense that it was an inside job, which left her family as possible suspects.

Josh hesitated for another moment, and he was standing so close to her that she thought he was going to kiss her, especially when he touched her chin. But he didn't lower his head or tip hers up like he used to. He just ran his knuckle along her jaw. "Be safe," he said. Then he turned and headed out the door.

"You, too," Natalie whispered. But it was too late. He was already gone.

"He's going to be fine," Sylvie said.

"How can you know that?" Natalie asked, and that fury bubbled up inside her again. Obviously, she cared more about him than his sister did. "How could you know five years ago that he would survive prison?" Because it hadn't been just a life-and-death situation for her, it had been for him as well.

Sylvie's pale, silvery eyes widened for a moment. "Oh, we're going to go there..."

"I just don't understand how you could let him take the punishment for something you did," Natalie said.

Tears filled Sylvie's pale eyes. "I didn't know what to do back then. I wasn't even in my teens when Luther made me start stealing to pay off my mother's debts. And he swore if I told anyone, he would kill them and me. Then when Josh was arrested, I didn't know how to get myself out of that situation, let alone how to get him out. I was just nineteen then. For so many years Luther convinced me that there was nobody I could trust, that he had the whole damn police department on his payroll and the DA's office." She blinked furiously at the tears that brimmed over into her lashes. "And maybe I was mad at Josh. He got to live with his dad and his grandma, and I got *her*. Our mother, the raging narcissist. All she cared about was herself, making herself feel better, whatever it took. And it took a lot..." She squeezed her eyes shut. "And maybe back then I was too much like her, too selfish and scared to do what was right for Josh or even for myself."

Sylvie started toward the door then, her hand on the strap of the bag she'd slung over her shoulder. "But now I know that he will be fine because he's not the one meeting with the person who has the actual lead. I am."

Natalie jumped up from the sofa and headed after her. "You can't—"

"I want to help get your son back," Sylvie said. "Don't try to stop me."

Natalie didn't want to stop her, if that was truly what she was doing. But she didn't trust Sylvie Combs. She couldn't trust someone who'd let another person, let alone her own brother, go to prison for something she'd done.

For all Natalie knew, those diamonds might be in Sylvie's bag. She might not be meeting the fence who had a lead on them, she might be fencing them herself.

And then their leverage to get their son back would be gone.

Milek jerked awake from the vibration of the desk where he'd lain his head. For a minute. Just a minute...

The vibration was from his cell, the screen lit up with a text of an address. Josh sent him an address. He reached for the phone just as it rang.

"Where is this?" he asked, his pulse quickening with excitement. "Did you find him and his grandmother? Are they there?"

"No. But the diamonds might be," Josh said. "Or at least a lead to them."

"What kind of lead?" Milek asked. "Is this a fence?"

"I think so. I don't know for sure, though," Josh replied, as if he'd been given information he couldn't trust. "But I'm going there to find out."

"Wait for me." Because whoever had those diamonds wasn't going to give them up without a fight.

With their current market value, the thief would have no compunction against killing to keep them.

Chapter Twelve

Josh pulled up to the alley behind the nightclub. This was where Sylvie had set up the meeting. Not inside the nightclub but in the alley.

It wasn't like the alley behind Croft Custom Jewelry. It was too narrow for him to drive into, so he had to park down the block, in the only free spot he'd been able to find. While the club was obviously busy, judging from all the vehicles parked around it and the music booming out of it, the street was dimly lit.

Only one light glowed next to the club's door, so the people waiting to get inside were lined up in the dark. Josh walked past them, probably as invisible to them as they were to him.

Was one of those people the one he was supposed to meet? Or were they already in the alley?

He just about walked past it like he'd driven past it just a short while ago. It was so narrow and dark, and as he started down it, he nearly tripped and gagged because it was so littered with trash. The acrid smell of it filled his nostrils. He could almost taste the garbage.

Or maybe that was the fear.

Fear that this wasn't going to lead anywhere, that it was a dead end. And not just the alley…

But he had to check it out, just in case it was a viable lead to those diamonds.

Not that he gave a damn about them, but whoever was holding his son and Marilyn Croft cared about them. And so he didn't dare wait for Milek in case whoever Sylvie had set up this meeting with took off with what was his only possible lead to those damn diamonds.

Maybe he would have waited for Milek if he thought it was going to actually be dangerous. Or that it was going to be anything at all.

But he didn't trust Sylvie. She was his sister, and he still loved her. But after what she'd done...

He wasn't sure he'd ever really known her. And maybe he hadn't. While Sylvie was just four years younger than his twenty-eight, they hadn't grown up together. His father hadn't even let him visit her or their mother that often. Every time he had, she would beg to come home with him, and he would be upset to leave her. So his father had started limiting those visits even more.

When they were older and had phones, they texted each other and had video calls. But they were both busy with friends and school. Or so he'd thought.

But she'd been doing other things. Stealing.

He wouldn't have believed her capable of that if she hadn't confessed to him after he'd been arrested with that package she'd asked him to hold for her. He'd been uneasy when he'd done that, wondering if there were drugs inside, but there had been jewels instead and some loose stones like the ones that were missing. And someone had been tipped off that Josh had had them.

Sylvie had been so upset when she'd come to see him in jail. She'd been apologetic then that he was involved, but she'd also obviously been afraid for her life and their mother's and for his. And when she'd confessed that Luther Mills was the one who'd forced her to steal to pay off their mother's debts, he'd understood that fear. And he'd been afraid, too, especially when the officer escorting him back to his holding cell after visitation with his sister had whispered to him that he needed to plead guilty or bad things would happen to a lot of people.

So he'd believed Sylvie. But even though she'd told him the

truth back then, that didn't mean she'd told him the truth now about this lead. Was it real or just a wild goose chase?

He and the rats that he could hear scurrying and squeaking in the dark were probably the only living things in this alley.

But then something else moved in the dark, its footsteps heavy. Before he could react, something jabbed into his back. Something cold and hard. The barrel of a gun.

And he realized that soon those rats might be the only living thing in the alley. Well, the rats and whoever was about to shoot him.

Fortunately Natalie had managed to use a charger of Sylvie's to charge her cell some because the minute Sylvie ran out of her apartment, Natalie opened the Uber app to order a car. It probably wouldn't have arrived in time to catch up with her if Sylvie had transportation of her own. But she was waiting outside for a vehicle, too.

Instead of standing in the shadows of the porch like Natalie, Sylvie paced in the street, obviously impatient to get away.

With the diamonds?

Josh wouldn't have come here if he hadn't had doubts about his sister, just as Natalie had doubts about her family. But would any of them risk lives for money?

She cringed as she realized how damn naive she was. So many people did exactly that. They didn't just risk lives, they actually killed for money. Sylvie was capable of stealing. Was she capable of killing?

A vehicle turned onto the street and then stopped abruptly, its brakes screeching. Sylvie didn't even appear to flinch as the headlights illuminated her. She could have been hit. But she didn't even move now. Then those bright lights flicked on and then off.

This wasn't a car for hire like the one Natalie had requested. This was someone else picking Sylvie up, someone who knew her.

The young woman ran around to the passenger's side and pulled open the door.

Natalie's stomach sank with dread that she was going to lose her. But her phone pinged.

Here.

A car pulled up right as the other one pulled away. She ran down the front steps and rushed to the vehicle. As she yanked open the door, she said, "Follow that car. Hurry!"

The older guy behind the wheel laughed. "Seriously? You're going to Charleston—"

She'd typed in her sister's address on the app. But she shook her head now. "No, please, follow that car."

"Why?" the guy asked. "Cheating spouse?"

"Cheating something," she suspected. "My little boy is missing, and I think that person might be able to help me find him."

"The kid from the news? The cute little guy with dark eyes?"

She nodded. "Yes, Henry Croft is my son."

The tires squealed as the guy's vehicle peeled away from the curb. "I have five kids and ten grandkids," he said. "I can't imagine what you're going through, lady."

"Thank you for doing this," she said. "But please don't get too close. I don't want her to see me."

"Sure, sure. Are you going to call the police?" he asked as he glanced back at her.

She shook her head. "And tell them what? That I have a hunch? I don't have anything more than that."

He nodded. "Okay. We'll follow them and see what's up. But I can already tell from the direction we're heading that it's not to any place good, any place safe."

She'd been right to follow Sylvie. She was meeting with the person who might actually have the diamonds or maybe she even had them herself.

So who was Josh meeting with and was he really in no danger like his sister claimed?

Sylvie had already risked his life once; she probably would have no compunction against doing it again. Sylvie had admitted to resenting her older brother when they were kids, so she might still resent him. Maybe even enough that she would do anything to hurt him.

Like take his son...

Was Sylvie leading Natalie to the diamonds or to her son? And if it was to Henry, then what the driver said scared her. Henry and her mother weren't anywhere safe.

And soon Natalie, and this very kind driver, would not be safe, either. She felt guilty for involving him, but she was desperate to save her son and her mother if it wasn't already too late.

Woodrow was used to getting calls at all hours, not that it was very late right now. But those calls were one of the reasons why he was planning to retire. The other reason was the woman lying next to him. He wanted to spend more time with her.

All the time that he had. He'd come close to dying just a few short years ago, and it had put into perspective for him what was most important. Family.

And love.

His love, Penny, released a shaky breath. "So they didn't find the boy yet?"

"No." The Amber alert had solicited a lot of calls, but so far all of those suspected sightings of the boy and the vehicle had proven to be of someone else and some other car. No one so far had seen the real boy, except on that recording his father had taken of the video call. And his grandmother and her vehicle were also nowhere to be found.

Penny sighed again. "When the phone rang..."

"I'm sorry that woke you up," he said, and he slid his arm around her, cuddling her close to him. She was so warm and soft, so perfect.

"I was awake," she said. "I don't think I will be able to sleep until that little boy is found safe and sound. I can't imagine the fear and pain his mother is going through."

"Actually, I think you can," Woodrow said. "All of our kids have been in dangerous situations before. We've been lucky that we haven't lost any of them."

"But they were older," Penny said. "They were all able to fend for themselves. He's just a little boy."

"A little boy that a lot of people are willing to do anything to find." Especially his father.

Josh Stafford had just risked his life and his freedom for a possible lead to either the child or the diamonds. He was convinced that he would need the diamonds to get the boy and Mrs. Croft back.

But as a former FBI agent, Woodrow knew that paying the ransom didn't always guarantee the safe return of the hostages. Most kidnappers killed their hostages rather than risk those hostages being able to identify them.

And in this case...

How it was all playing out...

The kidnapper almost had to be someone in the hostages' world. Someone who worked at the store and knew the family. Or maybe even...

One of the bodyguards.

What was certain was that in cases like this, it was really hard to trust anyone and really hard to hang onto hope that the hostages would be returned unharmed.

Chapter Thirteen

Once the police officer who'd nearly arrested him in that alley let him go, Josh headed straight for his sister's apartment. The officer, Sheila Carlson, probably wouldn't have released him if not for Milek showing up and calling the chief of the River City PD.

Officer Carlson had been nearly as desperate for a lead to those diamonds as he was. "Sylvie said you knew something about them."

"Sylvie told me you were the fence," Josh said. Clearly Sylvie had set them both up to waste their time. Or to distract them.

Why the hell was his sister so close with a police officer? And why had that police officer been so quick to pull a gun on him?

Like Sylvie had just reminded him, Luther Mills had had police officers and more on his payroll as part of his criminal organization. Just like that officer so long ago who'd escorted Josh back to the holding cell after Sylvie had come to see him. That police officer had threatened him into pleading guilty, so he'd been on Luther's payroll, too.

Josh really couldn't trust anyone.

He should have been relieved Officer Carlson hadn't pulled the trigger. But whatever the hell else his meeting in the alley had been, it had also been a waste of time. He drove so fast back to Sylvie's place that he was surprised he didn't have the police trying to arrest him again for reckless driving. Because he had a feeling that officer was probably following him...

She hadn't been happy about talking to Chief Lynch. After ending the call, she had made a remark as she uncuffed Josh about having a Get Out of Jail Free card.

Hell, if Josh had that, he would have used it long ago.

Chief Lynch was only giving him leeway because his son was missing. Milek had explained that to Josh and warned him not to push it and not to go off alone again.

But Josh had left his boss dealing with the irate officer and rushed right back here. Not just to Sylvie but to Natalie, too.

He shouldn't have left her with his sister. He should have insisted she go back to her sister's house. Or somewhere else, somewhere she would be safe.

She wasn't safe with Sylvie.

Once he pulled up to the curb outside the Queen Anne, he jumped out and ran up to the porch. He touched the intercom button for 2C, but nothing happened. The door didn't unlock. He pressed it again. Harder.

Still nothing.

The door remained locked.

So he pressed all the other buttons until, finally, someone unlocked it. He pulled it open and rushed inside, running up the stairs.

The door to Sylvie's apartment wasn't locked. It pushed open easily. And he stepped inside to find it empty.

The place was small, just an open area with a bed that folded from a bookshelf and a tiny bathroom. There was no place for anyone to hide in it.

Where the hell were they?

Maybe Natalie had gone back to her sister's. But somehow Josh doubted it, and he didn't want to waste time driving over there if she was somewhere else, somewhere she might need help, like their son and her mother needed help.

Had she been taken, too?

He didn't have her cell number. Why the hell hadn't he gotten it earlier?

So he couldn't call her.

But he had Sylvie's number from when she'd texted him earlier. He tried to call, but it went right to voicemail, a voicemail that hadn't yet been set up for this phone. Was it even her phone or a burner?

How badly had she betrayed him?

And once again he'd risked Natalie's life because of Sylvie. He had to find her and make sure she was all right. His hand shaking, Josh grasped his phone and tried another number. This time the person answered.

"Nikki, this is Josh Stafford," he said.

"I know," she replied. "And I promise I'm not going to stop going over this recording of your son until I can figure out where he and his grandmother are being held. If only—"

"Right now, I need to know where his mother is," he said.

"I thought she was with you," Nikki replied.

He cursed. "I screwed up. I left her alone to chase down a damn dead end. Do you have her number? Can you ping her location?"

"I've got her number and a great program. I'll narrow it down as much as I can."

He heard the stroke of the keyboard and then a curse.

"What?" he asked.

"Her phone must be off—"

Then he remembered that it had died earlier. That was why she had to try to call her sister and brother-in-law from the store phone. While she'd used Sylvie's charger, it must not have been long to keep the battery from draining again.

"I've got another number," he said. And he read off the one from his sister's phone. That was probably off, too, though. "I'm not sure they're together…"

But he had a horrible feeling that they were.

Nikki cursed again.

"That phone dead, too?" he asked. He wouldn't have put it past Sylvie to destroy it even if it wasn't a burner.

"No, I found a location," Nikki replied with a shaky breath. It wasn't good.

He knew that even before Nikki told him where it was. He

knew because of how tightly his stomach was clenching and how the short hairs on the nape of his neck were standing on end.

He'd made a big mistake trusting his sister. The last time he had it had cost him his freedom. This time it might cost a life. The life of the woman he'd never stopped loving and apparently had also never stopped hurting.

The driver wasn't wrong about the area. It didn't look safe. People congregated on sidewalks and in the streets, but they didn't do it under the few streetlamps; instead they slunk in the shadows.

"We need to turn around and get the hell out of here," the driver remarked.

"But if this is where my son is…" She didn't want to believe that, though, that her little boy and her mother were somewhere around here. Because it definitely was not safe. She felt bad about pressing the driver to keep following that vehicle, but if she lost it, she felt like she might lose the one chance of finding her son and mom.

"You need to call the police," the driver said. "But I don't think even they come down here. I know we shouldn't be here."

"Thank you for bringing me," she said. "Thank you…" Tears stung her eyes.

"I really want to turn around," he said, his voice trembling with the fear gripping her.

But then the vehicle they were following turned off the scary street. The driver released a slight sigh as he turned to follow it. It went down a few more roads, deeper and deeper into an industrial area.

"This is weird," he murmured.

And then the car they were following seemed to disappear. The lights went off, and it just dropped out of sight.

"I don't see it," he said. "Where the hell…" The road seemed to end at a dock of some kind. "Did it drive off into the water?"

"Where are we now?" she asked.

"The river," the driver responded. "It winds through the whole damn city, but I don't think I've ever been in this area."

There were buildings and shipping containers all around. But few lights and no people.

"We lost them," he said.

"No. No. They have to be here," she murmured. "In one of the buildings or…" Maybe even one of those shipping containers. It would be the perfect place to hide people where no one would see or hear them. Her pulse quickened. "I bet my son is here."

"Then we need to call the police," he said.

"I—I don't think that's a good idea…" If the kidnappers heard sirens, they might get rid of the hostages. She couldn't take that risk. "I'm going to get out," she said. "And just look around."

"Miss Croft, this is a really bad idea," the driver warned her.

She couldn't argue with him. And she couldn't put his life in danger, either, but she was so desperate to find her son and her mom. "You stay here. Or drive off if you want," she said. "I have to look. If my son is here…"

If she did nothing to save him even though she was so close, she would never forgive herself if something happened to him or her mother. She might never forgive herself anyway.

"Be careful," he said.

She pushed open the door and stepped out. Then she started walking toward the building. Maybe the sound of his car engine got quieter because she was walking away from him. Or because her heart was beating so fast and hard that it was all she could hear.

Or maybe the man was driving off like she'd told him he could.

Either way Natalie had never felt as alone or as scared as she did now. But maybe she wasn't alone. Maybe her son and her mother were here, too.

But how the hell was she, on her own, going to save them from their kidnapper?

Milek had just sat back down at Garek's desk when his cell rang again, but when he saw who was calling, he breathed a sigh of relief.

"Nikki, I was just going to call you," he said. "I need you to help me find Josh Stafford."

Josh had disappeared so fast from the alley that Milek hadn't even realized he was gone until Officer Carlson had pointed it out to him.

"You shouldn't let him go off alone like that," she'd admonished him. "That guy is so desperate that he's going to get himself killed."

That was what Milek was afraid of.

"Or he's going to get someone else killed," Carlson had added. "And I always heard that the Payne Protection bodyguards were the best."

"We are," Milek had insisted. "But he's not a bodyguard right now. He's a father whose child is missing." And from personal experience, Milek knew how desperate that made a dad, desperate enough to do anything to get him back.

Even give up his own life…

"He just asked me to find someone for him, so I have a pretty good idea where he is," Nikki replied. "And he's going to need backup."

Josh hadn't called for it like he had the last time, though. But he hadn't waited for Milek then, either. Or maybe he didn't trust him to get there in time.

Maybe, after his own sister set him up to either get shot or arrested in that alley, Josh didn't trust anyone anymore. Milek could understand that.

"Who did he have you track down?" Milek asked.

"First he had me try to find Natalie Croft, but her phone is dead," Nikki said. "So then he had me track down another number. The name the service provider has on the account is Sylvie Combs."

Josh's sister. That was who had brought both Officer Carlson and Josh to that dark alley just a short while ago. What the hell was the young woman up to?

She was the one who Amber suspected had really been the thief all those years ago. Was she still?

Or was she more than a thief now?

Was she also a killer?

Chapter Fourteen

God, Josh hoped he was wrong. He hoped like hell that Natalie wasn't with his sister, that she was with her own sister instead. That she was safe with her dad and her brother-in-law in that high-class house that probably had a great security system.

There was no security down here.

Especially not for Josh who couldn't even carry a gun, only the damn canister of pepper spray. Just driving through a neighborhood like this, with gangs and prostitutes and drug dealers, could be a death sentence.

Why would Sylvie have come down here? And why would she have brought Natalie with her?

He hoped like hell that she hadn't. But his gut, his clenched stomach, was warning him that she had.

His cell rang, then connected automatically to the speakers in the SUV.

"What the hell are you doing?" Milek asked him. "Down there? In that area on your own?"

"I'm trying to find my sister and Natalie," Josh said, although he figured that Milek probably already knew exactly what he was doing. "Nikki must be the one who told you where I am and that I'm here because I had her ping my sister's cell."

"Yeah, she also told me about a call she heard on the police scanner while she was on the phone with me," Milek said. "A rideshare driver called in and said that he dropped off a woman near the river just past the area where you are now. She claimed to be Henry Croft's mother."

Josh's blood chilled as his suspicion was confirmed. He shivered.

"He just left her and drove off?" he asked, his heart beating fast and hard with fear for her.

"He wasn't sure what to do," Milek said. "It's a dangerous area."

Josh could see that for himself. "But to leave her alone down here…"

"They were following someone," he said.

"Sylvie…"

"She thought the person might lead her to her son," Milek said.

A place by the river with shipping containers and warehouses. It would be a great hiding place for hostages, especially in an area like this where even if anybody heard or saw anything, they wouldn't tell anyone. They wouldn't want the police coming down here.

"Units are on the way," Milek said. "You need to just stay in your vehicle and wait for them to arrive."

Josh's lights shone on a sign for a shipping company, and he turned onto the street, following it down toward the warehouses, containers and the river.

"Wait in your vehicle," Milek said again. "The police are on the way."

They must have been coming with sirens off because when Josh shut off the SUV engine, he didn't hear anything. It was almost eerily quiet, so much so that he opened his door to listen.

Milek's voice broke the silence, "Josh—"

"What would you do if your son and his mother were in danger?" he asked.

Milek cursed, probably because he knew he couldn't argue with him. He couldn't convince Josh to do something he wouldn't have done himself.

Josh disconnected the call. Then he stepped out onto the cracked asphalt.

There were no other vehicles in sight. Obviously, the rideshare driver had just left her here, but at least he'd made that call to the police.

But where was the vehicle he'd said they followed? Sylvie's vehicle?

He had no idea what his sister might drive. He hadn't even known that she was still in River City for sure until Milek tracked her down. But Josh had had his suspicions when Sylvie stopped trying to visit him that she hadn't held up her end of the deal he'd made with her. Maybe she didn't have a choice, just like Luther Mills had given her no choice when she was just a kid. Or maybe it was all she knew.

Despite what she claimed about no longer stealing, she was all too aware of what was going on in the criminal world. Somehow, she even knew which officer was handling the theft at the jewelry store. And she knew a fence for stolen property, for items of as much value as those missing diamonds.

If that was who she was really meeting here…

At least she hadn't brought Natalie along with her. Natalie had followed her, apparently believing that his sister might lead her to their son and her mother.

Was the little boy here somewhere?

Josh wanted to call out for Henry, for Natalie…even for his sister. But that eerie silence kept him quiet, had him moving slowly toward those buildings. Whatever vehicle Sylvie had driven here had to be in one of the warehouses or maybe even a shipping container.

Some of the asphalt of the parking lot wasn't just cracked. It was crumbling, and the toe of his hiking boot hit a chunk, sending it tumbling ahead of him to roll against the side of one of those buildings. The bang as the asphalt struck the metal reverberated in the silence.

And then another bang rang out.

A gunshot. But no bullets struck the ground near him. The shot was echoing inside one of the warehouses.

Was he already too late?

Natalie had done her best to move quietly. To be careful. To draw no attention to herself as she searched the area for Sylvie and, more important, for her mother and her son. That was why it was a shock when the gunshots rang out, bullets ricocheting off the metal walls of the building she'd entered a short while ago.

Then lights flashed on, and an engine revved.

Natalie had found the vehicle that Sylvie had taken to this horrible area.

Then Sylvie stepped into the beam of the vehicle's headlights. She wasn't inside it anymore. And this time Natalie wasn't sure that it was going to stop for the young woman like it had in the street outside Sylvie's apartment earlier that evening. It seemed intent on heading directly for her.

Fear welling inside her, Natalie screamed, "Sylvie!"

And more shots rang out.

Sylvie fell.

Natalie screamed again. Then she realized that Sylvie had been knocked to the ground by a body and hopefully not a bullet.

A man with dark hair had pushed Sylvie out of the way of the vehicle that sped now out of the building, bullets pinging off it.

Natalie recognized the man's dark hair and muscular body. Josh had stepped in front of a speeding vehicle, in front of a barrage of bullets to save his sister. But had he once again sacrificed himself in the process of protecting Sylvie?

"Josh!" Natalie yelled from where she was hidden in the shadows on the other side of the warehouse from them. Her heart hammered with fear for him, fear that she might have lost him again. "Are you all right?"

At the sound of her voice, more shots rang out, chipping away at the wood of the crate she was crouched beside. But at the moment she didn't care about herself as much as she did him. He was the kind of man who kept putting himself in danger to save others. He was the kind of man she'd thought he was all those years ago.

And she wished like hell that back at his sister's apartment she had kissed him before he left. She'd thought for a moment that he was going to kiss her, but he hadn't.

And now he might not get the chance. To kiss her. Or to meet his son.

"Get down!" Josh yelled at her. Then to Sylvie who was struggling to get back up, "What the hell—"

"Let me shoot back at them!" Sylvie said as she pulled something from the bag she'd brought with her. Obviously his sister had a gun.

"Get down!" Josh yelled again.

Natalie wasn't sure if he was talking to her or his sister. And then more shots rang out. Some struck the wood crate, sending chips and splinters raining down on her. She lay flat against the cold concrete now, trying not to get hit. Her heart pounded so hard that she was surprised it didn't crack the concrete.

She wasn't afraid just for herself, but for Josh and Sylvie, too. Because the bullets were flying all around, pinging off the metal walls. Josh or Sylvie must have been firing some, too, because there were so many gunshots. They reverberated inside Natalie's head, ringing in her ears.

But despite the noise inside the warehouse, she could also hear sirens in the distance. Someone had called the police.

But would they get here in time? They had to because this time Josh might be sacrificing more than his freedom to save his sister and her. He might be sacrificing his life.

The shooting inside the warehouse suddenly stopped. She wasn't sure if that was because the shooter had heard the sirens, too. Or it was quiet because the shooter and maybe Josh and Sylvie, too, had been struck.

Was it already too late for help?

When Woodrow received a second call that night, Penny had been hopeful that the boy and his grandmother had been found. Woodrow had even seemed hopeful after dispatch let him know that someone called in saying that there was a possible location for the hostages.

Penny jumped out of bed and started getting dressed. She was eager to find out if the boy was okay. Woodrow was, too. He was putting his clothes back on as well.

But then his phone rang again. And as he listened to the caller, his whole demeanor changed. His body was tense again, and when he disconnected the call, he wouldn't meet her gaze.

"What is it?" she asked as she stepped closer to him. "What happened?" Because it was clear that something had. Something bad. She didn't need her sixth sense to tell her that; she could feel it. She could feel it in her husband, in his concern and his dread.

"That location," he murmured, his voice gruff, "where it was suspected the hostages might be..."

"Henry," Penny corrected him. "Henry and Marilyn." They weren't just hostages. They were people. *Real* people. Important people. People who were loved, who were needed, by their family and their friends.

Woodrow nodded. "Yes..."

"What happened?" she asked.

"We don't know yet," he said. "But there are reports of gunfire now at that location."

So if the hostages were there, their kidnapper wasn't giving them up without a fight. Or they were getting rid of them for good...

Chapter Fifteen

Josh couldn't stop shaking even now hours after the close call he'd had. And he wasn't shaking because of how close those bullets had come to him. Though they had come close.

He wasn't the only one who'd nearly been hit, though.

Sylvie had.

And Natalie...

She was shaking, too.

"We'll be safe here," he told her.

Or so that was what Milek had assured him. The condo was tucked away in a corner of the new Payne Protection Agency's office. Also somewhere in this remodeled warehouse was a space Milek used as his art studio.

Josh closed and locked the heavy steel door behind them. He still wasn't sure, despite the security in this building, that they would be as safe here as he'd just told Natalie they would be. But he wanted her to stop shaking.

Back at the river dock, Milek had convinced the police to take Josh and Natalie's statements first, so they could leave the scene of the shooting and get some rest.

Big dark circles rimmed Natalie's green eyes, nearly as black as the frames of her glasses, and she was deathly pale. And shaky...

He was, too, but Josh wasn't sure if he was shaking from fear and adrenaline or from exhaustion. But as tired as he was, he doubted he would be able to sleep. Not with their son missing.

"What the hell was Sylvie doing?" Josh asked. "And you... I can't believe you put yourself in danger like that!" He could have lost her all over again.

Not that he had her now.

But he wanted to have her, to hold her, to kiss her. He'd missed her so damn much, and tonight...

"You put yourself in danger, too," she said.

He snorted. "The meeting Sylvie set up for me was with an undercover cop, not a fence."

She smiled. "So she told me the truth about that. She assured me she wouldn't put you in danger again."

Something that had felt like a tight band around his heart eased slightly. Maybe Sheila Carlson wasn't one of the cops who used to work for Luther Mills then. Maybe that wasn't how his sister had known her. And she hadn't known that the cop would pull a gun on him like she had.

"But then you were in danger in that warehouse," Natalie said. "You're the one who knocked her down, who protected us both from whoever was shooting at us." She stepped closer to him and wound her arms around him. "I was so afraid..."

He pulled her closer and held her trembling body against his, which was trembling just as much if not more. "I was so scared, too. I was scared that you were going to get hurt, Natalie, seriously hurt."

Or worse. The thought made him shudder.

Her arms tightened around him. "I'm fine," she said. "Not a scratch on me."

He wasn't sure about that. So many of those bullets had seemed to come so close to her. That crate she'd been crouched beside had been riddled with holes.

"What were you thinking?" he asked.

"I was thinking that you sought your sister out because you suspected she might have the diamonds, and then when she hopped in a car with someone right after you left, I had to follow her and see where she was going."

"But you told that driver that you thought she might be leading you to Henry and your mom."

"I wasn't sure where she was going, but I was hoping it was to them." Tears welled in her green eyes. "But they weren't there."

Officers were still searching the area, but Josh doubted it, too. He released a shaky breath that stirred her hair. "And Sylvie claims the person in the car was the fence and the person they were meeting was whoever stole the diamonds." At least that was the story she'd told them and that she was probably now telling Officer Carlson.

Natalie nodded.

"But we have no proof since both the fence and the shooter disappeared before the police arrived."

"Then we need to go back out there," she said, but she didn't pull away from him. She stayed in his arms, almost as if she was leaning on him.

"We need to charge your phone and recharge our bodies," he said. "Food and a quick nap, or we're not going to be any help to find Henry and your mother or of any help to them when they are found."

He was just repeating what Penny and Milek had told him when they'd both showed up by the river. But this time he believed them. Because he was so tired, he could barely stand. Maybe he was the one leaning on Natalie.

"We need to find them," she said, her voice breaking.

"I know."

"You're not going to promise me that we will?" she asked. She stared up at him, her green eyes so intense behind the lenses of her glasses.

"I think we both know that I've already broken a lot of promises to you," he said. "I don't want to break another one."

"I don't want you to," she said.

He touched her chin then, tipping it up. "I'm sorry, Natalie. I'm so sorry...for everything."

Even if she hadn't already told him that it was too late for them, an apology wasn't going to be enough to make it up to her for how much he'd hurt and disappointed her. He had to do a lot more than just apologize. He had to find their son and her mother.

But he knew that he didn't have the ability to do that right now. He had no idea where to look and was so tired that he could not see…beyond her face.

Her beautiful face.

He wanted so badly to kiss her, but he didn't dare. He'd given up that right long ago.

But then she rose up on tiptoe and kissed him, her lips soft and silky as they brushed across his.

Maybe he was so tired that he'd fallen asleep on his feet because this couldn't be happening. He had to be dreaming. But the dream got more and more vivid. And the feelings, as always when it came to Natalie, overwhelmed him.

The fear she'd felt in the warehouse was nothing compared to the fear Natalie was feeling now. What had she done? The kiss went on and on like it had a life of its own. And the passion overwhelmed her. She opened her eyes, and she could see the same passion in his dark eyes.

He pulled back slightly and hoarsely whispered, "Natalie?"

It was as if he couldn't believe it was her, like he was dreaming. And maybe that was all this was. A nightmare at first and now a dream…

She didn't want the dream to end. She didn't want to wake up. "Don't stop," she said, and she reached up to kiss him again. And as she kissed him, she pulled at his clothes, undressing him.

It had been so long since she'd felt passion like this, and it had only ever been with him. After Josh had broken her heart so badly five years ago, she hadn't dared to risk it again. So she'd focused on her son instead, on being a mother to him and a daughter to her parents.

And she'd forgotten she was a woman.

Until that kiss…

Now all the needs she'd denied for so long took over, and after she finished pulling off his shirt, she reached for hers. But his hands were there, pulling up her sweater and then unclasping her bra. And his fingers stroked her shoulders and then moved lower, over her breasts. Her breath caught as need clawed at her. And she unbuttoned his jeans and then reached for the tab, slowly lowering his zipper.

He groaned as she released him from his boxers, stroking her fingers over his engorged flesh. "Natalie," he whispered. "Are you sure?"

"I need this," she said. She needed him. She needed a release from all this tension gripping her. She needed oblivion.

"I can't stop…" He finished undressing her quickly, but as fast as he moved, he also seemed to take his time. He touched every inch of skin he exposed and kissed her everywhere.

Somehow, they made it from the living area into the bedroom, and then he was inside her, and they were making love like they used to. Moving together in perfect rhythm, her meeting his thrusts like this was a dance they'd choreographed long ago and knew by heart.

And her heart… It beat furiously as that tension wound so tightly inside her. And then it broke as an orgasm gripped her. Maybe it was because it had been so long or maybe it was because of everything else, but the pleasure was even more intense as was the passion…

But not love.

She couldn't love him again. Not after how badly he'd hurt her. Maybe she just needed someone to hang onto, something to feel that wasn't fear and pain. But after being with him again, like that, she was even more afraid…that she was falling for Josh Stafford all over again.

His body tensed, and then he found his release. As always, he was considerate of her. Instead of collapsing on top of her, he rolled to his side and kept her clasped against him. The tension drained from his body, and he started to breathe slow and deep and steady.

And something about the rhythm of his sleeping lulled her to sleep, too.

She didn't know how long she slept, but it felt like hours when she jerked awake. But it wasn't like she was waking up from a nightmare but waking up into one as she remembered every-thing that had happened.

That her son and her mother were still missing, were still hostages.

While she had awakened, Josh continued to sleep. She eased away from his side. They'd fallen asleep in each other's arms. So maybe he'd needed someone to hold onto as badly as she had.

But he must have gotten up sometime after she'd fallen asleep because her phone was on a charger next to the big bed, and she didn't remember putting it there.

All she remembered was how he tasted, how firm his lips were on hers and then on her body. Heat rushed through her, but it wasn't just passion, it was embarrassment and shame. How could she do that when she didn't even know where her son and mother were?

But maybe that was why she'd had to do it, to get her mind off the nightmare of not knowing where they were. To stop thinking…

Apparently, she'd stopped listening, too, because as she reached for her cell, she could see all the messages and missed calls lighting up the screen.

What if she'd missed a call about Henry? What if he and her mom had been found?

Her hand shook as she grabbed it, but she noted the only missed calls and messages were from her sister. If anyone had found Henry and her mother, she suspected that they would have contacted her directly, not through Dena. They'd had enough trouble tracking her down just like Natalie had.

Why? What was going on with her sister because it was clear that something was.

Natalie's skin, naked beneath the sheets, chilled, goose bumps rising on her flesh. Could her sister actually be involved in the theft or the kidnapping?

Bracing herself, she opened a text message: You need to an-swer your damn phone.

And another: Where the hell are you?

And another: Why did you leave with him?

And then the last: Dad is missing now. This is all your fault.

Natalie gasped, not at the accusation but at the news.

"What?" Josh asked, and he sounded wide awake. "What's wrong?"

Everything.

Everything was wrong, and she'd been a fool to give in to her feelings last night. Or this morning…or whenever they'd made love.

Heat burned her face now. "My dad is missing." She was fumbling with her phone, trying to call Dena.

It rang several times, but her sister didn't accept the call. Was that because she was looking for Dad yet? Hadn't she been able to find him?

Or had she found him, and she was just too angry with Natalie to answer her call?

Josh wasn't the only one who had a sister who resented him. For some reason Dena resented her, too. Maybe just because she'd stopped being an only child when Natalie was born.

Then her cell rang, with Dena calling back.

"Yes? Did you find Dad?" Natalie asked her.

"Not yet," her sister replied. "Timothy is out looking for him."

"Dena, when did he go missing? What happened?"

"He was so unsettled last night that he couldn't sleep. He kept trying to get out of our house and was setting off the alarm, so we disarmed it," Dena said. "I don't know when he took off, but Timothy woke up and found the front door open."

"Dena, how could you…" Emotion choked Natalie as she was overwhelmed with concern. Now her father was missing, too.

"You shouldn't have left him here," Dena said, "and you shouldn't have left with *him*."

"My son is missing," Natalie said. "Our mother is missing. Can't you understand why I'm out here trying to find them?"

"Of course I understand, and I'm upset, too, but I don't know where to look for them and neither do you," Dena said. "You could have stayed with Dad. He's used to you being around. He's not used to being here with us."

"Did you call the police?" Natalie asked.

"No. I'm sure he's just off walking. Timothy is looking around our neighborhood for him. He can't have gotten far."

Natalie jumped up and started reaching for her clothes. "I'll find him." As long as nobody had taken him like her mother and Henry had been taken.

She disconnected the call with her sister and finished dressing to find Josh already dressed, the key fob for the SUV in his hand.

"I'll help you look," he said.

"I'm sure he's fine," Natalie replied. "He does this. He goes walking sometimes..." Especially when he was restless or upset. And not having her mother around made him both unless he was at work.

Josh nodded. "My grandma used to do that, too. She thought she was walking to school, but it was always in the middle of the night."

Despite the medication, night was the worst for her father, too. But she and her mother were used to dealing with him.

"We need to find Henry and my mom, too," she said. "You should focus on that, on them."

"I am. We are," he said. "But we don't have a lead right now. So let's find your dad."

And maybe looking for him was like what they'd done last night, something that would take their minds off their fears over Henry and her mom.

That had to be all that last night was...an escape from reality. Because she knew there was no chance of anything real or lasting between them. She couldn't risk her heart like that again. She couldn't risk getting hurt again.

"Claus," Mimi murmured in her sleep as she moved on the air mattress next to Henry. "Claus..."

That was Grandpa's name, kind of like Santa Claus, but with a funny-sounding difference, like people were speaking a different language when they talked to him. And people liked talking to Grandpa. He was always so funny and nice.

No wonder Mimi was calling for him.

Henry wanted to see Grandpa, too.

And Mommy.

But he didn't call out for them. He called out for someone else. "Daddy..."

That was who was supposed to find them. Where was he? Why wasn't he here yet? It had to be daytime now. Henry wasn't sure because that lamp was still the only light in the metal building. He just figured it was morning because he was hungry again.

Daddy had to get here soon. He had to get them out of here. Why wasn't he here? Hadn't he found those things he was supposed to find for the person in that mask?

The diamonds?

What would the person in the mask do if Daddy didn't find the diamonds?

What would that person do to Henry and Mimi?

Chapter Sixteen

Josh was furious Natalie's sister had lost Mr. Croft. The last thing they needed was someone else to find. Why hadn't Dena taken precautions to make sure that her dad didn't go wandering in the middle of the night?

It wasn't always possible to prevent that, though. He and his dad had tried with his grandma, but she had become quite the escape artist. When she'd slipped out, she'd always been going to school.

Since Claus had gone to school in another country, he wouldn't be walking there. Maybe he was headed to his home or to the store. Given the early hour, Josh was banking on the house.

As they pulled into the driveway, crime-scene tape fluttered near the side door of the house. Someone had broken it to get inside.

Natalie must have seen it, too, because she released a heavy sigh of relief. "He's here." She didn't jump out before he shut off the SUV like she had the day before.

In fact, Josh reached for his door first. "Are you okay?" he asked.

She nodded. "I don't know what to tell him," she said. "He's most aware in the mornings. He will know we're lying to him. He'll be able to tell something's happened here."

Josh drew in a breath and nodded, too, as he remembered

how little patience his grandmother had had when she was lucid and knew she was being humored. "Yes. We'll have to tell him the truth." And hope Mr. Croft could handle that his wife and grandson were missing.

"Thank you," Natalie murmured.

"For what?" he wondered.

"For being here."

He wished he'd been with her the past five years, like they'd planned. That she hadn't had to raise their son without him or handle her dad's diagnosis without him. And no matter how much Josh was with her now, he knew he couldn't make up for not being there then. For choosing to go to prison instead of honoring their engagement.

Even though he'd had his reasons, he didn't expect her to forgive him because he couldn't forgive himself. He pushed open his door and got out.

Natalie rushed around the front of the SUV first and stepped into the house, calling out, "Dad? Dad?"

Josh followed her inside and grimaced. Her dad had been upset with the mess the crime-scene techs had left in the store. But the kitchen was even worse. Since whoever had taken Marilyn and Henry had been inside in order to slip those sleeping pills in the coffee, they'd had to touch things. So most surfaces had been fingerprinted, and the place had been searched.

Natalie ran around the house, calling out for her father. But like the day before, they didn't find a person inside. She turned to Josh with wide eyes. "Where could he be? I thought he was here."

The broken crime-scene tape indicated that he had been. Or at least someone had. Maybe it wasn't Claus. It could have been whoever had taken Henry and Marilyn returning to the scene of their crime, making sure they'd left no evidence behind, or it could have been someone looking for those damn diamonds even.

"Let's check the garage," Josh suggested as he stepped out the patio doors into the backyard.

"We hid the keys to his car," Natalie said. But she followed him across the yard to the side door of the detached structure.

The crime-scene tape fluttered free here, too, broken in the middle. And the door stood open. Josh didn't see anyone standing inside the garage, though, until Natalie bumped his arm and pointed at the Cadillac.

Her father sat behind the steering wheel, his hands gripping it tightly almost as if he was imagining that he was driving. But no sound came from the engine, no exhaust from the tailpipe. It wasn't running.

"Good thing you hid the keys," Josh whispered.

Natalie nodded and drew in a deep breath. Then she crossed the garage, careful to avoid the spot that was marked off where the bloodstain was on the concrete. And she knocked on the driver's window.

Her father jumped and whirled toward her. But he couldn't lower the window since they were power and the vehicle wasn't running.

Josh joined them and opened the door. At least her father had left that unlocked.

Natalie dropped down to her knees, so that she was eye-to-eye with him. "Daddy, where are you going?"

He stared at her and blinked. "I—I…"

"The store is closed today, so you don't have to go to work," she said.

He shook his head. "I—I have to go…" Then he leaned back and pointed toward the passenger seat where some velvet pouches lay. "I have to put those back in the safe."

Natalie gasped in shock. "Daddy, do you have the diamonds?"

Josh silently cursed himself for not considering it earlier. After he and his dad moved his grandmother into a memory care unit at an assisted living center, they would often find things in her room that didn't belong to her. Like TV remotes, wheelchairs and even a few pairs of dentures, but Grandma had had all of her own teeth.

But diamonds…

How the hell would the older man have been able to bypass the security system and open the vault?

At the moment that was the least of Josh's concerns, though. The only things missing right now had been in a pouch like this, so these were definitely the diamonds.

"We need to get word out that we have them," Josh said, his pulse quickening with hope. He grabbed his phone and started texting.

Not just Milek and Detective Dubridge but also his sister. He wanted everyone to know, so that word would get back to the kidnapper. So that he or she would know that Josh had what they wanted now.

And if they wanted those diamonds, they would have to give him the clue they'd promised that would lead him to where his son and Marilyn were being held. He had to get them back.

While Josh was texting and making calls, Natalie dealt with her dad. She got him out of the car and into a folding chair next to it. Then she reached across the seat for those velvet bags. As she dumped each of them out onto the supple leather of the driver seat, she sucked in a breath.

"This is stuff that went missing before the security system was installed," she said.

These were things for which they'd already filed insurance claims and had been reimbursed. But apparently the items hadn't really been stolen. She dumped out the last bag of small loose stones. There were some diamonds but mostly rubies and emeralds. "This isn't the diamonds that have just gone missing."

"What?" Josh asked.

"They're not here." And she wasn't particularly surprised because she couldn't imagine how her father would have remembered the code to bypass the system. It was changed too often and was too long for her to remember without putting a note in her cell phone.

Josh cursed. "Are you sure? There are a lot of diamonds there."

She shook her head. "Not even close to what was taken." Or to what it would take to get their son and her mom back from the kidnapper.

"It's too late," Josh said. "I've already gotten the word out."

She shook her head. "It isn't going to work. People who actually saw the diamonds and knew how many stones and the size of them won't be fooled."

"I told the detective to let your family know, too," Josh said, "when I texted him."

Her stomach flipped with the fear that her brother-in-law or sister were responsible for Henry and her mom missing. Maybe that was why Dena wasn't as worried as Natalie was. Maybe she knew where they were and that they were safe.

Please, let them be safe.

"This could still be our best shot at getting them back," Josh said.

"Getting what back?" her father asked. "What are you talking about?"

"Nothing, Daddy."

"The diamonds," Josh said, turning toward her father now. He knelt on the floor in front of him.

Her father gestured to his Cadillac. "They're in there. All of it's in there."

"No, Daddy," Natalie said. "There is a big bag of diamonds missing from the vault, remember?"

His forehead furrowed as if he was struggling to find the memory. But then he shook his head. "No, honey. I can't..." He sounded so defeated, and he looked so tired, too, with his suit rumpled, and his white hair mussed. It was so unlike him to not have his hair neatly combed and his suit pressed. He must have slept in it the night before, if he'd slept at all.

Why hadn't Dena taken care of him? Why hadn't she found him some pajamas of Timothy's to wear? And given him a comb?

Maybe he wasn't the one who maintained his meticulous appearance after all. Maybe her mother had been taking care of him more than Natalie realized. Maybe the medication hadn't slowed the progression or reversed some of the damage as much as she'd thought.

She gasped at a jab of guilt with the realization that he hadn't taken his prescription. That was another thing her mother handled and without her there, Natalie had forgotten. Maybe she couldn't judge her sister as harshly as she had.

"Let's get you inside, Daddy," she said as she helped him up from the folding chair. "We'll get you something to eat." And his pills.

"Mr. Croft, where were you keeping these things?" Josh asked, pointing toward the driver seat.

Her father sighed. "The vault, of course."

Natalie shook her head. "No. This stuff went missing a while ago, Daddy. It wasn't in the vault."

He shrugged. "I don't know then, but we better get it back to the store."

"Tomorrow," she said. "It's closed today."

He nodded.

"Let's get you inside..." She pointed him toward the door, but before she could follow him out, Josh caught her hand.

"This isn't right, Natalie," he said.

"I know," she agreed. "I told you. The diamonds aren't there."

"No. This stuff wasn't in here yesterday. We would have noticed or the techs would have noticed when they processed the garage."

"Dad was in the house, too," Natalie reminded him. "Maybe he has a hiding place in there." It made sense. He'd grown up with family who'd gone through the Holocaust and had learned to hide their valuables. "I'll look for it after I get him his medication. Maybe we'll find them yet."

"If we don't, we have to use what we have here," Josh said. "We have to do whatever we can to get our son and your mother back."

She knew he was right, but she was scared they were making a mistake. That instead of getting their son and her mom back, they might piss off the kidnapper and he or she would make certain that they never saw Henry and his Mimi again.

Guilt weighed so heavily on Milek that he hadn't been able to bring himself to go home the night before. He wouldn't have felt right holding his son and his daughter when Natalie and Josh couldn't hold their child. Natalie had given Henry's picture to the police for the Amber alert, and Milek had a copy of it pinned to the corner of the canvas over which he swept his brush.

The photo was so flat, so two-dimensional. With paint and his brush, Milek could bring the picture to life. And by doing that, maybe he could somehow keep the child alive, too. Because he hadn't done anything else productive.

Garek and Candace were back now and in the office, going over everything with fresh eyes and their expert perspectives. They could do more than Milek could now.

A door creaked open, and he felt her before he saw her. The air seemed to shimmer around his wife; Amber was that full of vitality and ambition and intelligence. And with her vibrant red hair and sharp green eyes, she was stunningly beautiful as well. He still couldn't believe that she'd chosen to be with him.

"I'm sorry I didn't come home," he said. He'd texted her to let her know.

"I didn't expect you," she said. "I know you would be working hard to find the missing child and his grandmother."

Milek sighed. "I tried, my darling. I tried. But I don't know where to look in that world anymore." Last night, slipping back into the ugliness of it had affected him. That was why he was in his studio, with the need to make something beautiful again.

"You were doing everything you needed to," Amber assured him. "Running this agency and coordinating with the police department."

He grinned. "You were keeping tabs on me."

"I am always aware of you, my darling," she said. And she kissed him.

His lips clung to hers for a moment, and he wanted to deepen the kiss. To make love with her. But she was already dressed in a suit and ready for work. And he had work to do, too, more so than just painting. They stepped back, and both released a shaky sigh of regret at ending the kiss.

"How is Josh?" she asked with concern.

"Desperate," Milek said. "He texted. They found some jewels—"

"They found the diamonds?"

He shook his head. "At first he thought so, but Natalie said they weren't the correct ones. He wants to try to use them anyway to get the lead to his son."

"Of course he does. As you said, he's desperate."

"But it might get him killed."

"Josh Stafford has no problem making the ultimate sacrifice for people he loves," Amber said. "Just like someone else I know. He reminded me of you the first time I met him. That was why I knew he was a good man and wanted to help him."

Milek wanted to help him, too, but he didn't know how to save someone from himself. He had a terrible fear, the same one that Garek had shared with him at their grand opening party. He was afraid that they might lose one of their team.

That Josh Stafford would give up more than his freedom this time. He would give up his life.

Chapter Seventeen

Josh's phone vibrated, then lit up with a video screen from an unknown number. "It worked," he whispered to Natalie who stood beside him in her father's study.

If Claus had a secret safe or hiding place anywhere in the house, it would probably be here, but they couldn't find it. And they'd searched pretty much everywhere while Claus was sleeping. This was their second time going through his study.

Natalie rushed to Josh's side and pressed up against him. "Take it, take the call," she urged.

Josh swiped to accept and stared at the face that filled his cell phone screen.

Henry was pale yet with dark circles beneath his brown eyes, like he hadn't slept well. He probably hadn't.

"Hey, there, buddy," Josh said, his heart filling with love for this child he had yet to meet in person. "How are you and your grandma?"

"Daddy?" Henry said, and he blinked and peered at the screen. "Yes."

"I'm here, too, sweetheart," Natalie said.

"I miss you, Mommy," Henry said, and his bottom lip quivered. Then he glanced up, above the camera lens on the phone, probably to whoever was holding it. Then he looked down at the screen again and, as if he was following orders, asked, "Did you find the diamonds, Daddy?"

"Yes, I did."

Natalie tensed and opened her mouth, probably ready to tell the truth, like she always did.

But Josh grabbed one of her hands with his free one and gently squeezed. He hated that he was lying to his son, too, but they couldn't waste any more time. They needed to get him and his grandmother home.

"How is Mimi?" Natalie asked.

And Josh realized the boy hadn't answered his first question. He hadn't told him how they were.

"She wants Grandpa," Henry said, his voice breaking with tears. But then he glanced up, probably at the masked person again.

At least Josh hoped the person was still wearing their mask, that they hadn't let Henry or Marilyn see their face. As long as they couldn't identify them, their kidnapper didn't have any reason to kill them.

But that still didn't guarantee that he or she wouldn't. There were no guarantees even if Josh had the right diamonds for the ransom.

Henry's long dark lashes fluttered as if he was blinking away his tears, or maybe he was just that nervous. That scared. "Did you really find the diamonds, Daddy?" he asked.

Glad now that he'd brought in those bags from the car, Josh handed the phone to Natalie. He pulled the bag of loose stones from his pocket and spilled the diamonds into his hand while leaving the other stones in the bag, making it look full. Hopefully the kidnapper would think the rest of the diamonds were still in the bag.

He nodded at Natalie, who focused the camera on his hand and the bag. Her throat moved as she swallowed hard, as scared as he was that this might not work.

"I have them right here," he said, "but if that person with the mask wants to get them, they're going to have to let you and your grandma go." Then he reached out with his free hand and disconnected the call.

Natalie fumbled with his cell, as if trying to get the call back. "What the hell are you doing!" she exclaimed. "We're not going to get them—"

The cell vibrated, and a text lit up the screen: Don't play games with me.

"They know," she whispered as if the kidnapper could still hear them, as if Josh hadn't disconnected the call.

Hanging up on his son was like punching himself in the gut. He hated to do it. He wanted to stare at the little boy as long as he could. But he knew this was the best way to deal with the kidnapper, to keep them off guard, to make them mess up.

He dumped the diamonds back in the bag and shoved it in his pocket. Then he took back his cell and typed a response.

I have what you want. You have my son and his grandma. Give them back if you want the diamonds.

The phone was still for several long moments. Natalie began to cry, tears sliding down her face.

Then the text came back:

No police. No games. In an hour I will text you an address where you are to come. Alone. With the diamonds or the hostages die.

"It's too dangerous," she whispered again.

"It's too dangerous to bring the police and have the kidnapper run off without letting me know where our son is," he said.

"It's too dangerous to try to pass off that bag as the missing diamonds."

"Then let's add more to it," he suggested. "Let's get some of these other diamonds out of the settings and go to the store and get some, too. Whatever we have to do."

She sucked in a breath, but then she nodded. "Yes, whatever we have to do…"

They'd spent most of the past hour at the closed store with her dad, taking apart whatever piece of jewelry they could to add more diamonds to the bag. Though he hadn't understood what they were doing or why, her dad had helped.

And then Josh's phone vibrated. "This is it," he said. But he didn't pull it out. He didn't look at the address.

"Tell me where," Natalie said.

He shook his head. "No. And you can't try to follow me like you did my sister."

"But—"

"No, Natalie," he said. "You need to stay here with your dad. I can't protect myself if I'm worried about protecting you, too."

That was true. He could have died the night before in the warehouse, with the shooter firing at him, Sylvie and her. She didn't want him alone in a situation like that again. But she didn't want her son and mother in it, either.

Tears stung her eyes. "At least tell me where—"

He shook his head. "No. I can't risk you getting nervous and contacting the police."

"Josh—"

"I have to go, Natalie. I have to try…"

To get their son back and her mother. He had to try even though he was risking his own life for theirs. Damn him.

She was starting to fall for him all over again, no matter how badly he'd hurt her five years ago.

As he headed toward the back door and the alley where he'd parked the SUV, she stepped in front of him and kissed him. Their lips parted, their breath combined, and the passion ignited. But then she pulled back and whispered, "Be careful, please."

While she wasn't sure she could ever trust him again with her heart, she didn't want to lose him again, either.

He nodded. But he didn't promise.

And she had no doubt he would do whatever he had to in order to get their son and her mother back. As the door closed behind him, she felt like she had when she left the prison after visiting him that last time. Like she might never see him again…

The thought had a tear spilling over and rolling down her cheek.

Her father put his arm around her. "Don't worry about him,

honey," he said. "That man of yours is a good one. You can trust him."

Her father had no idea who Josh was and how badly he'd already broken her heart. But she hugged her dad tightly, taking the comfort he offered as well as giving some.

After he'd showered, eaten and taken his medication, he seemed like his old self again. Almost as if he knew what was going on, but she couldn't be sure.

"We better get this stuff back in the vault," he said, pointing toward the bags lying around that contained the stones and other items they hadn't used. The things that had gone missing before the new system.

"Let me get the lock," she said.

But he opened the middle drawer of the desk he had in the backroom. Then he pulled out some folded slips, sales invoices, but the numbers scrawled on them weren't item numbers or orders. They were the codes that changed every day or so.

"Dad," she gasped. "I didn't realize you were writing those down."

Every time it changed, she had shared the new code with him because she'd known he wouldn't remember it. It had seemed respectful to include him, to act like he was still running the store. He was already losing so much that she hadn't wanted him to lose his pride, too. So she'd just read them off to him, and while he usually had a pen on him and a pad of invoices nearby, she hadn't thought he would have been quick enough to write down the whole series of numbers.

"It's my vault," he said with that pride. "My store...until it's yours."

"Mine?"

"Your mother had the lawyer draw up papers to turn ownership over to you. I already signed, and she was waiting just a bit longer before she signed. I can't remember why."

"Mine—"

A floorboard creaked.

Natalie tensed, hoping that it wasn't Timothy or Dena out there. They must have unlocked the front door. Usually, they would have come through the alley, though, like Hannah, but it was her usual day off.

"Hello?" Natalie called out. "Who's…" She started toward the showroom door, but it opened before she reached it. She stumbled back a step as Sylvie Combs walked into the room. "What are you doing here?"

"Don't worry," Sylvie said with a smile. "I'm not here to rob you."

Her father chuckled. "You would be the prettiest thief ever if you were."

Natalie smiled at her father's flirting. Even if he wasn't trying to sell something, charm and flattery were such ingrained parts of his personality that she doubted even the progression of Alzheimer's would change it. "This flirt is my dad, Claus Croft. Dad, this is Josh's sister, Henry's aunt, Sylvie."

Sylvie let out a little gasp. "Oh, it didn't even occur to me that I'm an aunt."

"Yes, you are." Natalie hoped that the young woman would be able to meet her nephew soon. But most of all she hoped Henry would meet his dad. That Josh would bring their child and her mother back home.

And himself.

"I—I saw Henry's picture on that Amber alert," Sylvie said. "He looks just like Josh."

Natalie smiled and nodded. "Yes, he does."

"That must have been hard," Sylvie said. "After what happened…" She trailed off with a glance at Natalie's dad, as if wondering how much he knew.

Even before his early on-set diagnosis, Claus hadn't known much about Josh. But he was still pretty perceptive. "I'll leave you two lovely ladies to your conversation, and I'll spruce up the showroom." He stepped out the door that Sylvie had just entered.

"How did you get in here?" Natalie asked. She knew she'd locked up last night and had engaged the alarm on the front door. "Was someone else out there? Did someone let you in?"

Sylvie smiled. "Nobody has to let me in."

"That's a really good security system," Natalie said. It wasn't as high-end as other models Garek Kozminski had showed her, but it was the best they'd been able to afford. Apparently, it wasn't enough to keep out diamond thieves and Sylvie Combs. Were they one and the same?

"It is a really good system," Sylvie agreed.

"Have you been in here before?" Natalie asked with suspicion.

Sylvie shook her head. "No. I haven't. I was just curious how good the system was and what kind of thief it would take to bypass it. Now I've confirmed it would take either a really good thief or someone who didn't have to bypass it, someone on the inside."

That was Natalie's fear, too. She closed her eyes and nodded. "I know…" That her sister and brother-in-law were possible suspects.

"It could also be someone on the inside of the company that set it up," Sylvie continued. "The Kozminskis have a reputation in this town, Natalie. And Josh is the only one of their employees who didn't actually commit the crime he served time for."

"What are you saying? You think it's one of his coworkers or his bosses?" Natalie asked with sudden alarm. "They've been tracking his whereabouts." Even though he hadn't told her where he was going, his company would know. She wasn't going to get her son and mom back, she was going to lose Josh too.

Fear struck her so hard that she dropped into the chair behind her father's desk and knocked the sales slips onto the floor. "Oh my God…"

Sylvie knelt down in front of her. "What are you talking about? Where's Josh?"

"He left to make the exchange," Natalie said.

"He has the diamonds?" Sylvie asked. Then she glanced around the backroom, at the items strewn across the surfaces. "What's going on here? What is he really trying to exchange for the hostages?"

The kidnapper had to believe that he had the real diamonds. And Sylvie…

Could she still be part of it? Should Natalie trust her? Josh's sister had already put his life in danger before; Natalie didn't want her putting him in danger again. But he was already in danger, maybe more than Natalie had realized if he couldn't trust his bosses and coworkers.

"Tell me what's going on," Sylvie urged her. "You can trust me, and you can definitely trust my brother."

Tears stung Natalie's eyes now as all her doubts and uncertainties and fears overwhelmed her.

"Now you're scaring me," Sylvie said with a shaky sigh. "He's doing something stupid, isn't he?"

"Do you mean like when he took the blame for you?" she asked. Sylvie was the thief. Josh was a man who sacrificed himself to protect those he loved, like a child that he hadn't even known he had.

"Exactly like that," Sylvie said. "If he's trying to convince the kidnapper that he has the diamonds, his bluff is going to get called."

"Why are you so certain that he doesn't have them?" Natalie asked. "Do you have them?"

Sylvie shook her head. "No. You know I don't."

"I wouldn't be asking if I knew," Natalie said.

"You wouldn't be asking if my brother actually has them," Sylvie said. "And look at this mess..." She picked up the sales slip from the floor and used them to gesture around the place. "It's obvious what you're trying to do."

"I'm trying to get my son and my mother back," Natalie said.

"That's what my brother is doing," Sylvie said. "And I'm afraid he's going to get himself killed."

She wasn't the only one afraid...

"Because you know he doesn't have the diamonds," Natalie said. Maybe Sylvie had just figured it out from the mess in the backroom. But still... "On your brother and your nephew's lives, do you have them?"

"I swear I don't," Sylvie said. "I was with the fence who was supposed to be meeting with the person who actually has them."

"I don't really care about the diamonds," Natalie admitted, even if her father and mother were going to give her the store. "I just want my son and my mom safely back." And Josh.

Sylvie unfolded the slips she'd picked up from the floor, and her pale eyes narrowed. "What are these?"

Natalie snatched them from her hand. "Sales slips. My dad still uses the paper invoices. He hates the computer." So he had a pad of invoices…that had carbon between them for duplicate copies for the buyer and the retailer and in some cases the finance company. She unfolded each slip that was only the top sheet. What had happened to the other two?

Even if he'd thrown them out…

"What?" Sylvie asked. "What's wrong?"

Natalie let out a curse. "I think I know who has the diamonds."

But there wouldn't be time to get them back. Josh was already on his way to make the exchange. And when the kidnapper realized he'd lied, would that wind up costing Josh his life and their son and her mother's theirs as well?

Mimi was still sleepy today, but Henry was excited. Too excited to sit on that air mattress, so he walked in circles on the concrete floor, never going much beyond the glow of the lamp.

"Daddy's coming," he told her. "He found the diamonds. And now he's going to find us."

Mimi pushed herself up, but then she closed her eyes again, and her face scrunched up like she had a bad headache. She was even holding onto her head, like it was too heavy for her neck. "Sweetheart," she said, "we don't know for sure that person in the mask is going to tell your daddy where we are."

"But that was the rule of this game," Henry said. "Daddy had to find the diamonds, and then he would get a clue to finding us."

Mimi nodded, but then a little groan slipped out of her mouth. "I know. But sometimes people break rules."

"Like Chelsea Oliver." She broke the rules all the time. She cut in line. She never waited until she was called on, and she would just walk out of class without asking for permission to leave. He really wasn't sorry he'd accidentally spit his gum into her hair. But she sure had told on him quick even though she got mad every time someone told on her for breaking rules.

"Yes," Mimi said. "Like little Chelsea."

"Daddy won't break the rules," he said.

And his grandmother made that face again, like she was in pain, but she hadn't moved.

"He won't," Henry said. "He'll find us."

"I hope he does," Mimi said. "But we have to try to find our own way out, too."

Henry liked that idea. He really wanted to get out of this place. Even with the lamp, it was dark, and it was cold when he wasn't under those blankets with Mimi. He wanted to go home.

Chapter Eighteen

Josh didn't have to glance into the rearview mirror to know he was being followed. The kidnapper might be back there, but he knew for certain who else was following him. Someone from the Payne Protection Agency.

He wasn't so naive that he didn't realize that his phone was being monitored. Probably not just by the Payne Protection Agency but also the River City Police Department. Milek wasn't going to let him get himself killed like he nearly had the night before.

But their presence made that more likely to happen than if he went alone. Even worse, it might cause the kidnapper to get rid of their hostages.

So he called his boss now, who sounded a bit distracted as he answered with rustling noises more so than his voice.

"Milek?"

"Yes, what are you doing?"

"I think you know."

"Getting yourself killed?"

"Better me than whomever you have following me," Josh replied. "Tell them to back off, or they're not going to get just *me* killed."

"You're making an exchange for the hostages right now," Milek concluded.

"I hope so," he said.

"Or you're walking into a trap," Milek said.

"Either way I have to risk it. But I don't want to risk Henry and Marilyn's lives because the kidnapper spots someone else. Tell Dubridge that, too."

"He knows," Milek said. "He has a child now, too. He gets it."

Josh was only just *getting* it. He'd given up a lot for his sister, but that might have been partially out of guilt that he hadn't been there for her when she'd needed him. But with Henry...

It wasn't just guilt driving Josh, although he felt some of that, too. And it wasn't just love. It was something even more primal. He knew he would do anything for his son.

"Just please, keep everyone back and out of sight," Josh implored his boss. "Don't make it so that I lose my son before I ever get a chance to meet him."

Milek released a sigh that rattled the speaker. "Okay. Just be careful."

Josh wasn't going to make his boss a promise he couldn't keep—he'd already made too many of those. So he disconnected the call.

The area for this meeting wasn't as dangerous as where Natalie had followed Sylvie the night before. This was a hiking trail, but it was a busy one, with several vehicles parked at the head of it. People were coming and going, alone, in pairs and groups, with strollers and dogs.

This wasn't going to be dangerous at all. So maybe whoever was holding Henry and Marilyn wasn't dangerous, either.

Hopeful now, Josh jumped out of his SUV with the bag of diamonds zipped into one pocket of his leather jacket, and the pepper spray zipped into the other.

He started off, walking fast, hurrying past hikers to where the trail came to a fork. One side was the easy trail which was wide and obviously well trod. The other led uphill, over tree roots that made the ground uneven. This was where he had to go.

He was the only one who took that fork as the others continued on with their dogs and strollers on the easier path. He had to find another fork between this trail and what was essentially an animal track. And along that track, he was to leave the bag on the other side of a fallen tree.

Ordinarily he would have enjoyed the day, which was unseasonably warm this early in the spring. The sun beamed down through the trees that were just budding leaves. He missed the fork to the animal path at first and only turned back when he noticed a deer standing above him on the trail.

The animal path went uphill before going down to where a fallen log lay across it. Josh's heart was pounding hard with anticipation more than exertion, and he glanced around him. But even the deer was gone now. And the birds and squirrels had gone quiet as well.

He was close. Not just to the log but to the kidnapper, too. They had to be somewhere nearby, watching him. And so he did what he'd been ordered to do. He unzipped his pocket and pulled out the velvet bag. Then he crouched down and leaned over the fallen tree, tucking the bag onto the other side of it. He pressed his palms against the rough bark to push himself back up. But before he could stand, something struck him hard across the back of his head.

Pain radiated throughout his skull, but he clung to consciousness. He blinked and tried to clear away the black spots blurring his vision. And he rolled over to stare up into a hideous face… That mask…

The one his son had been talking about.

And he reached out, trying to grab the kidnapper, trying to hang onto them.

"Where is my son? Where…" Josh whispered, his voice draining away along with his consciousness. His last thought before everything went black was that he'd failed Natalie once again.

"Why hasn't he called?" Natalie asked as she paced the cramped backroom of Croft Custom Jewelry. She should have insisted on going with Josh, although she wasn't sure what she would have done with her dad if she had.

Claus had already set off the alarm twice since they'd arrived at the store. Maybe he wasn't doing as well as she thought. Or maybe her restlessness was making him restless.

"You said he left right before I showed up, so he hasn't been gone that long," Sylvie pointed out. "And you don't know where he was even going for the drop-off. It could have been a long drive to it."

Natalie had told Sylvie how he hadn't shown her the address. "But what if some of his team or his bosses aren't to be trusted?" she asked her deepest fear aloud. "Then he has no backup. He's all alone, just like he was in prison..." Her heart ached thinking of how it must have been for him, of how much he'd given up. And now he might be giving up his life.

Sylvie reached out then and clasped her hands. "I am so sorry, Natalie. What he did for me hurt so many more people than I knew." Tears shimmered in her eyes. "Not that it matters. Just hurting him was bad enough."

"It was," Natalie agreed.

"But you and Henry suffered, too," Sylvie said.

"And now my little boy is out there, and my mother..." Natalie was so scared for them, for Josh and for herself. She was falling for him again even though she knew she shouldn't.

"Josh is going to do his best to get your son and your mother back," Sylvie said.

"But what if the kidnapper knows that he doesn't really have the diamonds they want? What will they do to him?"

Sylvie released a shaky breath. "I don't know. But let's focus on what we do know." She tapped a finger on the sales invoices that sat on top of Natalie's desk now. "Your father was writing down the security codes. Whoever saw these or got ahold of the other copies of these invoices probably has those diamonds. Who could have seen them?"

Natalie felt that surge of urgency and anger again as she'd realized who the prime suspects were. "I think it has to be one of the other sales reps." She'd already called them. Timothy had been short with her, saying he'd been up all night looking for her father, so he was taking the day to rest. Hannah had promised to drop by before she headed to a class. This would have been her usual day off. And Natalie felt a pang of guilt for suspecting them. "But then I guess that even a customer might have wondered about those numbers, someone perhaps casing the place..."

Sylvie shook her head. "I don't know. I think Payne Protection would have picked up on someone casing the place."

"My brother-in-law thought that Josh was when he saw him on the surveillance videos from after hours."

"He was guarding it, though?"

Natalie nodded.

"He wanted to go into law enforcement," Sylvie said. "I'm glad that he is…in a way."

"Because the diamonds were stolen, I think he feels like he failed," Natalie remarked. "Like he felt he failed you."

"I failed me," Sylvie said. "Though it was easier to blame him. I guess I picked that up from my mother, not taking any responsibility for my actions and blaming everyone else."

Natalie's heart softened toward the younger woman.

"I failed him, too," Sylvie said. "And you and my nephew. And I really want to do whatever I can to help now."

"Then let's find him," Natalie said. Because the longer she waited to hear from him, the closer she was getting to losing her mind.

When the alarm went off again, she cursed and rushed out to the showroom. But it wasn't her father who'd opened the door this time; it was Hannah.

"I'm sorry," the young woman said. "I saw Mr. C and thought it was unlocked."

"No, we're closed for the day," Natalie said as she quickly punched in the code again to shut off the alarm.

Hannah tilted her head, and her long dark ponytail swung across her slender shoulders. "Then why did you want to see me?"

"Geez, you have to know about her son," Sylvie remarked as she joined them in the showroom. "How can you ask?"

"Who are you?" Hannah replied. "And I'm sorry about the kid and Mrs. C, but I don't know how to help."

"You can answer a question," Natalie said.

Hannah nodded. "Yeah, but I already answered everything the police and those bodyguards asked me." She yawned as if she was tired.

Natalie was tired, too, tired of people who didn't care about other people. Like her sister and brother-in-law and this young, carefree woman. "Well, I am damn sorry to inconvenience you, but two people I love are missing, and I will do anything to find them!" Three. Maybe.

Why the hell hadn't Josh called?

Hannah's thin throat moved as she swallowed. "I—I get that. I do, but I don't know how to help you."

"Tell me the truth," Natalie said. And she laid the sales invoices on the showroom case between them. "Do you have the other copies of these?"

Hannah didn't even look at them. "I do everything on the computer. Those are Mr. C's."

"I know. But the other copies are missing."

Hannah shrugged. "I don't handle the paperwork. You do."

"These aren't real sales," Natalie said. "They're the codes to the security system."

Hannah sucked in a breath. "Oh. I didn't know…"

She hadn't even looked at them, or she would have known that the figures jotted down on them weren't item numbers.

"So if the police are searching your place right now, they won't find copies of these?" Sylvie asked as she stared intently at the woman who was probably just slightly younger than she was.

Hannah snorted. "The police aren't searching my place. They have no reason to do that, and even if they were looking, they wouldn't find anything. I don't have the code to the vault."

"Maybe you didn't keep the copies," Sylvie began. "But—"

"If you really want to find out who's been taking things," Hannah said and she was looking at Natalie instead of Sylvie, "you need to look closer to home than me."

That was what Natalie had been afraid of. "So you do know something?" Natalie asked.

"I know that there are things happening around here that I don't want to be part of anymore," Hannah said. "Let's consider this my last day. I'm not coming back to work here even if you manage to reopen." She whirled around and rushed out the front door, setting off the alarm once again.

While Natalie was able to shut off the security alarm, another one kept raging inside her. Alarm for her son and mother and for Josh.

"What the hell did she mean by that?" Sylvie mused aloud. "Even if you manage to reopen?"

Natalie shrugged. "The store is the least of my concerns right now."

"I know," Sylvie agreed. "But she knows more than she told us or the police."

"But why wouldn't she share it?"

Sylvie sighed. "She's either afraid of incriminating herself or she's just afraid."

Natalie could relate to the latter. She was so very afraid.

Despite everything else going on around him, Milek was inspired to keep working on his painting of the little boy. Something about it called to him as if he could find answers within the portrait.

As if he could find the child and his grandmother...

"Are you going to the hospital?" Garek asked.

Milek hadn't heard his brother come into the studio, but he didn't jump. He expected him. "Josh won't be there long."

"He got knocked out. He needs a CT scan."

"He won't be there."

Milek's cell rang, but Garek was the one who answered it, putting it on speaker. They looked so similar that Garek was able to open it with face recognition.

"He's gone," Ivan's voice rumbled out of the speaker.

"Who?" Garek asked.

"Josh took off from the hospital. I thought he was in radiology, but he just left." The big man cursed. "First I lose sight of him on the trails, and he gets hurt, and that bastard kidnapper gets away, and now this."

"He wasn't going to get treatment," Milek said. "He's not going to do anything until he finds his child."

"And, boss..." Ivan continued, his voice gruff with either concern or embarrassment.

"What?" Garek asked.

"My truck keys are missing. I think Josh took it."

Milek chuckled. "Of course he did." Josh had taken his vehicle once, too, but he wasn't about to admit that in front of Garek. Josh was more resourceful than even Amber had realized. But then he'd probably had to be in order to survive five years in prison.

"What do I do now?" Ivan asked.

"I'll have Nikki see if she can track his phone," Garek said.

"He left it here," Ivan replied.

Garek cursed. "I'll get back to you," he said and disconnected the call. He stared at the portrait for a moment. "Man, you've really brought him to life. It's like he's here in this room with us."

"I wish he was."

"Do you think he's dead?" Garek asked. "Do you think it's too late for him and his grandmother? The kidnapper got away with the diamonds."

"Not the ones he or she wanted," Milek said.

"Yeah, exactly," Garek said. "Either way it doesn't look good for the hostages."

And it didn't look good for Josh Stafford, either.

Chapter Nineteen

Josh hadn't found the slip of paper in his pocket until he was getting ready to change into a gown for the CT scan. It was in the pocket where he'd had the velvet bag of jewels he had stashed in the fallen log.

The masked person had taken the bag after knocking him out. And they'd gotten away before the bodyguards and the police officer who'd been close to him had been able to see them. Ivan, Viktor, and Officer Carlson had all missed the person in the mask.

Was that possible?

Or was more than one person involved in the kidnapping? Maybe someone close to Josh or within the police department. He couldn't trust anyone.

There was definitely already more than one person involved since the person who'd stolen the diamonds and the one who'd taken his son and the boy's grandmother couldn't be the same. So maybe there was another...

Someone helping the kidnapper escape.

That was why Josh told nobody what he found in his pocket, and he left his cell behind, too. He regretted that now since he hadn't had a chance to talk to Natalie, to tell her what was going on. She was probably going out of her mind with concern for their son and her mother.

He needed to bring them back to her. It was the least he could do to try to make up for all the other ways he'd disappointed and hurt her.

She was such a loving and beautiful person that she deserved to be happy. He knew that she probably wouldn't ever find happiness with him again, if she could ever bring herself to forgive him, but he had to try to get her back the people who made her happy, the people she loved like he loved her.

So he slipped out of the hospital with that note in his pocket along with the keys to Ivan's vehicle.

It wasn't a Payne Protection Agency SUV. Because those were so easy to spot, Ivan had used his personal vehicle to follow Josh, an older truck with a lift kit and oversized tires on it. The thing was big and loud, which was unfortunate because the kidnapper was going to hear him coming.

If this was a trap...

It probably was a trap. But Josh didn't care. He didn't care about himself at all. He cared about Natalie.

No. He still loved her. He cared about her mother, too. And he loved his son already. He'd told his son that he would find him, so he had to try. He had to follow every lead to wherever he was being held.

But were the little boy and his grandmother here?

It was surprisingly close to where Josh and Natalie had spent the night, in the condo attached to the office of the newest Payne Protection franchise. The area had once been a booming industrial district but was pretty much abandoned now but for warehouses being converted into businesses and living quarters and artist studios.

But this wasn't an address for a warehouse, Josh saw as he drew closer. It was for an old storage facility. The place had been abandoned long ago, probably when the factories and other things had gone out of business around it.

It would be the perfect place to hold hostages. Or to kill someone.

The short hairs on his nape tingled as he feared that someone was watching him. But he didn't notice any other vehicles parked on the cracked asphalt. Unless it was parked inside one of the storage units like that car Sylvie rode in had parked in the warehouse the other night.

Was Sylvie part of this?

Did she resent him that much that she would hurt him like this? That she would hurt his son? He wasn't sure how she would have even known about him, though, but Sylvie had somehow known which officer was investigating the diamond theft. She had connections. Was it still through Luther Mills's criminal organization?

Josh shut off the loud engine of the truck, and an eerie silence enveloped him. He was just far enough outside the part of town that was starting to come back that there were no sounds here. No engines. No voices. Not even birds or animals made a peep around here.

He pushed open the truck door, which creaked slightly, and jumped down. The movement jarred his body and his head, and he flinched at the pain that shot through his skull. Whatever the masked person had struck him with had been hard enough to knock him out.

A branch or a gun?

Had nobody else really seen the person? Josh wasn't sure he could trust the other bodyguards or now even his bosses. But maybe the kidnapper had quickly taken off the mask and tucked it and the bag of diamonds inside one of those strollers. That would have been a great way to blend back in with the other hikers.

But around here there was no one to blend in with and escape unseen. There were just the metal walls of the storage units that cast shadows all around. Some of them had doors that opened to the outside. Those all stood open and were obviously empty. The other units' doors opened off a wide walkway that ran between the middle of two separate buildings. The walkway had a roof over it and a metal floor that creaked beneath his weight and echoed with his footsteps. If someone was here, they would hear him coming.

And just like them, Josh really had nowhere to hide.

But now, he realized, someone could be hiding inside one of the units, ready to jump out at him as he drew near. So he pulled out his can of pepper spray, the one he should have had ready back in the woods.

But each unit he passed was either locked or stood open and empty. Until...

Some light filtered through a hole in the metal roof and shone into the shadows of one unit, glinting off metal and glass. A vehicle. The same make and model of Marilyn Croft's missing vehicle.

This was where the kidnapper had brought them. Were they still here?

Unconcerned about his own safety, he called out, "Hello? Henry? Marilyn?"

His voice echoed off the metal. Maybe they weren't here anymore. Or they were tied up and gagged.

Or...

He didn't even want to consider the thought that flitted through his mind, that brought him such pain and dread. No. He couldn't consider that possibility...that he was too late.

That they were dead.

Natalie needed to find Josh and her son and her mother. After that conversation with Hannah a short while ago, she suspected her sister and brother-in-law might know how.

"Can you stay here with my father?" she asked Sylvie. He was in the backroom again, fiddling with some of the empty settings.

Maybe he was wondering the same thing Hannah had been, how they would open again with so much of their stock gone. The insurance company would probably reject a claim for those diamonds, and they wouldn't pay twice for the other items. So how would they replenish their inventory?

Sylvie narrowed her silvery eyes. "Why? Where do you think you're going?"

"I have to talk to my sister," Natalie said.

"Not alone."

"She's my sister," Natalie said. "She won't hurt me."

"If she's been stealing from you and has something to do with the disappearance of your son and mom, you can't trust her even though she is your sister," Sylvie said. Then she grimaced. "Yeah, I heard the hypocrisy in that."

Despite herself, Natalie smiled. There was something about Sylvie Combs…something that made it impossible to dislike her. "How are you going to protect me?" she asked the younger woman.

Sylvie wriggled her brows, which were a darker blond than her streaked hair. "I am the one who is armed," she said.

Natalie remembered that she'd had the gun the other night, the one that Josh had taken to fire back at whoever had been shooting at them. She'd seen him hand it back to her before the police arrived.

"I should have made him keep it," Sylvie said. "But if Officer Carlson knew he'd touched it the other night, he would be in violation of his parole. And she would probably be only too happy to put him back in prison."

Natalie flinched with the realization that not only had Josh gone off alone, he'd gone off unarmed. "I really need to find him."

The alarm rang out from the showroom again.

"Speaking of unarmed," Sylvie said. "You really should have just disarmed that thing."

She probably should have, but she'd wanted to keep the store closed and her dad safe. So maybe leaving him alone in a jewelry store with a thief wasn't her smartest option. She glanced at the monitor for the camera in the front and saw Mrs. Lynch standing inside, but she wasn't alone. A blond man messed with the control at the front door, and the alarm stopped.

Natalie rushed out to join them, anxious for news. That had to be why they were here. Something had happened.

"So someone else knows how to disarm that system," Sylvie remarked. She'd followed Natalie.

Garek Kozminski turned toward her, his silvery eyes narrowed. Then they widened with surprise. "Who are you?"

"Sylvie Combs," she replied.

"Josh's sister," Natalie said. "Why are you here? Has something happened to him?"

Garek tensed and cleared his throat.

Natalie turned to Mrs. Lynch. "Please, tell me what you know." She trusted the older woman to share everything with her. She'd been so empathetic and comforting the day before.

"We don't know much," Mrs. Lynch replied.

"Josh made the drop," Garek said.

"And?" Sylvie prodded.

But Natalie's stomach was tightening with dread. She knew. "He was hurt."

Mrs. Lynch nodded. "Yes. But not so badly that he didn't leave the hospital on his own before he was even treated."

"Treated for what?" Natalie asked.

"Was he shot?" Sylvie asked, her voice sounding as if she was being strangled.

Garek shook his head. "He got hit over the head during the drop. But he was well enough to steal a vehicle."

Natalie gasped while Sylvie chuckled.

"His coworker won't press charges," Garek assured her. "We just don't know where he went. He left his phone behind, so we weren't able to track his whereabouts through that. And Ivan's truck is too old to have GPS. He was using it instead of one of the company SUVs so the kidnapper wouldn't notice it."

So they had been following him, just like Natalie suspected. But to help him or to hurt him? He'd been hit over the head and the jewels taken, but even though he was injured, he'd rushed off again without telling anyone where he was going. Because he didn't trust them, either…

"I don't know where he went," she said. "He didn't call me." But she suspected they already knew that, too, that they were monitoring her phone calls. To help them? Or to make sure they didn't figure out what was really going on?

"We think he may have gotten a lead to where your son is," Penny said.

Garek's phone vibrated, and he pulled it from his pocket to look at the screen.

"What? What is it?" Natalie asked. "Have you found him?"

"Uh…someone might have spotted Ivan's truck," he murmured. "I'm going to check it out."

"I want to go—" Natalie began in unison with Sylvie.

But Garek ignored them both and rushed out the door. They started to follow him, but Penny stepped in their way. "He must think it's dangerous," she said. "And he doesn't want you getting hurt and anyone getting distracted. You need to stay here."

Natalie shook her head. It was dangerous because Josh couldn't trust his boss or coworkers, and now they knew where he was. "I have to go," she insisted. She had to follow Garek to make sure he didn't do anything to Josh or to her son and her mother.

"We can head down to the police department or the bodyguard headquarters," Sylvie said. "Maybe we can find out from someone there where Josh is headed. Or, after what Hannah told us, your sister and brother-in-law might know, Natalie, if they actually have something to do with all this."

"You should just wait for news," Penny said.

But Natalie had been standing around and waiting for news for the past two days. "No. Penny, can you stay here with my father? He's in the backroom."

But she didn't wait for the older woman to agree. She just rushed into the backroom, grabbed her purse and kissed her father's cheek. "I'll just be gone a little while, Daddy," she said. Then she pushed open the back door to the alley and started toward her SUV. Fortunately, she and Josh had taken separate vehicles to the store that morning.

She clicked the fob and unlocked it. As she jumped in on the driver side, Sylvie jumped in the passenger side.

"Kozminski was driving a long black SUV," Sylvie said. "Maybe we can catch up with him. But you need to hurry."

Her hand shaking, Natalie pushed in the ignition and then shifted into Reverse. She coasted back a bit before shifting into Drive and heading toward the mouth of the alley. The road it opened onto was a busy one, so she started braking. But the pedal kept going down…all the way to the floor.

And nothing happened.

"I can't stop!" she yelled.

The SUV kept going, directly into the traffic racing along the busy road. Either she screamed or Sylvie did. Then horns blared, brakes squealed, and metal crunched as they were struck…several times.

* * *

"Henry!"

That wasn't the person with the mask calling his name.

Henry didn't know why Mimi was holding her finger against her lips, shushing him like Miss Howard shushed their class when they were getting too loud.

"Henry, it's…" The deep voice trailed off for a moment before getting louder, closer. "Henry, it's your dad. Let me know if you're here. Help me find you."

Henry started to open his mouth, but Mimi covered it with her hand. And she shook her head. Then she used her other hand to shut off the lamp.

Didn't she want his daddy to find them?

"Mrs. Croft, Natalie sent me," the voice continued. "She and your husband are really worried about you both. He's confused and…"

She gasped then. "Josh?" she called out. "Is that really you? Josh Stafford?"

That was his daddy's name?

She slipped her hand down from Henry's face.

He called out, "Daddy?" Then he called out even louder, "Mommy?" Was she with him?

As much as he wanted to meet his daddy, he really wanted to see his mom. To hug her and have her hug him. Her hugs always made him feel better. Safer…

Happier…

Chapter Twenty

Josh could hear them, but he couldn't see them.

Henry banged on the door from the other side, calling out to him, "Daddy! Daddy! We're in here."

"There's a lock," Josh said. A padlock held the sliding door shut on what must have been one of the bigger storage units. "I have to find something to break this lock." Maybe Ivan had something in his truck, some tool that Josh could use to snap the padlock loose. "I'll be right back," he said. "I promise."

But when he started toward the exit, he heard the rumble of an engine. And another.

Then a shadow fell across the entrance.

"Damn..."

He had the pepper spray canister. But obviously more than one person had driven up since there was more than one vehicle. And they were probably armed with more than pepper spray.

What the hell was he going to do?

Whatever he had to in order to protect his son.

He headed the exit but kept close to the side of the walkway, in the shadow of the units. But then shadows blocked the exit, making it even darker around him. Despite the dim lighting, he noticed the glint of a gun.

He wasn't going to be able to do much to protect himself

against bullets. He didn't have Sylvie with him today. He didn't have her gun to use to fire back.

"Josh?" a familiar voice called out. "It's Garek and Ivan."

It sounded like Milek, but it was his older brother.

Josh would have preferred that it was Milek. Of everyone in the agency, he trusted Milek the most. But he wasn't going to be able to take out Garek and Ivan with his can of pepper spray. So Josh braced himself and stepped out of the shadows. "I'm here."

Garek's gaze went straight to the canister he clasped. "Did you think we were the kidnappers coming back?"

"Just because it's not, doesn't mean you're safe," Ivan said, his voice gruff.

Josh started to raise the canister. Ivan was the only one of his coworkers who was allowed to carry a weapon. Pepper spray wouldn't protect Josh from bullets, but it might buy him some time. "What do you mean?"

"You stole my truck!" Ivan said.

"You need to get better at your job," Josh said, and he wasn't really teasing.

But Ivan laughed anyway, and some of Josh's tension eased. There really was a kindness in the big man that made Josh want to trust him. And Garek was Milek's brother, and they seemed much more alike than Josh and Sylvie were.

Josh drew in a breath, then released it along with his mistrust. "Do you have anything in your truck that would break a lock?"

"You found them?" Garek asked.

Tears burned Josh's eyes as he nodded. "I found them." He headed back toward the big storage unit with the locked door. "We need to get them out."

"Daddy?" Henry called out, his voice quavery.

"Yes, I'm still here. Some friends are here, too. They're going to help me get you and your grandmother out of there."

Garek looked at his gun before holstering it again. He knew what Josh did, that the risk of one of the people inside getting hit with a stray bullet was too great. "I never met a lock I couldn't pick," Garek admitted. And he reached into his pocket and pulled out a small case.

Ivan ran back from wherever he'd gone, his big body hitting

the walkway so heavily that the metal bounced beneath Josh's feet. "I have a tire iron."

Garek snorted. "This'll be faster." A phone buzzed, but he ignored it while he used two small metal picks on the padlock. Within seconds, it popped open.

Josh's hands shook as he pulled at the handle. Ivan reached over his head and shoved it open.

The little boy standing on the other side stepped farther back into the unit, as if scared. He had every right to be after the ordeal he'd endured.

To seem less intimidating, Josh dropped down to his knees. "It's me, Henry. I'm your dad."

Henry hesitated another moment, his dark eyes wide in his dirt and tear-smeared face. Then he rushed forward and threw his arms around Josh's neck, clinging to him, as his little body shook.

Josh shook, too, with relief and with rage for the monster who'd put a child through such fear. Who'd put him and Natalie through such fear.

Henry pulled back to look over his shoulder. "Where's Mommy?"

"She's at the jewelry store with your grandpa," Josh said. "She can't wait to see you, though." Because he hadn't trusted his team, he hadn't brought his phone. But now that it seemed like Ivan and Garek were really here to help him, he would use one of their phones to call her.

The two of them had rushed over to Mrs. Croft, who was sitting on an air mattress in a corner of the unit. Her hair was stained with blood, and her face was deathly pale.

While his boss and coworker were checking her out, Josh cupped Henry's face in his hands and studied him. "Are you okay? Did that person hurt you?"

Tears welled in the little boy's eyes, but he shook his head. "No. Mimi got hurt though when she fell...or maybe that person pushed her..." His bottom lip quivered.

Josh hugged him again. "You're safe now, honey. You and Mimi are safe."

"Did that person get in trouble for making us play their stupid game?" Henry asked as his lip quivered again. "For Mimi getting hurt?"

"Not yet," Josh reluctantly admitted. "But soon. Soon." He silently cursed himself for letting that monster get away with the jewels.

"We're going to call in paramedics," Garek said, "For Mrs. Croft. We don't want to move her until we know how badly she's hurt." He pulled out his cell. As he glanced at the screen, his mouth fell open with a soft gasp.

"What is it?" Ivan asked.

Garek glanced at Josh and then at the boy. "Let me make this call..." He called 9-1-1 and reported Mrs. Croft's head wound and that she'd been held for a couple of days in an old shed and wasn't treated for her injuries. Then he added that he also had another person with a head wound.

Josh looked at him in alarm, concerned for Henry, but then realized that his boss meant him. His head was pounding, but he'd figured that was just with the adrenaline coursing through him. And the fear...

Ivan rushed out to his truck and came back again with bottles of water and some candy bars. While the big guy chatted with the little boy, Garek gestured Josh out the open door.

"What is it?" Josh asked with dread. Because he knew that Garek had seen something on his phone, either a text or a voice-mail transcript that had unsettled him before he'd called for help.

Garek's throat moved as he swallowed. "I left Mrs. Lynch at the jewelry store with Natalie and your sister."

"My sister? Sylvie was with Natalie?" That alone was cause for concern. The last time Josh left them alone together he could have lost them both. "What happened?" Because he knew from the tense look on his boss's face that something had.

"I think they were leaving to try to follow me here, and they were involved in an accident," Garek said.

"Accident? What the hell did Sylvie do now?"

"She wasn't driving. Natalie was," Garek said. "But I'm not sure how much of an accident it was. Mrs. Lynch thinks the brake line was cut. There was a puddle of fluid in the alley where her SUV was parked."

Josh bit back a curse. "Just...how badly are they hurt?"

"They're at the hospital. They're being treated," Garek said. Which meant they were hurt.

Josh's heart had filled with love and relief just moments ago when he got to hold his son. But now... Now fear gripped it again, so tightly that he could barely breathe.

"Daddy," Henry called out to him, as if he too sensed that something was wrong. Then he pushed past Ivan and ran out to join him in the walkway. "Daddy! I want Mommy. I want to see Mommy."

"Me, too, buddy," Josh said, and he picked him up, holding him close against his hurting heart. "Me, too."

She had to be okay. For her sake. For their son's sake and her parents' and for Josh's.

Natalie never lost consciousness. Maybe it would have been easier if she had, if she'd had a moment in which she wasn't worried about her son and her mom and her dad, too, and the store.

And Josh...

Maybe she was worried the most about him right now. He'd left the hospital with a head injury. He could have crashed, too, or worse.

Head injuries were so serious. She didn't have one. Just some bumps and bruises. The airbags had saved her and Sylvie from the worst of it. But the vehicle had been damaged so much that it had taken a while and the jaws of life for firefighters to extract them from the wreckage. She and Sylvie had talked a lot then, and Natalie understood her better.

But Natalie couldn't understand what had happened with her SUV. Just that morning the vehicle had been fine, but as they'd left the alley, the brakes had gone out, making it impossible for her to stop.

"We're really lucky we didn't get killed," Sylvie remarked from the gurney on the other side of a heavy curtain that separated her ER bay from Natalie's. Then Sylvie reached out and jerked back the curtain.

"I'm sorry," Natalie murmured.

"Sorry that I didn't get killed?" Sylvie teased.

"Sorry that it happened," Natalie said.

"You're really sweet," Sylvie said with a smile. "And like my brother, you try to take the blame for things that aren't your fault. Someone must have cut the brake line."

The thought had occurred to Natalie, too. It was the only thing that made sense since she kept her vehicle properly maintained. She wouldn't drive her son in a vehicle that wasn't. She wouldn't risk his safety in any way.

Yet Henry and her mother were in danger. She'd thought it was because of Josh at first, but now she realized it had to do with the store. With the jewelry and the money...

"Someone tried to kill you," Sylvie said.

What if Henry had been with her then?

"We need to get out of here," Natalie said.

"Go," Sylvie urged her. "I'm going to wait for that prescription for painkillers the doctor promised. I know when the adrenaline wears off tomorrow, we're going to feel like a semi hit us."

"I think it did," Natalie said. She already felt the pain as she swung her legs over the side of the gurney.

Her feet had just hit the floor when she heard a voice call out, "Mommy? Where's Mommy?"

There could have been a bunch of other mommies in that ER, but she knew this child was calling for her.

"Henry!" she yelled. Had she hit her head after all? Was she imagining this? Because all she could see in front of her was that curtain.

Then a small body wriggled under it, and Henry ran to her, winding his arms around her legs. "Mommy! Mommy!"

Her legs weakened, and she sank to the floor, clutching him in her arms while tears rolled down her face. "Oh, my sweetie, I love you so much! Are you okay?"

He leaned back and nodded. "Yeah, Daddy found me, Mommy. Just like he promised."

And more tears spilled over with gratitude and with love. She was falling for Josh all over again.

"Where is your daddy?" Sylvie asked, her voice cracking.

The curtain that Henry had crawled under was pulled back, revealing Josh standing there. He looked beyond exhausted with dark circles beneath his eyes and blood staining the collar of his shirt. He'd never looked better to Natalie. Just that he was here...

She picked up Henry in one arm and wrapped the other around Josh's neck, holding him close and said, "Thank you. Thank you so much."

Sylvie sniffled and muttered, "I'm not crying, you're crying."

Josh chuckled as he pulled back from Natalie.

"What's so funny?" Henry asked.

"Your aunt is funny," Natalie replied.

"Auntie Dena isn't here," Henry said, and he glanced around as if to make sure. Then his face twisted into a grimace. "And she isn't ever funny."

"This is your aunt Sylvie," Natalie said, pointing toward the woman on the gurney. "She's your daddy's sister."

"And she is funny," Sylvie said of herself. "Nice to meet you, little man."

Henry smiled shyly at her.

"My mom?" Natalie asked. "How is she?"

"She's here," Josh said. "She's being treated, but she was conscious and seems to be doing well."

Some of the pressure on Natalie's chest eased a bit. "That's good."

"What about you two?" he asked, his voice gruff. "I heard about the accident."

"That isn't what I would call it," Sylvie said.

"Detective Dubridge has some questions for you about that," Josh said.

"He probably has some for you, too," Sylvie remarked.

Josh nodded. "And for Henry. They need to figure out yet who the person in the mask is."

Henry shuddered at just the mention of his kidnapper, and he hugged Natalie tighter. "I didn't like that game, Mommy. I don't want to play it again."

"You're not going to play it," she assured him. "That person is not going to bother you again." But as she said it, she heard the hollowness in her own voice, the lack of conviction.

"If you see that person again, you scream your head off,"

Sylvie told him. "You kick them. You punch them. You don't go without a fight."

"Fight?" Henry asked.

Sylvie nodded.

"But I won't get in trouble?"

"No," Natalie replied. And she wondered now if this abduction was partly her fault, that she'd taught her son to be too polite, to play too much by the rules.

Sylvie nodded. "Don't ever let someone take you where you don't want to go," she said.

"But I'm little, and that person was big," Henry said.

"But you're tough," Sylvie said, and her voice cracked a bit. "You're really tough, Henry."

The little boy sent his aunt another shy smile. But then he whispered in Natalie's ear, "I was really scared, Mommy."

"That's okay," she said. "I was, too."

She was scared when he and Mother were abducted. And she was scared in that warehouse and when her brakes didn't work. And she was still scared that that person might come back for her son or for them.

She was also scared that Josh might leave again. Just as she was realizing how much she still loved him. But could they have a future if she couldn't bring herself to fully trust him with her heart again? Could they have a future with so much still up in the air about the diamonds and whoever had abducted Henry and her mom?

Or was that person going to come back and come after them again just like Henry seemed to fear?

Garek was pissed, not because his and Candace's getaway had been cut short but because his brother hadn't called him sooner. From the first moment they'd opened their own agency, he'd worried about something like this, about losing one of their employees. Or their family...

Family made him think of his dad, who'd died a few years ago serving time in prison for a crime he hadn't committed. Like Josh Stafford.

Patek Kozminski spent fifteen years in prison for murder

until a fellow inmate killed him, coerced by the man who'd really committed the murder. That was all over now. His father was gone. But for some reason Garek was thinking about him since meeting Josh's sister.

Sylvie Combs looked more like Garek's sister than she did Josh's. With her pale, silvery eyes, she looked more like a Kozminski, which made sense since Amber was pretty sure she was the one who'd stolen the stuff that Josh had gone to prison for stealing. While Garek's father hadn't been a killer, he had been a thief.

A thief was still on the loose now. The original bag of diamonds was missing as well as those other pieces Josh had used in exchange for his son.

But the thief was the least of Garek's concerns right now.

He was worried about the kidnapper and about the person who'd cut the brake line on Natalie's vehicle. It hadn't taken a crime-scene tech long to confirm what had caused the wreck. Nikki had pulled up the security footage from the alley that showed someone dressed like a vagrant in a ratty old parka lurking around Natalie's SUV. The vagrant had known to keep their face away from the camera, well aware of where it was, but it was clear they'd messed with Natalie's vehicle.

She and Sylvie Combs could have been killed. So yeah, a thief was the least of his concerns.

Garek had a would-be killer to find before the person tried to kill again.

Chapter Twenty-One

That first day when Josh and Natalie had searched her house for Henry and her mother, Josh had been looking for people, so he hadn't paid much attention to the furnishings and the decorations. But now, standing in the doorway to Henry's room, he could see that Natalie had taken care to make the place perfect for their son.

Henry had blue-and-green-striped walls decorated with *Toy Story* decals that matched his curtains and blankets. Stuffed animals took up more of the bed than he did, tucked as he was under the covers.

"I can stay in here with you," Natalie said.

"No, Mommy. I'm tough, like Auntie Sylvie says," Henry insisted. "I'm not scared."

Then he was the only one in the house who wasn't, because Josh was scared, and he could tell that Natalie was, too. Her parents were staying at the hospital. Her mother had a concussion and was seriously dehydrated and anemic. After his sleepless night and his worries, her father's blood pressure had been so high that they'd wanted to keep him for observation as well.

Natalie had considered staying at the hospital, but Penny Payne-Lynch and Sylvie had sworn that they would keep watch on them.

Josh still wasn't sure that he could completely trust his sister, but he loved her and appreciated that she was trying to help as much as she could. He just hoped that was out of love and not guilt.

"He's fallen asleep," Natalie whispered, and she backed slowly toward the door, as if worried that a sudden movement might awaken him. And after what the poor kid had been through, it might.

"Leave the door open," Josh said when she joined him in the hall. The two of them stood there for a long moment, just watching him. Love filled Josh's heart, but it wasn't just for his son.

Their son.

They'd made that perfect little boy together. And he could just about pinpoint the night they'd done it, probably the night they'd gotten unofficially engaged.

"I'm sorry," he whispered to her. But the words weren't enough, they would never be enough.

"You're sorry?" Natalie asked. "You found our son and my mother, just like you promised. You brought them back."

"I was talking about everything else." Everything Josh couldn't take back, that he couldn't undo. All the pain he'd caused her.

"Tonight…" Her throat moved as if she was struggling to swallow. "Tonight, let's just be grateful that we're all okay and that Henry is home where he belongs."

Josh nodded. "I'm staying, too," he said.

He knew that Garek had posted bodyguards outside, but he didn't care. He wasn't leaving Natalie and Henry. Not again. If he had his way, it would never happen again. But that wasn't his decision to make; that was hers.

"I want you to stay," Natalie said. And then she reached out and entwined her fingers with his. In her other hand she held a monitor that matched the one on Henry's nightstand. She clearly intended to make sure that she was always connected to their son now, no matter where they were.

"I want you to stay with me," she said, and she led him down the hall toward another bedroom.

With its soft pink walls and white lace curtains, this room was clearly hers. And instead of leaving the door open, like she had Henry's, she closed it behind him, shutting them inside together.

Natalie had so many reasons to be afraid. So many reasons to be upset and even angry after what had happened over the past couple of days. But at the moment, like she'd just told Josh, she wanted to focus on gratitude.

And on him.

"Thank you," she said, "for bringing back our son at the risk of your own life. And I'm grateful for your sister, too."

"You've nearly gotten killed with her twice now," Josh said with a shudder. "I don't think she's very good for you."

She smiled. "Actually, she is. She's made me laugh despite all the stress of the past couple of days. And she's staying at the hospital with my dad and mom. My own sister and brother-in-law can't be trusted to do that."

She couldn't trust them at all right now. She really couldn't trust anyone but Josh. But she had called Dena and Timothy and let them know their parents were at the hospital. She'd assured them there was no need to come down, that they could wait until morning, since their parents were sleeping. Timothy and Dena had readily agreed to wait.

And Natalie's doubts about them had increased. Where had her father found those missing jewels? Did he have a secret stash in the house? Or had he walked to the store first before going home?

But she didn't want to think about the store or her sister. Or even Josh's sister right now. She didn't want to think at all right now.

"Thank you," she said again. And she slid her arms around his neck, careful of the bandage on the back of his head, and stretched up his body to press her mouth to his.

His lips clung to hers in nibbling, caressing kisses, but he pulled back with a shaky sigh. "Natalie, you're hurt, and you must be exhausted."

She shook her head. "I'm a little bumped and bruised, but so are you. And I'm not tired at all." She was wound up from the rush of adrenaline from the crash but mostly from getting Henry back home.

Josh had done that. And she loved him for it. She loved him. If only she could trust him again...

"I don't want to take advantage of you," he said. "Of how high your emotions are right now. I feel badly that I might have the other night."

She chuckled. "If anything, I'm the one taking advantage of you..." She reached for the hem of his shirt, pulling it up over his washboard stomach. He was lean, but he was also all muscle.

So damn sexy...

His dark eyes got even darker as passion flushed his face. "I want you so badly, Natalie."

"Then make love with me," she urged as she stepped back and pulled her sweater over her head. She flinched as she did it, though, her sore muscles protesting.

Josh cursed. "I can see the bruises from the seat belt. I don't want to hurt you."

It was already too late for that, but she didn't want to dwell on the past anymore. She didn't even want to worry about the future. She wanted to be only in the moment, in the now. So she ignored the pain and her bruises, and she finished undressing until she stood naked before him.

"Natalie..." He groaned as if the sight of her brought him pain. She could see the tension in his face and his body. A muscle twitched in his cheek. "I want you so badly." He touched her then, running his fingertips along the bruise over her shoulder. "But you've been through so much."

She smiled and offered him the same assurance their son had offered her. "I'm tough."

"Yes," he said, his voice gruff with awe. "You are incredibly tough."

She wasn't, though. She'd nearly lost it so many times over the past couple of days. And she undoubtedly would have if he hadn't been there for her, for them.

He yanked off his shirt and shucked off his jeans and boxers so that he was naked, too. His body seemed to pulsate with the passion that coursed through her as well. He kissed her with all that desire, his mouth moving hungrily over hers. But he touched her gently, like she was made of glass.

But if she was, she would have broken before now. She would have broken five years ago when he went to prison. She hadn't entirely believed it herself when she'd claimed just minutes ago that she was tough, but she was. And even if Josh hurt her again, she would survive.

But she didn't want to miss another chance to be with him, to feel the passion and the ecstasy that he brought her.

Though his touch was gentle, it drove her mad. The way he ran just his fingertips over her skin, over her breasts, over her nipples which were so incredibly sensitive. She moaned as the tension built inside her, winding so tightly through her that she worried she might break.

Then his hands moved down her body, over the most sensitive part of her, and her knees began to shake. She moaned again, nearly reaching a release. But she didn't want to go without him. So she touched him as tenderly as he was touching her, gliding just her fingertips across his skin, over his muscles.

He groaned. Then he guided her toward her bed, laying her down atop her quilt. And he made love to her with his mouth.

She couldn't hold out. The tension broke as an orgasm quivered inside her. And she shook from the force of it. And then he was moving, sliding in and out again. Thrusting as gently as he'd touched her.

That tension built again, bringing back the desperation and the desire. She arched and moved, meeting those slow thrusts, clutching him with her inner muscles.

He groaned again. "Natalie…" He started moving faster now.

She matched his rhythm.

He lowered his head and kissed her lips, nibbling at them. Then his tongue slid into her mouth, mimicking the movements of their bodies.

A madness overtook her. She wrapped her legs around his body and held on as she moved her hips. The tension broke again, this orgasm more powerful than the last. She muted her scream of pleasure against his mouth.

She swallowed his groan as his body tensed and then convulsed.

He murmured something against her lips, something she wanted to pretend she hadn't heard. Something she didn't want to acknowledge even though her heart yearned to be his again. She loved him.

Natalie had never stopped loving him, and she didn't think she ever would. But that still didn't mean she would ever be able to trust him again not to hurt her or, worse yet, to hurt their son.

His bed was so soft and warm that Henry wanted to snuggle even deeper under the covers. He wanted to sleep and dream only good dreams.

But something was waking him up. Some noise, some movement.

And he opened his eyes to find that he wasn't alone. It wasn't Mommy or Daddy in his room, though.

It was the person in that mask.

He remembered what Auntie Sylvie told him. To scream. To kick and punch. To not let that person take him anywhere again without a fight.

But Henry didn't feel tough like she told him he was. He felt scared and almost as if he couldn't even move as that person reached out for him again.

Chapter Twenty-Two

As exhausted as Josh was from the past couple of days and from making love with Natalie, he couldn't sleep. Even though they had Henry back and Marilyn was being treated, Josh couldn't relax.

Because he couldn't be sure that, even with the bodyguards outside, they were safe. If only he hadn't lost that bastard on the trail. But he had, and then he'd nearly lost Natalie and his sister, too, when the brakes were cut on her SUV. Someone was deliberately targeting her.

But why?

Natalie was the sweetest, most selfless person he'd ever met. Such a good mother and daughter…and lover. As passionately as they'd just made love, he was tempted to reach for her again, but she'd fallen asleep. And he wanted to let her rest.

But he couldn't. He was restless instead, his stomach muscles tight, his nerves on edge. Then he heard something sputtering out of that monitor. A creak of a door or a floorboard.

Was Henry up?

The poor kid was probably having a nightmare after the ordeal he'd gone through, after that abduction. The thought made Josh more uneasy, and he slid quietly out of bed and quickly got dressed. He grabbed the monitor, taking it with him as he carefully turned the knob and opened the door just wide enough to squeeze through before pulling it closed behind himself.

He didn't want to disturb Natalie's sleep. She had to be exhausted, emotionally and physically. And yet she'd made love to him with so much passion.

And love?

Did she love him yet?

He'd told her he loved her, in that moment when he felt the pleasure he'd only ever felt with her, so intense that it was almost painful. So intense that it shook him to his core. He loved her. But he couldn't expect her to give him another chance. He couldn't expect her to ever trust him again after how badly he'd hurt her.

He closed his eyes for a moment and then opened them again. That was when he saw the shadow down the hall, standing inside Henry's open doorway. Had one of the bodyguards come inside the house to check on them?

"Hey," he called out softly, not wanting to wake up Natalie but also wanting to know what was going on.

The person turned toward him, and he saw the mask, the mask Henry had talked about, the mask Josh had seen for himself after he'd been struck over the head.

And then he heard Henry scream.

"I told you not to play games," the person said to Josh, the voice raspy and strange yet almost familiar, too.

"Who the hell are you?" Josh asked, and he rushed forward, closing the distance between them.

But the person was closer to the stairs and half fell, half ran down them and then through the kitchen and the open patio door.

Josh followed, reaching out, trying to catch them.

Where were the others? The bodyguards who were supposed to be guarding the place? Had this person hurt them? Had he or she hurt Henry? He'd screamed, but that had sounded more like out of fear than pain.

Still, Josh was torn between wanting to go back and check on his son and wanting to catch the kidnapper and end this once and for all.

* * *

Natalie wasn't sure if she actually heard the scream or if it was part of her dream. But then she heard the pounding footsteps on the stairs. "Josh?"

She reached for him, but the bed was empty and already cold on his side. How long had she been asleep?

And what had happened? Where was the monitor she'd put on the nightstand? It was gone with Josh.

She jumped out of bed, dragged on some clothes and then ran out into the hallway.

It was empty now. Those footsteps must have been pounding down the steps, not up. On her way to the stairwell, she stopped in front of the open door to Henry's room. The blankets were pulled back, some of the stuffed animals and pillows lying on the floor.

But not her son.

He was gone.

"Henry!" she shrieked. "Henry!"

Oh God, no…

That kidnapper shouldn't have been able to get to him again. There were bodyguards outside. They were supposed to be protecting them, though she should have known better than to trust them. But she had that monitor, too. How hadn't she heard the person on it? She never should have left Henry alone.

But maybe he wasn't alone. Josh was gone, too. He must have heard something before she had, or he'd reacted faster.

"Henry! Josh!" she yelled their names as she ran for the stairs. Where were they? What had happened to them?

Once she hit the bottom step, she felt the cold breeze blowing through the open patio door. The curtains danced on the wind, flapping against the walls and the glass. They slapped at Natalie as she passed through them, as if slapping her for being a bad mother, for putting her own desires over the safety of her son.

"Henry!" she called out again. "Hen—"

A big hand covered her mouth, muffling her cry. And a heavy arm wrapped around her, holding her, imprisoning her. This wasn't Josh's body; she knew his too well.

No. This was a stranger.

The intruder? The kidnapper? Was he going to take her now? Better her than her son.

Please. Henry had to be safe.

Milek had spent too many hours awake over the past couple of days. He wasn't sure if he'd ever slept at all, but even with the little boy found, he hadn't been able to rest. So he was driving over to check on the overnight guards who were making sure that Josh, Natalie and that precious little boy stayed safe.

Ivan and Viktor were there. They were bigger than he was. Younger. Stronger. But they hadn't been bodyguards very long. And their actual jobs were to protect things, not people, so he called them on the radio as he headed over.

"We just heard something down the street," Viktor said. "Sounded like a scream. Maybe somebody saw someone lurking around. I'm going to check it out."

"I can," Ivan chimed in on the radio.

"Just one of you," Milek said. "And I'll be there soon." He drove up just seconds later, but he didn't see anyone near the front of the house.

He called them up on the radio, but neither guard answered. Had they both gone to check out that noise? That could have just been a distraction to get them away from Josh and Natalie and Henry.

Milek knew it when he heard a scream through his open SUV window, this one coming from inside the house. He threw open the door and jumped out. As he was rushing toward the house, he tripped and fell over a long, hard body. "Ivan!"

He'd been so worried about losing Josh that he hadn't considered the risk to the others. To Ivan and to Viktor.

Milek felt the man's neck and found a pulse. He was alive, just unconscious like Josh had been earlier that day when the kidnapper had struck him.

Knowing how dangerous the kidnapper was, Milek drew his weapon from its holster. His finger slid off the safety because he knew he needed to be ready. He was a good shot, and he had no compunction against killing if it was to save someone else. As a teenager he'd killed…to protect his sister.

And he would do it all over again if he had to.

Anything for family. And his employees were family, too. He had to find Viktor and Josh and that little boy and Natalie Croft.

He started toward the house. The side door was closed and locked. But then he heard movement coming from behind the house. And he rushed around the corner, his gun drawn and pointed. He wasn't going to get hit over the head and disarmed. He was going to shoot to kill.

But when he stared down the scope on his barrel, the gun was pointed at a boy. A little boy whose wide eyes stared at him in horror and fear.

Chapter Twenty-Three

Josh had pursued the kidnapper down the stairs and through the backyard to an alley that ran between the houses in this area. He was gaining on him, and when he extended his arm, he was nearly able to reach him. But he grabbed the back of the hood instead, pulling it down, snapping the string of the mask that fell away to the ground. The hood slipped through his fingers.

Josh was so close. He nearly had him. He pumped his legs to run faster, to close the distance between them again.

But then he heard another scream. Henry's.

The little boy sounded terrified.

Josh had assumed there was only one kidnapper, only one intruder in the house. But it made more sense that there were two or even three. How else had the bodyguards been disarmed? Or were they in on it?

And Josh had left Natalie and Henry alone with them in that house. He turned around to run back toward them.

But he felt a flurry of movement behind him, like the person he was pursuing was going to become the pursuer again.

When Josh turned back, he caught a glimpse of a face before the man reaffixed the mask he'd picked up from the ground. But it was too late.

After hearing the terror in Henry's scream, Josh hoped that

it wasn't too late for Natalie and their son, too. He ran back toward them as fast as he could.

And he could only hope that he made it to them in time. He couldn't lose either of them, and he certainly couldn't lose them both and survive.

Natalie's heart was pounding so fast and hard that Henry had to be able to feel it, too, as she held him tightly in her arms. "Are you okay?" she asked him again.

His last scream had terrified her. And she'd managed to wrest free of the man holding her to find another man trying to hold her son.

"Mommy!" Henry had screamed before running into her arms. She'd been holding him ever since, and this time she never intended to let him go.

"I didn't know he was the one in the backyard," Milek said, and his face was nearly as pale as his silvery eyes. "After I found Ivan unconscious on the front lawn, I had my gun drawn and pointed it at him."

"Is Ivan okay?" asked the man who'd caught her as she slipped out the patio doors. "He offered to check out that noise down the street. I shouldn't have let him go alone. I knew it, I started after him..."

And that must have been when the man in the mask got into the house.

"Ivan has a pulse, but he needs an ambulance. You call for one, Viktor," Milek said. His hands were shaking.

"Where's Josh?" Natalie asked, her voice cracking.

"Daddy chased the person in the mask out of my room and out of the house," Henry said. And the little boy must have followed them both out.

"Of course Josh went after him on his own," another man said. He came around from the front of the house, holding his head.

Viktor smacked his shoulder. "You're all right?"

Ivan nodded. "Yeah...son of a..." He glanced at Henry. "Person got a jump on me."

"Did you see who it was?" Milek asked.

Ivan shook his head and grimaced. "I was walking toward

that noise we heard, sounded like a woman screaming. And then someone must have rushed out of the shadows, got me from behind like they got Josh. I didn't see anything."

"I saw someone in a mask coming out the patio door," Viktor said. "Josh was right behind them. And the boy and then someone else came after him." He turned toward Natalie. "I thought you were an accomplice chasing the kid."

So he'd been protecting her son from her. She nearly smiled. She would have if Josh was back. But he'd gone after the kidnapper alone.

Where was he?

"There's Daddy!" Henry exclaimed when his father ran into the backyard.

"Oh, thank God," Mommy said, her voice all soft and shaky.

Maybe she thought the person in the mask was going to take Daddy away like they'd taken Henry and Mimi. Was that why they came back tonight?

"Daddy protected us," Henry said. Because they were all here, and the masked person wasn't.

"Did he get away?" one of the big men asked. He had really, really short, really, really pale hair, and he kept rubbing his head and making the faces like Mimi had made after she fell. He was the one who'd helped him and Mimi at the metal building. He'd had candy bars.

Daddy nodded. "This time."

Henry's heart started beating as hard as Mommy's was against him. "Is he coming back?" he asked, and his voice was all shaky like hers. "I don't want him to come back." Tears filled his eyes.

He wasn't as tough as Auntie Sylvie said. After feeling like he was frozen at first, he had tried to fight off the person when they started reaching for him, trying to pull him out of his bed. But he knew that if Daddy hadn't shown up when he had, he wouldn't be here now. He would have been back in that cold building, on the hard concrete floor. And Mimi wouldn't have been with him this time because she was with Grandpa and Auntie Sylvie.

"He's not coming back," Daddy said, and he reached out and

patted Henry's back, rubbing it like Mommy did when he didn't feel good. "He's going to go to prison where he belongs."

"He?" Mommy asked. The other men said it at the same time she did.

"You saw him," said the man who had eyes just like Auntie Sylvie's. And he was smiling like he already knew Daddy's answer.

Daddy smiled back, but then he looked at Mommy and his smile slipped away.

"I don't care who it is," she said. "I just want them behind bars where they can't hurt us anymore."

Josh nodded, and then he walked a short distance away with the other men. And they lowered their voices, probably so that Henry wouldn't hear them. They didn't want him to be scared. But he was.

Especially when he heard Daddy say, "He knows I saw him. He's going to run. We have to hurry."

"If he knows you saw him, you're in danger," the bigger guy with the longer hair said. "You need to lie low with protection. Let us handle this."

But Daddy shook his head. "No, I want to see this through. I want to watch them put handcuffs on him and take him away."

Henry would have wanted that, too, but he really didn't want to see that masked person ever again. He just wanted him gone.

And for Daddy to stay forever.

Chapter Twenty-Four

Josh did as Milek told him—he called Detective Dubridge. But they were already in Milek's Payne Protection Agency SUV, heading over to the house the masked man owned to make sure that he didn't get away before the police arrived. They were definitely going to beat the detective there, which was good because Josh was really tempted to beat the man who'd terrorized his son.

"Don't do anything stupid," Dubridge warned through the speakers of the SUV as if he'd read Josh's mind. Or maybe he just knew what he would do if someone had done to his child what this bastard had done to Josh's.

The masked man had put Henry and Natalie through hell.

Milek drove the SUV up to the monstrous concrete-and-glass house at the end of the cul-de-sac. Instead of pulling into the driveway, he pulled across it, blocking the entire width of it so that the Lincoln parked in the open garage wouldn't get past them. The trunk lid was up, some things spilling out of it like someone was packing in a hurry.

Just Timothy, or was Dena involved too? Viktor and Ivan had heard a woman's scream; it was what had lured them away from the house. So Timothy had to have a female accomplice.

Josh reached for the door handle.

"Stay here," Milek said. "Let's wait for the police like Detective Dubridge told us to."

"But he could run."

"I've got him blocked in, and he won't get far on foot," Milek said.

"You don't know that," Josh said. He'd barely been able to catch the guy earlier that evening. Timothy was much faster and stronger than Josh would have thought. "He could call an Uber. We need to get out. We need to hold him until the police get here." Because he wasn't letting him get away again.

He wasn't giving him another chance to abduct his son.

And he wasn't wasting time arguing with his boss about it, either.

So Josh opened the door and stepped out onto the driveway. Just as he headed toward the Lincoln, the door to the house opened, and Timothy, arms loaded with suitcases, stepped into the garage. He must not have been able to see over the pile of luggage because he kept coming toward the open trunk and dumped the load onto the other stuff.

"Going somewhere?" Josh asked.

Timothy fell back against the car. "You son of a bitch."

Josh shrugged off the insult. It was the truth, after all. "It's over, Timothy."

Timothy turned and reached into the trunk. And Josh heard the sound of a gun cocking.

"I will shoot you," Milek said almost matter-of-factly. "I've killed before, another creep like you who terrorized a kid."

Josh glanced at his boss, and he could see that Milek wasn't bluffing. He would kill, and he very clearly had.

Timothy must have realized it, too, because he pulled his empty hands out of the trunk and held them up. "You've got this all wrong," he said. "I didn't hurt anyone—"

"Was it your partner who hurt Mrs. Croft then?" Josh asked.

"Partner?"

"You can't have done this all on your own, Timothy," Josh said. "Who are you working with?"

"With or against…" Milek muttered.

"I don't know what you're talking about," Timothy said, and he was clearly bluffing. "You have no proof of anything."

"We won't find those diamonds you took off me on the trail around here somewhere?"

"Those weren't the right ones," Timothy said, his voice shaking with fury as his face flushed. "You think you're so damn smart playing that sick joke on me..."

Sirens wailed in the distance.

"Who are you working with?" Josh persisted. Because clearly Timothy wasn't smart enough to have pulled off the kidnapping on his own. He was barely making any sense right now.

"I'm not saying anything else without a lawyer present," Timothy said.

"We're not the police," Josh said. "It doesn't matter what you say to us."

Timothy snorted. "No, it doesn't. So I'm not saying another damn word to you." But then he must not have been able to help himself because he continued, "She'll never forgive you, you know."

"Forgive *me*?" Josh asked. "What are you talking about?"

"Natalie, she's never going to forgive you."

"For figuring out that you kidnapped our son and hurt her mother?" Josh asked. "I don't think she needs to forgive me about that."

"For breaking her heart," Timothy said. "She was devastated and embarrassed. Her baby daddy went to prison as a thief, leaving her to raise her son alone. She had to live with her parents. She had no life, nothing, after you left. You think I'm the bad guy here? You're the bad guy, Josh Stafford. And while she might be happy with you now for finding Henry, it won't last, not when she remembers how horribly you disappointed her."

"I guess you would know something about disappointing people," Josh said.

Timothy nodded. "I do, and I know how it feels to be disappointed by people. It's not something you get over easily if ever at all."

The sirens grew louder as the police vehicles turned onto the cul-de-sac and drowned out whatever else Timothy was going to say.

But Josh didn't need to hear the rest of it to know that the guy might be right.

Natalie might never forgive him.

Natalie wanted to get Henry back to bed, and she wanted to be alone for a moment. But the two big bodyguards were both still here, inside the house with her. She wished they would have gone with Josh and Milek instead.

But Josh and Milek were going to call the police. They'd promised. Had they?

"You should take him to the hospital," she told Viktor as she pointed at Ivan, who had one hand on the back of his head as he grimaced. "Head injuries are serious."

Her mother was still in the hospital because of hers. And Josh probably should have stayed as well after he got hit over the head earlier today.

But instead he'd been here with her and Henry, saving them both again.

"I'm fine," Ivan insisted.

"No, you're not," she said. "But I am. Henry and I will be okay. Timothy won't come back here." Before they'd left, Josh had told her whom he'd seen. And Timothy knew that Josh had seen him, that he knew who he was. He had to be on the run now.

A knock rattled the side door that opened onto the driveway. Henry, who'd been nearly falling asleep at the table, gasped. And the two men tensed. Then the knob started to turn. Was it unlocked?

Or did this person have a key?

The door opened. But Natalie couldn't see who'd entered because Viktor and Ivan put themselves between the door and her and Henry. Just like Josh, they were willing to give up their lives for her.

She'd been wrong to doubt them. They were good men.

Like Josh…

"Who the hell are you?" Dena asked. "And where's my sister?"

"I'm here," Natalie said. "And this is my sister," she confirmed for the guards.

"I wish it was Auntie Sylvie," Henry muttered. He'd only met her once, but he'd had an immediate connection with her like he had with his father. Like Natalie had had with his father all those years ago, a connection that heartbreak and five years apart hadn't severed.

"Who's Auntie Sylvie?" Dena asked. "Some female body-guard?" She shrugged. "Never mind. I don't actually care."

Of course she didn't.

"I want to speak to my sister alone," Dena told Ivan and Viktor.

But Ivan shook his head, which made him wince again.

"I will be safe with my sister," Natalie said, though she wasn't totally sure about that. "Henry, why don't you take Mr. Viktor and Mr. Ivan upstairs and show them your stuffed animals?"

"I am a big bear guy," Viktor said. "And maybe a teddy would help Mr. Ivan feel better."

"You can lay down in my bed," Henry offered. "Mimi slept a lot after she fell in the garage." He took one of Ivan's big hands in his and tugged him toward the stairs.

Natalie smiled as she watched the three of them climb the stairs. She didn't have to worry about anyone getting close to Henry, not with those two gentle giants guarding him.

"What the hell is going on, Natalie?" Dena asked.

"You tell me," Natalie challenged her sister. "I am really curious how much you know, how involved you are."

"Involved in what?"

"Henry and Mom's kidnapping," Natalie said. "The diamonds—"

"Like I told the police, I have no idea about any of that, and I still don't know what's going on," Dena said. "Timothy grabbed his passport and is throwing all of his stuff in his car right now, and he won't answer any of my questions."

"And you thought I would have the answers," Natalie said. "So you must know—"

"He told me to come here, that you would be able to explain everything," Dena said.

"He's the one," Natalie said. "He took Henry and Mom. He hurt her."

Dena shook her head. "No. That makes no sense."

"Josh caught him in here tonight, trying to take Henry again."

"He doesn't even like kids," Dena said.

"No, but he likes money," Natalie said. "Or maybe you're the one who likes money."

"Most people like money, Natalie," Dena said. "Stop being so naive for once."

Natalie had been through so much the past couple of days that her patience had run out, leaving her temper to snap. "Stop being such an uncaring bitch for once, Dena."

Instead of being offended, Dena smiled. "You should be more like me," she said. "Then you wouldn't get hurt so much."

"Just once," Natalie said. Just Josh.

"But it was enough that you never tried to get in another relationship," Dena said. "You were afraid to get hurt again. But you wouldn't if you just wouldn't care…"

"But I want to care," Natalie said. "I want to be able to love, to care about the people close to me, like my son and our parents…and you."

Dena chuckled now. "I'm surprised you managed to spit that out. We've never been close."

"Whose fault was that?" Natalie asked.

"Mine," Dena admitted. "I hated you from the day you were born because Mom and Dad loved you so much."

"They love you, too."

"They're not giving *me* the store."

"You've never shown any interest in it," Natalie said. Then she stepped back. "You knew it. You knew about their plans."

Dena snorted. "Mom warned me because she was worried that I would be mad at you. That I would think you put them up to it. She didn't want to cause any more friction between us."

It had always bothered her mother, much more than it had ever bothered them, that they didn't have a close relationship. But because of who Dena was and how she'd always treated Natalie, Natalie had given up trying to have a close relationship with her sister.

"She didn't want you to be spiteful," Natalie said. And she remembered how many times Dena had ruined the cake for

Natalie's birthday, how many times she'd ruined the surprise about what her present was. "I'm shocked you didn't tell me what they were doing."

Dena shrugged. "I didn't care."

Natalie snorted now. "Yeah, right. Is that what this is all about? You and Timothy stealing from the store and then kidnapping my son when those diamonds disappeared before he could get to them."

"I told you *I* didn't care," Dena said.

"But you knew what he was doing," Natalie surmised.

Dena shook her head and then laughed. "I actually thought he was having an affair. The late nights, the sneaking around..." She laughed again.

"And you didn't care about that, either?" Natalie asked.

Dena shrugged. "It would have been kind of hypocritical of me."

"You're having an affair, too?"

Dena smiled now, and her blue eyes lit up. "Yes. I was planning to divorce Timothy anyway. But I really had no idea what he was doing, that he was even capable of such things. I guess that just goes to show that you really can't trust anyone."

Natalie understood that all too well.

Dena studied Natalie's face for a moment. "I actually thought Timothy might be having the affair with you."

"What?" Just the thought had bile rising up the back of Natalie's throat.

Dena shrugged. "All he does is work. Who else is at his work besides you and Dad?"

"Damn!" Natalie and Sylvie had been right to suspect Hannah.

"What?"

"Maybe you should have spent more time at the store," Natalie remarked. Because her and Sylvie's instincts had been right. No matter what she'd claimed, Hannah was involved in the thefts and probably with Timothy as well. Co-conspirators or ex-co-conspirators who had double-crossed each other?

If the latter was the case, then surely Timothy would give

her up, would provide evidence against her, and this would all be over soon.

If Timothy had been caught...

Had Josh and Milek arrived in time to stop him from getting away? Timothy had already had his passport and been packing his things when Dena left their house.

"Mommy!" Henry called down from the top of the stairs. "Mommy!"

Scared by the urgency in his voice, she ran halfway up toward him. "What? What's wrong?"

"The big guy fell down," Henry said. "He's sleeping like Mimi was."

"We do need that ambulance," Viktor called down from behind Henry. He stood at the top of the stairs with his cell phone pressed to his ear. "And you and Henry are going to need to come to the hospital with us," he said, "so that we can make sure you stay safe."

"We'll be fine," Natalie assured him. "My sister is here with us."

"No, she's not," Henry said as he peered down the stairs. "Auntie Dena left."

For where? To go back home? Or to her lover?

Or to find her husband's lover?

Because if that was the case, Dena was putting herself in danger. And while her sister made her crazy, Natalie still loved her and didn't want anything to happen to her.

Milek hadn't expected to be brought down to the police station along with the suspect he and Josh had stopped from fleeing the country. But when he arrived at Timothy Hutchinson's house, Detective Dubridge insisted that both Milek and Josh give their statements immediately and in person at the police department.

Milek could understand needing Josh's statement since he was the one who'd seen the intruder without his mask and could identify him. But Dubridge had also wanted Milek's.

He'd put them in separate rooms, and he hadn't asked them about just tonight but all the events that had gone on leading up to tonight. Dubridge started with his and Garek's agency being hired by that insurance company to investigate all the claims they'd had recently.

Clearly Dubridge suspected that Timothy wasn't the only guilty party in this case. And Milek had no doubt that he was right about that.

Someone else was definitely involved. They'd stolen the diamonds that Timothy wanted, and he'd been so desperate to get his hands on them that he'd kidnapped Josh's son to get them.

So who had stolen the diamonds?

And was that the same person who shot at Natalie and Sylvie in that warehouse?

Was it the person who'd cut the brake line on her car?

Even with Timothy in jail, Natalie and her son were still in danger. So Milek and Josh needed to get back to them and out of the police department before something else happened to them.

Chapter Twenty-Five

Josh hadn't realized when he'd gone to the River City PD to give his statement that Timothy might not be the only one who needed a lawyer. He probably needed one, too, because Detective Dubridge was keeping him there, drilling him with questions that had more to do with the thefts than with the abduction of his son and Marilyn Croft.

And he even left Josh sitting in that interrogation room while he questioned Timothy, too. Like he was checking to see if their stories matched.

"What's going on?" Josh asked when the detective returned. "Do I need to call a lawyer?"

"That's up to you."

"I didn't do anything wrong," Josh insisted. Though he had gone a bit rogue a couple of times, it had been to make certain he got his son back safely. "Timothy is the one you need to be questioning."

"I have been questioning him, too. We found enough evidence in his car and house to link Timothy Hutchinson to the abductions," Dubridge agreed. "But we didn't recover the real diamonds. He admitted that's why he went back tonight to grab Henry again because you didn't give him the diamonds he thinks you'd taken. You gave him back the things he already stole that disappeared from his house when you were there a couple of nights ago with his sister-in-law and father-in-law."

Josh sucked in a breath. "That's where those came from... his house."

"What?"

"Natalie's dad came up with the jewelry that had gone missing before the Payne Protection Agency was even hired, the jewelry the insurance company had already paid them for," Josh said. "He must have found them in Timothy and Dena's house."

"Hutchinson admits to taking them," Dubridge said. "After he learned that his in-laws were going to give the store to his sister-in-law, he was hell-bent on getting everything out of it that he could."

Josh cursed. "To hurt her. That must be why he took Henry, too."

"He took Henry because he really believes you have the diamonds," Dubridge said. "You're a convicted jewelry thief, and you had the security codes to the store. That's why he's convinced you have them."

"He's wrong. I don't have them."

Dubridge stared at him through narrowed dark eyes. "I'm beginning to believe you."

"I really don't care whether you believe me or not," Josh admitted. "I care about finding out who tried to hurt Natalie. Her brake line was cut. You confirmed that. And someone shot at her and my sister the night before that. Was that Timothy?"

Dubridge sighed. "I really don't think so."

"But he resented Natalie getting the store," Josh reminded him. "Maybe he thought he would inherit it if something happened to her."

"But he wouldn't inherit it, his wife would," Dubridge said. "And it doesn't sound like they're on good terms. She wasn't at the spa the other day. She was in a hotel with another man. I personally confirmed her alibi with him and the hotel staff."

"Natalie's relationship with Dena isn't good," Josh said. It was even worse than his relationship with Sylvie. "Even though she had nothing to do with the abduction, Dena could have been the one who tried to hurt her. And who might still try to hurt her…" He jumped up then. "I have to get out of here and make sure Natalie is safe. If you want to keep me here, you're going to have to arrest me."

Dubridge didn't stop him from walking out. Josh found Milek waiting for him in the hall outside the door. The older man looked tense and exhausted.

"Are you okay?" Josh asked. "What's going on?"

"Ivan passed out," Milek said. "The head injury was worse than he would admit."

"Is he okay?"

"He's at the hospital getting treated. An ambulance brought him there, and Viktor followed it with Natalie and Henry, too, to make sure they stayed safe."

The pressure on Josh's chest eased a bit. "That's good." They still had protection.

"But they disappeared on him once they all got to the hospital," Milek said. "He can't find them. And in the rush to leave with Ivan being hurt, they left Natalie's cell at the house."

Josh cursed. But then he remembered the last couple of times that Natalie had gone off on her own that she hadn't actually been alone. "Do you still have my sister's cell number?" Josh asked.

Milek nodded.

"Call her."

When Sylvie picked up, she sounded groggy like she'd been sleeping. "Hello?"

Milek had his cell on speaker, so Josh spoke, "Are Natalie and Henry with you?"

She hesitated a moment.

"Sylvie? Are you there?"

"Yeah," she said. "I didn't want to wake up the Crofts. I'm out in the hall now. What's this about Natalie and Henry? I haven't seen them since they left with you."

"You're still at the hospital?"

"Yeah, Mrs. Lynch was exhausted, so I told her I had this watch. But I fell asleep, too."

"So you didn't see Natalie and Henry at the hospital?"

She gasped. "Are they hurt? What happened?"

"They were fine, but Natalie's brother-in-law tried to grab him again tonight."

"Son of a bitch!"

"He's in police custody now." And Josh had nearly been as well.

"That's good."

"But I don't think he's the one who cut the brake lines or shot at you both," Josh said. "So someone else is still out there trying to hurt her. I think it could be her sister, trying to stop Natalie from inheriting the store."

Sylvie whistled. "And I thought I was the worst sister ever..."

"Sister?" Milek asked. "Viktor said Natalie's sister was at the house when Ivan passed out. But then she just disappeared."

That didn't mean that Dena had left, though. Maybe she'd hung back and followed them to the hospital.

Josh cursed. "We have to find them."

Because he had a horrible feeling that Dena was going to kill Natalie and Henry both. That way she could make certain that she was the only heir left to the jewelry store.

Had she made a big mistake leaving the hospital with her sister? Viktor was with Ivan in radiology, so Natalie hadn't had the chance to tell him where she was going.

She probably should have woken up Sylvie, though, but the young woman had been sleeping so hard in a corner of the room that Natalie's parents shared. Even Henry, as happy as he'd been to see her, hadn't wanted to wake her up. And Natalie hadn't felt comfortable leaving him with her while she was sleeping. Her parents were sleeping, too.

So she and Henry had gone back into the hall with Dena, who'd been standing in her parents' room when Natalie and Henry had come by to check on them.

"They're getting so old," Dena had mused.

Natalie hadn't known if she was surprised or appalled or sympathetic. "Midsixties isn't old," she'd said. Mom looked great, usually, but she'd been through a hell of an ordeal. And sixty-seven was much too young for her dad to already be getting dementia. She hated that, hated that they were already starting to lose him.

"It is, really," Dena had insisted. "I always thought Timothy and I would be like them and stay together forever."

But Timothy was going to prison. On the way to the hospital, Viktor had confirmed that Natalie's brother-in-law had been taken into custody. He couldn't try to hurt Henry or her again. He had to be the one who'd cut her brake line and shot at her and Sylvie in the warehouse, too. He had to be furious that she was going to get the store that he worked at for so long.

Dena wasn't, though. She wasn't mad at her or jealous, so Natalie had no reason to suspect her of anything anymore.

"Who is he seeing? You know," Dena had prodded her.

"If what you say is true, and he only works and comes home, it would have to be Hannah."

"Hannah?"

"She's a young woman who works as a salesperson," Natalie had explained. "Worked. She quit the other day." When she and Sylvie had confronted her with those sales slips with the passcodes on them.

Dena nodded. "She must have known that Timothy would screw up and get caught. She's probably already out of the country."

"With the diamonds," Natalie said. "She must have been the one who took them and then double-crossed him."

"Let's go to the store and find out where she lives," Dena said.

"Why? She's probably already gone."

"What if she's not?" Dena asked. "And I want to see the woman my husband was having an affair with. You must have a photo ID or something of hers around the store, something with her picture on it."

"I thought you didn't care," Natalie reminded her.

"I'm curious."

Natalie should have reminded her that curiosity killed the cat, but she didn't want to say that in front of Henry. He was so tired that he was nodding off. She'd sighed and agreed to go to the store as long as Dena brought them home after so that Henry could go back to sleep in his own bed.

But once Dena parked her vehicle in the alley, Natalie had an overwhelming sense of foreboding like she'd made a mistake. A horrible mistake.

Was the mistake leaving the hospital with Dena? With trusting her? Or in coming to the store?

Dena herself had called Natalie naive and admonished her for trusting anyone. Had she been warning Natalie to not even trust her?

Dena pushed open her door and then glanced across the console at Natalie. "What's wrong?"

"This is probably a mistake."

Dena shrugged. "Why? I'm not going to fall apart seeing his affair partner. I just want to know what she looks like, how young she is..."

Natalie sighed. "What do you care when you have an affair partner of your own?"

"He's old," Dena said dismissively. "He's rich. But he's old. And I just... I don't know." She shrugged again. "Yes, I know. As you and Mom would point out, I'm vain and shallow. And I just want to know..."

"Dena, you're beautiful..."

"And impatient," Dena said. "Just let me in, and you can come back out here."

Natalie glanced at Henry who was sleeping in a booster seat in the back. Apparently, her sister knew someone with a kid. Maybe her affair partner. "Okay. Henry is exhausted. Let's leave him here."

Dena glanced in the back, as if she'd forgotten he was even there. "Sure."

"Just lock him in." Natalie did not want to risk losing him again. That was why she wanted him in the vehicle. In case this was a mistake. In case Dena wanted to do more than look at a picture of her husband's affair partner. She stepped out of the car and waited until Dena locked it before she opened the back door to the store.

"There's a picture of Hannah on the wall in the showroom," she told Dena. But then she turned on the lights and found the woman herself standing in the backroom. The vault door was open, and she was emptying it out.

"God, you're a pain in the ass," Hannah said. "If only I would have killed you when you and that blond woman messed up my meeting with the fence." She reached for something else in the vault and then turned back toward them with a gun in her hand. "I'm not a great shot at distances, though. But up close..." She stepped closer to them.

Dena moved closer to Natalie. "Hey, what's going on? Who is this?"

"This is her," Natalie said. "The woman having the affair with your husband."

Dena snorted. "No, it's not."

Natalie's heart was beating even faster and harder with fear. What was her sister doing? Were they in on this together, Dena and Hannah?

Had it been a setup bringing her here?

"This woman is too young for Timothy, too pretty," Dena said, and she edged a little closer to Natalie.

She felt the tool that Dena was slipping into her hand, behind their backs. It was one of the sharp chisels Natalie, Josh and her dad had used to get some of the diamonds out of their settings.

Hannah smiled. "And he said you were a bitch."

"Oh, I am," Dena said. "I'm just not stupid. There's no way you would ever fall for my idiot husband. You were just using him."

"Yes, but he's not such an idiot that he must not have had some doubts. He held onto everything we stole, saying we'd cash it all out at once and run away together."

"That's why you took the diamonds," Natalie said. "You didn't want to wait for him."

"I didn't want to go away with him, especially not where he's going now," Hannah said. "He's such an idiot. He hasn't figured out I've had the diamonds the whole time I've been *helping* him try to get them back. Like tonight, I distracted the bodyguards, and he still nearly got caught trying to abduct your son again. He knows he was seen and that he will be arrested if he sticks around."

"That's why you're here," Natalie surmised. "You're taking everything you can to run away."

"He promised he won't implicate me," Hannah said. "But I knew you were already figuring out what he hadn't."

"That you stole the diamonds."

Hannah laughed. "He really believes your baby daddy has them. He told me all about him when he saw him on the security footage."

Josh hadn't taken them, just like he hadn't taken the things he'd gone to prison for stealing.

"Maybe whoever finds your bodies here will believe the same thing, and nobody will be looking for me," Hannah said with a smile.

"You think you'll be able to blame our murders on a guy who isn't anywhere around here?" Natalie asked.

"I don't care who they blame as long as it's not me," Hannah said. Then she swung her gun barrel toward Dena. "Now hand over the keys to your vehicle."

"Why?" Natalie asked, thinking with horror of Henry sleeping in the back seat. If Hannah was heartless enough to kill her and Dena, she wouldn't hesitate to kill him as well.

"Well, I know your vehicle is out of commission after I cut the brake line," Hannah admitted. "You should have died in that crash. You and your blond friend. Where the hell is she?"

"At the hospital still," Natalie said. "But why do you want my sister's vehicle? Didn't you drive yourself here?" She didn't want Hannah anywhere near the alley and her son.

"It's getting light out," Hannah said. "I don't want anyone to see me leaving the front of the store. I'm going out the back, and since that's where you came from, you must be parked in the alley."

"Who cares why she wants it?" Dena asked. "Let's just hand her the damn keys." She reached behind Natalie again and took the chisel from her. Then she stepped toward Hannah, like she was going to hand her the keys. But instead Dena swung her arm, with that tool in her hand, toward the girl's face.

Natalie didn't know if Dena hit Hannah or not…before the gun went off.

The blast echoed off the walls of the small room and knocked Dena back into Natalie. And she didn't have to wonder if she'd been hit or not. Her sister had obviously been shot.

And now Hannah swung the gun barrel toward her.

The sound of a blast woke Henry up to darkness. "Mommy!" he cried out. "Daddy!"

But they hadn't been with Daddy. He'd gone after the person in the mask. He was going to make sure that person didn't ever play games with Henry again. But Henry felt like someone was playing a game now. Cops and robbers?

That was what Chelsea played with him sometimes, and she pointed her finger at him like it was a gun. Then she yelled really loud, "Bang, bang, you're dead!"

He wasn't sure that she sounded like a real gun, though. She didn't even sound like the ones on TV. But whatever he just heard had sounded like the ones on TV.

Was that what that noise was? Not Chelsea but a real gun?

Lights flashed in his face as another vehicle pulled into the alley. It was that long black vehicle that Daddy had left in with his boss.

"Daddy!" he yelled. Henry unbuckled his seat belt and went to the door, but it was locked. So he had to scramble over the seat to the one in the front, behind the steering wheel to unlock it. Then he pushed open the door and jumped down. "Daddy!"

He was right. Daddy was here, and he wasn't alone. Auntie Sylvie was with him. He was so happy to see them, but he wanted Mommy, too.

And so did Daddy. He hugged Henry tight and asked him where she was.

"I don't know. But I heard something… I think I heard a gun…"

"You stay here with Auntie Sylvie," Daddy said. And he handed him over to her, like Henry was a baby that couldn't walk.

Henry didn't care, though. Auntie Sylvie was warm and smelled really good. And he snuggled close to her.

"You can't go in there if someone has a gun," Sylvie said. "Let me. I'm armed."

Daddy took Aunt Sylvie's purse and said, "Now I'm armed. Get in the SUV and call the police."

"Just wait for them—"

Another *bang-bang* echoed around the alley. Daddy pulled open the back door to go inside the store. That had to be where someone had a gun.

And it also had to be where Mommy and Auntie Dena had gone when they left him sleeping in Auntie Dena's car. But Mommy didn't have a gun.

Did Auntie Dena? Or was there someone else inside with them?

Someone like the person in the mask who played games that weren't fun and hurt people?

Chapter Twenty-Six

Screaming and swearing greeted Josh the second he stepped inside the back of the jewelry store.

"You bitch!" a woman shrieked.

But it wasn't Dena. It was the younger woman, the salesclerk, and she held a gun, pointing the barrel at Dena with one hand while she held the other over her eye. Blood trailed down from beneath her hand.

"You already shot her," Natalie said as she leaned over her sister who was lying on the floor. "Twice."

"The first shot didn't kill her because she got me again!" the woman said. "She got my eye!" She gestured toward her face with her gun before swinging the barrel back toward Dena and toward Natalie, who was much too close to the object of Hannah's wrath.

"You'll shoot your eye out," Dena muttered and then laughed.

"She's crazy!" Hannah shrieked. "She's a crazy bitch! No wonder Timothy cheated on her with me."

It was all making sense to Josh now, though he wasn't sure why or how all the women had wound up here. But Sylvie had been right when she'd figured that this was probably where they were.

"Somebody will have heard the shots," Natalie said. "The police will be on their way. You should get out of here."

"She never gave me her keys," Hannah said. "But it doesn't matter now. You're going to have to drive me. Get her keys and the bag."

A big bag lay on the floor next to her, jewelry spilling out of it. She must have dropped it when she fired at Dena or when Dena had attacked her.

"But before we leave, I'm going to put a bullet in this bitch's brain," Hannah said, and she stepped even closer to them.

"No!" Natalie screamed. "I won't drive you anywhere if you hurt her."

"You're going to do what I tell you," Hannah insisted. "I am the one with the gun."

"You're not the only one," Josh said, and he stepped out of the shadows with Sylvie's gun clutched in his hand.

But he hadn't moved fast enough because Hannah grabbed Natalie with her bloodied hand and kept her between them. "Put it down, or I'll kill her right here!" she yelled.

Josh didn't lower the weapon, not yet, but he moved farther into the room, trying to get closer to her. Trying to get between them.

But Hannah was moving, too, jerking Natalie with her toward the door he'd stepped through just moments ago, like the three of them had done a little turn to switch positions in the room.

"Let her go," Josh urged Hannah. "I'll drive you. My vehicle is right outside."

"Give her your keys," she said.

"They're in it. It's running," he said. "I think you could drive yourself. Leave her here."

"If I leave her here, she'll be dead. Just like you and that bitch on the floor," Hannah threatened.

But if she took Natalie with her, she would definitely kill her, too, once she no longer needed her. He willed Natalie to duck, to do anything to let him take a shot.

But Hannah held the gun so close to Natalie's head as she dragged her to the door. It must not have shut tightly behind him because it was open now. Before Hannah could step through it, though, something swung. Something long and shiny and hard. It struck Hannah's head, and she fell to the ground with a clank.

"I know, I know," Sylvie said. "You told me to wait in the car with Henry." Instead, she'd gotten a tire iron out of it. "I locked him inside it, and I did call the police."

Sirens wailed.

Natalie was back on the floor next to her sister. "Help's coming, Dena. Hang in there."

Dena nodded. "She just hit me that first time," she said. "It hurts like a bitch, though. Guess it takes one to know one…"

Sylvie chuckled. "Henry's wrong," she said. "Auntie Dena is pretty funny, too. And pretty tough."

"Henry has a lot of strong women in his life," Josh remarked with awe over how fearless they'd all been.

He was also awed by how much he loved Natalie. He hoped so damn much that Timothy was wrong and that she would be able to find a way to forgive him for hurting her and give him another chance to prove how much he loved her and that he would never hurt her again.

Natalie had never been so afraid as when she'd stared down the barrel of Hannah's gun. She'd thought for sure that she was going to die. But that hadn't scared her as much as the thought of that heartless monster leaving with her son sleeping in the back seat of Dena's car. Hannah would have killed him, too, just as she'd tried to kill Dena.

Dena had been wrong—Hannah had struck her twice. Once in her side and the second time in the shoulder. But she'd probably already been in shock and hadn't felt it. Both bullets had gone straight through her, and while the surgeon had to stop some internal bleeding, he had assured them that Dena would be fine.

Natalie wasn't fine. She was still scared. And not just over what could have happened but over what would. It was all over now.

Hannah had been treated and taken into custody. Timothy was already in jail. It was over.

Did that also mean that Natalie and Josh were over? She was pretty sure that he would want to stay a part of their son's life. They were together now while Natalie had stayed at the hospital with Dena and their parents.

Natalie left her parents standing over Dena's bed and stepped out into the hall. She needed a breather. And she needed to see her son and Josh.

She wanted him to not just be part of Henry's life but part of hers, too. But she'd been grappling so much with her own feelings, with falling for him all over again, that she wasn't sure what he wanted.

"There's Mommy!" Henry said, and he let go of Josh's hand to run up to her.

She dropped down to gather him into her arms and hug him tightly. "I thought you two went home," she said. That was what she remembered telling Josh to do when the ambulance arrived. She'd ridden in it with Dena to the hospital, and she'd told Josh to take Henry home.

"We wanted to be here for you," Josh said, answering for them both.

But did he mean it? Did they both want to be there for her or just her son?

"Hey, Henry," Sylvie said as she walked up behind Josh. "Your daddy's boss is painting a picture of you, and he wants to see you up close to make sure that he got you just right." She held out her hand. "Let's go talk to him."

Henry wriggled away from Natalie to rush over to his aunt. But Sylvie pointed him back toward the waiting room. "He's right there. The one on the left." She made an L with her left hand to show the boy which was which. "Cuz they both look so much alike."

"They look like you," Henry said.

"Uh...yeah..."

Once the little boy scampered away, Sylvie turned back toward them. "Milek has time yet. He could add the two of you to that portrait and make it a family one. Please, don't let my mistakes mess up the rest of your lives. You belong together." Then she blinked furiously and turned away, heading off after her nephew as she muttered under her breath, "I'm not crying. You're crying."

Natalie smiled, but her heart was beating fast and hard after

Sylvie's pronouncement, especially with the way Josh was looking at her. So intensely. "What?" she asked.

"Could you do it?" he asked.

"Do what?" Be a family with him and their son? She would
love to do that.

"Could you ever forgive me?" Josh asked. "Could you ever
trust me again after what I did?" He sounded so tortured, like
he was in more pain than Dena after she got shot.

"I didn't think I could," Natalie admitted.

He flinched. "Giving you up was the hardest thing I've ever
done. But I didn't know how to save Sylvie. She was working
for a monster who threatened her life and our mom's…"

"And yours," she said. "That was why she didn't take the
blame because he said he would kill you. And why she kept stealing. He told her that if she didn't, he would get to you in prison.
Someone else she cared about died in prison, so she knew he
could do it." Sylvie had explained all that to her while they'd
been trapped in the wrecked SUV.

Josh sucked in a breath. "That explains her actions. Can you
understand and forgive mine?"

"I know that you were worried about the same things she
was, about her life and yours and even mine," she said. "But
you could have told me the truth."

"You never would have let me go to prison for something
I didn't do," Josh said. "And if you had started making noise
about the charges and the conviction, I was sure that he would
go after you next."

Josh had already told her as much, but she needed to confirm.
"So, you were trying to protect me, too?"

He nodded. "I would rather lose you that way, to never see
you again, than for you to lose your life."

"It wouldn't have been just my life," she said. Henry would
have died, too. She'd been pregnant then. "You did the right
thing. We're all alive. You, me, Henry, Sylvie…"

He released a breath like he'd been holding it a long time,
maybe five years. "Yes, that is all that matters. That we're
all alive."

"And you're out now," she said. "You have a chance at a new life."

"I want a chance at the life we would have had," he said. "I want to marry you. I want to be a family. I love you, Natalie. I never stopped loving you."

"I never stopped loving you," she admitted. "Even when I hated you for what you'd done, I still loved you."

"And now?"

"Now?"

"Do you still hate me?"

She closed the distance between them and wrapped her arms around him. "No. Now I love you more than ever."

"So you can forgive me?"

She nodded. "Can you forgive me?"

"For what?"

"For not telling you that I was pregnant."

"I didn't give you much of a chance to talk that day," he admitted. "I had to get you to leave before I told you the truth."

"The truth is that everything you did, you did out of love," she said. "I was angry."

"You had every reason to be."

She kissed him. "You are the most amazing man, Josh Stafford, and I can't wait to be your wife."

"I hope Sylvie is right and Milek has time to add us to that portrait of Henry. We all belong together," he said. "For the rest of our lives." And then he kissed her back.

"Are we crazy?" Garek asked his brother. He'd come so close to having all his fears realized about starting his own branch of the Payne Protection Agency.

Their employees had been hurt and could have died. They could have lost members of their team. Now they were considering adding another one.

Milek let out a shaky breath. "No. It has to be her. She looks exactly like Stacy."

"Oh God, we have to tell Stacy," Garek remarked.

"Who is Stacy?" Sylvie asked. "And why are you two talking about me like I'm not here?" Her nephew had run back to his parents, but she'd stayed in the waiting room with Garek... because he had asked to talk to her.

But all he could do now was stare at her.

"Stacy is our sister," Milek replied.

She nodded. "Okay...what does any of that have to do with me?"

"Because we think you're our sister, too."

She chuckled. "I'm Josh's sister."

"And yet you look more like us," Garek said.

"Well, Josh and I had different fathers. He looks like his dad, and I..."

"Look like yours," Milek said. "Our father."

"I don't know," Sylvie said. "I was really little when he went away, so I don't remember much about him...except his eyes." She looked at the two of them then. "My mom didn't tell me much either except that he was a criminal who went to jail. Even on her deathbed, she wouldn't tell me his name, just that he died in prison."

"He was murdered," Garek said.

"I know that," she said.

"How?"

"Luther Mills told me that," she said. "He also knew who my father was. And he mentioned the name to me once, but I was never certain if he was telling the truth or just messing with me."

"Patek Kozminski was our father," Milek said. "I think he was yours, too."

She shrugged. "I don't think it matters much. He's dead."

"It matters to us," Garek said. "You're family."

"Josh is my only family. And Henry...and hopefully Natalie will be soon."

"We're family, too," Milek said.

"But you don't even know me."

"We'll get to know you when you're working with us."

"What are you talking about?"

"We're offering you a job with our branch of the Payne Protection Agency," Milek said.

She laughed. "That's like having the fox watch the henhouse, isn't it?"

"We've heard that before," Garek admitted. "We're former foxes ourselves. That's what you are, too, right? You told Josh that you're not stealing anymore."

"Not since Luther died," Sylvie said. "I swear."

"Yeah, we'll have to work on that," Garek teased her. "You do swear a lot. We'll have to give you some training, too. I hear you're a lousy shot. But we do need some employees who are actually allowed to carry firearms. Most of ours would violate their parole if they did."

She laughed. "Okay, I'm beginning to see the family resemblance now. You're both smart-asses."

"And so are you," Garek said. "You're very smart. Josh told us that you already figured Hannah was involved. And then you were the one who knocked her out. You'll be an asset to the team, Sylvie."

"So, this isn't a pity job offer?"

"I didn't know there was such a thing," Milek said.

"Uh, that's why you work for the Payne Protection Agency, out of pity," Garek teased. "God knows you couldn't support yourself let alone your family on what you make as an artist."

Milek was probably a millionaire several times over, but he just nodded. "That makes sense," he agreed. "Because I'm not very good with firearms, either. We can work on that together, Sylvie." He held out his hand.

She shook it. Then she shook Garek's. "All right," she said. "I'll take this job. I just hope we all don't come to regret this."

Garek remembered his fear from the opening, that he would lose one of his team. With Josh and Ivan getting hurt, he had come close, but they'd all survived.

But what if something like this happened again? Now their own sister was a team member, they could lose her again after they just found her.

They wouldn't put her right on any cases, though. They would train her first.

And they would focus on the rest of the team. On Blade and Viktor and Ivan...

Josh had already earned some time off to be with his son and the woman who would hopefully be his wife soon.

* * * * *

Don't miss the stories in this mini series!

BACHELOR BODYGUARDS

Hostage Security
LISA CHILDS
January 2025

Personal Security
LISA CHILDS
March 2025

MILLS & BOON

Breaking The Code
Maria Lokken

MILLS & BOON

A cozy reading chair and a romance novel are all **Maria Lokken** needs to have the perfect afternoon. The perfect evenings are spent with her husband— her real-life romance hero. Both her husband and her large family are inspirations for many of her stories. Besides being an avid reader, she loves popcorn, movies and walking around museums. You can find her at marialokken.com or on Instagram, @maria_writer_lokken.

Books by Maria Lokken

Harlequin Romantic Suspense

Breaking the Code

Visit the Author Profile page at
millsandboon.com.au.

Dear Reader,

This is a story about family and second chances set against the backdrop of cybersecurity.

Growing up in a tight-knit family, I've always been fascinated by the bonds that tie relatives together. That sense of unwavering support and camaraderie served as a major inspiration for me in telling Rafe and Mallory's story.

Their chance at love and a fresh start hinges on their ability to uncover the identity of a mysterious threat to Mallory's daughter.

Because cybersecurity is becoming increasingly critical in our daily lives, I felt it had to be a central theme to the story. And when it comes to second chances, I mean, who doesn't love them? We all yearn for redemption, and the opportunity to rewrite our stories, and Rafe and Mallory are no exception.

In *Breaking the Code*, my characters face many challenges, but throughout, there are two things they can rely on, and that's each other and family.

I hope you enjoy Rafe and Mallory's journey. I know I enjoyed writing it.

Happy reading!

Maria

To my amazing family for everything you do.

And to Carly and Magda, who helped shape
this story when my hero was a mechanic.

Chapter One

The death of a husband would devastate most women. But Mallory Stanton wasn't like most wives. When two men from Interpol arrived on her doorstep with news that her husband, Blake, had perished in a plane crash over international waters, she dutifully played the grieving widow and let the tears flow freely. But inwardly, every fiber of her being wanted to celebrate. Finally, she was liberated from a marriage that had almost destroyed her spirit. If not for his continual threat to take away her daughter, she would have left years ago.

For the last month, she'd been slowly claiming her life back. With Blake gone, so was the feeling of having to look over her shoulder or walk on eggshells, trying to anticipate her husband's sudden mood shifts or angry outbursts. At last, the house was peaceful, and she relished her newfound freedom, doing what she wanted, when she wanted—like creating a playlist of her favorite songs from her single days.

The warm, early afternoon sunshine streamed through the window, and Mallory sang out loud and danced through her spacious kitchen. With her hips swaying to the beat, she piled on layers of creamy cheddar cheese over cooked noodles.

While her husband was alive, she never dreamed of serving mac and cheese, even with a gourmet recipe. Blake considered it too ordinary to be served in his house. Well, it was her home now, and making her daughter's favorite meal without fear of retribution from her maniacal husband filled her with euphoria. She laughed and performed another twirl to the music. Strands of shiny coal-black hair from her messy bun came loose, and she blew them off her face. She sashayed over to the speaker and pumped up the volume. Nothing could ruin this perfect late-August day.

When the doorbell rang, she quickly shoved the casserole into the oven. "Coming. Just a minute." Mallory lowered the music, wiped her hands on the dish towel, and hurried to the front door. She'd been expecting the delivery of a new chair for the family room to replace the one she'd thrown out. Day by day, she removed reminders of her husband. Her latest purchase would replace the stuffy, dark leather chair he loved. The thought made her smile.

Mallory opened the front door, but there wasn't anyone there. She raised an eyebrow. *Odd.*

She stepped onto the walkway and glanced right and left but saw no one, not even a car driving away on the wide, tree-lined street with its spacious McMansions. As she stepped back, she noticed a manila envelope inside the threshold that she hadn't noticed when she opened the door.

She picked up the envelope and pressed back the metal clasp, then pulled out several black-and-white photos. Adrenaline coursed through her veins as she studied one image after the next of her daughter at yesterday's playdate. The neatly typed note on unremarkable plain white paper held an ominous threat that had Mallory letting out a shuddering breath.

GIVE US THE INFORMATION ON THE HARD DRIVE OR WE TAKE HER. DON'T CALL THE AUTHORI-TIES. WE'RE WATCHING.

Mallory dropped the photos and flew up the stairs to Justine's bedroom. A deep breath of relief whooshed out at the sight of her precious five-year-old still napping. "Oh, thank goodness," she whispered, slumping against the doorjamb. Justine's soft brown curls were splayed out on the pillow. Her tiny fingers curled into relaxed fists, and the sound of her gentle snore signaled Mallory's world was still intact.

Closing her eyes, Mallory willed her heart back into her chest and focused on slowing her breathing. The ringing phone startled her, and she hurried into her bedroom to pick it up before it woke Justine.

"Hello?" Mallory said into the receiver.

"We want the drive."

The raspy voice on the other end made her skin crawl.

"Your daughter's pretty."

"You leave my daughter alone. I don't know what you want, but whatever it is, I don't have it."

"Well, you better figure it out," the raspy voice said. "'Cause Blake was holding it for us, and now we want it back. You don't have much time. The clock's ticking." The line went dead.

A cold sensation swept over her. She'd never let them get close enough to touch her daughter. Not Justine. Not her baby. She wrapped her arms around herself and began to rock back and forth, her mind trying to understand what was happening. Mallory had no clue what drive they wanted, where to find it, or how much time she had. *Damn you, Blake.*

The world thought of her dead husband as a financial genius. They'd dubbed him the Wizard of Wall Street. But she knew better. He was a criminal dressed in thousand-dollar suits. Blake kept her out of his business, but she wasn't stupid. She knew he associated with powerful men who didn't play by the rules. And it would seem he had something they wanted.

Mallory spent most of the night frantically searching the house and Blake's home office for anything that resembled a drive. All she recovered was a hidden laptop and some cash taped to the underside of his desk chair. She'd tried desperately to get into the laptop but had no luck with the passwords she tried. A trip to the local computer store hadn't helped her get any closer to discovering if the laptop was what the men were after. There seemed to be no way into the password-protected computer without wiping out all the contents on the internal hard drive.

Dejected, Mallory drove home, wondering how she would find what these men were after. Deep in thought, she hadn't fully realized her front door was slightly ajar as she came up the walkway.

"What in the world?" she whispered and held on tight to her daughter's hand. She motioned for Justine to keep quiet by putting an index finger over her lips. Tentatively, Mallory peeked inside. "Hello?" Her rapid breathing was the only sound. "Hello? Anyone here?" There was no response. If she were smart, she'd step back onto her walkway with her daughter and call the police. Instead, she stepped over the threshold and into the foyer, where she came to an abrupt stop. With her mouth open, her gaze took in the scene.

She couldn't believe what she was seeing. Slashed sofa cushions, drawers dumped onto the floor, closets emptied with their contents strewn about, furniture turned upside down, and holes punched into the walls. Shock slowly crawled through her like an unwelcome visitor.

"Mommy?" Justine began to cry.

Mallory swooped Justine into her arms, rushed out of the house, and phoned the police.

Hours later, when they could find nothing had been stolen, they labeled it vandalism.

To Mallory, it didn't matter what they labeled it. She knew with certainty it was no longer safe for her and her daughter in Westchester County. It was time to flee.

Mallory's hands had finally stopped shaking as she gripped the steering wheel. The knowledge that her daughter's life was in danger made her sick. How could her husband still be controlling her life from the grave?

"Mommy?"

"Yes, Punkie?" Mallory glanced at the rearview mirror. Her eyes met her daughter, who was sitting in the back seat.

"I thought we weren't going to Grandpa's house until next week?"

"Well…change in plans. It'll be fun, you'll see." Mallory tried to keep the tremble out of her voice.

She'd driven over two hundred miles, and exhaustion was beginning to seep into her bones. The night was coming on fast, and Mallory hadn't planned on stopping, but she wasn't sure how much farther she could safely drive through the winding roads of the Catskill Mountains in the dark. Holding the wheel in a death grip, she leaned forward, looking for an exit sign. She needed to find a place to stay for the night. The once familiar area had undoubtedly changed in fifteen years, and in her hurry to put as much distance between her and the people who trashed her house and threatened her daughter's life, she hadn't even thought to check on possible places to stay. The plan had been to get straight to her father's house in Rochester. She shook her head. There was no way she'd make it tonight. But she remembered a small motel she hoped was still in business. The Sunrise. That was the name. Sunrise, how ironic. She hoped she would see one of those again.

She glanced at the large onboard screen mounted into the dashboard—a lot of good it did. The screen was blank. Dead. Nonoperational. It should have come on when she started the car—but nothing. Unable to make it work, she couldn't get directions or the address of a nearby motel. She scoffed. *Some fancy car.* Once she got to the exit, she'd look it up on her phone.

This was her first time behind the wheel of the brand-new, special-order, top-of-the-line Tesla. The dealership phoned, saying it was ready for pickup. Its arrival had been unexpected. Blake never mentioned he'd ordered a new vehicle. But then, Blake rarely told her anything. Now, he was dead, and she needed a car that wouldn't be recognized. The timing was perfect. Almost too good to be true.

The Uber had taken her directly to the dealership. She signed the necessary papers and drove out of Westchester County as fast as possible, hoping no one followed her. There had been no time to get a demonstration of how the car worked or what buttons to push to get the onboard navigator to work.

As she looked for an exit, she rounded a curve and approached an incline. The car slowed. She increased the pressure on the accelerator but failed to pick up speed. Instead, the car stuttered as if she were tapping on the brake. She slammed the pedal to the floor—and nothing. "No. No. No." She banged her hand against the dashboard. "You brand-new piece of crap. Don't stop! Come on, don't stop!"

"What's the matter, Mommy?"

Mallory closed her eyes for a moment and let out a breath. The last thing she needed was a wide-awake five-year-old. She glanced at her daughter in the rearview mirror. Curly brown strands escaped her baseball cap, and the quiver in her lower lip broke Mallory's heart. "Oh, honey…sorry. Um…it looks like this car has a mind of its own." She worked at keeping an even voice. "But don't worry, everything's going to be fine." Focusing on the road ahead, she willed the Tesla to keep moving, but her intention wasn't enough. She had no choice but to pull onto the shoulder and put the car in Park.

"Mommy, why are we stopping?"

Forcing a smile, Mallory turned to face her daughter. "The car's acting a little funny." She tried not to sound as alarmed as she felt. "I'm going to step outside and see if I can find out what's wrong. I won't be long."

"Mommy?"

"Yes?"

"I'm really hungry."

"I know, Punkie, and as soon as I can get this car started, we'll find somewhere to eat." Mallory reached between the seats and squeezed her daughter's knee. "In the meantime, how 'bout a pretzel?" She pulled out the snack from her oversized leather tote bag and handed it to her daughter. "Okay, I'm going to check on the car."

"Is everything okay, Mommy?"

"It will be," Mallory lied. All day, she'd managed to convince Justine they were on an adventure, but she wasn't sure how much longer that story would hold. "Just wait here, Punkie."

She jammed a baseball cap over her head, walked to the front of the Tesla, and peered down the road. There wasn't another car in sight. In fact, she hadn't seen another vehicle for the last thirty miles. Strange. Very strange.

Her shaking hands managed to raise the hood. In the dwindling light, it was difficult to see. Even if she found something, she wouldn't have a clue what to do. Her extensive knowledge of automobiles began with putting the key in the ignition and ended with pressing down on the gas pedal. And this car had a keyless ignition, so she was already off on the wrong foot.

Exhausted and frazzled, she studied the engine while muttering unintelligible swear words. Hadn't she already been through enough? Five hours ago, she'd left her home in Pelham, New York, first driving into New York City, then maneuvering onto the New York State Thruway, doubling back onto the Taconic Parkway, and finally taking a back road in an effort to lose whoever might be following her, only to be stuck on the side of the road where she was an easy target. She only hoped she'd put enough distance between her and the people who wanted the drive.

Her father would know what to do if she ever got there.

For the next several minutes, her gaze focused on the horizon as the remains of the day turned to twilight. Mallory bit her lower lip, working out what to do. The fear of being stranded outweighed the fear of getting help, and she swiped open her phone and pulled up a travel app. She waited, but no browser appeared. "Perfect. No signal." Holding it above her head, she walked a few feet away from the car, hoping a different position would at least produce one bar. But still, nothing.

Think, damn it! She kicked at the dirt and turned her attention back to the car. Exhaustion made it difficult for her to concentrate, and she studied the engine as if the answer would magically present itself. "I have no idea what I'm doing," she said under her breath.

A low rumbling sound coming from the road startled her. Oh, God, had they found her?

She wiped her sweaty palms against the front of her jeans and cautiously inched her head around the hood. A single headlight appeared in the distance. *A motorcycle?* Mallory knew only one thing about motorcycles—gangs rode them. This cannot be happening. *Please, keep on riding—nothing to see here.* She tried to push away her panic and hoped she'd get lucky. But luck left Mallory three days ago, and despite her will for whoever it was to keep moving, the motorcycle slowed and pulled off to the side of the road.

The rider hit the kickstand and straddled the bike. He took his time removing his helmet, the fading light giving his silhouette an ominous look. She couldn't make out his face as he headed toward her.

"Hey, what's the trouble?" the mysterious man asked.

Adrenaline coursed through her body, and her pulse hammered hard. *Deep breaths, deep breaths*, she ordered herself as she folded her arms across her chest to keep from shaking. "Justine, stay right there. Don't come out."

"Hello? Are you okay?" the stranger asked as he continued toward her.

Mallory pulled the bill of her cap lower. "I'm, I'm…not sure," she managed to get out. "My car. It…it…just stopped." Sweat began to pool at the base of her neck, and her mind raced. Leather jacket, motorcycle, long hair, dark stubble. With the brief assessment of his appearance complete, she quickly fixed her gaze on the ground. Had she fled one dangerous situation only to find herself in another?

"Do you mind if I have a look?"

Mallory hesitated. She could barely hear him above the roar of blood pulsing in her ears.

"It'll only take a second," he said.

Reluctantly, she stepped back and indicated, with an outstretched trembling hand, that he was free to look under the hood. She hadn't a clue if she was doing the right thing, but she was stranded and officially out of options.

The rider pulled a mini flashlight from inside his leather jacket and leaned under the hood to examine the engine.

While he was preoccupied, Mallory slowly inched herself closer to the road, hoping an SUV carrying a family would come by. She'd feel safer asking them for help.

Several minutes passed, and she held her breath, watching from a relatively safe distance while the stranger poked around, holding his light over different parts of the engine.

"Looks like one of the cooling hoses is loose," he finally said.

Mallory stepped several feet back. Her gaze focused on her daughter. "That doesn't sound good."

"It's not great, but it's not the worst thing. I know about cars—

but electric isn't my specialty. You'll need a mechanic for that. Either way, it doesn't look like you'll be going anywhere in this car tonight."

"Damn," she said under her breath. "Can you tell me how far away we are from Hollow Lake?"

"It's the next exit. Five miles down." He slammed the hood shut.

"Mommy, are you okay?" Justine called out.

"Yes, Punkie, I'm fine. Stay where you are."

The rider walked toward the passenger door, peering into the car. "She's cute. But it looks like you and your kid are stranded."

Except for the rasp in his voice, he almost sounded familiar. But his words made her uneasy, and she didn't dare look him in the eye. Keeping the bill of her cap low, covering her face, she inched her way back toward the car. "Don't worry." Mallory stiffened, ready to reach in, grab her daughter, and run if necessary. "Thanks for your help."

"Listen, if you need a place to stay—"

"N-n-no. We'll be fine." Mallory quickly got into the driver's seat, slammed the door, and hit the locks.

"Mommy, what's happening?"

"We're waiting for another car to come and help." Mallory hoped. But what if the next car held the men who were chasing her?

"Isn't that man gonna help us?"

"I'm not sure. I'm not sure he can." Mallory faced straight ahead and squeezed her eyes shut, trying to work out a solution. When he tapped on the window, she jumped, and for a moment, her heart stopped before it began to race uncontrollably.

The stranger made a rolling motion with his hand, indicating she should lower her window. But Mallory shook her head in vain.

"Listen, I'm not going to hurt you," he said, loud enough for her to hear. "Let me help get your car towed."

Mallory stared at him through the glass between them. Something about him seemed familiar. A sense of warmth in his eyes almost had her at ease. She knew those eyes. She shook her head again, warding off fatigue and possibly her lack of judgment.

This man was a complete stranger, and she needed to remind herself that she wasn't a good judge of character. That had been proven the day she'd married Blake.

"Okay. Look, stay put," the man said.

Stay put? Where was she going to go? How had she allowed herself to be so trapped? Keeping an eye on her side mirror, she watched him walk back toward his motorcycle. *Please get on that thing and go.*

But that was too much to hope for. She watched as he leaned against the seat, crossed his legs at the ankles, and pulled out his mobile phone.

Oh, God, what is he doing now? Who's he calling? How does he even have a signal? She leaned closer to the mirror and squinted. *Is that a satellite phone? Who is this guy?* Mallory tapped the steering wheel with the palm of her hand. *Think. Think.*

"Mommy, what's the matter? How come we're not moving?"

Mallory turned to face her daughter. "Something's wrong with the car. It's going to take a few minutes for me to figure this out."

"Are you scared?" Justine's brown eyes were wide.

"Oh, Punkie. No. Everything's fine," Mallory said, trying to keep the muscles in her face relaxed. "I need a minute to think."

"When you're finished thinking, then can we get something to eat? I'm really hungry."

"I know, and I'm sorry it's taking us so long to get to where we're going. But I promise I'll feed you as soon as we get there." Her voice quivered, and she quickly turned. She didn't want to lose it in front of her daughter. Once they were safe, she promised herself a good cry.

Mallory put her attention on her side mirror as she tugged on the heart-shaped pendant hanging on her necklace. Twenty minutes passed, and her daughter finally dozed, but the rider hadn't moved. What was he waiting for?

Sweat dripped down her back, and she rechecked her mobile—still no signal. She tossed the useless device onto the passenger seat.

The next ten minutes were spent with her focus moving from the nonexistent traffic to the unmoving rider resting against his bike. She was beginning to seriously wonder if she'd stepped into another dimension. How could she have found herself on a road with no traffic?

When lights from a few yards away finally filled her rearview mirror, she decided to take her chances, threw open the car door, and jumped out, waving her arms. "Oh, thank God. Finally, another human being."

As the headlights came into focus, she could make out two vehicles. They both pulled up behind the stranger's motorcycle. *Ohgodohgodohgodohno! What's going on?*

The rider called to her, "Ma'am, that's your tow. Let's go ahead and get you hooked up."

"Hold on." Mallory thrust her palm out, facing him in the universal stop-right-there sign. "I don't know you, and I don't know whoever is in that...that...truck. So don't come any closer."

"It's a tow truck," the rider said.

The headlights from the truck and the motorcycle blinded her, and she shaded her eyes with her hand. Someone walked toward her, and Mallory took a step back.

"Hey," a woman's voice called out. "I hear you need some help."

The figure of a petite woman came into focus. "Who are you?" Mallory asked.

"I'm Abbey Ong. I own the B&B in town. Rafael here called and said you needed some help and a place to stay for the night. He also said you're not too easy with strangers. He thought if I came out with the tow, you might be more apt to let us help you. Sorry it took so long. But there's a bad pileup down at the last exit. State troopers aren't letting anything through. We had to take the back roads."

"But why?"

"Sorry? I don't understand the question," Abbey said.

"Why are you helping?" Mallory's words came out on a sob. She'd become so accustomed to protecting her daughter with no outside help that the offer nearly made her weep.

Abbey pulled her jacket tight across her chest. "You've got car trouble and a little girl. We're not going to leave you out here on this back road. The night's getting colder."

It had been so long since anyone had been kind. Her instinct was to reject the help. But it was dark. She was stranded, and she'd run out of options. Taking a deep breath and a mental leap of faith, Mallory decided to go with it. "Okay. Thanks."

"Do you have any bags?" Abbey asked.

"In the trunk."

"Okay, we'll put them in my car. You get your daughter."

Mallory nodded and opened the back passenger door, helping Justine out. "You okay?"

"I'm okay, Mommy, are you?"

Mallory smiled at the genuineness of the question. "Yes. These people are going to help us."

"Because our car's broke?"

Mallory nodded, put her hand on her daughter's shoulder, and walked toward the trunk as their luggage was removed.

"The short, rangy guy with the tow, that's Mickey. He'll hook up your car. And this guy here is Rafael," Abbey said, nodding in the rider's direction. "He's the one who called me."

At the second mention of his name, Mallory dared for the first time to really look at the rider, whose features were now illuminated by the tow truck's headlights. He was as drop-dead gorgeous as she remembered. "Oh my gosh. Rafe? Is that you?" Her first reaction was shock. The next thought had her wondering why she hadn't recognized him.

Rafe took a step toward her.

Mallory pulled off her cap.

His gaze scanned her face. "Mallory? Mallory Kane?" He pulled her into a hug.

His arms wrapped around her, and she nearly collapsed in the cocoon of his embrace. Old feelings flooded back in a rush. Oh, how she missed that. She had no idea how much she'd missed him. Quickly stepping out of his arms, her gaze scanned the ground as she tried to collect herself. "Wow. This is a surprise. I never expected to see you." She swallowed back the tears pooling at the sides of her eyes and swiped her nose with the back of her hand.

"I could say the same thing. You…um…look so different."

Rafe ran a hand through his hair. "I mean, you look great." The words stumbled out of his mouth. "You...you cut your hair?"

Heat crept up her cheeks, and she self-consciously touched the back of her neck. It felt clammy. The hair that was there yesterday, now gone, made her feel exposed.

"Mommy. Who is that?" Justine tugged on Mallory's jeans.

"Oh. Rafe, this is my daughter, Justine." Mallory took her hand. "Punkie, this is...an...old friend. His name is Rafe."

"That's a funny name. How do you know my mommy?" Justine tilted her head, looking up at Rafe.

"We went to school together." He looked around. "But that was a long time ago."

"You went to school with my mommy?"

Rafe chuckled. "Yes, we were in high school—"

"It was a lifetime ago." Mallory pulled Justine toward her. The less said, the better. She couldn't trust what Justine would say if they continued any conversation. Right now, she needed a place to stay and a new plan.

"Hey, Rafe," Mickey, the tow driver, called out. "We're all set. The car's hoisted."

"That was fast," Mallory said. "Thanks. I'm not sure what we would have done if you hadn't come along." Mallory focused on the tips of her sneakers. "I'm sorry. I didn't recognize you. Must be the beard."

Rafe rubbed the side of his face. "I forgot I had this. Just back from a fishing trip in the woods. A couple of weeks with no razor. Kinda heavenly."

"Anyway, I can't be too careful with my daughter," she said apologetically. "But thanks so much. You saved us."

"Yeah, thanks," Justine piped up.

Rafe crouched at eye level with Justine. "You are most welcome."

"You ready?" Abbey asked. She opened her car door. "Do you need help getting your daughter in the back seat?"

Mallory shook her head.

Rafe smiled. "Well then, I'll be taking off. But you're in good hands. I'll check on you tomorrow, and we can catch up."

"Sure." Mallory gave a thin-lipped smile. The hope was that

her car would be ready first thing in the morning, and there would be no "catching up."

But her gaze lingered as he rode off. Seeing him again stirred up feelings she forgot she had. She shook her head as if that would help rid her of the memories. This was not a reunion, and involving him in her situation was not an option. Rafe didn't deserve her troubles. She nearly emotionally destroyed him once; she wouldn't do it a second time.

Chapter Two

Rafe switched off the ignition, pushed the kickstand down, and took off his helmet. His mind was spinning. After so many years, seeing Mallory again knocked the wind and the sense out of him. In a half daze, he strode toward his brother's house and rang the doorbell.

"Bro. You're back. How was the fishing?"

"Hey, Zack." Rafe gave his younger brother a weary smile.

"You look rough, man. Everything okay?" Zack opened the door wider.

Rafe didn't respond or wait for an invitation. Instead, he breezed past his brother into the well-appointed two-bedroom cottage with wide white-planked wood floors.

"Sure, come on in," Zack said, his tone laced with sarcasm. "*Mi casa*...and all that."

"Yeah, yeah." Rafe waved a hand and didn't look back. "Came to drop off your keys."

Like his home, Zack was neat, trim, and concise. Eighteen months younger than Rafe, they bore a remarkable resemblance and, in high school, had often been mistaken for twins. Their deep brown hair highlighted their chocolate-colored eyes. Their most striking feature was a dimple in the center of their chins. As the years passed and life happened for both of them, their styles changed. Rafe wore his hair past his neckline and was comfortable in jeans and T-shirts, while Zack preferred suits and ties and wore his hair in a professional cut.

"I've got a bit of a thirst," Rafe said and walked through the large living room, past the breakfast bar separating the kitchen area. He headed straight for the refrigerator and grabbed a beer. "Want one?"

Zack smirked. "Sure. I'll have one of *my* beers. Thanks for asking. Something on your mind? Or did you come back from a two-week fishing trip worse than when you left? 'Cause I thought you took two weeks at my lake house to give your attitude a little vacation. You know, chill from all the hard work over the past year before we start new projects. Me and Max definitely took the two weeks to vacate—body, mind, and spirit. Sandy beaches. Blue oceans." He cocked his head to the side. "I'm gonna take one of my always correct educated guesses and say you decided to skip the chill. So, spill. What happened?"

Rafe shook his head, grabbed the bottle opener from the drawer, opened the beers in silence, and handed one to his brother. "Well...hold that thought." He took an extra-long pull from the bottle.

Zack made a face. "Whoa. What's going on? I sense we got a problem here. *Dimelo.*"

"That's the criminal defense lawyer in you. Always digging."

"Nuh-huh." Zack wagged his index finger while holding onto the beer. "This isn't about me. I'm not the one walking in here looking like someone smacked me, walked away, came back, and smacked me again. I could've been perfectly happy sitting on my couch watching *Amor de mi Vida*."

Rafe barked out a laugh. "Sorry, I didn't mean to interrupt your very important *telenovela* viewing."

"Go ahead. Make all the fun you want. You'd be surprised what you can learn from these Spanish soap operas. They're helping me develop my next career as a writer."

"For real?" Rafe said, skepticism showing on his arched brow.

"One hundred percent. With all the intrigue, multiple plot twists, villains, and people rising from the dead, you can't beat it. Anyway, it's my thing. It's how I unwind from our work. So don't knock it till you try it."

"I did try it. Remember when *Abuela* Carmen babysat us? That's all we watched. Not a cartoon in sight." Rafe smiled, remembering his maternal grandmother. Even now, he could vividly recall her signature rose-scented perfume and the warmth he felt whenever she hugged him. Thinking about her took the edge off his taut emotions. He exhaled, letting go of the tightness in his chest. "You know the funny thing about plot twists and people coming back from the dead? Sometimes real life is like that."

Zack gave him a pointed look. "Stop talking in riddles."

Rafe let out a long exhale and leaned back against the kitchen counter. "Dang it, bro. I don't even know where to start."

"Like I tell all our clients. Start at the beginning."

If he were going to tell anyone how he was feeling, it would be his younger brother, Zack. Not that he didn't love and respect the eldest of the three, Max. But Zack was slow to rile. Slow to react. He listened first. Digested. He could quickly untangle facts from emotions. It had served him well for the ten years he worked as a criminal defense lawyer for a major Manhattan law firm, handling white-collar crime and getting CEOs off the hook for embezzlement, money laundering, and fraud. He was good at it. Too good. When he realized helping the bad guys win wasn't the reason he went into law, he packed up and joined Rafe in his start-up cybersecurity business. Zack handled the security, Max oversaw the strategy, and Rafe handled the technology. On the side, Zack worked on his first novel.

"So. What gives?" Zack pulled out a stool from underneath the breakfast bar and sat.

Rafe brushed his hair back and placed his beer on the counter. He didn't really know where to start. With so many emotions bubbling up inside, he launched in at the beginning. "Do you remember my senior year in high school?"

Zack placed his elbows on the breakfast bar and leaned forward. "Is there something specific I should be remembering about your senior year?"

Rafe let out a huff. "Do you remember Mallory Kane?"

"Your girlfriend?"

"She was more than just my girlfriend. I was in love with

her. But—" Rafe jutted out his lower lip "—she wanted different things. Or maybe I should say her mother wanted her to have different things." Rafe paused. "And... Mallory went along with it." Rafe tried to hide the hurt. When she broke it off, it nearly crushed him. *Leave it*, he told himself. *That was a lifetime ago.*

Zack sat back and crossed his arms over his chest. "Uh-huh. I remember her mother wasn't your biggest fan. Didn't Mallory end up moving to the city after college and marrying...what's his name?"

"Blake Stanton."

Zack snapped his fingers. "That's the guy." He tilted his head and looked up to the corner of the room. "Didn't they call him the Wizard of Wall Street or something like that?"

"Yup. That's the one. Imagine, of all the people in the world, I ran into her tonight. Car trouble. Stuck out on Route 23 with her little girl. Thing is, we didn't recognize each other, and...well... her behavior was...strange, like she was afraid of something." Rafe scratched the side of his face. "Yeah. Something was off."

"This just happened?" Zack asked.

Rafe nodded.

"So, let me get this straight. A woman who you were in love with, what? Fifteen years ago? Right? Is stranded on the side of the road, and it's getting dark. Here you come riding on your motorcycle, looking like that—" Zack pointed a finger at him "—I mean, I'd be scared of you, too."

He put his head in his hands when he realized what the problem was. "Oh, man. She was afraid of *me*." Rafe scrubbed his face with his hands. "Oh, man." He looked up. "You think she knew?"

Zack grabbed Rafe's forearm and gave it a gentle squeeze. "Nah, man. You were exonerated. She probably doesn't even know what happened to you."

"I'm not so sure about that. Once she knew who I was... I can't explain it. There was a sense of... It... She was uneasy. Nervous."

"And this is important, *por qué* why? I think you're overreacting. What did you expect on a dark road after all these years?"

"Yeah, I get all that. But what I don't understand is why she's on a road outside Hollow Lake. Think about it. Her father doesn't live here anymore. Where's she going?"

"Now look who's talking like a criminal defense lawyer." Zack took a swig of his beer. "Sounds like running into your lost love got you all in a state."

"I wouldn't say I'm in a state. But I won't deny it stirred up feelings. My gut tells me something's off."

"And my gut tells me it's time to eat." Zack stood, walked to the refrigerator, and pulled out a plastic Tupperware container. "I've got leftover *empanadas* and more beer. I can't talk about important matters on an empty stomach."

Rafe gave a wry smile. "Okay. Let's eat. Then you can tell me what to do about Mallory."

"Sure thing. But listen to me. I bet Mallory doesn't know about your past. It's been forever since you've seen her. She got married and had a kid. I'm not being mean, but it looks like she moved on. And as far as your problem is concerned—I keep telling you, there are a lot of people in this town and in our family who know you could never have committed a crime. That's all I'm going to say."

"Yup. I feel you. A lot of people, except for Pop. For whatever reason, our father doesn't believe I'm innocent. Mom tried to tell him, but he wouldn't listen. She was the great equalizer." Rafe paused. "I miss her."

"Me, too. Every day." Zack shook his head. "Man, cancer sucks."

"It really does." Rafe swallowed hard. "Listen, I wish it were different between me and Pop. But it's not."

Mallory checked the time on the dashboard. Barely nine o'clock and the streets were already tucked in for the night. She was certainly back in Hollow Lake. Grainy snapshots flashed through her mind—images of her time with Rafe. Friday night football, eating burgers at the diner, district math competitions, their magical night at the prom, and the summer they spent before she went to college. So many memories.

She swallowed hard remembering how she broke it off. Why

had her desire to live up to her mother's expectations been greater than her love for Rafe?

From the day they began dating, Sharon Kane had been relentless in her objections. *You're too young to be serious. You have your whole life ahead of you. Rafe's a nice boy, but he's got no ambition outside of Hollow Lake. Don't make the same mistakes I did. I married too young and got stuck. Get out of this nowhere place while you can.* For the longest time, Mallory didn't listen, but when she came home for winter recess and discovered Rafe had quit community college to figure out his life, doubts began to creep in. She wasn't sure they were after the same thing anymore. Maybe her mother was right. Maybe she was too young to know if this was a forever thing with Rafe. And the idea of ending up like her parents scared her.

Even though she loved him, she pulled back. *Who are you kidding? You didn't just pull back. You were harsh.* For the remainder of the semester, she answered only a few of his calls, rarely responded to his texts and found reasons for him not to visit campus. When she finally told him it was over, it was the worst night of her life. She'd seen in his eyes how she'd hurt him. At the time, she honestly thought she was doing the right thing for both of them.

Mallory let out a wry laugh.

"Everything okay?" Abbey asked.

"Yeah." Mallory nodded and thought about how her mother once ruled Mallory's life. But after her parents divorced, Sharon Kane couldn't get away from small-town life fast enough. She traveled throughout Europe for a while before marrying a rich Italian who owned a villa in Sardinia. If not for the yearly Christmas cards, Mallory would never hear from her.

She lowered the car window and inhaled deeply. The woodsy scent brought her back to her senior year and those precious summer days she and Rafe spent together before she listened to her mother. Before she went against her own heart.

She closed her eyes against the night breeze and tried to forget everything that brought her here. Even if only for a moment. But her mind wouldn't still. There was a time when Rafe was her entire world. He'd sweep her into an embrace, look into her eyes, and kiss her. She was lost to him. To his kindness and humanity and his dreams. But all that ended when he chose a different path. A simpler path.

She wanted to put all the blame on her mother, but the truth was she'd been weak. She always had a choice, even if her mother had made it harder for her to choose. She'd allowed herself to be convinced Rafe wasn't enough.

Years later, when Mallory brought Blake home, her father cautioned her to take it slow. Her mother, however, had been thrilled. And, like always, she'd been swept up in her mother's enthusiasm. Blake was everything Sharon Kane had wanted for her. Even then, Blake was an important person in investment and political circles. The day her wedding announcement was featured in the *New York Times*, Sharon Kane purchased dozens of copies, distributing them to all her friends.

The photo in the announcement featured two people with large smiles who seemed happy. And at the time of the photo, they were. Once they were married, Blake changed. He went from harsh to cruel, and Mallory wanted out. When she soon realized she was pregnant, she decided to stay, believing things would change. They never did. They only got worse. And then it got to the point where he would only allow her to leave if she left Justine behind. And she would never do that.

The car pulled up to a three-story red brick building. "This is it," Abbey announced.

Mallory dragged herself out of her past and looked at the familiar building. "This used to be Dr. Roberts's house. Right?"

"Yeah. He retired about five years ago. So I bought it and turned it into a bed-and-breakfast."

Mallory stepped out of the car and reached into the back seat to wake her daughter. "Hey, my little Punkie, you ready to continue our adventure?"

"Uh-huh." Justine sat up, rubbing the sleep from her eyes. "Mommy, I'm hungry."

"I know." She lifted her daughter out of the car. "We're going to take care of that very soon."

"This way," Abbey said, ushering them toward the front door.

Mallory's eyes adjusted to the warm glow of the foyer. Watercolor landscapes dotted the pale yellow walls. With Justine in her arms, she followed Abbey down a wide corridor that opened onto a parlor with a butterscotch-colored sofa and several strategically placed chairs. The elegant yet inviting room made Mallory want to curl up and sleep, but that was not an option. Instead, she gently laid her sleepy daughter on the couch, headed straight for the wide French doors overlooking a patio, and jiggled the handle. The doors were locked, and she leaned her forehead against the glass in relief.

"I can open those doors if you want to go outside," Abbey said. "It's the next thing on my handyman's list. I've been keeping them locked because the springs are broken, and the darn things won't stay closed. The last thing I need is field mice getting in."

"No, it's fine. I was only looking." Mallory leaned against the door. Her body felt like lead, and fear was the only thing keeping her upright.

"I bet you're exhausted. My husband will take your bags up while you and I take care of the registration. He's in the kitchen—" she took her phone out of her pocket "—I'll just text him."

Mallory crossed the room toward the small mahogany counter that served as the reception desk.

"Unfortunately, I can only offer you this one night. I've only got five rooms, and I'm booked up for the rest of the week through the weekend with a family from Connecticut. They'll be in town to celebrate their grandparents' sixtieth wedding anniversary." Abbey blew out a breath. "Can you imagine? Sixty years together. Amazing."

The last thing Mallory could imagine was a happy marriage, let alone one that lasted six decades. All the hype about growing old together was for greeting cards. As far as she was concerned, she'd grow old by herself. She didn't need a man for company. "Uh, yeah. Well, that shouldn't be a problem. I'm expected at my dad's, and Rafe said it was some sort of hose connection. I don't know anything about cars, but it didn't sound like a big deal."

Abbey shrugged. "Seems simple enough. So, how do you know Rafe? That was a bit of a surprise."

Heat crept up her cheeks, and Mallory bit her lower lip. "Yes.

I didn't recognize him right away. You know…it was dark…and that beard. Anyway, it was fifteen years ago. We went to high school together."

"What a coincidence running into him after all these years."

"Hmm," Mallory murmured.

"So where you headed?"

Under normal circumstances, Mallory would have found the question harmless—simply idle conversation. *How are you? Where are you from? Where are you going?* All perfectly innocent. But not tonight. She was aware any seemingly innocuous revelation on her part might mean her daughter's life.

Whatever answer she gave, it was safer to stick as close to the truth as possible without giving away too much. "We're on our way to see my father," Mallory offered without looking Abbey in the eyes.

Abbey took a registration card from the drawer under the computer and handed it to Mallory. "Sign here, please." She handed her a pen. "Going farther north, then?"

"Yes."

"Where about?"

"Uh… Rochester. He was transferred there some years ago."

"Oh, I've been there once, on my way to Toronto. My husband's family lives there."

Mallory grinned, hoping her smile was friendly but not encouraging—she had things to do, and more small talk wasn't on her agenda. Concentrating on the registration card, she wrote Mallory S and stopped short, quickly changing the *S* of her married name to *K* and signing her maiden name, Kane. She left the address line blank and pushed the registration card back toward Abbey. "How much do I owe you?" She reached into her purse.

"Two-hundred-twenty-five dollars for the night, plus tax. Comes to two-hundred-fifty-six dollars and fifty cents."

Her hand tightened around her wallet. The amount was more than she'd expected for a small town. Using her credit card was out of the question. Without a doubt, the person or people who ransacked her home were the same people who sent the threatening notes. And she was certain they were professionals who were now trying to find her. She wouldn't help them by leaving a financial trail. Blowing out a breath, she loosened her grip and opened her wallet, counting tens and twenties from the stash she found hidden under the chair in her husband's home office.

Abbey's eyes widened at the crisp bills on the counter.

Mallory kept a neutral expression. *Nothing to see here. I'm not a fugitive or a criminal.*

The moment passed, and Abbey tucked the money in a drawer.

Mallory let out a slow, shaky breath. "Can you tell me where we can get something to eat? I'm afraid getting stuck on the road interrupted our dinner plans."

Abbey shook her head. "I'm sorry. At this hour, nothing's open in town. Most folks go to Ravena, the next town over, for a late-night supper."

"I was afraid of that." Just her luck, streets rolled up and she was stuck in a B&B. Not even a vending machine in sight.

"Mommy, I'm awake!" Justine sat up on the couch. "Can we eat now?"

Mallory pursed her lips and tightened her fists.

Abbey must have recognized the frantic look of a mother with a hungry child.

"Hey there, Justine," Abbey said. "How 'bout a grilled-cheese sandwich? Would you like that?"

Overwhelmed at the offer, tears welled in Mallory's eyes. She was nothing but a bag of raw nerve endings, and the gesture nearly put her over the edge. But she needed to keep it together for her daughter's sake. "Thank you." Swallowing the tearful lump in her throat, Mallory picked up Justine, brushed her curls from her forehead, and kissed her. "Grilled cheese sounds good, doesn't it, Punkie?"

Justine nodded enthusiastically.

"Okay, let's follow Abbey."

After they'd eaten, they said goodnight to Abbey and headed to their room. Mallory was bleary-eyed and unsteady on her feet as she trudged up the stairs to the second floor. On the other hand, Justine, now satiated and apparently wide awake, skipped up the stairs, ready for the rest of this adventure.

The elegant furnishings in the room matched the foyer, giving Mallory a measure of comfort that they weren't staying in a dive. If it had been otherwise, it might have broken her. The room featured a queen-size canopy bed with an array of colorful pillows and, mercifully, a private bath.

Mallory locked the door behind her, hauled the suitcase onto a luggage rack, and began rummaging through her things for their toiletries. "Come on, let's get your toothbrush and get you cleaned up and ready for bed." Mallory thought if she tried to maintain some normalcy, then this nightmare she was living wouldn't take over.

"Aha! I knew it was hiding somewhere." She handed Justine the toothbrush and toothpaste. "You know the drill." Mallory forced a smile and pointed her toward the bathroom. When she was sure Justine was fully occupied, she double-checked the window locks and dragged a chair across the room, pushing it under the door handle. Wiping the sweat off her brow, she took a deep breath. "You need any help?" she called out.

Justine came into the room with a smile, "Nope. All done. I brushed all my teeth. Even the back ones."

"That's my Punkie. Come on, let's get your pj's on." Mallory got Justine changed and into bed. "You, button nose, are going to sleep. It's way past your bedtime." She tucked her under the covers. "I'm going to sleep right beside you."

"But where's Teddy? I can't sleep without him." Justine pouted.

Mallory recognized that tone and didn't want to end the day with a full-out crying jag from an overtired five-year-old. If Justine cried now, without a doubt, Mallory would lose it. She leaped off the bed and dug through everything in the duffel bag until she retrieved Teddy.

Holding the bear triumphantly, she smiled. "See, here he is, and I expect both of you to be asleep in two minutes." She tucked him under the covers next to Justine and kissed her daughter on the forehead.

"Give Teddy a kiss goodnight, too." Justine shoved the bear toward her mother.

Mallory hesitated. She never liked kissing that smelly, bedraggled excuse for a stuffed animal. Justine's attachment to Teddy went beyond what Mallory could understand. In recent months, she'd worked on getting Justine to grow out of the Teddy phase but was unsuccessful. After today's events, she knew she needed to drop the subject until things returned to normal. If they ever returned to normal. She kissed her daughter again, blew Teddy a kiss, and turned off the bedside light.

Tempting as it was to crawl under the covers and lie beside her daughter, she had work to do. Men were after her, and she needed to find out what they wanted. Now was not the time to get comfortable.

Mallory grabbed her oversized shoulder bag and pulled out a small silver laptop. Silently edging toward the window, her gaze swept the empty street. Satisfied no one was watching, she slipped into the bathroom, closed the door, and flicked on the light.

She leaned against the white tiled wall and slid down to the floor. Once the laptop was powered up, she began typing letters and numbers. She'd already tried several possible combinations with no luck. What confusing password had her husband created? Whatever it was, she needed it. She was convinced information in this laptop would tell her who was threatening Justine's life and why. If only she could hack her way in.

Rubbing her forehead with the palm of her hand, she took another deep breath. *What password would a devious mind create?* She placed her fingers on the keyboard and typed in passwords she'd already tried, with the illogical hope they'd miraculously work this time. Putting in her husband's birthday backward, she hit Return, and nothing. Next, her wedding anniversary backward, a date she wished never happened. Again, she hit Return, and…nothing. "Shoot!" She tilted her head toward the ceiling and closed her eyes. "Think, think, think!"

All these years, she managed to hang on. Managed to tell herself she'd find a way out. And here she was, literally free from her abusive husband. He was dead, and you couldn't get much freer than that. She groaned, realizing there was no getting away from Blake Stanton. Until she could get into the laptop, she'd be connected to him. It was as if he were reaching her from the grave. The thought made her whole body go cold.

Mallory stared into space, trying to come up with a solution, but she was exhausted and getting nowhere. She needed a few hours of sleep. She turned off the light and stepped into the bedroom. Smiling at Justine's sprawled-out sleeping figure, Mallory stretched her arms over her head and yawned. She turned to the window and pulled back the curtain. Across the street, in the shadows, she thought she saw someone looking up at her window. Quickly, she dropped the curtain and pressed herself against the wall. Her mind raced. *Don't be afraid. Breathe.* Clenching her jaw with a determination she didn't feel, she inched her way back to the window and peeked out, but the street was empty. Mallory shook her head, trying to clear her thoughts, wondering if what she saw was real or if her exhausted mind was playing tricks.

Chapter Three

Rafe punched in the code to the front entrance of the offices of RMZ Digital Fortress. On any given day, he'd be the first to arrive, but when he crossed the threshold this morning, the rich scent of freshly brewed coffee told him Max had beaten him to it. His older brother couldn't kick-start his workday without his hands wrapped around a cup of black gold.

The large antique railway clock on the wall read 6:30 a.m., and Rafe chuckled. Max must have been as anxious as he was to handle what was probably a mountain of work after a two-week vacation. He passed the all-glass reception desk and headed straight back toward the rec room.

The company offices were housed on the top floor of the old post office building on Main Street. The whitewashed brick walls, exposed-beam ceilings, and massive windows allowed natural light to pour into the large space. The concrete floors and open architecture gave it a modern look.

The redesign had been Rafe's doing. In today's world, most clients never came to the office, preferring video chats. So, he made the space comfortable for the people who worked for his firm. In addition to the low sofas and plush chairs, there were cutting-edge tech stations with high-resolution monitors, ergonomic keyboards, and noise-canceling headphones. The rec room at the far end of the floor resembled a combination coffee bar slash adult playroom.

When the analysts, techies, and office personnel weren't staring at their computer monitors, they could grab a snack or relax with a game of ping-pong, foosball, or air hockey.

Rafe slid a puck across the hockey table, walked past the pool table, and toward the barista counter where Max was making his morning cappuccino. The hiss of the milk steamer and the smell of the chocolatey espresso dripping from the porta-filter filled the air.

"Hey, bro. Let me have one of those."

Max turned and smiled. "Make your own."

Rafe ignored the tease and held out his hand, wriggling his fingers. "Come on."

Max gave a half eye roll, handed him the steaming cappuccino, and proceeded to make another.

"Thanks. So, how was your trip?"

Max closed his eyes and smiled. "What's not to love? White sandy beaches by day, candlelight by night."

Rafe thought he detected a blush creep up his brother's neck. "So, you and Gloria had fun?"

The quizzical expression on Max's face told Rafe everything he needed to know. "So—not Gloria?"

"Nope."

"Who then?"

"No one you know."

Rafe laughed. His brother had been a quantitative analyst on Wall Street, and he'd brought all that brain power to RMZ Digital Fortress. At work, he was a genius and all business. But when it came to relationships, being smart wasn't his forte.

"Oh, man." Rafe shook his head. "At some point, all that messing around with a different woman every week is going to catch up to you."

Max raised an eyebrow. "Do I look worried?" He poured the steaming milk into the espresso. "But there is something that has my concern antenna tuned in real fine. I spoke to Zack this morning. He told me you ran into Mallory Kane...or should I say Stanton."

"You spoke with Zack this morning? When it's not even seven o'clock."

"Good morning." Their receptionist, Brittany, walked toward them, stopping their conversation. "Welcome back. Hope you all had a good vacation."

"Thanks." Rafe checked his watch. "But what are you doing here so early?"

"Zack has a video conference with a new client in London, and I wanted to get the conference room all set up."

"Oh, shoot. I forgot we arranged that before we left. I wanted to be on that call." Max turned to Rafe. "I need to get a sense of what IT systems they have in place before the meeting. Let's talk later." Max grabbed his coffee and headed toward his office.

Rafe nodded. It seemed he wasn't the only one with Mallory on his mind. Last night, he'd dreamed about her, and when he woke, he had the same uneasy feeling that Mallory was hiding something. Whatever it was, he was going to find out. But first, he needed to start his workday and put out any potential fires that were likely brewing after he'd been completely off the grid for two weeks.

The private offices at RMZ Digital Fortress lined one long wall. Tall windows on one side and all glass on the other allowed light to filter across the bullpen area where the analysts and techies worked.

The number of emails and voicemail messages waiting for Rafe almost made him wish he'd never taken his fishing trip. After ten years in business, the brothers had developed a solid reputation among Fortune 100 companies and several government agencies. They were in high demand. In fact, none of the brothers had taken more than a day off in over eighteen months. And now he knew why it had taken so long to go on a vacation. Rafe loved his work and the company he created, but reentry sucked.

An hour passed, and he wasn't halfway through his emails. Rafe sat back, stretched his arms over his head, and put his feet on the desk.

Zack stuck his head into Rafe's office. "The meeting went

well—London's on board. And, hey, *Tía* Ellie called. She needs you to go over and fix that leaky faucet in the upstairs bathroom."

Rafe rolled his eyes. "I love her, but why doesn't she call a plumber?"

"With three strong nephews living in the same town? Pfft. Never gonna happen, man." Zack rapped his knuckles against the doorframe. "Get to it. It's your turn. I got rid of the squirrel in the attic last month."

"Ha! You called animal protection services. Not the same thing."

Zack stepped back into the hallway. "*Adiós*, bro," he called over his shoulder.

Rafe sighed and looked out the window. He sat straighter and squinted when he saw Mallory and her daughter crossing the street toward the diner. He checked his watch. "Maybe I'll have a little breakfast first."

Hollow Lake's picturesque Main Street featured one-and two-story shops and office buildings set back from a tree-lined boulevard. Except for the addition of several specialty artisan shops, the town hadn't changed much.

The slight breeze and the crystal blue, cloudless sky reminded Mallory of the late August mornings of her childhood, when she played from dawn to dusk, squeezing every last drop of freedom before school started.

The memory was bittersweet. Her life had been so simple then. Full of promise. Why hadn't she listened to her father all those years ago? How often had he warned her about Blake against her mother's insistence? One more issue her divorced parents hadn't agreed on.

"I should've listened," she muttered.

"What did you say, Mommy?"

"Nothing, Punkie. Talking to myself."

"What did you say to yourself?"

"Nothing important. Are you hungry?"

Justine nodded. "I'm so hungry I could eat twelve whole donuts."

For the first time in days, Mallory let out a laugh. "I know

just the place." Taking Justine's hand, they crossed the street and
headed for Fritz & Dean's diner. She hadn't been inside since
she was seventeen. She'd loved its 1950s vibe, complete with a
picture window and a red-and-white-striped awning. It was the
kind of place where a person could drown their problems in a
bottle of maple syrup drizzled over a stack of pancakes.

Before heading in, Mallory scanned the block. Nothing looked
out of the ordinary, but then, she didn't know what she was
looking for. Trusting her gut, she held onto Justine's hand and
walked in.

As they entered, the bell above the front door rang. The unexpected sound caused Mallory's stomach to drop, and her throat
went dry. *It's a bell, Mallory. Get a grip.* She took a deep breath,
and her eyes adjusted to the light. The place hadn't changed.

The morning rush buzzed all around her, with the chatter of
diners, the ring of the cash register, and the waitstaff taking orders and pouring coffee. The red leather stools at the counter
were taken, and the tables in the middle of the room were equally
occupied. Scanning the far wall, Mallory noticed a couple leaving a booth and headed straight for it.

She slid into the booth and tucked her shoulder bag between
herself and the wall. "You good over there, Punkie?"

Justine grinned. "Yup!"

A server arrived, cleared the dirty dishes, and wiped down
the table. Her name tag read Penny, and every inch of her youth-
ful face was covered in freckles. "Would you like coffee while
you look over the menu?"

Mallory nodded.

"And how about a booster seat for your little one?" Penny
asked.

"I don't need another seat," Justine answered.

Penny smiled and looked Justine in the eyes. "Got it. No
booster. How about a phone book?"

Justine tilted her head to the side. "Huh?"

"They still have those?" Mallory asked.

"Yeah, welcome to Fritz's, where nothing gets thrown out.
You need a 1956 mixer?" Penny laughed and turned back to Justine. "Before computers, before the internet, if you needed to

find someone's phone number, you looked it up in a big book. Anyway, we don't use those anymore, but they're pretty thick. Thick enough for you to sit on. It'll make it easier for you to reach the table. You wanna try it?"

Justine closed her eyes for a moment. "Okay, thanks."

Penny winked. "Coming right up."

Once Justine was settled and they'd ordered, Mallory took another look around for anything that might be out of the ordinary.

The low hum of conversations competed with the Muzak pumping out of the speaker above the register. The seats were filled with several men and women in business casual and others who looked like retired regulars. A family of four sat at a center table, backpacks hanging over their seats. Tourists, she thought, and felt a prick of envy, wishing she could be that carefree.

Her gaze rested on the counter area, and Mallory recognized the wiry man behind the register with the graying temples as Fritz, the owner. With a ready smile, he seemed to know everyone by name and greeted them with an effusiveness that had small town written all over it. A sense of nostalgia overcame her like a wave. The familiarity of the diners' voices merged with the clinking of plates and glasses. Memories flooded her mind—all the Sunday nights she spent here with Rafe sipping an ice cream soda. She smiled.

Stop it. Don't get comfortable, came the silent warning in her head. Too much needed to be done. First, she'd make sure her daughter had a good breakfast. Then, she'd locate the garage that had her car. Once all that was sorted, she'd search for a computer store. Getting into her dead husband's laptop was a priority.

The bell above the front door rang, and Mallory glanced toward the entrance. Rafe stepped through the door. Their eyes met before she could look away, and Mallory had no choice but to acknowledge she'd seen him and gave a small wave.

"Who you waving at, Mommy?"

"Rafe. My friend who helped us with our car last night."

"I wanna wave at him, too." Standing on the booth's bench, Justine turned and put both hands in the air like a cheerleader at a varsity game. "Hey, Rafe. Come sit with us."

Several diners turned to stare.

"Sit down," Mallory urged.

"Come over," Justine said, ignoring her mother. "We're having breakfast."

Rafe nodded, and diners stared as he strode toward their booth. He cut an imposing figure dressed in a black shirt and black jeans that accentuated his tall, athletic body. He was difficult to ignore, and his effect on Mallory was almost instantaneous. An electrifying surge shot through her—and a longing she hadn't experienced in years. Her cheeks grew hot, and she turned to gaze at the pictures on the wall. She didn't want him to know that his appearance flustered her.

"Hi," Rafe said.

"Sit down. Mom says it's not polite to stand at the dinner table."

"Justine!" Mallory raised an eyebrow.

Customers continued to stare. Mallory couldn't afford to be noticed. "Please, Rafe, eat with us." Mallory slid several inches to the left, making room on the bench, hoping the other diners would get back to their own business.

"Mornin', Rafe." With quick, practiced movements, a cup and saucer were placed in front of him, and Penny poured him coffee. "What can I get you?" She took a pad from her apron pocket.

Rafe smiled and ordered.

"Be right back with your food," Penny said.

"So." Rafe cleared his throat. "I'm glad I ran into you. We didn't get much chance to talk last night, I—"

"One more thing." Penny placed a coloring book and crayons in front of Justine. "Enjoy."

Justine clapped her hands.

"That was nice," Mallory said.

"That's Hollow Lake for you. Welcome back." Rafe smiled. "So, we didn't get much of a chance to talk last night. Did we?"

"Yeah, I know." Mallory chewed on the inside of her cheek, looking past him, watching the front door.

"I didn't expect to see you…again." Rafe took a swallow of coffee. "What's it been? Sixteen years?"

"Fifteen." She shifted her focus and really looked at him for the first time. The snake tattoo on his inner left wrist was new, as was the small crescent-shaped scar above his right eyebrow. Apart from that, he was the same but older. Lines marked the edges of his deep brown eyes. The soft, ready smile on his full lips was as she remembered. Despite her circumstances, he could still make her stomach behave like a circus performer executing multiple somersaults. She cleared her throat. "You shaved." Of all the things she could've said, it was the only one she could think of that would keep the conversation neutral.

"Yeah." Rafe rubbed his chin. "Mountain man wasn't exactly a good look for the office."

Just as she thought, he worked here and never left town.

They smiled at each other, and the conversation, such as it was, lulled into nothing. Mallory didn't know what to say or ask. Her situation was so untenable she remained cautious and close-mouthed. The silence was punctuated by an incessant rhythmic beat, which Mallory soon realized was coming from her foot tapping against the floor. *Nerves.* She put a hand on her thigh to stop the motion. *It's Rafe. Keep it light. Act casual. And get through breakfast.* "So you work around here?"

"Yeah." Rafe pointed straight ahead. "The building across the street."

"You work at the old post office?"

Rafe let out a laugh. "Well, yes and no. I bought the building a few years ago. I have a company with my brothers. You remember Max and Zack?"

Mallory nodded.

"You have brothers?" Justine put her crayon down.

"Yes. Two brothers."

"And you went to school with my mommy?"

"Yes, I did." Rafe chuckled. "Your mom was a math genius," he said in a conspiratorial whisper.

While Justine peppered Rafe with questions, Mallory wondered what her life would have been like if she'd never left Hollow Lake and stayed with Rafe.

Justine's laugh pulled her out of her reverie. She hadn't seen Justine this animated in a very long time. Her daughter's non-stop curiosity had driven her husband crazy, but Rafe seemed to be totally engaged.

Mallory pursed her lips and mentally juggled whether she should confide in Rafe. Maybe too much time had passed. Too much unsaid. Too much to undo. There was no denying that she'd dreamed of Rafe over the years, especially when everything turned sour in her marriage, but never imagined she'd see him again. *Was it fair to involve him?* No. The right thing to do was get her car fixed and get to her father's house. Leave the past in the past.

"Here you go." Penny placed a stack of pancakes in front of Justine with a glass of milk. A bacon, egg, and cheese sandwich for Rafe and a single English muffin for Mallory. "More coffee?"

Mallory nodded, pushing her cup toward Penny with one hand and grabbing the syrup bottle from Justine with the other.

"Mommy, I'm not finished," Justine protested.

"I think your pancakes may just float away. Why not eat what's on your plate and see if it's enough before you pour anymore?"

"Oh-kaaay." Justine sighed. She picked up her fork, dug into the pancakes, and took a bite. "Mmm, these are good. Like yours, Mommy."

"I'm glad. Now, don't talk with your mouth full." Mallory gave a quick smile, then went back to surveying the people in the restaurant from the corner of her eye.

"So, what have you been up to? What brings you back?" Rafe asked.

"Uh…" She shrugged. "I'm on my way to see my dad." Unable to look Rafe in the eye for fear he'd see that nothing was as it seemed, she began cutting Justine's pancakes.

"Mommy, I don't need any help. I can cut my own pancakes."

"Oh, sorry, Punkie."

Justine took a long gulp of her milk. "Hey, Rafe, you know what?"

"What?"

"I don't have any brothers. But I have Teddy."

"Who's Teddy?"

"He's my best friend. We sleep together." Justine put a bite of pancake in her mouth.

Mallory leaned in and whispered to Rafe. "It's her stuffed animal."

"Oh." Rafe's smile widened. "He must be very special."

"He is. And you know what? We slept all night. We were cozy, and we didn't wake up once." A note of pride rang through her voice, "Right, Mommy?"

"Well, yes. That's right." For the first time in a year, Mallory realized her daughter hadn't woken up once with a bad dream. A tightening sensation pushed against her chest with the knowledge that Justine felt more comfortable in a strange place than she had in her own home. Her heart ached for what she'd put her daughter through. Her husband had been an abusive bully, and she should have figured out a way to leave long before he died.

"Do you want to, Mommy?" Justine said, tapping Mallory's hand.

"What? Oh, sorry, I was thinking about…something else."

"I was suggesting when you're finished here, I could give you a lift to the garage, and we could find out when your car will be ready."

The bell over the door chimed again, and Mallory's heart raced as she lowered her head and raised her eyes to see what looked like a nonthreatening teenager enter. Would she ever feel safe again?

"Hey, so how about that ride?" Rafe asked.

"Uh, yeah, that—that would be great. Thank you."

Rafe waved Penny down for the check, and Mallory pulled out her wallet, but he put his hand over hers. "I got this."

His touch sent a shiver through her, and she closed her eyes for a moment to get focused. "You don't have to do that."

"It's just a friendly gesture."

"All right. Well…thank you." Relieved not to shell out any more cash, Mallory put her wallet away. She had no idea when or if she'd be able to access her bank account or use her credit cards. In the meantime, she needed to be cautious with the money she had and be ready to run at a moment's notice.

Chapter Four

Rafe helped Justine into the back seat of his truck. "Can you buckle your seat belt?" he asked.

"Yes." Justine smiled.

"Here. Let me." Mallory reached in front of him to help.

Rafe was momentarily unable to move. The subtle fragrance of her familiar citrus scent called to mind warm summer nights by the lake when he held her in his arms, and it was only the two of them with an endless future.

"Excuse me, Rafe. I need to get in so I can reach the buckle."

"Sorry." In a daze, he stepped to the side. He hadn't expected to have such a reaction.

"Punkie, lift your arm. I'll snap in the belt," Mallory said.

Rafe stepped further back and observed Mallory as she helped her daughter. It was the only time she seemed halfway relaxed. Otherwise, her entire demeanor indicated something was off. He'd listen if she wanted to talk, but he wouldn't pry.

After his release from prison, Rafe made it a firm policy not to get involved in other people's business or their lives. It was better for everyone if he kept to himself. But this was Mallory. She'd once been the love of his life, and after fifteen years of no contact, it surprised him how much he cared. Even more startling was the realization that his desire for her hadn't lessened. He took a deep breath as he walked to the driver's side and tried to tamp down old feelings threatening to push to the surface. "All secured?" he asked.

"I'm good," Justine said.

"Yes," Mallory said.

"Okay, then." Rafe put the key in the ignition and waited for Mallory to get in.

"How far is the garage?" Mallory asked as she buckled her seat belt.

"Not far. A few miles away. Right before you hit the county road." Rafe double-checked Justine was buckled up in the back seat, then put on his turn signal and pulled his truck onto the main road.

They drove several blocks before he glanced at Mallory, who was staring out the passenger window. Last night, she'd been so skittish he'd barely seen her face. In the light of day, at the diner, he'd gotten a better look. Physically, not much had changed. She was as beautiful as she'd been when they first met. At five foot seven, her lean, statuesque frame gave her the stance of a runway model. Her once long, coal-black hair was now a pixie cut, and he thought it was hot. The most significant change was the fear in her sea-green eyes. He spotted it last night, and it had only intensified this morning.

While serving time, Rafe developed an antenna for sensing trouble that was 99 percent accurate. His breakfast with Mallory had set off all kinds of alarm bells. For one thing, her husband's death had been all over the news, and she'd never even mentioned it. He'd also observed how her gaze darted toward the front of the diner each time the ringing bell signaled a new customer. Her anxiety only seemed to intensify as they drove. In the short time they'd been in the car, she'd turned her head more than once to check behind them. He noticed the constant bouncing of her leg and her continual glances at the side mirror—all of it indicated something wasn't right. Whatever the reason, there was no mistaking she was afraid.

It was a palpable fear, and he wanted to wrap her in his arms and make her feel safe. But Rafe tried to push the thought from his mind. He couldn't make anyone feel safe until he cleared his name of his wrongful imprisonment and found the person who framed him.

Once more, he glanced at her. She seemed so vulnerable. After everything they'd once meant to each other, could he leave her on her own?

Several minutes later, they pulled up to a single-story building. "This is it," Rafe said.

Chip's Garage and Auto Body sat at the edge of town, just before Main Street turned onto County Road 385. There were several cars and trucks of various makes and models parked along the left side. The front of the building featured three wide openings, and inside the last two bays were a car and a pickup hoisted on lifts.

"Hey, Mickey, how's it going?" Rafe asked as he walked inside the first bay.

Mickey came around from underneath the hood of a truck, wiping his hands on a rag. His five-foot-five frame carried an extra twenty pounds right at his midsection.

"You remember Mallory and Justine from last night?" Rafe asked.

Mickey nodded. "Hi there, how ya doing today?"

"Hi." Justine waved.

"I'd be a lot better if you told me my car was ready." Mallory bit her lower lip.

"Well, about that." Mickey took off his cap. "It looks like there is something wrong with the coolant hose to the battery."

"Can it be fixed fast?"

Mickey shrugged. "Not sure. Depends."

"On what?"

"On how fast they can ship the part. But honestly, you should call the dealer and let them handle it." He looked over at the car parked in the last bay. "That's a new car. There's barely five hundred miles on it." Mickey shook his head. "I'd call and give them hell. For sure."

"If I…" Mallory cleared her throat. "If I don't go to the dealer, how long for the part?"

Mickey shrugged again. "If that's the way you wanna go, but I took the liberty of checking the glove compartment, and the paperwork's all there. The car's from Leonard Devane's and from what I hear, he's one of the biggest luxury dealers on the East Coast." He scratched the back of his neck. "I'm sure they'd help you out. So, you wouldn't have to pay us."

"Let's not call them. Can't you just call the manufacturer and have them overnight the part?" Mallory wiped her upper lip with the back of her hand. "I mean, that's probably what Leonard would do anyway."

The perspiration on her face made Rafe wonder what she was so nervous about. Why wouldn't she call the dealer? It would save her from shelling out any money.

"I'd need to make some calls," Mickey said. "But with the current supply chain issues, I'd guess at least two weeks."

"Two weeks!" The sound of the whirring air compressor from one of the bays ceased, and her voice reverberated around the garage.

"Wait a minute." Mickey put up a hand. "That's purely a guesstimate. I won't know exactly until I make some calls."

"I can't believe this." Mallory paced in a circle, clenching her fists. "I can't be stuck here. Isn't there anything you can do to get it faster?"

"Mommy, why are you mad?" Justine took a step back.

Mallory stopped pacing. "Oh, Punkie, I'm not mad. I'm… I'm…just surprised." Mallory took in a breath and looked around.

"I'm sure Mickey will do everything he can to get the part and get you on your way." Rafe gave a sympathetic smile and put his hand on Mallory's forearm for reassurance. The feel of her made his pulse race, but she jerked her arm away, and her reaction hurt. Maybe the fear he saw in her eyes did have something to do with him. He clamped down on his emotions and forced himself to shrug it off. It wasn't the first time someone steered clear of him, but he didn't expect it from Mallory. It seemed his past would always be a present-time problem until he cleared his name. The more he thought about it, the more it made sense to help Mallory get her car fixed and out of town. "Maybe calling the dealer is the best plan. Maybe they can get the part faster," Rafe said.

"Nah, man," Mickey said. "The dealer doesn't have the part

laying around. They'll go directly to the manufacturer. I suggested the dealer because it's their problem and wouldn't cost Mallory a dime. Maybe even give her a replacement car for her troubles."

"Mickey, I want you to go ahead and make the call to the manufacturer for the part," Mallory said. "I'll just have to wait."

Her response surprised Rafe. Not less than two minutes ago, she needed to leave Hollow Lake as fast as possible. Now, she had time to wait. It didn't make sense.

"I'll get you a card with the number for the garage. I'll be right back." Mickey headed for his workstation when a tall man with black-framed glasses perched on the tip of his nose opened the office door. "Hey, Mickey."

"Yeah, boss?"

"Oh, hi, Rafe, I didn't know you were here."

"Hi, Chip." Rafe lifted his chin, acknowledging the garage owner.

"Mickey, you finished with the Explorer SUV already?" Chip asked.

"Yeah. In fact, as soon as I'm done here, I'm gonna head over to the Bailie's place and drop it off."

Chip slid the glasses on top of his shining bald head. "That was fast."

"Yeah, well, it's their first family vacation in five years," Mickey said. "They're heading out to New Mexico to see his sister. I wanted to help them out."

"You sure did. Let me know when you get back, and we can schedule the rest of the week."

Mickey gave a thumbs-up and turned back to Mallory. "Okay. Let me get you that card."

"Thanks." Mallory's cell phone buzzed, and she retrieved it from her pocket, swiping it open. "Hey, hold on a sec," Mallory said into the phone, then turned to Rafe. "Do you mind if I take this outside? And…uh…could you watch Justine? It'll only be for a sec."

The flick of her eyes toward her daughter and then toward her phone told him she didn't want Justine to overhear.

"Please? Really, it won't take long. I have to take it."

Rafe hadn't a clue what was going on. In the span of five minutes, she'd seem to run the emotional gamut from jumpy to angry to fearful to—he didn't even know how to describe this current manifestation. All he knew was that someone was on the phone, and when she answered it, she looked desperate.

Of course he would watch her daughter, but he was determined to unravel some truths when she finished the call. "Okay. Sure," Rafe said. "Hey, Justine, you like LEGOs? 'Cause the owner keeps a box of them in the waiting room."

Rafe's soft-spoken kindness toward Justine made Mallory smile. At least that part of him hadn't changed. But the tattoos and motorcycles—that was different, and something she never could have imagined. Not the Rafe she knew. But for some reason made him all the more attractive. She shook her head. Now wasn't the time to focus on him. She put her head down and walked quickly out of the garage.

The moment she stepped into the open air, Mallory carefully scanned her surroundings and headed toward the bushes on the side of the building. When she was fully out of sight, she spoke into the phone. "Dad, hi! I was just going to call you."

"Oh, thank God, you answered."

"What's the matter?"

"Two men came to my office this morning, and they were asking a lot of questions about you. They wouldn't tell me who they were and why they were asking, but I can tell you they weren't friendly. I know this has something to do with that dead husband of yours. Am I right?"

Mallory didn't respond. Couldn't. She was too busy trying to breathe. Her world was crashing in all around her.

"Mallory? Mallory? You still there? Because something's very wrong, and I'm about to call the police."

"No! You can't do that," Mallory shouted before she could stop herself. "Sorry, Dad." She let out a breath. "Just, please, tell me what they said." This was so much worse than she could have imagined. She paced back and forth, unconsciously picking tiny leaves off the hedges along the side of the garage.

"They wanted to know where you were and when I'd last seen you."

Damn it! The one person she'd tried to shield from her troubles, and now she'd brought them right to his doorstep. She hadn't planned on telling him about the threats or the vandalism of her home until they were face-to-face. "What did you tell them?"

"I told them it was none of their business, and I told them to leave. I had security escort them out. But since then, there's been a black sedan parked outside our offices all morning."

She kicked at the dirt beneath the bushes. "Listen carefully, Dad. Me and Justine will be fine as long as no police get involved."

"Don't go to the police? That's crazy. I can't agree to that."

"Dad, I can't get into it right now," Mallory said, gripping her mobile, "but I'm begging you. The only way for us to be safe is if you don't get the authorities involved."

There was a brief silence. "Mallory, what is going on? You're scaring me."

"It does have something to do with Blake, but I honestly don't know what. Some people—I don't even know who—think Blake left me something that belonged to them. And they've made threats about Justine if I go to the police." Mallory lowered her voice and scanned the area again. "Listen, Dad, I promise to explain everything. For the time being, it's best if I don't come straight to your house. Especially if men are watching. I think I'm safe for now. But I need some time to think this through."

Mallory quickly considered her limited options. In all this madness, she was certain that keeping her father in the dark was for the best. The less he knew, the safer he was. Maybe her best option was staying in Hollow Lake and finding a way into that computer.

"I can't believe this is happening. That husband of yours... well, that's not going to help the situation."

Mallory turned her face toward the cloudless sky. Her father had never been one for I-told-you-so's, but he was right. He'd warned her and tried to get her to see Blake for what he was. If only she'd listened before it was too late. "Dad, you're right. You were always right where Blake was concerned."

"I'm not trying to be right. I only want you safe."

"Well, the best thing for all of us is if I stay where they'll least expect to find me. At least until that black sedan is gone and we're sure those men aren't coming back. I need some time to find out what they're after. If I can figure that out, maybe this nightmare will disappear."

"Are you sure you know what you're doing?"

The truth was, she didn't have a clue what she was doing. All she knew was she needed to keep her father as far away from this as possible. And considering she no longer had wheels and couldn't use her credit card, staying put was looking better and better. "Dad, I'll be in touch. But…not by phone. You know what I mean?"

There was another long silence.

"Hello, Dad? Did I lose you?"

"No, I'm here. I understand."

Mallory heard the tremble in his voice and tried not to react.

"This is all so hard for me to take. You're still my little girl, and it's killing me to know you're in trouble, and there's nothing I can do."

"Try not to worry. I love you. I'll see you soon. I have to go." Mallory swiped off the call, leaned her forehead against the cool brick of the building, and stifled a sob. The situation couldn't be bleaker. She was stranded, broke, and scared.

It had been two years since she'd seen her father—a separation not of her choosing. There'd always been a reason she couldn't see him or he couldn't come for a visit. Blake had seen to that.

Too soon after her marriage, she'd become a simpering, subservient doormat. Love, ha! For whatever reason, maybe it was pride, she wanted to believe she hadn't been a total fool. There must have been some love at the very beginning.

When they met, he'd been the perfect gentleman, romancing her with his charm and seducing her with his larger-than-life way of taking on the world. With a snap of his fingers, he could get the hottest tickets on Broadway, the best table at any restaurant, or seats in the owner's box at a Yankees game. Anyone who mattered in New York was part of his circle of friends and business associates. Blake wasn't the most handsome man in any room, but his six-foot, trimmed frame struck an imposing figure in his expensive suits and slicked-back dark hair. Theirs was a whirlwind fairy tale that got ugly fast.

They'd gotten married five months after their first date. Ten months later, Justine was born. Soon after that, everything changed. Blake changed. What began as small criticisms and urgent requests turned into cruel remarks and total control. From hiring a stylist to dress her to a personal trainer to get her body back in shape after giving birth to cooking lessons so she could throw lavish dinner parties for his clients. She went along with these decisions to keep the peace—anything to keep Blake from becoming upset.

After the second year of their marriage, her husband was rarely home. When he deigned to make an appearance, he was either verbally abusive or spent the evening locked in his study.

At one point, Mallory suggested they get counseling. But that conversation hadn't gone well. "You have to realize things have changed since Justine was born," she said one night when he came home early. "Maybe if we talk to someone, a neutral party, we could get back to where we were."

Blake scoffed. "You have everything you could possibly want. All you need to do is smile and look pretty. And when I tell you to show up at a fundraiser or a dinner, be there and play the part of a loving wife."

His words were like a knife piercing her heart. That night, she decided her only course of action was to leave.

"You want to leave—there's the door," Blake sneered—the smell of whiskey on his breath. "But you go the way you came. With nothing." That night had been a barrage of threats. He promised to take everything away from her, including her daughter. While she didn't care about his money or possessions, losing Justine wasn't an option. In his twisted mind, he wanted the world to see a picture-perfect family.

The verbal violence turned physical, and she tried leaving many times, but he was always one step ahead of her.

A shiver shot through her as she stared at her phone. *How stupid.* The people chasing her were probably like her ex, powerful enough to track her. And what better way than through her mobile phone? Her panicked mind hadn't thought of getting rid of it when she fled from home two days ago. The only objective had been to put as much distance between her, Justine, and whoever the hell was after them.

"I hate you, Blake," she shouted.

Overwhelmed with emotion, she squeezed her eyes shut, forcing herself not to break down. Not here. Not yet. But she was unable to hold in her anger and ran toward the back of the building, where there was nothing but an empty field and a railroad track. Taking a deep breath, she screamed into the air, the sound instantly muffled by a passing freight train. She screamed until her throat was hoarse and her head hurt.

Breathing hard, she leaned against the wall, pondering her next move. If they were tracking her now, she needed to send them in the wrong direction.

The wrong direction. Think. Her mind buzzed, and an idea formed. Hadn't the garage mechanic, Mickey, said he'd fixed an Explorer and was taking it to a family headed out West?

Mallory hurried from the back of the garage toward the only Ford Explorer parked out front. Looking around, she cautiously opened the back door of the SUV and jammed the phone underneath the back seat. "Have a good trip," she murmured, her heart beating like a jackhammer as she walked toward the open bay at the front of the garage.

"Hey, Mom, look what we made." Justine skipped toward her, holding a motorcycle made of LEGOs.

Mallory gave a tight smile. With her heart racing, she used every ounce of energy to appear normal.

"And Rafe says I can keep it."

"Oh, Punkie, those aren't yours—"

"She made it all by herself, and I know the owner. He's got boxes of those things. He'd be happy if she kept it."

"Thanks. Thanks for everything," Mallory said, her tone weary.

Rafe smiled. "I'll drive you back."

"Appreciate it," Mallory said without looking at him.

What she really wanted to do was wake her husband from the dead and then kill him herself. Enough was enough. She had to stop running and think.

Chapter Five

Rafe pulled the car keys from his back pocket. "All right. You ready to take off?"

Justine raised her hand and hopped up and down. "I am, I am."

In contrast, Mallory remained silent, never taking her gaze from the road in front of the garage. She seemed frozen in place and hadn't heard him.

This wasn't the confident person he remembered. He couldn't quite figure her out, which was unusual because Rafe could read most people in the time it took to shake their hand—his year in prison taught him a lot about secrets and hiding.

While Mallory hadn't given him any idea what was going on, something happened between the time she took that phone call and now.

His gut was telling him he couldn't afford to get involved. He could think of a dozen reasons to let her go, her secrets intact, and act like this little interlude was simply an old friend passing through town. To put his company and brothers in the middle of whatever this was would be reckless.

Despite the warning signs, his heart told him otherwise. Damn. Mallory could always get to him. They were once inseparable. The feelings he'd had for her were singular, and he hadn't felt that for another woman since. He could not let her go without trying to help. Somehow, they'd have an honest conversation between now and when her car was ready. Maybe he could do something. He'd take her back to the B&B and invite them to dinner this week.

"Ready?" He gently touched Mallory on the shoulder.

"Mmm." Mallory stepped away.

"Mallory? Mallory? You ready?"

She turned to face him and blinked as if she were waking up. "Sorry. Was thinking."

"You seemed a million miles away."

"More than that," she said.

The comment was strange, but he chose to ignore it. "Okay, let's get in. I'll take you back to Abbey's."

Rafe chose the back roads to town, hoping Mallory might chill and enjoy, or at least notice, the perfectly cloudless late-August day. The scenic route did nothing to ease the tension in the car. While Justine played with her LEGO motorcycle in the back seat, Mallory played percussion on the armrest, her nervous fingers tapping out a consistent beat, her gaze never straying from the side mirror.

When they got to town, Rafe turned down Avery Place and stopped at the red light. At the corner, a tall woman with a gray bob, wearing jeans and a light blue sweater, waved and walked to the car.

Rafe pushed a button, and the window slid down.

With a wide smile and eyes that seemed to sparkle, she leaned in and kissed him on the cheek. "*Hola*, Rafael. You just passed my house. Aren't you coming in?" She paused and looked inside the car. "Oh, I see you have company."

Rafe smiled. "*Tía*, what are you doing out here?"

She held up a small brown paper bag. "I was at Judy's hardware store. I got a washer because you'll need it to fix the leak in the upstairs bathroom. I didn't want you to have to go out and buy one."

Rafe chuckled. "You think of everything." He turned toward Mallory. "Do you remember my aunt Ellie?"

Mallory smiled. "Hi—"

"Wait," Justine said from the back. "I wanna meet your aunt."

"Who do we have here?" Ellie leaned in further.

"I'm Justine. What's your name?"

"Ellie. It's nice to meet you."

Rafe turned to see Justine give a shy nod. "So, *Tía*, I'll drop them off and be right back."

Ellie placed her hand on his forearm. "Absolutely not. You'll come over and fix my faucet, and we'll all have lunch together. Besides, I haven't seen you since you came back from your vacation."

"Yay! I'm hungry," Justine piped up from the back seat.

"Punkie, you can't possibly be hungry. You just ate breakfast," Mallory said.

Rafe checked the clock on the dashboard. It was nearly noon. They'd been at the garage longer than he thought. As much as he felt a pull toward Mallory and wanted to try to help, he did not want to bring whatever troubles she had to his aunt's home. But before he knew it, the back passenger door flung open, and Ellie was making herself comfortable in the seat next to Justine.

"I'll ride with you." Ellie buckled her seat belt and smiled at Rafe. "Drive around the block and then park in front of the house."

"Mallory," Ellie said. "It's been ages. How are you doing?"

"Just fine, Mrs. Chavez."

"Call me Ellie," she said, laughing. "We're both adults now."

Rafe parked in front of a yellow Victorian with a wide wrap-around porch, sitting atop a small incline.

"Well, here we are." Ellie got out of the car.

Instinctively, Rafe knew this was a bad idea. He turned to Mallory. "If you don't want to come in, I'll tell my aunt you need to get back to Abbey's Bed and Breakfast." Rafe cleared his throat. "You know, she lost my uncle last year—"

"Oh, I'm so sorry." Mallory looked away.

"Yeah, it was rough. But we're all getting through it. Anyway, my cousins live in the city, so she's on her own now. My brothers and I have lunch with her at least once a week. But we haven't seen her since we were all on vacation."

"It's fine. It would be rude to refuse," Mallory said.

That wasn't the response he was expecting or hoping for. Figuring this woman out was proving to be a challenge.

At the sound of the back passenger door slamming, Mallory turned. "Justine, wait for me."

"Oh, it's okay. I've got her," Ellie called from the porch as Justine climbed the stairs.

In a flash, Mallory was out of the car after her daughter.

Knowing there was no way to stop this little get-together, Rafe decided to go with it.

Once inside, Mallory could feel her shoulders drop. It had been a while since she'd been here, but nothing had changed. The bright, open foyer featured a center staircase with a mahogany railing. She breathed in the familiar scent of furniture polish and Pine-Sol. It reminded her of Saturday mornings when she helped her parents with the weekly cleaning. She'd put old rags on her sneakers and glide around the wood floors, polishing them until they shone. The memory soothed her, and she unclenched her hands.

The dining room was to the right of the foyer, and on the left was a parlor with turn-of-the-century pocket doors and a baby grand piano. The rooms were flooded with natural light streaming through the oversized windows at the front and sides of the house.

"Why don't we all head back to the kitchen?" Ellie said. "I've got some lemonade. And today, I've got tuna sandwiches."

"I don't want to put you out." Mallory held onto Justine's shoulders.

"It's no trouble," Ellie said, ushering them on. "Rafe and I have a standing lunch date on Mondays. There's plenty of food. Really."

Mallory followed Justine, whose mood was suddenly buoyant at the sound of a cold glass of anything, her ponytail swinging from side to side as she skipped toward the back of the house.

Glasses, fresh lemon slices, and a tall pitcher filled with ice and lemonade were placed on the table. Mallory remained quiet as Ellie poured the drinks. "So, what brings you back to Hollow Lake after all these years? It's been a long time." She opened the refrigerator, pulling out a large bowl covered in plastic wrap.

"*Tía*, let me help you with that." Rafe rose from his seat.

"*Siéntate*. I'm not too old to make sandwiches for company."
She waved him away. "Justine, how many pickles would you
like?" Ellie twisted open the cap on the jar.

"These many." Justine held up two fingers.

The smile on Justine's face eased Mallory's rising anxiety.

"Go on, Mallory. I'm listening." Ellie smiled, spreading tuna
on slices of bread.

"Well…we were on our way to see my father. And…um…"
Mallory slid the heart pendant up and down on her necklace.
"You see, my husband recently died."

Ellie turned to face her, knife in hand, the corners of her
mouth dipped. "I am so sorry for your loss."

"Yes. I'd heard," Rafe said. "My condolences."

Their sympathy took her by surprise. Rafe probably wondered
what took her so long to mention it. They had no way of knowing she was lying through her teeth or that she was relieved her
husband was dead or that she was running for her life. Mallory
felt her face grow hot and she lowered her head. She was already
so deep into the deceit she reasoned she had no choice but to
continue. She looked up, hoping her face held the appropriate
amount of sadness for a recent widow. "That's why we needed
a change. An adventure." She plastered on a reassuring smile
in Justine's direction.

Justine nodded. "An adventure to Grandpa's house."

"That's right. Part of this trip was to visit with my father and
show Justine upstate New York. It's been forever since I've been
here, and…well, you know… I thought it might be fun to show
her the different sights. Like…like…the…um…the Hampstead
farm with the horses, cows, and chickens."

"We're going to see chickens?" Justine asked. "Will we be
able to see them lay their eggs?"

"Oh, sorry. I don't think you'll be seeing any egg laying," Ellie
said. "That place has been abandoned for years. Although, when
I was at church last week, I heard they're planning on making
it a Piggly Wiggly."

Mallory saw the disappointment in Justine's eyes. Her daughter didn't know she'd never had any intentions of visiting farm
animals. She was simply trying to fudge her way through what

she hoped would come off as a believable story. "Justine, we can probably find another farm before we reach Grandpa's house."

"Can I pet the horses?" Justine smiled.

"Sure you can," she said, knowing she needed to stop talking before she dug herself deeper into this complicated lie she was weaving.

"So when are you taking off?" Ellie asked.

"Well, our car is in the shop and needs a part. And the funny thing is…even if we could get another car…well… I… I spoke with my father this morning, and on top of everything else, he was remodeling his basement when they found asbestos. So he's moving into a hotel, and we need to postpone our trip." She nearly ran out of breath, trying to keep up with the story she was telling on the spot.

"That's awful. Why didn't you say something?" Rafe leaned forward.

"What's ass-bess…ass-bess-toes?" Justine asked.

Ellie laughed, "Oh honey, sorry, none of this is funny. Asbestos is a material they used to put in walls to keep your house warm. That is until they found out it was very bad for you."

Mallory nodded, keeping her focus on Ellie. The kindness in her eyes reminded her of her father. How could she lie to this woman? *You're keeping Justine safe. That's all that matters.* Mallory sat straight and cleared her throat. "So it looks like we'll be here for at least a couple of weeks."

"Really?" Rafe put his glass of lemonade down.

Mallory kept her gaze on her lap as she spoke. She couldn't dare look Rafe in the eye and lie. "Yeah. Looks like it."

"So, will you be staying in town?" Ellie asked.

The question gave Mallory a jolt. Where would she be staying? She remembered Abbey's B&B wasn't available. "Actually, Abbey's place is all booked up with a sixtieth wedding anniversary. I guess I'll have to find something else in town or at least close by. I don't have a car."

Ellie placed the sandwiches on the table. "Unfortunately, Abbey's B&B is the only game in town."

"Ooh, potato chips!" Justine reached for the bowl and then stopped short. "Can I, Mommy? Can I? Mommy!"

"Oh…sorry, Punkie. Wasn't paying attention."

"I know. I said, can I have potato chips? Pleeeeeease."

"Oh, sure. But only a few. And only after you take a few bites of your sandwich." Mallory felt sick to her stomach. Using her credit card to rent a car so she could find a place to stay was not an option.

"Well, I have plenty of room," Ellie said.

Surprised at the offer, Mallory's eyes widened. "Really? But… but…but this is so random. You haven't seen me in years. Goodness, opening your home? Isn't it an inconvenience?"

"Mallory, you're hardly a stranger. As I recall, you and Rafe were once quite close." Ellie smiled at Rafe. "And that's good enough for me. Besides, I'm alone in this four-bedroom house. It could use a little more life."

Mallory noticed Rafe lean toward his aunt, eyebrow raised.

"I couldn't impose. Really." Mallory kept her gaze on her hands neatly folded on her lap, not daring to look at Rafe. She'd seen the look of incredulity in his eyes. He wasn't wrong. She shouldn't be staying here.

"*Tía*, let's finish lunch. Then Mallory and I can have a chat. After that, we'll figure out where she'll be staying."

Rafe's words sliced through her.

Ellie gave a soft laugh. "*Mira*. Just because you own a cybersecurity firm doesn't mean you have to be suspicious of everything and everyone." She tsked. "This is Mallory and her daughter—no need to run a security check, for goodness' sake. They are perfectly welcome here. And that's that."

Mallory looked up. *Cybersecurity?* "Rafe, I thought you were…well, honestly, I didn't know. I do remember how much you loved science and computers."

"It's true. My handsome, genius nephew was a nerd. He still is." Ellie smiled. "When his brothers and my boys got together, they played touch football in my backyard." She waved a hand toward the back door in the kitchen. "It didn't matter if it was raining or a hundred degrees. But not Rafael. Sure, he'd tag along, but he'd be studying at this table or at the computer in the den."

Rafe coughed.

"Sorry, don't mean to talk about you like you aren't here. But, *sobrino*, I'm proud of you. Your company's a big deal. Mallory, did you know they have some of the largest government contracts?" She squeezed his forearm.

"So, you're involved in cybersecurity?" Mallory cocked her head. This couldn't have been more perfect if she'd planned it. She had the urge to spill her guts and tell Rafe everything. "You know—"

"What's saber secure?" Justine asked, popping another potato chip in her mouth.

Again, Ellie laughed.

"What's funny?" Justine reached for another potato chip.

Mallory moved the bowl. "Punkie. Please eat your sandwich."

"It's cy-ber-se-cur-ity." Rafe pronounced it slowly. "You know how in your favorite superhero stories, there are good guys who protect everyone from the bad guys? And you know how we have locks on our doors at home to keep us safe from strangers?"

Justine nodded, her mouth now full of tuna.

"Well, when we use computers, phones, or tablets, there can also be bad guys who try to sneak into them to steal or mess with our stuff."

"What kind of stuff?" Justine asked.

Rafe gave a one-shoulder shrug. "Oh, you know, like our pictures, games, or even important information about us. So, cybersecurity is like the superheroes or the locks on our doors but for all our gadgets. It's all the things we do to keep bad guys out of our computers and keep our digital stuff safe. We use passwords, just like keys for our doors, and sometimes we use special programs like superheroes to guard our computers."

"Cool," Justine said.

Passwords. If there were a soundtrack that went along with her thoughts, the chorus would be singing "Oh Happy Days." There was a strong possibility that he could help her get into Blake's laptop.

Rafe stretched and pushed away from the table. "Uh, *tía*. I… uh, need to talk to you for a second."

The glances exchanged between Rafe and his aunt were unmistakable. He wasn't keen on her staying with Ellie. Mallory stood. "Go ahead," she encouraged them. "I'll clean these up. Can I put them in the dishwasher?"

Ellie rose and took off her apron. "You don't have to do that. You're a guest."

"That's exactly why I want to. Punkie, come on. Help me clear the table."

"I'll hang up my apron and be right there," Ellie said.

Rafe stepped onto the back porch and leaned against the railing, looking out at the expansive backyard. Two ancient oak trees with flat green leaves flanked his right. Several tall maples stood on his left, marking the plot of land belonging to his aunt and deceased uncle. A thin smile crossed his face as he remembered the many happy family barbeques and Sunday dinners they'd had before all the harsh words were traded between him and his father. Oh, how he wished he could turn back time and take back everything he said.

He heard the screen door slam shut, and Ellie was beside him. *"¿Qué te pasa?"*

Rafe turned to face his aunt. He loved her for her endless supply of kindness. He saw the love in her silver eyes now. It didn't surprise him that she'd offered Mallory a place to stay. Ellie opened her arms and her heart to anything that was hurt. His cousins would bring home all sorts—from injured birds, lost puppies, and baby squirrels to neighborhood kids looking for some of her famous *flan* and a glass of milk. It was common knowledge that Eloise Chavez would take care of them. She never asked questions and only believed the good in people, and Rafe loved her for it. But this time, regardless of the feelings Mallory stirred in him, he was worried.

"¿Qué te pasa?" Rafe raised an eyebrow. "You're asking *me* what's the matter? You haven't seen her in fifteen years. She's practically a stranger to you. We have no idea what she's been up to."

"We know her husband is dead. And you and I can see something's not right—*¿verdad?*"

Rafe huffed. "Exactly why you should be cautious before opening your home."

"*Sobrino*, you are so protective, a quality I don't particularly like, but in you, I forgive." Ellie smirked and crossed her arms over her chest. "You know, this old house is so big, I only ever use three rooms on a good day. Your friend looks like she could use some taking care of—looks a little lost. She's got a little girl and no place else to go. I can't *not* help."

At that, Rafe smiled. "You're as stubborn as ever."

Ellie stepped back. "*Exactamente.* Now we're on the same page." She winked and gave a little head nod.

Rafe raised a hand. "Hold on a sec. Max and Zack would have my head if I didn't investigate her before she settles in here."

Ellie's mouth went slack, and an expression of shock crossed her face.

"Don't look at me like that."

"*¿Pero me qué estás diciendo?* Investigate? That's ridiculous—"

"Let me explain." Rafe gently placed a hand on her shoulder. "It wouldn't be prudent to let her stay here without at least asking some questions."

"Well, then ask." Ellie poked him in the chest. "Go in there and tell her you want the truth. If you're satisfied, we'll leave it at that."

His aunt was probably right. He should have a conversation with Mallory. The idea made him nervous, and he wiped his brow. She'd once been his everything. Now, she was a stranger with a situation. "I can't just ask her what's going on with her kid sitting right there." The words came out more defensively than he intended. "Sorry. I'm a bit rattled."

"*¡Ay mijo!*" She stomped her foot. "You and your brothers run a company with big government contracts facing down crime every day. This is one woman. A woman, I might add, who you used to love. And from what I can see, it looks like you still have some feelings."

Rafe flinched.

"So, she's got an issue. So, help her, for god's sake." Ellie put her hands on her hips. "Now, I'll go in there and tell her about the room. Once her daughter is settled, tell Mallory you want to talk. Take her for a walk by Sullivan Park. Or better yet, go to your apartment where there are no prying eyes. I'll watch Justine. We'll bake cookies." She turned. "Let's go."

Rafe held the screen door open and followed his aunt back into the kitchen.

"So—" Ellie clapped her hands together "—why don't I give you a tour?"

"Do we have our own room?" Justine asked.

"Yes, you do, and it's on the second floor. Follow me." Ellie walked out of the kitchen and toward the center hall staircase. "It faces the back of the house and has wonderful early sunlight. So, I hope you're a morning person."

"What's a morning person?" Justine asked as she held onto the banister and hopped up one step at a time, following Ellie.

"Well, it means you like to get up early. You know, greet the day."

"Oh." Justine stopped hopping, sticking her tongue into the side of her mouth, and looked up. "I'm not a morning person."

Ellie chuckled, glancing at Mallory. "That's okay. I think you'll like the room anyway."

At the top of the stairs was a wide hallway with five doors. Ellie led them to a large room overlooking a vegetable garden at the back of the house. The queen-size bed featured a quilted headboard, and the duvet cover was sage green with a leaf pattern along the edging. A tall dresser flanked one side of the window, and a writing table sat opposite. There were two comfortable chairs against the far wall.

"I'm assuming you'd like to be in the same room as your daughter?"

"Yes."

"Okay, good. The room has its own bathroom," Ellie said. "I hope you'll be comfortable here."

"It's perfect," Mallory said.

Ellie crossed over to the one closet in the room and pulled out a blanket. "The nights get cold," she said, placing the blanket on the bed. "If this isn't enough, there are more in the linen closet at the end of the hall. Just help yourself."

"Thanks. I think we'll be fine."

Justine sat on the edge of the bed and began bouncing up and down.

"Justine..." Mallory gave a raised eyebrow in her daughter's direction.

"Look at the time," Ellie said, glancing at the watch on her wrist. "I was hoping you wouldn't mind if Justine helped me bake some cookies?"

"Yes! I wanna. I wanna." Justine leaped off the bed and raced toward the door.

"Hold on, Punkie." Mallory caught her by the waist. "Ellie, staying here is one thing. But I really don't want you to, you know, take care of us."

Ellie waved her hand. "I'm baking them anyway. Might as well have a helper." She headed out the door, and Justine followed her, silencing any further argument.

No sooner had Justine left than Rafe turned to Mallory, a solemn look on his face. "Mallory, we need to talk."

Chapter Six

The drive to Rafe's apartment on the east side of town was silent, except for Mallory's continuous finger drumming on the middle console. The converted paper mill housed seven luxury condos on an embankment fifty feet from the Hudson River. Rafe had moved into the penthouse a year ago.

The apartment was large and airy. Oversized, multicolored abstract paintings decorated the ten-foot Sheetrocked walls. Moveable dividers separated the kitchen and dining area from the living space. Beyond that, a long hallway led to several bedrooms. The entire east wall of ten-foot windows overlooked the broad, sparkling Hudson.

Rafe tossed his keys into a bowl on a table near the entryway. "Want something to drink?"

Mallory looked around. "Uh...water?" She made it sound like a question.

"Sure thing." Rafe opened the refrigerator and pulled out two bottled waters. "Come on. Let's go upstairs."

Mallory gave him a quizzical look.

"Roof garden." Rafe glanced upward. "Follow me."

He led her toward a spiral staircase that opened onto a landscaped terrace. Complete with flower gardens, gravel paths, benches, and patio furniture.

"This is all yours?"

He let out a one-syllable laugh. "Yes. The apartment. The roof. All mine."

"You hired someone to do these gardens?" Mallory's eyes widened. "They're amazing."

"I wish." Rafe shook his head and put the bottle of water on the wrought-iron table. "Did all the work with these." He held out his hands. "Some tools, and of course, my brothers chipped in with hours of manual labor." Rafe scanned his work admiringly.

When he was released from prison, he wanted a place with lots of open space. He chose the apartment because the barren roof had so much potential. He created this garden terrace, which had been a labor of love. "It took some doing, but I'm happy I did it. I get to enjoy this space so many months out of the year. Sometimes, even in the winter, I grill if it's not snowing or raining. Nothing like steak on the grill—" Rafe cut himself off and put his hands in his pockets. "Look, we didn't say more than two words on the ride over here, and now we're talking about my terrace. You and I both know that's not what we're here for."

Mallory stared for several seconds. The expression on her face told him all he needed to know.

"You sure Justine is going to be okay?" Mallory looked down. "Your aunt—I mean, I know she's very nice—"

Rafe nodded. "Please don't worry." He patted the phone in his pocket. "If anything's wrong, Ellie will call."

Mallory let out a long breath. "Okay."

He wanted her to feel comfortable, so he casually lowered himself into one of the chairs, put his legs out in front, and crossed his feet at the ankle. Keeping his expression neutral, he waited. Whatever was going on, it was clear she needed to tell someone. She'd been acting like a powder keg about to burst since the night he found her on the side of the road. Somewhere in the depths of his soul, he'd already decided to help her take refuge or just be there for her. He knew that trapped look because he'd been there. He didn't want that to be Mallory's situation, no matter what she was about to say. "All right then." Rafe held out the flat of his hand toward the table and chairs. "Why don't you have a seat."

* * *

Rafe was giving her the chance to spill her guts. Instead, she froze. Her back felt stiff from days of bottled-up fear and tension. She studied the flowers, tresses, and lanterns strewn overhead. She was stalling. Was she crazy for thinking she could trust Rafe?

Nervously, she twisted the water bottle cap back and forth until she finally removed it and gulped greedily, not realizing how thirsty she'd been. She took a deep breath and slumped into the chair opposite Rafe. "I guess there's no point in pretending I'm not hiding from someone."

"Nope." Rafe's voice was clipped.

She pressed her lips together, and for a minute or so, she looked anywhere but at Rafe.

"Hey, you've already established something is going on." He leaned forward. "Just spill it."

Easier said than done. Where to begin? Closing her eyes, she tilted her head toward the sky. And then, she began to laugh. Not the ha-ha funny kind of laugh, but the uncontrollable, on-the-verge-of-hysteria laugh.

Rafe laughed lightly in response. "What's so funny?"

"You…wouldn't…believe me…" Mallory couldn't speak through the laughter. The release felt better than a good, long cry.

"Try me."

Tears rolled down her face, and the uncontrollable laughter made her sides hurt.

"Mallory, you okay?"

She nodded, but just barely. *He must think I'm mad. Maybe I am.*

"What could possibly be so funny?"

It took several minutes, but Mallory finally got a grip on her emotions. She took a deep breath, stood, wiped her cheeks with the back of her hand, and walked toward the roof's edge. Looking out over the railing, she tried to compose herself and focused on an embankment on the far side of the river. The leaves on the trees glistened in the sunlight. She couldn't hold it in any longer. She didn't want to. Rafe was asking her to tell him. It was now or never.

She kept her back to him. Telling him her story was one thing. Facing him was another. "Nothing's funny," she said. "In fact, what I'm about to tell you is probably the most unbelievable story you've heard in a while."

Rafe rose and stepped beside her.

"Please don't ask any questions until I'm finished." She paused, hoping she was doing the right thing. "I don't even know where to start." Mallory stared at the view, her knuckles white from gripping the railing, afraid she'd lose her nerve.

"How about at the beginning." He placed his hand gently on her forearm, and Mallory had to steel herself from the overwhelming feeling of desire from his touch.

Squaring her shoulders and without any preamble, she began at the beginning.

"All right. Here goes. I worked at a top-ten accounting firm in New York City. I'd just made Vice President of the Forensic Accounting department. The company bought a table at a charity event, and I was invited to attend. That's where I met Blake Stanton. Some people might say it was love at first sight. Looking back, I'm not sure what it was." Mallory hung her head. "Let's just say I was consumed with everything about him. So was the rest of New York. I mean, he wasn't simply a popular hedge fund manager. He was trending in all the right circles. There wasn't a celebrity, banker, or even a government official he couldn't reach with the touch of his phone. Everyone wanted his opinion, and he was envied for his charmed life."

"That wasn't the case?" Rafe asked.

She swallowed hard, preparing to say words she'd never spoken to anyone. "Hardly," Mallory scoffed. "Our life together was not the Camelot he portrayed. Blake was a master at manipulation and had everyone fooled. Before I knew what was happening, I quit my job, a career I'd worked hard for, and I found myself isolated from all my friends and family." Mallory banged her fist against the railing. The words poured out. She couldn't stop if she wanted to. "Rafe—" she turned her head, still holding the railing "—you have to believe me. I tried to leave him when Justine was just two years old." She let out a tired laugh. "I got as far as the airport when he found me. In the steely voice he reserved for business negotiations, he assured me he would always find me and that he'd take Justine. I believed him. Blake's connections included all the power brokers in New York and DC. He had the best lawyers in the city on retainers. I wouldn't have stood a chance."

"That's awful." Rafe took a step closer.

"I'm not done." But Mallory stopped. A war still raged in her mind, battling whether to tell Rafe or let him live a life that didn't involve her and her problems.

Rafe leaned against the railing. "Like I said, I'm listening."

She could feel his expectant gaze, and she cleared her throat. "When Interpol came to my door to tell me that my husband's plane crashed in international waters and no bodies were recovered, I thought I'd been given a second chance at life."

Mallory smiled at the memory. Moments after the Interpol officials left, she slumped against the door and wiped the tears of joy from her face. Then, she blasted the stereo and danced around the living room. When Justine came home from school, she delayed telling her the news. Instead, they ate hot dogs and French fries off paper plates while they sat on the floor watching *Frozen*.

"That look on your face," she said, pointing at his raised eyebrow. "You're surprised because I'm smiling. Right?"

"Yeah. A little."

"Well—" she shrugged "—that was my liberation day. I knew I would never have to be perfect or do things the way Blake demanded ever again." She shook her head. "But, damn it, I was foolish to believe I was ever really…free." The last word came out as a sob.

Rafe placed his hand on her back. It felt good. The warmth of his hand made her want to wrap her arms around him. Instead, she stopped herself and stiffened. Getting help was one thing. Leaning into the comfort he offered would only be the first step in a downhill slope of relying on a man again. She wasn't sure she could let that happen. Her daughter needed her to stand on her own two feet and stay strong. Ultimately, the only person Mallory felt she could ever really trust was herself.

"Mallory? What's going on?"

She hadn't realized she was crying until the teardrop landed on her hand.

"Hey there. Let's sit." Rafe took a few steps to the table. "Here." He handed her the water. "Take a sip."

Mallory took the offered water. "You don't need to hover."

The look on Rafe's face registered hurt. She hadn't intended to make him feel bad—she simply needed some room to breathe. "Thanks. Really. I'm fine," she said, softening her tone.

He sat across from her, leaning forward with his elbows on his knees, chin cupped in his hands. The kindness in his eyes made her relax. "You okay to keep going?"

Mallory nodded and let out a breath. "A month after his death, I received a note and a threatening phone call. In both instances, they claimed Blake was holding a hard drive they wanted. They warned me not to go to the authorities or they'd hurt Justine." A chill ran down Mallory's spine, remembering that afternoon.

Rafe raked a hand through his hair. "My god. Why didn't you call the police?"

"The note included photos of Justine at school, in the playground. Clearly, they were watching us, and…and… I believed they would hurt her."

"This is unbelievable." He reached for her hand.

The panic that consumed her when she read the note hadn't left because her mouth went dry, and her heart stuttered with the memory. It was his nearness and the warmth of his hand that kept her steady. "I had no idea what they were talking about, but I searched the entire house, including Blake's home office."

"Did you even know what you were looking for?"

"No. But I was certain if I could find something, anything that looked like a disc, I'd give it to the company attorney and let them handle it."

"I'm confused. Did you find the disc or not?"

"No. At least, I don't know." She scrubbed her face with the palms of her hands. "I found a laptop and ten thousand dollars in cash strapped to the underside of his chair."

Rafe let out a low whistle. "Do you think it's the laptop they're after?"

"It's all I have to go on." She blew a breath out through her nose. "The note said 'hard drive.' I searched every inch of Blake's home office and couldn't find anything else. The laptop has a built-in hard drive. If I had to guess, that's what they're after. Otherwise, why would Blake go through the trouble of hiding it?"

"Sounds about right."

"I tried to get into the laptop, tried every possible password combination. I was never locked out of the computer, but I didn't have any luck getting in. Before I left, I took the laptop to the computer store in town. The techie said the only reason I'd been able to attempt so many passwords was because Blake never changed the factory setting on the computer. He also said that without the password, the only way in was to wipe the hard drive."

"Yeah, that sounds about right."

"Well, I couldn't let that happen. I need the password because I think whatever is on there is going to save my daughter's life. But I don't trust whoever's after us to leave us alone once they get what they want."

"Your ex was a powerful man indeed, but what makes you think they wouldn't leave you alone?"

Mallory shivered and ran her hands up and down her arms. "When I came back from the computer store, my house had been ransacked—furniture turned over, pillows slashed, closets emptied onto the floor. Even though they warned me not to go to the authorities, I finally succumbed and called the police." Mallory pulled on the pendant around her neck. "A lot of good that did me. They found no fingerprints and no evidence anything had been taken. The police labeled it vandalism and left."

"Maybe it was?" Rafe shrugged.

"No. It couldn't be. I live..." Mallory shook her head. "I *lived*, past tense, in a gated community. There's nothing but miles of expensive homes and everyone has CCTV. And these so-called vandals left not a single fingerprint, and not one camera captured an image?" She raised both eyebrows. "How is that possible?"

"Sounds like professionals."

"That's exactly what I thought." She sat back in the chair. "Not to be melodramatic, but I sense those types of people would want to make sure that whatever was on the laptop was for their eyes only. If they even suspected I knew what was on it, I think they'd for sure want to get rid of me. I couldn't take a chance. I knew I had to get out. I had to protect my daughter."

"How in the world did you end up here, back in Hollow Lake?"

"Well, it was on the way to my dad's new place in Rochester. I thought I'd be safe with him. I'd get into the computer and then figure out my next step."

Rafe pursed his lips. "Okay, so far, I'm tracking with you."

"Well, the day before they vandalized my home, the Tesla dealer phoned. Evidently, some new car Blake purchased had arrived. I didn't know anything about it. Apparently, he'd ordered a custom model, and it was already paid for. That's when the lightbulb went off. I could get out of town in a car I wasn't associated with. Which meant maybe I wouldn't be followed. I hoped by the time they realized I wasn't home, I'd be long gone and far away." As she recounted the details, her adrenaline levels began to surge.

"I was scared to death, but I had to act fast. I cut my hair and threw on jeans and a baseball cap. I packed what I could, took the laptop and the ten thousand in cash, and called a cab. I knew whoever photographed Justine was watching, so I had the cab meet me in town. I snuck out the back door and somehow managed to walk along the back roads with Justine and the luggage about a half mile into town. I took the cab to the dealership, got the car, and drove. Several hours later, that's when I met you, stalled out on County Road 385."

Rafe was silent.

"I know. I know." Mallory shook her head, eyes downcast. "It almost sounds like a reenactment of a true crime series." Mallory let out a bitter laugh and slumped back in her chair. The weight of what she was carrying, finally out in the open, afforded her some relief. But at the same time, she felt ashamed that she'd lived for so many years with a monster, unable to escape. She covered her face with her hands. "I'm so god-awful tired…of everything." Mallory got up and started pacing along the gravel paths. "I'm scared."

Rafe didn't move.

"Ironically, when Blake went on this last trip, I'd already had an appointment with a divorce attorney. I was going to leave him. Somehow, I was going to figure out how to escape with my baby." She wanted Rafe to know she did have some spine left.

"I'm not sure what to say."

"I know." She stopped pacing and saw the disbelief in his eyes. "Imagine me, a trained forensic accountant, and I couldn't trace the lies Blake fed me from the very start of our marriage. I thought the nightmare was over when he died. How foolish of me. It was only beginning." She stood in front of Rafe. "I need your help. I have to get into that computer because until I do, that bastard will still torment me and my daughter even from the grave."

Rafe took her hands in his. "Mallory, he isn't here. He can't hurt you."

"Oh no? Haven't you heard what I've been saying? That's exactly what's happening."

"When was the last time you were contacted by those men?" Rafe asked.

"Not me."

Rafe frowned. "What do you mean, not me? Is that some kind of non sequitur?"

"I mean, I haven't been contacted again. But this morning, two men showed up at my father's office asking questions. That's what this morning's phone call was all about. He said they wanted to know when I'd last visited and when I would be returning. They're trying to intimidate me by stalking my father. They're waiting for me to show up. I know it." Mallory sucked in a breath. "My poor dad. He doesn't deserve this."

"Is your father all right?"

"For now. No doubt he's out of his mind with worry. But he's strong and trusts I know what I'm doing."

"What are you doing?"

Mallory hesitated. The more she thought about her situation, the more she knew what her next move needed to be. She'd already taken pains to disguise herself by cutting her hair. And now that she'd stuffed her phone in the back of a car going to New Mexico, her instincts told her she had a week, maybe two, to hide in plain sight. "I need to get into that computer. Something in there must be why my daughter's life is being threatened."

Mallory stepped to the side of the round wrought-iron table, picked up her large leather shoulder bag, and reached in. She pulled out the small silver laptop and handed it to Rafe. "Help me. Please."

Chapter Seven

Rafe pulled up to Ellie's house and waited until Mallory was safely inside. He put the car in Park and kept the engine running while he stared at the empty porch. He needed a moment. So many emotions were bubbling to the surface it was difficult to know exactly what he felt—anger, hurt, worry, maybe even desire. *Damn.* What had he gotten himself into? He banged his hand against the steering wheel and looked at the laptop resting on the passenger seat.

Yesterday, he'd been happy to see Mallory. Today, he was afraid. There wasn't a doubt in his mind she was in serious trouble. The kind of trouble that could get a person killed. Rafe closed his eyes, realizing he'd brought danger to his family. He should have sent her packing the moment she told him the truth. That's what he *should* have done, but that wasn't what he was going to do. After all, they had a shared history that couldn't be denied. Against his better judgment, he'd already opened himself up to feeling things for her that he thought were buried. Leaving her to fend for herself didn't seem like an option.

Once more, Rafe banged the steering wheel with the palm of his hand. It felt good momentarily releasing some of his frustration. He checked the clock on the dashboard. It was late, and he hadn't been back in the office since early morning. His brothers would be wondering what happened.

He pulled the phone from his pocket. The battery was dead. How had he let that happen? Hopefully, Ellie hadn't tried to reach them. He plugged it into the console. As it came to life, it dinged several times, alerting him of the five missed calls, two voice-mails, and ten text messages from Max, the perpetual worrier, and Zack, the other worrier. None from his aunt. He didn't bother to read any of the messages. He quickly sent a group text to his brothers, letting them know he would be there in ten minutes. He threw the gear shift into Drive and took off down the street.

The elevator doors opened, and Brittany greeted Rafe. "There you are." Her toothy smile faded. "Max is looking for you. He has been for the last hour. Why'd you turn off your phone?"

He smiled and ignored the question. "Is he in his office?"

"No. He said to meet him in the large conference room."

"Thanks." Rafe stopped by his office and popped the laptop into the bottom drawer of his desk. He locked the drawer and his office door and went to the conference room.

Max sat at the head of the long glass table with a sour expression. The oldest of the brothers, Maximo Jesus Ramirez, resembled their father in looks and attitude. He was the consummate rule follower. His chiseled features were set with tight lips and an arched brow.

Rafe slid the door closed, and Max hit a button on the built-in console, darkening the all-glass wall and shutting out prying eyes.

"So. You want to tell us what's going on?" Max pushed his light brown hair from his forehead.

"We got a little worried," Zack said. "I mean, it doesn't take hours to fix a leaky bathroom sink, so we called *Tía* Ellie, and she gave us a little bit of the tea. You know, the 411."

"But we'd love for you to fill us in," Max added.

Rafe was at a loss. *Where to start?* He strode to the far end of the room, opened a small refrigerator, and pulled out a bottle of water. "Anyone want?"

"Nah. Well hydrated at the moment," Max said.

"Yeah, I'm good." Zack waved him off.

"Bro. You're stalling." Max's tone turned serious. "Having

trouble remembering who you spent your morning with?" He pushed closer to the table. "You know who I'm talking about? Right? Woman, slender, pixie cut, car needs repair, curly-haired little girl? Oh, and you—" he pointed at Rafe "—you were in a serious relationship with her back in high school. Am I right?"

"Yeah. Want to fill us in on what you talked about?" Zack joined in. "*Tía* Ellie says it looks like she's in some kind of trouble. And if I'm correctly recalling our conversation from last night, I believe you suspected something, too. In fact, I thought we discussed you were going to let her go her own way."

Rafe made a motion with his hands as if he were patting something down. *"Cálmate."*

"Oh, I'm calm," Max said, sliding his seat further from the table and crossing one leg over the other. "What about you, Zack? You calm?"

Zack put his feet up on the table. "Feeling real relaxed."

Despite their sarcasm, their eyes held an intensity that said they were not joking around. It only reinforced how much danger he'd brought to the family.

"Have a seat, bro." Max pointed to the chair next to him and opposite Zack. Rafe sat, forming the familiar triangle at the head of the long conference table where they held staff meetings.

Max spoke first. "Seems your long-lost love is on the run."

Rafe opened his mouth to answer.

Max held up a hand. *"No me hables.* Don't say a word." He pointed to himself and Zack. "Neither of us are recent graduates in the investigation game. It took us less than the time it takes to make a *jamón y queso* sandwich to find out that your girl, Mallory, is running from something. Her house was ransacked, and she left yesterday in a brand-new Tesla purchased by her husband before his death."

"Yeah," Zack said, sitting forward and rolling his chair closer to the table. "So the husband, who happens to be…wait for it—" Zack pointed to Max.

"Blake Stanton," Max said in a deadpan voice.

Zack snapped his fingers. "That's the one. Anyway, he dies mid-Atlantic. All mysterious like. You know? His plane bursts into flames in the middle of the ocean, and guess what? No bodies are recovered. Fascinating, don't you think?"

Rafe shook his head, not sure what to say. Clearly, his brothers had done some digging. And while it annoyed him, he understood because they did it to protect him. "Well, I appreciate—"

"¿Pero qué te pasa? ¿Acaso no piensas?" Max tapped his temple.

"Yeah, what *were* you thinking? Did you somehow leave your brains back in the cabin when you went fishing? Why'd you take her to our aunt's house? *Tía* Ellie doesn't need this." Zack raised an eyebrow.

Max scoffed. "Believe it or not, we worry about you."

"Yeah, I know," Rafe said. *"Pero no te preocupes."*

"Hold up," Zack said. "We've earned the right to be worried. You were framed once before. Remember? We don't want you getting hurt, and this guy, Blake Stanton, may be dead, but he's got a past I don't like."

His brothers were right. Whoever was after Mallory was on the wrong side of the law. And going back to prison wasn't an option. He needed to be careful. More importantly, he needed to protect his family.

"I see the wheels turning in that head of yours," Max said. "You're thinking you can do this all by yourself." He slapped a palm on the conference table. "No!"

"I second that." Zack raised his hand. "We're brothers. We're in this together."

"Hold up. I'm not totally on board with whatever this is yet. I need more information," Max said.

His older brother was always the skeptic. Anally analytical. Most times, Rafe loved him for it. Today, not so much. For once, he wished Max would just go with it. Rafe sighed. He supposed Max was right. Get all the facts. Then make a decision. Helping Mallory would require his brothers' help.

"Miralo." Zack pointed at him. "I know that look. You're going do what you want to do because that's what you always do."

"Nah." Rafe shook his head. "When it comes to family it's a

democracy. This involves all of us, and I won't make the decision on how we move forward unless we all agree."

"Qué milagro." Zack smiled. "A zebra can change his stripes." Rafe grinned.

"So start. Tell us everything she told you," Max said.

Rafe ran a hand through his hair. "Mallory and her daughter are being hunted."

"Hunted?" Zack sat forward. "You got my attention."

Rafe told Max and Zack everything he knew, including the need to hack into Blake Stanton's computer and the fact that Mallory's daughter would be in danger if she went to the police. And that, as of this morning, at least two suspicious men were asking questions at her father's office.

When he finished, a silence descended. Rafe looked from one brother to the next. "Well, aren't you going to say something?"

Max pursed his lips.

"Ah, man. Don't give me that look," Rafe said.

"What look?" Max asked.

Rafe pointed his finger. "The one that's taking over your face right now. The one that screams Rafe's stepped in it again."

Max stood abruptly and strode to the far end of the conference room. He stared out the window for a few moments and then whirled around. "Honestly? I'm trying to remain calm."

Rafe didn't understand. "I get that you're upset—"

"Nah, man. Not upset. Nope. Scared." Max dug one hand into his pocket. "Let me break it down for you. This is *the* Blake Stanton you're talking about. And if his ex is being chased and her daughter's life is in danger, there's a reason." Max sat. "I need to think." He put his head in his hands.

Zack took out his phone and began to scroll.

Rafe didn't know what to say. When he was arrested for crypto-jacking, his brothers had been there for him. Through their efforts alone, the dark net hacking crew behind the illegal mining of cryptocurrency was discovered. RMZ's reputation had taken a hit, but together, they'd tirelessly worked to restore it. He would go along with whatever they decided. He owed them that much.

"Hate to break into your private thoughts. But we got a problem." Zack stared at his phone screen.

"What now?" Max moved around the table, looking over Zack's shoulder. "Oh, man." Max slapped the table with a palm.

"What?" Rafe stood.

Zack looked up at him. "News alert." He turned his phone's screen to face Rafe.

"I can't read that from here."

"Looks like the black box on Blake Stanton's plane has gone all Bermuda Triangle. It's gone. Vanished." Zack put his phone down.

"If we were analyzing this as a case, with all the information we have now, let's be real, we'd probably pass. Particularly since the main event, one Blake Stanton, was devious at best and an out-and-out criminal at worst." Max paced.

"Hell, that guy had back channels up into the White House. He was well protected," Zack offered.

"Even in death?" Rafe asked.

"Well, you tell me. How does a black box disappear?" Zack asked.

"But we're not protecting the dead husband," Rafe countered. "We need to protect Mallory and her five-year-old daughter. When did we stop caring about individuals? We've all been so busy stalking cyber criminals and the harm they do to big corporations and government agencies. But this is real. This is a person. Not some nameless government agency. Not a bunch of zeros and ones hiding in the dark web. Dammit. She needs our help. Let's not overthink this. The clock is ticking."

Max crossed his arms over his chest. "'Cause Zack and I know this guy's reputation from working on Wall Street. And Blake Stanton, alive or dead, isn't someone I would choose to mess with. Word was, he knew the kind of people you don't want to meet in a dark alley on a moonless night, if you get where I'm going with this."

A shiver crawled up Rafe's spine. He hadn't experienced that sensation since prison, where watching your back was part of daily life. He tried to shake it off by getting up and walking to the windows. His gaze traveled up and down Main Street just as a black sedan pulled up in front of Fritz & Dean's diner.

Chapter Eight

"Mommy's back. Mommy's back!"

"Don't open the door, Justine," Mallory heard Ellie admonish. "Let's see who's there first."

From the corner of her eye, she caught the flutter of the living room curtains and turned to see Ellie looking out and waving and Justine right beside her, smiling.

"We'll be right there," Ellie called through the closed window.

Justine barely gave Mallory a chance to get through the door with her packages before giving her the details of her afternoon. "Mommy, you won't believe what we made. I only got to eat one 'cause Ellie said I had to wait till after dinner or I'll spoil my appe…appe…"

"Appetite," Mallory finished for her.

"Yeah. Appetite," Justine said proudly.

"I'm happy to hear that," Mallory said.

"What happened to Rafe?" Ellie asked.

"Thanks for taking care of Justine." Mallory flashed a grateful smile and continued down the hall toward the kitchen. "Rafe said he had to get back to the office. He'll be by later with our luggage." She placed the bags on the counter and checked the clock above the sink. She'd been gone for more than three hours.

"What's all this?" Ellie said, pointing to the grocery bags.

"Rafe took me to the supermarket. I did a little shopping for dinner." It had taken a herculean effort on her part to convince Rafe to let her go to the local market. At first, he refused. They'd already stopped at Abbey's B&B so Mallory could pack. He'd been in a hurry to get back to his office and talk to his brothers. And he didn't want her walking around by herself. But Mallory was just as stubborn, insisting she had to do something special for Justine, who'd been shuttled around and disoriented. And she didn't want to take advantage of Ellie. He'd finally acquiesced on the condition he went into the market with her.

"It's spaghetti and meatballs as a thank you for the room and lunch and for watching Justine."

"Yay! I love spaghetti and meatballs." Justine clapped.

"I know you do. Hopefully, it's something Ellie likes, too." Mallory looked up expectantly.

"First of all, no thanks necessary. Justine and I had a wonderful time making cookies. Reminds me of when my grandchildren visit. And as lovely as dinner with the two of you sounds, I can't tonight. Tonight is book club night with the girls. It's Grace's turn to make the appetizers, and they're a meal in themselves." Ellie took off her apron and hung it up behind the door. "I'm going to go up and change."

"Oh, okay." Mallory was somewhat relieved Ellie would be out. Now, she wouldn't have to spend all evening pretending her life was normal instead of feeling like a mouse caught in a cat's playpen. She began unpacking the groceries and looking around the large kitchen for things she needed to prepare dinner. "Well, Punkie, it's just you and me tonight. How 'bout helping me make dinner."

"Sure. But when do we get to eat dessert?" Justine asked.

"The sooner we get dinner on the table, the sooner you can have one cookie." Mallory held up her index finger, emphasizing the number one. Her motherly instincts told her that in addition to the cookie already eaten, there'd been a healthy sampling of cookie dough and licking of spoons. Any more sugar and bedtime promised to be a struggle. She bent, put both hands on Justine's face, and kissed her nose. Her daughter's face made her heart ache with joy and trepidation.

"Owww. Mommy, you're squeezing too hard."

"Oh, sorry." Mallory kissed the top of her head.

A dozen times this afternoon, Mallory had vacillated about flying to her father's house and handing over the damn computer to the men who were after her, hoping to end this nightmare. But then the rational portion of her mind would kick in, cautioning her that these men were like her husband. They weren't honorable, and there'd be no guarantee she and Justine would ever escape danger.

No. Her only recourse was to get into that damn computer. Instincts told her if she could get the information these men were after, she'd have some leverage.

For now, she needed to stay put and hope that placing her trust in Rafe had been the right thing to do. Glancing up at the clock again, she wondered what he was doing now. Had he told his brothers? Would they help? When would she ever stop worrying? She blew out an exaggerated breath—time to make dinner.

Before long, Mallory had all the burners on the stove working, and the aroma of freshly made tomato sauce filled the room.

"That smells delicious. Tempting enough to make me miss my club meeting," Ellie said from the kitchen doorway. "But then I'd miss out on all the gossip, and it would take weeks to catch up." Ellie laughed. "I wrote my cell phone number on the pad next to the phone if you need me. But you should be fine. And I'm usually home by nine thirty or ten. Do you need anything before I go?" Ellie asked.

Mallory smiled and shook her head. "No, we're good."

"Yup, we're good," Justine echoed.

Ellie chuckled. "Well, all right, see you in a few hours." She headed out the kitchen door toward the garage.

Mallory checked to make sure the door was locked, then she lifted the lace curtain hanging over the door's window and scanned the backyard. Satisfied no one was lurking about, she went back to the stove. She lifted the lid on the pot and took in the rich aroma of tomato and spices. Her shoulders dropped a little. The kitchen was homey, and she was cooking a meal for Justine. She could almost believe her life was normal. She put up the water for the pasta and gave the sauce another stir. She began to hum the tune to one of her favorite songs and danced over to the refrigerator before she mentally slapped herself back to reality. This wasn't the time to feel as if she'd found *Good Housekeeping* nirvana. Blending in was one thing. Being relaxed, losing her edge, was altogether reckless. She had to stay alert. Period. She squared her shoulders and stood a little straighter.

"Punkie, it's almost time for dinner. You'll have to put that coloring book away and help me set the table."

Mallory put out the plates and grabbed some forks, handing them to Justine along with napkins. "Set those next to the plates."

"I remember, Mommy." Justine sounded a little exasperated, and it tugged at Mallory that she'd put her daughter through so much.

The meal was nearly ready when the doorbell rang. *Who could that be?* Mallory's heart went into overdrive.

"I'll get it," Justine said, dropping the forks on the table. She took off toward the front door.

"Don't open it until I see who's there." Mallory was right behind Justine.

"Yeah, I know. Ellie already told me." Justine's voice came in a singsong.

With shaking hands, Mallory parted the living room curtains and saw Rafe standing on the porch with their luggage. She dropped her shoulders. "It's okay. It's Rafe with our stuff."

Mallory opened the door and stepped aside to let him in. "Hi. Thanks for bringing over our bags."

"Mommy, did you remember to pack Teddy?"

"Of course I did, silly." That stuffed animal was more than security to Justine, and Mallory thought she needed it now more than ever.

"Is my aunt here?"

Mallory shook her head.

Rafe snapped his fingers, "That's right, it's Monday. Tonight's *Tía* Ellie's book club."

"She only left a few minutes ago." Mallory couldn't understand why he was being so casual. She knew he'd spoken to his brothers, and she was anxious to find out what they said. But Rafe acted like everything was normal.

"Where would you like these?" Rafe pointed to the luggage. "I can bring them upstairs if you like."

"Please, don't bother. I can do that after dinner."

"I thought I smelled some deliciousness coming from back there," Rafe said, giving a nod toward the kitchen.

"It's sghetti night," Justine said.

"Spa-ghetti," Mallory corrected.

"Well then, I'll take these upstairs. Spaghetti is one of my favorites, and I rarely say no to a favorite. That okay with you?" He gave Mallory a pointed look.

She felt a flow of intensity radiating from Rafe. He wasn't purposefully being casual; he was being guarded to avoid saying anything in front of Justine.

"After dinner, we can discuss the plan." Rafe turned to head up the stairs with the bags.

"After sghetti we get to have cookies. And I helped make them."

"Can't wait," Rafe called over his shoulder.

A plan. It seemed that Rafe and his brothers would be able to help.

"So it's just the three of us. My aunt doesn't know what she's missing," Rafe said as he entered the kitchen. "How can I help?"

"Oh…well, maybe you could pour Justine a glass of milk and then, I guess, have a seat because dinner is about to be served." She placed the bread on the table, followed by a big bowl of pasta and a green leafy salad.

"Is that bottle of wine for the meal?" Rafe's gaze turned toward the counter. "Would you like me to open it? I know where the corkscrew is."

Mallory gave a half nod, uncertain if opening it was a good idea. Being around Rafe made her feel things she'd buried long ago, and she needed to stay sharp. There was no sense in prolonging dinner. She wanted the meal to be over as soon as possible. She'd give Justine a bath and put her to bed. Then she'd be able to find out from Rafe if he and his brothers found a way into Blake's laptop. From there, she'd figure out what to do next.

He moved through the kitchen effortlessly like he belonged

there. As if the three of them having dinner was an everyday occurrence, like a normal family. The picture-perfect family scene, false as it was, almost overwhelmed her. She lowered her eyes and felt a physical sensation that could only be described as a deep ache in her soul for something she'd lost a long time ago.

Rafe took two wine glasses from the cupboard, glanced up at her, and smiled as he easily pulled out the cork. His dark brown eyes and barely-there stubble added to his attraction. She noticed the tattoo on his wrist again. Who had she ever known in her life who had a tattoo? Blake would have called it "common."

For that reason alone, she decided she liked it.

At six foot three, Rafe was taller than Blake. His frame was muscular but maintained a sleek athleticism. His dark brown hair was longer than she was used to seeing in a man. Blake had been conservative in his looks, and while his attire screamed money and power, it was all very understated. His appearance belied the maniacal bully underneath the expensive clothes. With Rafe, all you really noticed was his kind face.

"To old friends," he said, giving Mallory a lingering look and then clinking his goblet against Justine's milk glass.

"Okay, let's eat." Mallory placed the paper napkin on her lap.

After the initial spaghetti slurping, Justine looked up. "Delicious."

"Thanks, Punkie. I'm glad you like it." Mallory smiled.

"I second the declaration. Delicious." Rafe broke a piece of bread in half. "I can't remember the last time I had spaghetti."

"Me either," Justine added. "I wish we could have it every day." Her wide tomato sauce grin nearly covered her entire face.

Mallory relaxed her grip on the fork. She hadn't seen her daughter this carefree in a long time.

Rafe's easy conversation with Justine reminded her of his unending kindness. In high school, his care and compassion drew her in. If she'd stayed in Hollow Lake and married Rafe, her life would have been different. But she wouldn't have Justine. As much as she despised Blake and every single day of their marriage, her precious baby was the only worthwhile thing to come out of that union.

"So, Justine, tell me about Teddy," Rafe asked. "How long have you two known each other?"

Justine giggled. "He's one of my best friends. Do you have a best friend?"

"Yup, I have two."

"Two?" Justine tilted her head. "Can you have two best friends?"

Rafe shrugged. "I don't know that there's any rule that says you can't. Anyway, I have two. My brothers Max and Zack."

"Are they clean?"

"Clean?" Rafe furrowed his brow.

"Mommy says Teddy smells, but I can't give him a bath, or he'll fall apart."

Rafe threw his head back and let out a belly laugh. Justine joined in.

"I'm pretty sure my brothers take a bath every night." He winked.

"I don't have brothers," Justine said. "I'm an only child."

He pointed his fork at Mallory. "Ask your mother. I come from a very, very, very big family. We're all really close. And most of the time, I love it." He smirked. "Most of the time."

Mallory remembered Rafe's relatives as a tight-knit Puerto Rican clan. At school, no one started trouble with any of the Ramirez brothers or their Chavez cousins. It was unspoken—if you messed with one, you essentially messed with all of them.

And with scores of aunts, uncles, cousins, and grandchildren. The Ramirez family's annual July Fourth BBQ was the talk of Hollow Lake.

Rafe's mother, Maria, had two sisters, Ellie and Claudia. Each one moved to the area from the Bronx and married. When Mallory and Rafe were dating, she met and socialized with at least fifty members of the combined families living in and around the Hudson Valley. Now, fifteen years later, she could only imagine how many were in the family after even more marriages and births.

"Rafe's right, Punkie. He does come from a big family. By the way, how are your parents?"

Rafe looked down at his plate. "Uh, my mother passed." His voice was barely above a whisper.

Mallory leaned forward. "Oh. I'm so sorry."

"Me too," Justine said.

Rafe cleared his throat. "Thanks. As for my father, well, let's just say we're having a rough patch." Rafe straightened. "For now, I'm just enjoying this delicious meal and exceptional company." He smiled at Justine. "You'll have to introduce me to Teddy later."

Justine giggled.

Despite the sad news, sitting here with Rafe and her daughter, having a conversation and a meal, felt more intimate than anything she and Blake had shared outside of giving birth to Justine.

Mallory smiled, the kind of smile that came from within, and her body relaxed. Not for a minute did she believe this was at all normal. But she decided this one moment, this small window of time, she would enjoy.

And then, in an instant, her small bubble of happiness seemed to deflate when Justine reached for a piece of bread and knocked over her milk. Simultaneously, they heard a loud bang outside.

Rafe sprung from his seat and flew out of the kitchen.

"I'm sorry, Mommy. I'm sorry. It was an accident," Justine said, as tears welled in her eyes. Her hand trembled over her mouth, and she began to cry.

Mallory's stomach churned. "Stay right there, Justine."

"Mommy, I'm sorry." Justine continued to cry.

Mallory stood and eased her way to the kitchen window, her pulse racing. "Please, Justine. Stop crying." Standing on the tips of her toes, she peered out the window and into the backyard. There was nothing there. She jumped when a man came around the side of the house.

Rafe looked up and waved.

She gave a weak smile and tried to put her heart back in her chest.

He jogged up the back porch steps. "It's nothing," he said, closing the door.

"Nothing? What in the heck was that loud bang?"

Taking Mallory's hands, he gave a gentle squeeze and looked her in the eyes. "I guess we're all on edge. Must have been a raccoon. The lid of the garbage can fell to the ground. I'm sure it was loose, and raccoons are scavengers. It was probably looking for food. It's fine. I swear." He held up a hand and crossed his chest like a Boy Scout. He turned toward Justine. "Hey now, what are all the tears for?"

Justine sobbed and pointed to the spilled milk on the table. "I'm sorry. I didn't mean it."

"That's nothing. This is an easy fix."

"I won't do it again. I'll be careful," Justine cried.

Rafe grabbed a dish towel from the counter and patted the table dry. "It's fine. Really. I'm going to pour you another glass of milk, and then we'll start all over. No harm done."

Hiccupping between sobs, Justine asked, "Am I in trouble?"

"Trouble? Not in this house. Really, you don't have to worry about it. See—" Rafe poured her a fresh glass of milk "—problem solved."

Grateful for Rafe's ability to diffuse the situation, Mallory breathed again. "Yeah, don't worry, everything is fine, Punkie," she managed to get out, a slight tremble in her voice. She gave Rafe a sideways glance and could clearly see from the expression on his face that he understood what she'd endured in the Stanton household over the last six years. It was obvious this little milk drama spoke volumes.

"Now, where were we?" Rafe said.

While she appreciated Rafe's attempt at keeping the atmosphere light, Mallory put her fork down. She'd lost her appetite. The rest of the meal was fairly silent, and when Rafe finished, she announced bath time for Justine.

"I don't want to go upstairs and take a bath." Justine's pout was so big it practically devoured her face.

"Justine." Mallory gave a raised eyebrow.

"But I don't wanna. I wanna stay here and talk to Rafe."

"Well, it's kinda close to my bedtime, too," Rafe said, giving an exaggerated yawn. "While you're getting ready for bed, I'll clean up down here."

"Oh, please don't do that. I can take care of it later."

"Not gonna happen. In my family, whoever cooks doesn't clean. And really, there isn't much here." Rafe turned to face her, his demeanor suddenly not so carefree, as he gave her a pointed look. "Go. I'll be here waiting. I have news, and we need to talk."

Chapter Nine

Twenty minutes later, Rafe put a mug of coffee on the table in front of Mallory. "It's decaf."

"Mmm…smells good."

"I know where Ellie keeps the primo stuff." Rafe smiled and pushed the milk and sugar over to her side of the table. "Take a load off."

"Thanks." Mallory nearly slumped back in her chair. "So you spoke with your brothers. You want to tell me what they said? Were you able to get into the laptop?"

Rafe stared into his cup. "Let's face it. Your ex knew a lot of people in very high places. The kind of people who could make anything or anybody disappear."

"I already know this, and you're stalling."

"Okay. Whatever you have, or whatever it is they think you have, is important enough for them to threaten you. And to me, that means you need the kind of help that doesn't simply begin and end with a hacker. I say that because my brothers worked on getting into the laptop. They're thinking you need the kind of help we can't give."

"You mean like the police?"

Rafe shrugged. "Maybe."

"I'm afraid of taking the wrong step."

Rafe stood "Come here." He came around the table and pulled

Mallory out of her chair and into his arms. The top of her head reached just under his chin, and he caught a whiff of citrus. He closed his eyes and drank her in. Her body felt small and soft, and on instinct, he wanted to protect her.

Mallory relaxed into him. Her arms slowly wrapped around his waist. He held her and knew he was hugging her as much for himself as for her. Moments passed before she lifted her head and looked at him. She was beautiful. He brought his face close to hers, and when she didn't move away, he lowered his lips onto hers and heard her sigh.

The kitchen door burst open. Ellie swept in with Zack and Max trailing behind.

Mallory stepped out of Rafe's embrace. Her eyes were wide.

"Hello, Mallory. Long time," Max said, then looked at Rafe. "Coffee fresh?"

Rafe nodded. He knew why they were here.

"Get me a cup too, bro," Zack said, pulling a chair up to the table. "Hi, Mallory."

"I'll get some pie," Ellie said. "Just made an apple this morning." She got the pie stand from the pantry. "Rafe, please get the plates from the cupboard."

Mallory clutched at her throat, unable to understand what was happening. She tried to remain calm as Rafe's family filled the room but found it increasingly difficult. They were all acting normal, as if they'd been invited for social hour at a neighborhood gathering. But it didn't take a genius to know something was terribly off. Her heart beat like she was on a treadmill with the speed turned up to nine. "Why do I get the sense you're all here because of me?"

Max turned around, coffee mug in hand, and leaned against the counter. "Because we are."

"Let me. Okay?" Rafe tapped Zack on the shoulder. *"Muévelo."*

Zack rolled his eyes and vacated the chair.

Rafe turned the chair to face Mallory and sat. "So, look. Zack picked Ellie up early from her book club and told her everything."

"Everything. But why?" Mallory twisted the heart pendant on its chain.

"Because we don't think it's safe for you and your daughter to stay here," Max said. "And now it's not safe for *Tía* Ellie either."

"Oh, my god. I never meant for this to happen. Ellie, I'm so sorry." Mallory put a hand over her mouth.

"No te preocupes." Ellie put a piece of pie in front of Zack. "Really. Don't worry. I trust my nephews. And you need help. And that means we're going to have to move out of here tonight."

"Tonight." Mallory shook her head. "This is all happening so fast. I don't understand. All I know is that I've caused you all enough trouble." She stood. "I'll get Justine and go."

"No!" came the chorus of voices.

Stunned, she turned to Rafe. He'd known all along and yet behaved like nothing was wrong throughout dinner. "How could you have acted so normal? How could you just...just...just... The entire evening you never let on." Mallory began to shake. Her anger quickly turned to rage, and she pummeled Rafe on his chest. "Why? Why didn't you tell me the minute you walked in the door?" Her hands slapped at his chest for all the times she didn't get to stand up to Blake. For the pain she'd put her daughter through. For the trouble she'd caused this family. She finally collapsed against his chest and sobbed. The warmth of Rafe's arms as they encircled her made her cry harder.

"By the time I left the office, I didn't have all the information. While you were putting Justine to bed, I got a call from Max."

"I... I...put you all in jeopardy. This can't be right." Tears began to stream down her face. Rafe held her tighter, and she buried her face in his chest.

Ellie sat. "Mallory. Mallory. Please sit. Please."

Rafe released her, and Mallory wiped her face with the back of her hand.

"I know this is hard." Ellie pressed her lips into a tight line. "Hell, it's not something I've ever been involved in. But here we are. And there's not a person related to me who would let you go through this alone without giving our best shot at helping you get out of it. So, my nephews have a plan. And I'd like you to listen to it."

After a moment, Mallory sat and nodded.

"Mallory, we pulled out the latest tech we had, and it took

some doing, but we finally got into the laptop." Max crossed his arms over his chest.

Mallory almost stopped breathing.

"You never would have gotten into it, even if you'd tried a thousand passwords," Zack said. "It had encryption the likes of which we see being used only by government agencies. So, whatever is on there must be important to the people who are chasing you." He held up a hand. "Before you say anything, no we don't know what's on it."

"But didn't you just say you got into the computer?" Mallory asked.

"Yes. We did," Max said. "We also tripped some sort of signal."

"What?" She couldn't believe what she was hearing.

"Don't panic." Rafe put a hand on her forearm. "They were able to dismantle it within fifteen seconds, so we think we're okay. But no sense in taking chances. That's why we have to get on the move tonight."

"What we did see," Max continued, "were a lot of numbers on a spreadsheet that don't mean anything. At least not on the surface. We think it's a second encryption."

Mallory perched at the edge of her chair. "So, what you're saying is we're back to where we started." She pursed her lips. "I should give them the damn thing and tell them I don't know anything."

Rafe scratched the back of his head. "Well, about that. We think—" he looked at his brothers "—that if you give it to them now with the first encryption breached, they'll think you must know something."

"But I don't." Mallory raised her voice.

"We know that." Rafe squeezed her hand. "But from what we could discover, we think with your training, you can probably decipher those numbers and figure out what's put your life in jeopardy."

"How? I don't know anything."

"Because you were a forensic accountant," Rafe said.

"And how does that help?" Mallory furrowed her brow. She was trying to keep up with what they were saying, but the rising panic was making it difficult to concentrate. She dug her nails into the palms of her hands and forced herself to focus.

"This goes beyond cybersecurity and what we typically deal with. From the information we're able to see, that second encryption is what we would call a trick. You look at it, and you see nothing but a sophisticated general ledger. To the naked eye, it looks like it could be Blake's bank accounts or stock portfolio. But if you put your cursor on the last column, which is blank, it asks for a password. It begs the question, why encrypt it if all the information is already on the spreadsheet?"

"To keep me from getting his money?" Mallory said.

Zack tapped the table with his hand. "No. Because it's not real."

Mallory shook her head several times. "I'm not following."

Rafe let out a breath. "There's something more to it than meets the eye. In cybersecurity terms, it's called steganography."

"Steno—what?" Mallory squinted, trying to understand.

"Steganography. It's when something appears as one thing but is something altogether different. Like, in this case, a seemingly innocuous general ledger, but is actually concealing something else. Something your husband didn't want anyone to find out about. It's like a puzzle, only we don't know how to unlock it."

Mallory raised a hand. "Please, let's not call him my husband or my ex. I have a name for him, but I can't say it in front of Ellie."

"Oh, I've heard worse," Ellie said. "Believe me. And right now, I could probably go one better than what you're thinking."

"For now, let's refer to him as Blake." Mallory crossed her arms forcefully over her chest. She didn't think she could ever feel this much hate for one person. "So what do we do now?"

"That's where you come in," Max said. "With whatever knowledge you have of Blake, together with your forensic accounting background, you may be able to decipher what the steganography is hiding."

Mallory didn't know what they were talking about, but it appeared they were counting on her for the next move. This family she'd once been close to was willing to help her, despite the danger. She closed her eyes for a moment and felt a sense of strength she hadn't felt in too long. Maybe it was the Ramirez family in the room, willing to help. Maybe she'd had enough. Running scared wasn't going to save Justine. Right now, her daughter needed her to be strong. She sat up straighter. "I'm ready. What do I need to do?"

"For now, let's get you and Justine packed and out of here," Rafe said.

"Do you think they'll find us?" Mallory looked at the kitchen door.

"We're going to take every precaution so that doesn't happen. But the first encryption was government-grade. For that reason, we don't think getting the authorities involved is safe. So, we need to be super cautious, particularly since we have no idea who's involved. For now, we'll keep it among the family." Rafe nodded toward his aunt.

"My sister Claudia's kids are in law enforcement in Manhattan. We can trust them." Ellie put her hand on Mallory's shoulder.

"We contacted them and had them check the area." Max put his cup down and stepped up to the table. "At this point, there's nothing suspicious or out of the ordinary in Hollow Lake or the surrounding area. But these guys are smart, and it's only a matter of time before they figure out Blake purchased a Tesla, and you drove it off the lot."

"When they do figure it out, we do not want to be in the same town with that vehicle," Rafe said. "And to hedge our bets, Zack contacted Chip, the owner of the garage, and told him if anyone asks, they found the car vacant on the side of the road."

"Where will we go?"

"From what you told Rafe, there are men at your father's office. He moved to Rochester, correct?" Max asked.

Mallory nodded.

Rafe took Mallory's hands in his. "Well that's west of here, so we'll be heading north. First, we'll drop Ellie and Justine at our *Tía* Claudia's house. Then you and I will head farther north to Zack's lake house."

"I'm not dropping Justine off with anyone. Sorry." Mallory pulled her hands away.

Rafe raised his eyebrow. "Let's go into the living room and talk."

"I don't need a conversation. Justine comes with me, or I'm not going anywhere. And that's final."

"Mallory." Rafe's voice was firm. "We know what we're talking about. And if you want to keep your daughter alive, this is how it has to be done." Rafe placed his hands on her shoulders and put his face inches from hers, forcing her to look at him. "Are we good?"

There was a long silence, and Mallory lowered her gaze. "Yeah," she finally said, but down deep, where Justine was concerned, regardless of what Rafe said, she would make the final decision.

Chapter Ten

Rafe turned on his blinker and took the Saratoga Springs exit. They were ten minutes out from *Tía* Claudia's house.

"You're sure your aunt is expecting us at this time of night?" Mallory bit her lower lip.

"Yes. Everything's fine." Rafe put his hand over hers to still the nervous tapping. "Really, we got this."

"I'm anxious about leaving Justine."

"Staying with my aunts is the best alternative. *Tía* Claudia's sons, Jack and Andres, were able to get emergency leave from the NYPD. They'll be here in a few hours. Don't worry. They'll make sure Justine is safe."

Mallory pulled her hand away and shifted in her seat.

Sensing she was upset at having involved his relatives, there was no need to stress Mallory any further by telling her there were other family members helping.

Given the time pressure and the way in which Blake encrypted his files, the Ramirez brothers needed reinforcements. Even now, Rafe knew Zack was on his mobile with Ellie's kids, Carlos, Javier, and Marisa, who owned a small software development company and had provided many of the apps RMZ Digital Fortress used. Max decided to ask them to look into the encryption. The more eyes on this, the better.

"It's not that much farther." Rafe kept his focus ahead, following closely behind Max's BMW. With its hairpin turns, the two-lane back road was nearly impossible to navigate at night unless, like the Ramirez brothers, you practically grew up here, driving this road thousands of times. Only long-time residents ventured on this road at night. Everyone else took the highway. By taking the back roads, they hoped to arrive at *Tía* Claudia's house completely undetected.

Twenty minutes later, Rafe pulled into the driveway of his aunt's home. He put the car in Park and turned off the ignition. The living room lights went on, showcasing a sleek structure of wood and glass. The large front door opened, and there stood *Tía* Claudia in her white silk robe. Her long black hair cascaded over her shoulders. The youngest of his mother's sisters, she was in her late fifties, a statuesque figure with carved features and a Roman nose.

"You made it. I was beginning to worry. *Ven aca.*" Claudia held her arms out.

Ellie was the first to climb the four wide steps to the front door, embracing her sister.

"*Ay mija*, you must be exhausted," Claudia said.

Max and Zack followed with hugs for their aunt, while Rafe picked up a sleeping Justine from the back seat. He wrapped her in a blanket, shifted her to his left arm, and put his right arm around Mallory's shoulder. He leaned in and whispered, "It's going to be okay." He pulled her in close.

"*Hola, Tía Claudia.*" Despite their reason for being here, he smiled. As a child, she always made him feel safe and loved.

"*Ay, pobrecita.* The poor little girl. Come, come. Hurry." She planted a kiss on Rafe's cheek. "Put her in the first bedroom, second floor. She and her mother can sleep there." Claudia embraced Mallory. "Welcome to my home. Please, please come in. I'm so sorry for your troubles."

"Thank you," Mallory said.

Rafe stepped into the large open living room and smiled. Claudia's husband, Gene, an architect, had died suddenly five years ago. He'd been so young. It had shaken the family to its core. He'd built this home for Claudia as a wedding present. It had been an homage to his architectural inspiration, Frank Lloyd

Wright. The open plan, low lines, the vast expanse of glass, natural woods, and muted tones gave the home a feeling of being one with the nature surrounding it. It sat ringed by woods, giving the impression it was part of the hillside.

"Okay. It's late," Claudia said in a soft voice. "I'm glad you're all safe. If you're hungry or thirsty, you know where the kitchen is. Help yourself. I'm going to bed, and we'll talk in the morning." Claudia locked arms with her sister. "*Vamos a dormir*, Ellie." And the two women marched through the living room toward the back of the house, where the primary bedroom was located.

Rafe knew no matter how tired his aunts were, they were going to grab a whiskey and talk. And this time, there was a lot to say.

"Okay then. Everyone knows where they're headed?" Max asked.

The cousins had spent many summer vacations and holidays at their *Tía* Claudia's house with its eight bedrooms. Over the years, they'd each unofficially claimed a room. And now as adults, whenever they visited, they stuck to the room they'd chosen when they were kids.

"Come on, Mallory, I'll show you where you're sleeping."

"I'll get the bags," Zack offered.

They climbed the suspended staircase to the second level and headed toward the bedroom on their immediate left. Rafe pressed a button on the wall, and the recessed lights along the perimeter of the room gave a soft glow to the muted tones in the room. With the press of another button, curtain sheers slid across the wall of glass, providing privacy. On the opposite wall, the queen-size bed held several pillows and a matching duvet in various shades of yellow and eggplant.

Mallory pulled the covers back, and Rafe carefully laid Justine in the bed.

"Mommy?"

"Yes, Punkie?"

"Where are we?" Her voice was sleepy.

"We're visiting Rafe's aunt."

Justine rubbed at her eyes. "Ellie?"

Rafe shook his head. In the last seventy-two hours, Mallory and her daughter had slept in three different places. No wonder Justine was confused. She'd gone to bed in Ellie's house, and in the middle of the night, she found herself in a different town, in a different bed.

The soft light reflected Mallory's anguish, and Rafe stared as she nervously played with the pendant around her neck. The only consolation was that they were doing this for Justine's safety.

"Sleep, my little Punkie." Mallory brushed a lock of hair from Justine's forehead, leaned in, and kissed her on the cheek.

Justine yawned and stretched. "Goodnight, Mommy. Goodnight, Rafe."

The corners of his mouth lifted into a smile. In such a short time, this little girl had grown on him, and he would do everything in his power to make sure she stayed safe. "Come on," Rafe whispered. "She's fine. She's asleep already." He led Mallory out of the room, turning off the lights and silently closing the door.

They headed down the stairs.

Like the rest of the house, the kitchen area was sleek in design. Rafe tapped a button, and again, recessed lighting around the perimeters of the room glowed. "Want something to drink?" Rafe asked.

Mallory sat on a stool at the stone-topped island that separated the kitchen from the dining room. "I need something to calm my nerves. Uh…does your aunt have any herbal tea?"

"Yeah, I'm pretty sure you'll find that in this house." With a gentle push, the pantry door slid open, and Rafe walked into a spacious room with shelving on three walls filled with glass containers holding pasta, oats, rice, and dozens of other non-perishable goods. On the middle shelf to his left, he found the coffees and teas. "What's your pleasure?" he called from inside. "Chamomile, lavender, lemon balm, or passion flower?"

"I'll have the chamomile. Thanks."

He reappeared, putting the small canister of loose tea on the stone countertop. He filled the kettle with water and placed it on one of the burners. "I didn't take you for a tea drinker. I've only ever seen you drink coffee." He opened the cabinet above the stove and pulled out a transparent teapot.

"The last thing I need right now is caffeine. I've enough nervous energy to light up an entire city. I think it's better if I stay alert but calm."

Rafe filled the filter chamber with tea leaves. He turned to find Mallory's eyes wet with tears. He went around to the other side of the kitchen island and gently held her shoulders. "Listen to me, please. You've made it this far. None of us will let anything happen. *I* won't let anything happen." His voice was forceful, but his hands were gentle as he placed them on either side of her face. "Look at me. Mallory. I promise you. Justine will be safe. I'll do whatever it takes to make sure of that." He leaned in, pressed his lips to her forehead, and whispered, "I promise." He breathed her in and kissed her temple, then her cheek, then softly pressed his lips against hers. When she parted her lips slightly, it was all the invitation he needed, and he deepened the kiss. Sliding his arms around her, he lifted her from the stool until they were pressed against each other, and his hands were wrapped around her waist, pulling her in even closer. When Mallory sighed, he was lost to her.

At the unexpected blast of the kettle's whistle, Mallory jumped back.

Rafe rubbed at his jaw. "Sorry," he half muttered to himself. He walked back around the island and yanked the kettle off the stove. After all these years, his desire for her hadn't lessened, but the timing and circumstances were all wrong. Mallory's cheeks were flushed, and he sensed she, too, wished the timing were different. He poured the boiling water into the teapot.

"Are you going to join me?"

Rafe shrugged. "I'm in the mood for something…a little stronger." He went into the pantry, pulled out a bottle of bourbon, and poured himself a thumb full. He silently raised his glass in a mock salute, then drained it. He lifted the bottle to pour himself another shot but thought better of it. After placing the bottle back on the counter, he walked toward the glass wall on the dining room's south side and pushed back the curtain an inch. In the daylight hours, the view was spectacular, looking out over the valley and the lake beyond. Rafe sighed and moved over to the west wall, again parting the curtain ever so slightly. The full moon amplified the eeriness of the surrounding forest.

"Looking for something in particular?"

"Nah, just checking," Rafe said and turned to face her.

"You want to tell me what's going on?" Mallory's voice was low. "You want to tell me why the hell we're acting almost normal? That kiss? Drinking tea and bourbon? And now, you're casually looking out the window as if everything is fine. You and I both know nothing about this situation is normal. When we left Ellie's, you promised to tell me when we got here what happens next. I've been patient, but time's up. Please, Rafe. I can tell there's something you're not saying. Stop trying to protect me."

Rafe put his hands in his pockets and let out a sigh. "My cousins Jack and Andres did some checking and called in some favors with people they know in Rochester. From the intel they got, there are men still hanging around your father's place of business and his home."

Mallory gasped and let out a sob. "My father's home?"

Rafe rushed to her and held her hands. "I'm not finished. My cousins' friends are watching both places. Making sure nothing happens to him." The tears flooding Mallory's eyes tore at him. He had to help her end this nightmare.

"We can't waste any more time. I need to see that laptop." Mallory pushed Rafe away and paced.

"You will."

"No. I mean now." She slapped a hand on the counter.

Rafe shook his head. "It's not possible. At this moment, Max is working with Marisa, Carlos, and Javier, trying to clone the laptop."

"Ellie's kids are involved, too? Why?"

"When Zack told you it was government-grade encryption, he wasn't using the term lightly. It's going to take all of us to try and figure this out. They want to run a couple of newly developed apps that may get us past the fake wall. But they needed to clone it first. We can't take any chances. You were able to try hundreds of password combinations in order to log into the laptop. But now we're at the encryption wall, and there may be a limit to how many times you can put in a wrong password before it either sends out a signal or permanently shuts down."

"You should have told me that in the first place. You've been holding back a lot of information tonight. I don't like it."

"It's complicated." Rafe rubbed the back of his neck. "Can you please stop pacing and sit, and I'll explain?"

Mallory raised an eyebrow. "All right." She sat on the edge of the stool. "Start talking."

Rafe told her about the software company his cousins owned. Over the last two years, they'd helped RMZ develop proprietary apps, keeping them ahead of the competition. Tonight, they were using a new software that would hopefully clone the computer remotely and then try to get past the encryption.

"What happens if it doesn't work?" Mallory asked.

"Well, that was plan B. If it doesn't work, we'll have to go back to the original plan, which is using your forensic expertise. We'll know in the morning."

It was nearly midnight, and Mallory was past exhausted. Her body and mind felt numb. Stealing away from Hollow Lake in the middle of the night, coupled with the flood of information from Rafe and his brothers, seemed to have shut down her ability to feel anything. Even fear.

As exhausted as she was, she knew she wouldn't be able to sleep until she found a way to contact her father and reassure herself that he truly was safe. She trusted that Rafe's cousins, Jack and Andres, were looking out for him, but she had to be certain.

A year ago, desperate to see the only family she had, she secretly booked a flight to Rochester during the same week Blake would be away on business. While waiting to board, Blake unexpectedly appeared at the gate, and instead of going into a tirade, he smiled and kissed her on the cheek. He picked up Justine and hugged her, and for one foolish moment, she thought he would board the plane with them. His smile broadened, and in a calm voice, he said, "Listen, Mal, if you need to see your father that badly, go. But you're leaving Justine with me."

His words hit her harder than a smack across the face. There was no mistaking the underlying threat. He had the money and the connections to take Justine away from her. And that's when she created a way to get in touch with her father without Blake knowing.

"Rafe, I need to reach out to my dad."

"How? Is that even wise?"

"I have a special way. All I need is a computer. Surely, your aunt has one." Mallory wasn't about to let anyone stop her. She needed to know her father was okay. "Look, when that bastard of a husband wouldn't let me visit my father or let him come see me, I created a secret email account at the local library."

Rafe scoffed. "Well, that's hardly safe."

"You have another idea?" Her voice was rising.

"Come on, Mallory, keep it down." Rafe shoved his hands in his pockets. "Let me think."

Less than a minute later, Rafe grabbed Mallory's hand, took her out of the kitchen, and past the floating staircase to the back of the house. A small hallway led to two rooms, one on either side. Rafe put an index finger over his lips in the universal sign for quiet. Then he mouthed the word *aunts* and pointed to the closed door.

Across the hall from where his aunts slept, he opened the door to a home office with built-in bookcases and another wall of glass looking out toward the front walkway of the house. The left side of the room held a built-in desk with an open laptop.

Rafe pulled out the chair and sat at the desk. Mallory watched as his fingers flew across the keyboard. Several screens popped up and then disappeared. The screen went black, and green fluorescent numbers and letters wrote themselves onto the screen.

Screen after screen popped up and then disappeared. It was taking too long, and she was about to say something when he stood and, with a wave of his hand, indicated she should sit.

She gave him a questioning look, wondering what he'd done.

He whispered, "I created a VPN."

"A what?"

Rafe put his hand up. "Shhh. A virtual private network. It encrypts your internet connection and hides your IP address. Makes it so you can't be traced. I'll give you some privacy. I'll be back in a few."

Mallory sat, heard the door close, and stared at the screen.

What would she say? She bit the inside of her cheek, thinking of what to write. "Don't think. Just do it." She had to know if he was okay. With her knee bouncing under the table, she logged on to her account and thought of how to word the message. Not knowing whether the people looking for her had the capabilities to break through the encryption Rafe set up, she purposefully kept the message almost indecipherable.

Dear All Care Printing—
Punkie and I we are needing invitations of five.
Boxes of blue if you think that will work. Please use box letters, okay? Nothing flashy, cause we love plain. If there's a problem, you can provide a different option.
Thanks, M. Kane.

The note would appear strange to anyone but her father, who excelled at puzzles. The fifth word in each sentence, when put together, would reveal the message-*Are you okay? Love you.* The answer would tell her if anyone was still watching him and waiting for her. Using her maiden name would get him to read the message and know it was from her.

Mallory re-read the email one more time and then hit Send. She cleared the cache and was closing the browser when she felt a hand on her shoulder. Her heart sped, and she stiffened.

"Sorry. Did I scare you?" Rafe whispered, his breath sweet and warm.

Mallory turned and looked up at him. "If near heart failure counts, then yes, you scared me. I didn't even hear you come in," she said in a whisper. The constant fear of being found by the men who were after the hard drive was taking its toll.

"You should go to bed. If my cousins can't break through, then we'll have a long drive tomorrow," Rafe said.

Mallory rose and reached for his hand. A tingling sensation shot through her, and even though she knew it would be reckless, she wanted to be with him tonight.

"You go ahead. I want to double-check that the cache is fully cleared." He gently squeezed her hand before sitting at the computer.

"Rafe?"

"Yeah?"

"How much time do you think we have before they find us?"

He turned, and their gazes locked. "Let's not think about that now."

Mallory had no doubt Rafe would do whatever it took to protect them all. But she sensed there was something he wasn't saying, and that scared her more than anything.

Chapter Eleven

"Good morning, everyone." Rafe kissed both his aunts as he entered the kitchen.

"What about me?" Justine said, dropping a chocolate chip onto a half-cooked pancake in the pan.

Rafe patted her on the head and kissed her forehead.

"We're making pancakes. And they're going to be delicious," Justine said.

Rafe wiped some batter from Justine's cheeks. "I have no doubt. And I want to be the first customer."

"Okay." Justine tugged on Claudia's sleeve. "Rafe wants to eat first."

"I bet he does," Claudia smirked. *"Vaya, él es mandón."*

"I am not being bossy. I thought I'd be a test case." Rafe slid into the chair beside Mallory at the dining table and whispered, "We'll leave after we eat." His hand caressed her cheek. "We want to make sure Justine feels at home so she'll be okay when we go."

Mallory nodded her understanding. "Where's Max and Zack?" She poured herself a coffee from the thermal carafe on the table. "Want?"

"Yeah. Thanks." His gaze went to the ceiling. "They're upstairs on the phone with Marisa. Their app didn't work. She and Max are talking through what we'll need to take with us so you can work on getting past the steganographic wall."

"Hey, Mommy, look. I made a cow." Justine giggled. "This one can be for you."

"Ay, que bonita," Claudia said. "You make a fine sous chef." She gave Justine's shoulders a squeeze. "Ellie, *mira.* Look what our little *chiquita* made."

"Excellent. A culinary artist in the making," Ellie exclaimed.

The attention her daughter was receiving from these two women warmed Mallory's heart. This is what she'd hoped for when her daughter was born. A large extended family who would love and care for her. She could only hope that this was what Justine's future would be like. Mallory remembered how confident and content the Ramirez brothers seemed in school. Their many family members filled the bleachers, cheering them on for the school basketball and baseball games. Her own family had always been small. And now it was just her dad and Justine. She had to keep them both safe. They were all she had.

"Mommy, look at my cow."

"That's great, Punkie." But Mallory didn't get up to look. Her mind was on her father. With Rafe's help, she'd checked Claudia's laptop first thing, but still no answer from her dad.

"Mommy, look."

"That's nice, Punkie." Mallory chewed on her bottom lip. What could be keeping her father? He checked his emails as often as most people checked their social media. It didn't matter what time of day. She was certain she would have heard from him by now. His lack of response only managed to allow her mind to paint horrific images that something bad had happened.

"No. Come here and look," Justine urged.

"Okay." Mallory forced a smile and stood, coming around the breakfast bar. She peeked over Justine's shoulder and immediately saw why Justine had been excited. "Wow. That really is a cow. You're an artist, Punkie."

"That she is indeed," Ellie said, mixing more batter in a white bowl.

"Thanks," Justine said, grinning from ear to ear.

Mallory heard the pride in her daughter's voice and couldn't help but note—despite their being on the run—her daughter, surrounded by encouraging people and not the suppressive traits of a maniacal bully, had become noticeably confident.

The sudden chiming sound had Mallory looking for her phone before remembering she'd sent it out west. She looked up to find Rafe fishing his phone from his back pocket.

"I think you got a message." His voice was soft.

"How do you know?" Mallory tilted her head, straining to hear his words over the constant chatter of Justine, Ellie, and Claudia.

"I set my phone up to alert me if an email came in."

Mallory nodded. "Punkie, I have to go check on something. I'll be back soon, and we'll eat all your pancake cows."

"Okay, Mom. This one right here—" she pointed to the one in the pan "—I'm making it special for you."

Mallory couldn't help but genuinely smile. In the middle of all this madness, her five-year-old, who'd been dragged through it all, was still a ball of sunshine—standing on a step stool in a too-big apron, enjoying herself. It was another reminder of why she needed to get into that computer and find out what Blake had hidden.

The home office looked different in daylight. The room featured light gray and soft cream colors against blonde wood. The wall of glass looking out on the walkway was alive now, with the sound of birds flitting between the bushes and trees that lined the intersecting stone paths. The architecture was extraordinary, and she imagined the three families spent many a wonderful holiday here. She yearned for a life like that. If only she could go back and do things differently. She'd missed out on so much. Mallory released a heavy sigh. This was no time to dwell on what wasn't. What couldn't be. She had to focus on getting out of the situation she was in.

Rafe stood at the desk, opened the laptop, and typed a series of keystrokes, and her email popped up. "Have a seat." He pulled out the chair.

Mallory sat and positioned the laptop's cursor over the email from All Care Printing and double-clicked. She leaned forward. She felt the blood drain from her face as she read her father's response.

Hello, Ms. Kane-The item you requested is still out of stock. It's a popular item and people are here waiting for it. They inquire daily.

There's no need to follow up. I'll contact you directly when we have it.

"Look at this." Mallory turned the screen to face Rafe.

He rested his hands on the desk and leaned in.

"What does it mean?" Rafe asked.

"It means you were right. No one has found me because they're camped out at my dad's place, waiting for me to come there. Shit. My poor father."

"Mommy, you said a bad word."

Mallory turned to find Justine in the doorway.

"Why'd you say a bad word? What's wrong with Grandpa?" Justine fiddled with the strings on her apron.

"What are you doing here? I thought you were making pancakes." Mallory deflected with a weak smile.

"They're ready. The aunts told me to come and get you. But what's wrong with Grandpa?"

She didn't want Justine worried. "Nothing's wrong with Grandpa. Remember I told you we couldn't move there yet because of the asbestos?"

"I think so."

"Well, the people who were supposed to help him aren't there yet. So, he's been doing a lot of the work himself. That's all. He's fine, though. Don't worry."

"Can we make him a card?" Justine asked.

"A card?"

"You know, like a get-well card, so he feels better about having to do all that work."

Mallory smiled at Justine's genuine kindness. "That's a great idea," she said, feeling terrible about lying to her daughter.

"Come on, Mommy." Justine rocked against the door jamb. "Let's eat before the cows get cold."

Mallory closed her eyes and tried not to scream because that was the only release that would give her a modicum of satisfaction. "I'll be right there." Her father's email made it crystal clear that he was still being watched, and time was running out.

From Claudia's back deck, Mallory watched Justine and Zack. They were fishing in the lake at the bottom of the hill. Justine seemed so happy, and it was nearly crushing Mallory to leave her, but she had no choice. Rafe's cousin Marisa hadn't been able to break the second encryption. It was now up to Mallory to try and decipher the puzzle. She could almost bear leaving her baby, knowing she was being looked after by Rafe's family.

She pushed the heart pendant up and down her chain, willing herself to stay strong.

"I know it's hard not to worry, but she's in good hands." Rafe handed Mallory her large travel tote, along with a shopping bag. "I packed your things."

Her eyebrow raised. "You didn't have to do that."

Rafe took a step back. "I see that look in your eyes. I'm not him, and I wasn't trying to control you. I wanted to give you extra time with Justine before we left."

Mallory relaxed her face. "Thanks. What's this for?" She held up the shopping bag.

Holding an identical shopping bag, Rafe pulled out a fake beard.

She furrowed her brow.

"Check out yours."

Shrugging the straps of her tote onto her shoulder, she opened the shopping bag to find a blond wig and sunglasses. "Are you serious with this?"

"As serious as a heart attack." Rafe began putting the fake beard on his face.

For a moment, she couldn't find the words. This wasn't a joke, and that scared her more than anything. "I thought you said no one followed us."

"I did say that."

"So...so..." Mallory scoffed, "What's this all about?"

"It's called being safe. We're driving a long distance, and we don't need anyone on our tail." Rafe pointed to the trees on the west side of the house. "You see that mini forest over there?"

Mallory nodded.

"About a mile from here, Jack and Andres left us a car. We can walk through the woods to where it's parked."

"Why didn't they come to the house?" Mallory asked.

"They're doing their surveillance thing at the moment."

Mallory nodded that she understood, but she didn't.

She leaned against the deck railing and turned her head to gaze at her daughter. Her heartbeat ticked up a notch. If she were being honest and took a step back from her life, she would have to admit that the last few days resembled a bad TV movie. Was she doing the right thing?

Blowing out a breath, she rubbed the side of her face, still trying to make sense of it all. "I'm not trying to be difficult. I know how much you and your family are working to protect us. But I don't understand the need for the disguise. I thought your cousin Marisa said we weren't being tracked. And how does she even know that?"

"Marisa's ex-military. She knows a thing or two about trackers and tracing people. So far, she says we're in the clear. But she's as cautious as the rest of us because it involves Blake Stanton."

Mallory's eyes widened.

"Come on. Can you blame her? Or any of us? The family is out in full force on this, and we're not taking any chances. Especially if this goes as high up as we think it does."

It took a moment, but it finally dawned on Mallory why they all insisted she go farther north. How could she have been so dense? It wasn't only about having the quiet time to decipher the code. They wanted her away from the aunts. Sure, the brothers and cousins would look after Justine. But they were also here to make sure nothing happened to Ellie and Claudia. She'd put their lives in danger just as much as her daughter's. The realization hit her in the face like a bucket of ice water. This wasn't a choice. She had to leave. To protect these people. She closed her eyes to keep the tears from spilling.

Rafe's arms were around her before she could pull away, and she didn't want to resist. With his musky scent and his strong arms wrapped around her, it was like coming home. It felt safe.

She allowed herself a moment in his arms before she pushed

back and wiped her face with her hands. "I'll go put this on, and then we're out of here." Her steely determination came from the hatred she felt for Blake Stanton, and she would focus on holding onto that feeling until this bad dream of a life was over.

Chapter Twelve

With their new looks firmly in place, they began walking. Claudia's house was fairly secluded, surrounded by two acres of woods. With a compass in hand, Rafe led them for a little over a mile until they came to a nondescript dark gray SUV parked in a small clearing at the side of a dirt road. "Here's our ride. The fact that they think you might be headed west to Rochester to see your dad and we're going north gives us a little time to figure out what we've got." Rafe hoisted the backpacks with the laptops, his software case, and Mallory's travel bag into the back seat.

"Let's hope," Mallory said, climbing in on the passenger side.

Rafe reached under the driver's seat and pulled out a soft-sided case. Placing it on his lap, he unzipped the case to reveal two burner phones and a set of walkie-talkies. "Take these." He handed Mallory a phone and a battery. "Don't attach the battery unless you have to make a call. And then be quick." He un-strapped the walkie from the case and handed it to her. "Don't turn it on for any reason unless we're separated."

"Rafe, you're scaring me. Do we really need all this? The wigs, a different car, burner phones?"

He noticed the tremble in her hand as she held the walkie. "In a word, yes. We don't take any chances, and we stay safe." Rafe pressed the ignition button. "You ready?"

She chewed on her inner cheek and nodded.

He wanted to tell her it would be all right, to stop worrying. If only he could. In truth, he wasn't exactly confident everything would work out. Not since Zack and Marisa called at seven in the morning with their data mining search results on Blake Stanton's missing plane.

"Okay. We're off." Rafe put the car in gear and pulled out onto the dirt road. His mind stuck on the conversation with his brother and cousin.

It gnawed at Rafe that Zack and Marisa had a more difficult time than usual getting any information on the last flight Blake Stanton had taken. The man seemed to have covered his tracks well, which was in and of itself suspicious. Due to Marisa's unrelenting tenacity, they'd finally managed to get a hit through a backdoor channel and into the private airport's manifest. The document revealed the first names of the other passengers on board. With a little more data mining, they were able to come up with the surnames of the other three passengers on the doomed flight. The information, while startling, didn't come as a big surprise, knowing the circles Blake traveled.

On board was a prominent aide to the head of national security. Oddly, there had been no mention of his name in the news or online as being on the same ill-fated aircraft as Blake Stanton. The aide seemed to have mysteriously disappeared, just like the black box. The other two were executives from the Mason Corporation. The Ramirez brothers were very familiar with the company that had government contracts to manufacture long-range missiles. It was a passenger manifest that reeked of possible unsavory dealings. This new revelation put the family on high alert.

The idea of keeping all this information from Mallory seemed wrong. She had a right to know. But Max and Zack thought she had enough to worry about. They needed her to focus on getting the information from the laptop.

"You've been awfully quiet for the last half hour. What are you thinking?" Rafe asked.

Mallory sighed. "I miss my daughter. And I'm worried about her." She faced him. "I know she's in good hands, but I still miss her. I can't help it. I'm a mother."

The fake beard was itchy, and he scratched the side of his face. "Look, I've never been a parent, but I know how worried my mother was when they sent me to prison. It almost broke her. The only consolation was that she lived long enough to see me released." The words had simply tumbled out. That part of his life he didn't share with anyone but his family. What possessed him to tell her now? To make her feel better? It no longer mattered. The words couldn't be taken back. The only sound was the tires slapping against the road. Keeping his gaze straight ahead, he waited for her response.

"Are you joking?"

The tone of her voice cut him. Instead of being offended, he let out a wry, single syllable laugh. "I wish I were. But I'm as serious as a judge's gavel."

"What did you do?"

Now her tone infuriated him. The question hit him square in the chest. It told him that she didn't really know him if she could believe he'd done something to deserve prison time. It felt like all the air in the car was sucked right out. "Mallory, I know it's been years since we've seen each other. But do you honestly believe that I could commit a crime for which I would have to go to prison?"

"I don't know what to think." She threw up her hands. "I only know what you tell me, and this is the first I'm hearing of it."

"Well," Rafe scoffed, "I thought you should know. I mean, we are spending all this time together. Until now, it's not like we've had much time to get reacquainted. We've been dealing with your issues."

"Exactly. My issues. And my issues are because I was married to an awful human being, who I'm sure committed enough crimes to put *him* away for years. I'm sure that's what's in that laptop. His crimes and anyone who colluded with him. And that's who's after me." Mallory hit the passenger window with the side of her hand. "So, forgive me if I'm a little curious. If I'm asking what in the world they put *you* away for. Being involved with one criminal this lifetime is quite enough. Thank you very much." She let out a huff.

"I was framed." Rafe delivered the words in a matter-of-fact way. There wasn't a hint of defensiveness in his voice. He was done defending himself.

"You going to tell me what happened?"

He heard the tremble in her voice and hated that he scared her.

"It's complicated."

"So, *un*-complicate it."

What the hell? He drew in a sharp breath. He didn't expect to be on trial. Not again. He shifted in the driver's seat, working to tamp down a sense of rage coupled with injustice. He'd volunteered the information, and now she was grilling him. He hadn't expected that from Mallory. He understood how wounded she was by her marriage, but he was the wrong target. She shouldn't be on the attack with him. "You wouldn't understand."

"Rafe—"

Silence followed. He waited for her to say something more, but nothing came. The unspoken questions hung in the air. What happened? Who did it, if you didn't? Why were you the target? The same questions he and his brothers had asked dozens and dozens of times. Each time, coming up empty. No matter how many leads they chased. The fact that he'd been cleared wasn't a true vindication, not without finding the person or people who framed him. Without that, he didn't think he could ever be free. Without that, living a normal life was out of the question. He would forever be looking over his shoulder. So he knew exactly how Mallory felt. He also knew regardless of his feelings for her, he couldn't act on them. There was no future for them. Once this was behind them, she'd move on. And rightly so. In his current situation, he could offer her nothing but more looking over her shoulder.

Gripping the steering wheel, he quickly glanced in Mallory's direction. Her eyes seemed to bore into him.

"Rafe. I don't want to play games. I don't want to be afraid. And I don't want to pull out of you what you should have already told me. I just want you to tell me what happened."

Rafe let out a slow breath. "It's a long story."

Mallory scoffed. "Start at the beginning. We have a long drive. I'm a captive audience and all ears."

Her sarcasm cut, and Rafe could have done with a bit more

empathy. Whatever he felt, he knew she was hurting, and her life was upside down. This was another hit she clearly wasn't expecting. He let out a long breath. "About twelve years ago, I worked as an IT analyst at a state agency in Albany. You know. All the perks, short working hours, good vacation time, health benefits, and pension. My parents were happy I finally settled down."

Mallory frowned. "What do you mean finally settled down?"

"Oh, man. We've got a lot of catching up to do." Fifteen years was a long time to be out of touch. So much had happened it would be difficult to fill in all the gaps. It almost seemed ludicrous being on the run and telling her his life story after she left Hollow Lake. Well, they did have a long drive, and part of him wanted her to know if only to cement the fact that they had no future.

"I finally stopped messing around and went back to college. I spent my senior year as an exchange student in Prague. I got mixed up with a group of people I should have stayed away from. They were…well…let's just say they didn't like playing by the rules and operated on the outskirts."

"Outskirts of what?" Frustration rang through in her question.

"We skirted around what was legal, what wasn't. Fooled around in the dark web."

"You?" Mallory's voice held astonishment. "You were senior class president. You were the guy who went to the library and the nursing home to help with their computers for free. I mean, you were like a model high schooler."

"Things changed." Rafe gave a one-shoulder shrug. "My dad, you remember him. When you knew him, he was a lawyer."

"Yeah."

"Well, he got bumped up to county judge. And the higher up the judicial system he went, the more play-it-by-the-book he got. I guess I rebelled."

"You got involved in the dark web?" She sucked in a breath. "I'd say that was a bit dissident."

Rafe gave her a sideways glance. He didn't blame Mallory for her flippancy. She'd been lied to by her dead husband, and now he was confessing things he'd never intended for her to hear. "I never thought we'd get caught. But we did and I was sent home."

The memory of what he'd done brought back old feelings of shame. He could feel his cheeks flush. "We pirated movies and games and sold them." The words rushed out. "It was wrong. I knew it was wrong. My father wanted to kill me. I never finished my last year of school. He kicked me out of his house and refused to pay for the education of a criminal. He unceremoniously handed me all my student loans and told me I was on my own."

While neither spoke for several minutes, he could almost sense Mallory's mind whirring with a hundred questions. He checked the highway mile marker. They were another seventy-five miles from Lake Placid, and dark clouds hung low ahead. They seemed to match his mood.

"That can't be the end of the story. What does Prague have to do with being framed and going to prison?"

"I was sent to prison for cyber theft. But that was years later. And I was innocent. But the fact that I had a prior record didn't make my case an easy one." He paused. "I don't like reliving the past, so I'm going to say this fast." He held up a hand while keeping his eyes on the road. "Don't say anything or ask any questions until I'm done."

"Okay."

Rafe glanced at Mallory, who was staring straight at him. He would tell her his story, and either she would believe him or not. His hope was that she still had faith in him. "My first offense, which was really my only offense, was hard on my father. My mother tried talking to him. Tried convincing him I could make amends. That one bad thing shouldn't affect my entire life. But Judge Ramirez is a proud Puerto Rican. Came from nothing, worked his way up, and he expected his sons to do better. So, he wasn't exactly in a forgiving mood."

Rafe shifted uncomfortably in his seat.

"At my father's insistence, I did community service. Became a part of the Big Brothers program. And I got a job in Albany working for an IT company developing software. I was good. It's the one area in life where I've always excelled. You know, all those zeros and ones, the programming, the software. Without an actual degree, I started at the bottom, but it wasn't long before I was promoted. I would come in early and stay late to help fix bugs and develop new software, and before long, I started climbing the ladder."

Rafe stopped talking and put on his blinker, pulling into the exit lane.

"Why'd you stop talking? Are we here already?" Mallory looked around.

"Not yet. Soon. This is the last exit with any food. We can go to a drive-through. Grab a coffee and a sandwich. Then we're about an hour away."

"But why stop at all?" Mallory rubbed at her eyes. "You're confusing the heck out of me. I thought we were in a hurry to get to the lake house. Not to mention we're in the middle of a very heavy conversation. What is going on?"

Rafe pulled off the exit and checked the rearview mirror. "I spotted a dark blue pickup that I think may be following us. If it follows us off the exit, then we may have a problem."

Mallory turned in her seat.

"Please don't do that. Just keep your eyes ahead and act normal."

When they were through the toll, Rafe turned left. He rechecked his mirrors but saw nothing. "We're in the clear."

Mallory sat back. "I don't know how much more of this my heart can take."

"Since we're off the Thruway, let's grab something quick, then be on our way." He looked over at Mallory. Squeezed her thigh. "You going to be okay?"

"I'm not going to lie. I'm feeling uncomfortable on a number of levels."

Her words weren't a surprise, but he'd handle her feelings later. Right now, his gut told him to be on the lookout for a blue pickup.

As they pulled away from the drive-through, Mallory placed both coffees in the center console cup holders. Then reached into the paper bag and retrieved an aluminum-wrapped egg sandwich, pulled back the corners, and handed one to Rafe. "Here."

"Hold on to it for a sec."

Mallory furrowed her brows but didn't comment.

Rafe made a U-turn and drove in the opposite direction from the Thruway. By the looks of it, they were headed into town. "Where are we going?"

"I know a place where we can stop and eat," Rafe said.

"But I thought this was going to be a quick pit stop?"

"It still may be. I'm being cautious. I want to make sure we're in the clear."

Mallory turned and looked out the rear window.

"I wish you'd stay seated and not look back." They drove a few more miles into the center of town. "We'll park for a few minutes." Rafe pulled the SUV into an open-air municipal parking lot containing about a dozen available spaces.

"Why here? And why are we stopping?"

With the SUV now parked, they faced Main Street. "See across the street, over there?"

Mallory turned and looked at the one-story brick structure. "Why in heaven's name are we parked across from a police station?"

He took the sandwich from Mallory and bit into it. "Seems like this is the perfect place to park in case anyone's following us. Let's sit and eat for ten minutes." He chewed and then swallowed. "Looks like rain anyway."

"Are we seriously going to talk about the weather now?" Mallory stared at him. The energy running through her nearly made her body vibrate. She was like a coiled spring about to pop. She needed answers, and Rafe was being way too nonchalant. She wanted—no, she needed to know two things: Why was he sent to prison? And were they really being followed? In no particular order because both unanswered questions were freaking her out.

"I'm not going to discuss the weather with you. I'm going to tell you what happened and why I served time," Rafe said.

When he turned to face her, she saw the fatigue in his eyes and dark shadows under them that weren't there two days ago. With the realization that she was responsible for his exhaustion, and that her situation put his family in peril, the pent-up anger and frustration she'd been feeling dissipated. "I'm listening. No judgment." She held up her hand. "Promise."

"All right. Then I'm going to give it to you straight up, no chaser."

About time, she thought. She had to know what kind of man Rafe had become. But once she knew, would it matter? She was miles away from her daughter. She was carrying a laptop with what she imagined held highly incriminating information. Damaging enough that her life was in danger. All things considered, she was well and truly at his mercy.

Besides, once this ordeal was over, and she hoped like hell that would be soon, she'd be on her way to live with her father and probably never see Rafe again. To her surprise, the thought produced a pang of sadness. It had to be the lack of sleep and too little to eat in the last forty-eight hours. She took a healthy gulp of the coffee, nearly burning her tongue. But she said nothing. She needed to hear what he had to say.

"Where was I?"

"You were moving up in the company," Mallory said.

Rafe nodded. "Yeah. So, as I moved up, I started working on bigger projects. Without getting too technical, I helped create personalized antivirus programs for our clients. I got really good at it until one day, one of my programs was compromised, and I had to figure out why, which led me to find out about cyber-security. It was way more interesting than developing antivirus software. Anyway, as technology got more sophisticated and more companies began using cloud-based systems, there was a need for my services." Rafe took one last bite of his sandwich and wiped his mouth with the paper napkin. "One thing led to the next, and I thought, why should I make money for someone else? Why not start my own business? So I did."

She smiled to herself. Her mother had been wrong about him. He had been ambitious. "So, what happened?"

"I quickly became in demand, and in a few months, there was more business than I could handle. I hired a couple of technicians, some analysts, and a receptionist. It was proving to be a real business." Rafe turned toward her. The glint in his eye was unmistakable.

"I was on top of the world. My father actually invited me to Sunday dinner. My future was bright, and the past was behind me."

She could hear the *but* coming before it was out of his mouth.

"I got too big, too fast. There were too many balls in the air. It was hard to keep track of every project. Next thing I know, the FBI marches into our offices, and I'm arrested for crypto-jacking."

"Crypto-what?" Mallory's brow raised.

Rafe scoffed. "The short answer is stealing someone's cryptocurrency by hijacking their computer."

"And did you?"

Rafe hit the steering wheel with the palm of his hand. "Oh, man! Mallory. Not you, of all people." He clenched his jaw. "Of course I didn't do it. I was set up." He paused and pressed his lips together. "Look, me and my brothers tried to find out for the better part of a year who was behind it and why they would want to frame me."

Mallory didn't understand what he was trying to say. How could he know he was framed when they couldn't find out who framed him? She didn't want to doubt him. But she also didn't want to be with yet another man who was a liar.

Crack!

She jumped at the sound of the unexpected thunder. People on the street began scurrying into the various shops to get out of the sudden driving rain. Across the street, a woman with a purse over her head rushed into the bakery that butted up against the police station. Mallory wondered if the woman led a normal life. Or was she, too, carrying the weight of the world? She sank back into the leather seat, concentrating on the downpour. Within seconds, the rain on the windshield was like an open fire hose on full blast, obliterating any view.

"What are you thinking?" Rafe's voice was hoarse.

She fixed her gaze on his face. She'd ask him the question, and his eyes would tell her everything she needed to know.

"How'd you know you were framed if you can't find out who framed you?"

Rafe nodded. "Logical question. And an easy one to answer. I wasn't the only person accused of the theft. In fact, several other companies around the country, like mine—small, individually owned cybersecurity firms—were in a similar situation."

He didn't look away. His eyes were clear, the kind, honest eyes she remembered.

"The FBI thought we were a ring of hijackers. But we weren't. I mean, for the most part, we'd known of each other's existence. But that was it."

Mallory couldn't believe it. "Were you all arrested?"

Rafe nodded. "Eight of us."

"Oh, my god." Mallory put a hand to her chest. "How did you prove you were innocent?"

"We hired good lawyers. But mostly, it was Max and Zack. They believed in me, and they were unrelenting. They coordinated the investigation. They didn't work for me at the time. But they are my brothers. They wanted to help. And with Zack's legal background and Max's knowledge of securities trading, they were able to poke enough holes in the government's theory so that the case could be reopened on appeal."

The Ramirez brothers always seemed to be there for each other—a quality she admired. Even in high school, they stuck together. As an only child, she didn't have that luxury. She looked at him with a mix of regret and envy. Regret over what they once had and envy of the life he had with his family. "So, what did they find out?"

"There was no physical or cyber evidence that the eight of us collaborated. But they did find a virus in each of our systems. A company in Chicago sent all of us a request for a proposal. It was for a two-million-dollar contract. The information needed to create the proposal was sent on a link. We all downloaded it within days of each other."

"Why would you download a link? Don't they tell you never to do that?" Mallory thought there was a flaw in his thinking.

"This was a reputable company." Rafe made air quotes and took a swallow of his coffee. "The fact is, that link put a worm in our system, and that was it. It siphoned off money from people's accounts. People we didn't even know."

Even though she knew Rafe would never commit a crime, try as she might, it was difficult to wrap her mind around what he was saying.

"The FBI had no case against us. But it took a year to prove it, and I spent that year in prison. The currency was never found. Poof. Into the ether."

Another crack of thunder, and the rain came down harder.

"Looks like we'll sit a bit longer. I don't want to drive in this."

Mallory agreed.

"All this time, my brothers and I have been working to find out who framed me."

"Why, when the charges were dismissed?" Mallory turned her whole body to face him.

"Because I can't rest until my name is cleared. I don't feel I can fully be free if I'm not one hundred percent exonerated." Rafe looked away. "It kills me because breast cancer took my mother before I could prove it. My dad went back to forbidding me in his house. It stings because I lost both of them." Rafe sucked on his teeth. "But my brothers are by my side and committed to helping me find the truth. They're also committed to helping me repair the relationship with my father. But that's for another time." He let out a long, exaggerated exhale. "So. Now you know."

The sadness in his voice pierced her. She remembered his parents well. And if she were being honest, his family was another reason she'd fallen for him—his big, boisterous, loving family. Sunday dinners at his house were a big affair, and she cherished her invitations to join the aunts, uncles, and cousins at a table filled with plates and plates of food. His parents' home was bursting with life, music, and oftentimes spontaneous dancing. But it was that desire never to be far from his family, to never leave Hollow Lake, that eventually split them up. Now, she ached for him, knowing the many hits his life had taken over the last fifteen years. His business troubles, his mother's death, and his father disowning him.

"Looks like the rain's letting up. Maybe we should head out."

Mallory repositioned her seat belt and stared out the passenger window but wasn't really looking. Her mind was otherwise occupied by thoughts of Rafe and her feelings for him. The truth suddenly overwhelmed her. They could never go back to what they had. Her life was nothing but uncontrolled chaos. And when this was over, she'd leave and give him a chance to find someone with a clean slate and no baggage.

Rafe started the car and turned on the wipers. It bothered him that Mallory hadn't said anything after he'd filled in the missing pieces of his life. He wished he knew what she was thinking. But right now, he'd have to put his feelings for her on the back burner. His attention was focused on making sure no one was following them.

The SUV eased out of the parking spot, and Rafe didn't turn on his blinker. He didn't want to signal which way he would turn. He rechecked his rearview mirror. All clear. He headed straight for the Thruway.

Twenty miles from Zack's lake house, they stopped at a local grocery store for provisions. Only three days ago, he'd been at this very store for a coffee on his way back from his fishing vacation. So much had happened since then that it seemed like another lifetime.

Rafe exited the car, pulled a cap from the back seat, and pushed it down over his forehead. "Be sure to keep your sunglasses on. And never look up. There are probably CCTV cameras in the store. Keep your head down and be as quick as you can."

He held the door open for Mallory and pulled the bill of his cap lower. The market was small, with only four aisles and two registers. Rafe pulled a cart from the stack while sizing up the few customers milling about in the aisles. "Honey, I'll get us some steaks for dinner. Why don't you pick up some potatoes and salad stuff." His voice was loud enough to be heard. If anyone were listening, they'd have to assume they were a married couple shopping for dinner.

Rafe's attention was pulled toward a man a bit taller than six feet, with a couple of days' worth of stubble, dark sunglasses, and an expensive Barbour jacket. The loafers on his sockless feet screamed money. Immediately, his antennae went up, and his gaze frantically searched for Mallory. He bit his tongue, trying not to call her name.

The man headed over to the register with a loaf of bread. "Hey, Maureen. How's it going?"

"It'll be better once my shift ends," the thin redhead said.

"I hear that." And they both chuckled.

Rafe took in a deep breath and tried to slow his heart rate. It appeared the guy was a regular. But the incident had him looking over his shoulder for the duration of the time spent in the store. He'd feel safer once they were inside Zack's lake house.

By the time they arrived at the house, Rafe was stiff from the long drive. They climbed the slate path, and under the mat by the large mahogany door was the spare key. It took three trips to get everything into the house, and when Rafe locked the door behind him, he let out a breath. "Well, we made it."

Zack's house was the perfect retreat; over the years, Rafe had come here for long weekends to forget his troubles. He never dreamed he'd be here with Mallory. The large open floor plan seamlessly connected the living, dining, and kitchen areas. The one bedroom was off to the right of the living area. He felt his face sag when he remembered there was only one bedroom.

"What's the matter? Is someone out there?"

Rafe pulled off the fake beard and, took a step down into the living room and stood inches away from her. "No. Sorry, didn't mean to scare you. It's…well, I was so busy trying to get us up here and away from Hollow Lake, I forgot there's only one bedroom."

Mallory opened her mouth, presumably to say something, but Rafe heard no words. Nervous himself, he scratched the back of his neck. Yes, he was still attracted to Mallory, and he wanted her with an intensity he'd never had with any other woman. But now was not the time. Was he crazy for even thinking that? Their lives were in danger, and he needed to get himself in check. "Li-listen…uh…" Rafe stumbled over his words. Nerves getting to him. "I'm going to take the couch and sleep out here. So please don't worry."

Mallory's response was a high-pitched laugh. Rafe thought it bordered on the hysterical.

"Rafe. For goodness' sake. I'm not even sure we're going to get any sleep. We have work to do." Mallory slowly turned three-hundred and sixty degrees. "Why don't you set up the computer and software on the dining room table while I unpack the groceries? Then we'll switch places. I'll start working on the computer, and you can make dinner." She paused and tilted her head. "You do know how to cook?"

Rafe nodded as the heat of embarrassment crept up the sides of his neck. "On it." He walked to the backpack, pulled out the burner phone, put in the battery, and sent a text to Max. Here. The response was swift with a simple thumbs-up emoji. The entire transaction took less than fifteen seconds. He removed the battery and put the phone away.

"Everyone back at *Tía* Claudia's is fine." He looked around and swallowed hard. A strange sensation pricked at the back of his neck. His instincts told him time was running out.

Chapter Thirteen

Forty minutes passed, and Mallory was still staring at the laptop screen. The spreadsheet Zack told her about had dozens and dozens of numerical entries. The sheet was divided into four columns, with the fourth column blank. When she moved her cursor to that column, a pop-up would request a password.

The spreadsheet, with its various numbers and letters, appeared to be a jumbled mess. Nothing related to anything else. That would be so unlike Blake, who was anything but disorganized. This was the steganography she was told about. This was the puzzle she needed to crack in order to get answers.

Cautiously, she scrolled down the sheet, studying each number, looking for a clue. Anything she could start with that would tell her what type of puzzle this was. The answer was here, even if it was proving to be a bigger challenge than she had imagined. Mallory rubbed her temples hoping to release some of the tension crawling up from her shoulders to her neck like a web. There had to be a way to approach this problem.

"Hey, Mallory," Rafe called from the kitchen area. "I know we're not on vacation. But we do have to eat. So, the potatoes are almost ready. I'm going to cook these steaks on the grill."

"Uh-huh." Mallory heard the sliding doors to the deck open but was too engrossed in what was on the screen to look up.

"Be right back," Rafe said.

"Sure." For several minutes, she stared at the screen to see if a pattern would emerge. When that didn't work, she moved her index finger across the trackpad, highlighting each row one by one in an attempt to find similar sequences. Some rows began with letters—others with numbers. So far, she hadn't been able to make sense of the randomness with which the numbers were placed.

When she thought she might have spotted a pattern, she grabbed a notebook from the backpack and drew lines on the paper, mimicking the columns on the screen. She wrote, erased, and wrote again. She continued, hunched over her notebook, adding and subtracting numbers. Nothing seemed to make sense. She ripped the paper from the notebook, crumpled it, and threw it on the floor. She started from the beginning, drawing columns on the notepad, writing, rewriting, and writing again. Each time, she returned to the screen, checking her numbers against those in her notebook. In frustration, she kicked the leg of the table. *Come on, Blake. What's in here? There's something. I know I'm close—* She jumped when she felt hands on her shoulders.

"Sorry. Didn't mean to scare you."

"Rafe!" Mallory put her hand over her heart. "You can't keep coming up behind me like that. I didn't even hear you come in."

He squeezed her shoulders in response. "Sorry, but I made enough noise opening and closing the deck door that I thought you heard." Rafe didn't take his hands away and instead began massaging her shoulders. "You're tense."

"You should be worried if I wasn't."

"Ah, there's that sarcasm I've grown so fond of."

"Really, Rafe, stop." She put her hand over his. "One more squeeze, and I may just fall unconscious." She groaned. "And we need me awake."

Rafe began massaging her upper back, ignoring her. "Simply providing a little relaxation," he said.

It felt delicious, and for a moment, she could imagine him caressing her entire body, but they were treading on dangerous ground, not to mention they had other priorities. She needed to change the course of where this was headed. "I don't know what it is, but when it comes to numbers, especially puzzles, I go into a… I don't even know what to call it. I shut everything else out."

"I believe the phrase you're looking for is *in the zone*." He continued kneading her tight shoulder muscles.

"Huh. Maybe you're right." Mallory looked up at him. "I do tend to shut it all out." She placed her hands over his and stilled his motion. "I'm good. Thanks." She patted his hands and pushed her chair from the table.

"Well, whether you realize it or not, you've been sitting here for two hours."

"Are you serious?" Mallory turned her head and looked up at him. "That can't be."

Rafe smirked. "Told you—in the zone. Anyway, I stopped cooking the steaks as soon as I saw that concentrated look on your face. But it really is time to take a short break and eat something."

Mallory hesitated. So much was riding on her. She rubbed at her eyes, stood, and stretched. "Maybe a short break."

"I didn't want to disturb your papers, so I set us up outside. It's a nice night, and I've put the heat lamp on. We're not facing the road, so I think we'll be safe." Rafe pointed to the deck where the outdoor table was set with plates and silverware.

Reluctantly, Mallory agreed. Between sitting in the car for hours and sitting in front of the computer, her body was feeling the strain. And the aroma of the grilled steak made her stomach rumble. "I suppose I'm hungry after all."

Rafe slid open the deck doors, and Mallory stepped outside. This far north the late summer air was crisp, and the glow of the lights from the houses across the lake reflected in the water. This would be a nice romantic setting if she weren't running for her life. But that was so far from what they were dealing with it made her laugh out loud.

"What's funny?" Rafe asked as he took a seat beside her.

Mallory shook her head. Embarrassed to even be thinking such thoughts. "Nothing. Let's eat." She cut into the steak, took a bite, and moaned. "Amazing." She closed her eyes and chewed.

They ate their meal in silence, and the quiet agreed with her.

When she finished her last bite, Mallory's gaze settled on the lake, and her mind seemed to still of any thoughts.

"Did you get enough to eat?" Rafe asked, invading the void in her mind.

"Yes. Thanks. It was very good. This is the first moment I haven't thought about Blake or that stupid laptop, even for only a few minutes. Being out here is almost soothing. I wish... I wish..." Mallory waved her hand. "Oh, never mind. I have no right to want anything. Not until my life is normal again. Whatever that is."

She paused, thought for a moment, then twisted her mouth and slammed her hand on the table. "Actually," she glared at Rafe, "I know exactly what normal is. Me and Justine living a life without fear, without anyone telling us what to do and how to be." She blew out a heavy breath. "Oh, god. Rafe. Sorry, I didn't mean to direct that at you. You've been nothing but... Without you, I'm not sure Justine and I would still be safe." She put her head in her hands. "Thank you. If I haven't said it before, I'm saying it now. Thank you."

His hand touched her shoulder. "No need to thank me. Besides, we've got a little way to go yet."

"Yes, and I need to get back to it." Mallory groaned. "My body doesn't want to move. What's waiting for me seems insurmountable. I don't know if I can solve it."

"I'm betting on you. I know you'll get there." Rafe began clearing the table.

She pursed her lips and looked at the shining lights in the distance when, out of nowhere, the hint of an idea popped into her mind. "Wait. Don't go. When I was young and couldn't figure out a puzzle, it helped if I talked about the different possibilities for a solution with my dad. It helps if I can talk through what I'm thinking."

In one fluid motion, Rafe put the dishes down, turned his chair, and straddled it, resting his chin on his arms. "I'm all ears."

With that simple movement, once again, Rafe showed her what kind of man he was. Interested. Concerned. Willing to be there and help. He stared and calmly waited for her to speak. While his gaze was intense, she didn't look away. Nothing about

Rafe was threatening, and it was something she'd have to get used to. Not every look was disapproving.

In fact, she could see now there was a distinct difference. Her husband's glare had the purpose of intimidation. Whether it was showing his displeasure over the way she cooked his dinner or his annoyance that Justine was still awake. Or unhappy with the way the house or she looked. Or a million other things.

The difference between Rafe and Blake made it impossible to think of the two of them in the same breath.

When she was dating Rafe, he would always listen to whatever problem she had. At this moment, the kindness on his face reminded her of what they once had. It was more than love; it was mutual caring and concern. That's what she'd been missing all these years. She stared into his eyes.

"You okay?" Rafe asked.

Mallory felt the tears in the back of her throat for what she'd lost, but now was not the time for regrets or should-have-beens. There was work to do. A relationship wasn't in the cards for her. *Focus, Mallory. Focus.*

She cleared her throat. "Okay. So, all this time, we've been thinking about how to crack the password and the second encryption."

"Yeah. So?"

"Well, I don't want this to be a conversation about Blake, but there's something there. I know it."

Rafe reached for her hand, and she forced herself not to pull away.

"Tell me."

"I was thinking that when Blake and I started dating, he would spend hours asking me about my job. At the time, I honestly thought he was interested in what I did. He said understanding how I spent my days made him feel closer to me. He said it was important that, as a couple, we could talk to each other about our work. He reasoned that most couples drift apart when they aren't interested in what the other person does. I found his attentiveness attractive. You know how the beginning of a relationship is? You want to know everything about each other."

Rafe gave a half nod, encouraging her to go on.

"But it was pretty much one-sided."

"How so?" Rafe leaned in.

"After each question about my family or my childhood, he'd always ask about my work. At the time, I was rapidly moving up at the firm and working in some capacity on high-level cases. Blake would specifically ask me about cases involving securities fraud and embezzlement. I was the one forensic accountant at the company who had a thing for puzzles, and it somehow made me faster at solving cases. Maybe because I didn't just look at the numbers, I viewed each case like an intricate maze that needed to be navigated. Puzzles and math are my favorite topics to tackle. Remember how I never let you finish the Sunday crossword, and I always helped you with your calculus homework?"

Rafe smiled. "How could I forget? Sunday afternoons were my favorite, and you won the regional math competition, so why wouldn't I ask you for help with math?"

She wondered if life had ever been that simple and shook away the thought. Dwelling on her past with Rafe wasn't going to get her any closer to solving her problems and keeping her daughter safe. "Anyway, I told him countless stories of my 'brilliance—'" she made air quotes "—and how I discovered hidden money trails and mistakes the perpetrators made." Mallory tilted her head and looked up in thought. "Funny, he'd always ask me how I would do it differently if I wanted to get away with it. And I always had an answer."

Rafe let out a breath. "Oh, man. So, without knowing, you inadvertently taught him how to hide a money trail."

"Exactly." Mallory shuddered. She closed her eyes at the sheer stupidity of her supposed whirlwind romance with Blake when she realized he'd used her from the start. First, to gain the knowledge she had. And later, by holding on to her and Justine as props for photo ops. Always presenting the picture-perfect couple at the latest political fundraiser, charity ball, or any number of events he insisted she attend. Her presence afforded him a respectability he didn't have on his own. "What an idiot I was." She spat out the words.

"Don't be so hard on yourself. You were dealing with a pretty evil guy."

"Well, that's over. I'm going to beat him at his own game." Mallory sat up straight.

"Tell me how."

"I was thinking of all the passwords I've tried on the first encryption—birthdays, anniversaries, graduations—" Mallory ticked each one off on her fingers "—and none of them worked, and they probably won't work on this second encryption. And you know why?"

Rafe shook his head.

She took a moment to answer. When she did, her words were halting. She was still working out how everything fit together. "Blake knew everything, I mean, he knew everything about me. I… I had no…secrets from him. At least not at the beginning. You know?"

"I suppose so." Rafe cocked an eyebrow.

"Well, it was as far from a two-way street as you could get because I knew precious little about Blake or his family. Even after six years together." Mallory scoffed. "After Justine was born, that's when he changed. He got mean. He was gone a lot, and when he was home, he was annoyed and impatient. Nothing I did was right. He became jealous of the time I spent with my father and was even jealous of the time I devoted to our daughter. Stupidly, I attributed his horrific behavior to his heavy workload and the important people he was working for." Mallory gave a wry chuckle and looked toward the sky. "Who was I kidding? I made excuses—one after the next, after the next. For the longest time, I refused to see what was right in front of me. I ignored the news reports of his alleged illegal dealings."

Rafe reached out and put his hand over hers.

Mallory stopped talking. The warmth of his hand made her close her eyes. "Don't," Mallory said. "Let me finish." She abruptly got to her feet and began pacing the deck.

"I'm telling you all of this because, during our marriage, we barely spoke to each other. About anything. Except for one thing, and that was his father's suicide. And that wasn't even a conversation. It was mostly a rant about how his stockbroker father took his own life because of the big bank failure of 2008."

She stopped pacing and looked at Rafe. "You remember when the government bailed out the banks for trillions of dollars?"

"Yeah, I remember." Rafe furrowed his brow. "Why?"

"Well, every couple of months, Blake would get on a jag about it. He'd start off talking about how deceptive banks were, and within minutes, he'd work himself into a fury."

"And what does this have to do with passwords?" Rafe asked.

"I know it sounds crazy, but I think that Blake's father's death in 2008 has something to do with getting past the second encryption and opening up some of these folders."

"You think the password is two, zero, zero, eight?" Rafe said.

"Not all of it, but a piece of it." With that, Mallory marched back into the house and sat in front of the laptop. She picked up the pencil and wrote the year on the tablet. "Think, Mallory, think," she said aloud. Tapping the pencil on the notepad, she tried to come up with more numbers that stood out from her time with Blake.

Rafe was right behind her now, pulling up a chair to the dining table. "Can you remember the date of his suicide?"

Mallory put her head in her hands. "I'm thinking. I usually tried to block him out during his fits—wait. October! Yes. His father died in October because I love that time of year, and Blake always made me feel bad for being happy in the fall." She wrote the number ten next to the year.

"Can you remember anything else?"

Mallory shook her head.

"Let's try what you have," Rafe said.

Mallory took a deep breath. "I'm afraid. Zack said we only get a few tries before the computer either sends up a signal or we are permanently locked out."

Rafe bit his lower lip. "We have to start somewhere."

"Okay. Here goes." She leaned forward, studying the spreadsheet on the desktop. She clicked on the first row in the fourth column, and a pop-up box appeared requesting a password. Carefully, she typed in 102008 and hit Enter. Nothing. Perspiration began to form on her upper lip.

"I really hoped that would work. Too much to ask for." Mallory slumped back in her chair.

"Wait." Rafe pointed to the screen. "Try not typing in the whole year."

"Huh?"

"Try 1008," Rafe said.

Mallory took another breath and typed in the numbers. When she hit Enter again, nothing happened. She could feel more sweat collecting at the base of her neck. She had no idea how many times they could type in a wrong password before they were locked out. They needed to be cautious. "We have a month and a year. We've got to be missing the date. I don't know when he died. If only we could try all 31 days of the month of October." Mallory kept her fingers hovered above the keyboard.

"Yeah. If only," Rafe said. "Can you think of any possible date that would make sense?"

Mallory laid her head on the table. "I hate him. I hate him. I hate him." Mallory sat up and looked at Rafe. "His cruelness lives on." She took in a breath. "So. What would an evil person like him do?"

"You're scaring me. You have a strange look on your face."

"Because I think I've finally beaten him at his own game. If I were Blake Stanton, and I didn't want to create an obvious password like the exact date of my father's suicide, but I still wanted a reminder, what date would I choose?"

Rafe pursed his lips. "I'm clueless. You tell me."

"Halloween, of course." Mallory laughed, then quickly typed in the number 10312008. She expected nothing to happen when she hit Enter. To her surprise, up popped a swirling rainbow-colored ball. In seconds, the spreadsheet transitioned into a checkerboard pattern that disappeared, revealing three folders.

"That worked!" Rafe slapped his hand against his thigh.

"Hmm. Let's not pop the champagne yet. I don't know what I was expecting, but I have no idea what this is." Mallory ran her index finger over the trackpad. "I guess I'll start by opening each folder and see what I find."

Two more hours passed while Rafe watched Mallory at the computer. It seemed as if her expression never changed, and her eyes never left the screen as she opened each folder, one after the other. He did what he could, offering her something to drink and eat. But she refused each time, barely noticing him. Her laser concentration never left the screen.

Rafe wasn't sure what he expected, but he didn't think it would take this long to find something that would give them a clue. The nervous energy pulsing through his body had him pacing the length of the living room. Twenty steps in one direction and then twenty steps back. Each time he reached one wall, he checked the time on his phone.

The pacing wasn't helping; all it managed to do was leave Rafe alone with his thoughts. Thoughts that were becoming dimmer by the moment. He could no longer deny that he'd become attached to Mallory and to Justine. His feelings for Mallory weren't just rekindled; they were on fire. Regardless of the mess she was in, he wanted to be with her. The whole thing added up to an impossible situation. He couldn't ask her to be with him because he needed to clear his name. Any type of relationship outside of the friend zone was off the table. Besides, he rationalized that when this was over, she was going to live with her father. Sadness enveloped him like a heavy overcoat. He tried pushing through it by pacing from wall to wall faster.

When he couldn't take it another moment, he stopped at the head of the dining table. "Did you find anything?"

"Lots of numbers and letters," Mallory replied without looking up.

"Looks like this is going to take a while," Rafe muttered to himself.

"Uh huh," Mallory said as she scribbled something on a pad.

Once again, he paced. There was nothing else to do. Like a metronome set at a steady pace, he walked back and forth for what seemed like hours, but when he checked his phone, only ten minutes had passed. He didn't know how much longer he could continue to do this. He was either going to pass out from fatigue or lose his mind waiting for Mallory to decipher the spreadsheets.

"I'll be right back," Rafe said on a long breath.

"Where are you going?" Mallory asked, looking up for the first time.

"Outside, check around."

Mallory half stood as if she were ready to bolt. "Is everything okay? Did you hear something?"

"No. No. Nothing's wrong. I'm sorry. I didn't mean to frighten you," Rafe said, walking to the kitchen area. He opened a side drawer and pulled out a flashlight.

"What's that for?"

"Truth is, I'm a little antsy. There doesn't seem to be anything I can do to help you decipher the spreadsheets." Rafe shrugged. "I just want to take a look around. I need to do something."

"Why not rest? You must be exhausted."

"Not yet. I'll rest once I have a look outside."

"You think that's wise?"

Rafe waved the thought away. "If someone were following us, we'd know by now. And if someone were tracking the laptop, Max would have alerted us." At least, that was his sincere hope. While he didn't want to worry her, he also wanted to check the area to ease his own mind.

"All right. But please, don't be long, and don't go far," Mallory said.

"I won't."

"And be careful!"

The look in her eyes and the concern in her voice warmed him. Made him feel wanted. He hadn't felt that in a long time. "I'll be back soon."

The night air held a chill. He zipped his jacket closed and headed toward the wooded area on the side of the house. The tall trees surrounding the property allowed only a sliver of moonlight to reach the path. He pulled the flashlight from his back pocket and let the slender beam of light lead him as he walked a wide perimeter around the cabin. He couldn't see much, so every few feet, he stopped to listen. It was dead quiet, and yet a cold shiver traveled up his spine. He couldn't shake the feeling someone was watching him. Tightening his grip on the flashlight, he pointed it in several directions when a slight rustle in a bush to his right got his attention. Rafe held his breath and slowly walked toward where he'd heard the sound. A twig snapping beneath his own feet echoed in the silent night and stopped him dead in his tracks. Whoever was behind the bush knew he was coming in their direction. The leaves in the bush rustled once more, and he wished he had more than a flashlight in his hands. Inching closer to the sound, he lifted the flashlight above his head, ready to use it as a weapon, when a large buck burst forth, knocking Rafe to the ground as it took off. "Holy mother of..." Rafe's heart was in his mouth.

He lay on the ground for several minutes, trying to catch his breath. Over the years, he'd seen plenty of deer, moose, even bears. And not once had he been this afraid. His teenage years spent at his aunt's house had been filled with dozens of dares by his cousins as they traipsed through the woods at night. But tonight had been different, and until now, he hadn't realized how wound up he was. Mallory, her daughter, and his family were all at risk.

Dusting himself off, he took in a heavy breath and searched for his flashlight. Retrieving it from a nearby fallen log, he picked it up and realized his hand was shaking. It took two more walks around the perimeter of the cabin to still the whooshing sound of blood rushing in his ears.

Before going in, Rafe stood at the front door surveying the area, again pointing the flashlight in several directions. It was a few minutes before he sensed a stillness within himself and around the cabin. Only then was he satisfied they were alone and went inside.

Quietly, he hung his jacket on a nearby hook and bolted the door behind him. "How's it going?" Rafe asked as he raked his hands through his hair.

"I'm still looking," Mallory said.

Rafe saw worry etched in the furrow of her brow.

"Do you need anything? Coffee?"

"God, no. No more caffeine, please." Mallory arched her back and stretched.

"Maybe you should take your own advice and get some sleep," Rafe said.

Mallory shook her head, unconsciously tapping the tip of the pencil on the paper and jiggling her knee up and down. "There's no time. I'll rest when this is over. It shouldn't be much longer. I feel like I'm getting close."

"Really?"

"Yeah." Mallory picked up the pencil and wrote on the pad.

Rafe came closer and put his hand on Mallory's shoulder. "Don't let me keep you. But if you need anything, I'm right here."

"Thanks," Mallory said, and went back to the papers in front of her.

Rafe dug his hands in his back pockets, wishing he could help, but there was nothing for him to do but keep watch over her. It wasn't safe to call Max or Zack. He needed to stay off anyone's radar. He was edgy and bored and needed something to do. Glancing around the one-bedroom house as if it were his first time there, instead of his hundredth, including just a few days ago under very different circumstances, his gaze finally settled on the shelves in the corner. Running his fingers across the books on Zack's shelf, he picked out a mystery, perched himself on the couch and attempted to read. After reading the first paragraph a dozen times, he tossed the paperback onto the coffee table and focused his attention on Mallory.

Hunched over the laptop, she chewed on her lower lip. He smiled, remembering that same look whenever she took a math test. They'd been so in love back then. What would have happened if they'd stayed together? The memory of her soft lips and her small, firm breasts gave him a warm sensation. He wanted her despite all the craziness since she'd stumbled back into his life. He wanted her.

Rafe gave himself a firm mental shake. They had things to take care of right now. She hadn't pushed him away, but she hadn't encouraged him either.

He continued to study her. She looked tired. But she was still as beautiful as ever, and he was as attracted to her now as he'd been all those years ago. Rubbing his eyes with the heels of his hands, he stifled a yawn, willing himself to stay awake. The need to protect her was strong.

Coffee, he thought. Caffeine would keep him awake. He rose from the couch and, as unobtrusively as possible, he made a fresh pot. Rafe paced some more, then finally perched again on the edge of the couch and watched and waited until his eyelids grew heavy and fluttered closed.

"Rafe, I think I found something!"

Chapter Fourteen

"Rafe! Wake up."

Mallory's voice sounded distant, and Rafe realized he'd fallen asleep. He opened his eyes, sat up, and regrouped. He stamped his foot on the ground to rid it of the pins and needles sensation. "What did you find? What time is it?"

"It's three o'clock."

"In the morning?" Rafe wasn't sure how long he was out.

"Rafe? Wake up. Come here. I found something."

He gave a grunt and stood. His legs felt heavy, and he was a bit unsteady on his feet as he walked toward the dining area. Scrubbing a hand over his face, he walked up behind Mallory and squinted at the laptop screen.

Mallory turned toward him. "Turns out my suspicions were correct. Blake paid very close attention to everything I said about my job and how to hide money. He even took it a step further. It's all right here in black and white." She tapped the edge of her pencil on the papers.

Rafe picked up one of the spreadsheets she'd printed out and glanced over the rows of numbers. "Mallory, I'm not an accountant. Hell, you know I wasn't that good at crossword puzzles. Please tell me exactly what you've found. Step by step." Rafe pulled up a chair to the table.

"Sit. I'll show you." Mallory took the paper from his hand.

"Each line represents an account. But the numbers aren't account numbers. They represent something else."

"Something else? They look like numbers and letters to me."

"Stick with me. I'm about to explain. Each one of these initials represents a country: GC is for Grand Cayman, SC is for the Scottish Isles, OK is for Okinawa, and so on."

"How do you know that?" Rafe asked.

"Because these are all places where you can store money offshore."

"But as far as I know, that's not illegal."

"No, it's not. Not unless you're using these accounts to launder money, and that is illegal." Mallory put her pencil down and sat back.

"How can you tell this is a money-laundering scheme?" Rafe asked.

She let out a heavy sigh. "That's where I'm stuck. I can't prove it. There's a missing element. If I'm right, there's a key that opens these folders and shows the next layer of encryption. The key must be the drive. They must be one and the same. And on it is the information that could prove the money has been laundered, where it went, and who benefited. It could put important people behind bars. I'm sure of it."

"How can you be so sure?" Rafe asked.

"Remember, I'm trained to find the one mistake in a million. Look at this account here." Mallory pointed to a line on the spreadsheet. "This account number is eight digits long." She picked up another page. "This account here is five digits long—nothing out of the ordinary. But the account with the eight digits was the longest on any of the pages, so it was easy to spot. As I looked through the sheets, there were other accounts with eight digits. Again, no big deal. Except each of those accounts looked similar in some way, but I couldn't place my finger on exactly how. And when I took a really close look, I realized they all held the same numbers but in a different order."

"I'm totally not following you," Rafe said.

"Look, here. This account is 71228903." Mallory turned the page. "And here, it's 12289037." Using her index finger, she moved further down the page. "And here it's 22890371. And look here—28903712." She turned to Rafe. "What do you see?"

He studied the sheets for several minutes. "They're the same numbers, only each time the first number listed moves to the end of the sequence," Rafe said.

"Exactly. It's too much of a systematic coincidence not to be the same account. I tracked this one account through pages and pages, and each time it appears, the amount decreases from five million to three million two hundred and fifty thousand dollars."

"So that means one million seven hundred and fifty thousand dollars is missing." He stopped to think about it. He was a cybersecurity expert. Not a money-laundering expert. But in his mind, criminals were criminals. In the last ten years, he'd dealt with so many different nefarious schemes in his line of work that he'd learned to think like them. He folded his hands on the table and looked at her.

"What? What are you thinking?"

"Mallory, what you've managed to uncover is amazing. But does it prove anything? To the naked eye, it could appear that whoever owns these accounts simply decided to cash in."

"No." She slammed a hand on the table. "How could it? Look." She pointed to the sheets. "The missing amount appears here in a totally different account. Each time there's a withdrawal from an eight-digit account, the exact amount appears in a different account. That's moving money from one account to another in smaller amounts, so no one knows where it comes from when you buy things like, say, arms to finance a terrorist organization. It's money laundering 101."

"You know this for sure?" Rafe asked.

"No. Not for sure. It's a hunch."

Rafe pushed back from the table. "We can't go on hunches."

"You're right, but it's more like an educated guess. Right now, all I have are a bunch of numbers and initials that I believe are offshore accounts that are part of a money-laundering scheme, with initials that belong to the names of people and corporations. But these files, by themselves, prove nothing. The missing drive is the key that will unlock the whole system. I'm sure of it. Once that's unlocked, we'll know exactly what Blake did that has me and my daughter running for our lives."

Mallory looked drained. Rafe pulled his chair close and took hold of her hands. "You did a great job. You've found out a lot tonight."

"Come on, you and I know the truth," Mallory said. "The men after me aren't going to stop until they get what they want. They probably already have this. What they don't have is the drive that opens the next layer of folders. Those folders will be the most incriminating. That's the evidence. Because I'm positive the next layer names the names."

"We need to find that drive," Rafe said.

"I know you're right, but I have no idea where it could be. I tore my house apart looking for it. When I found the hidden laptop, I thought that was the drive. It's the only thing I could find. Believe me, I looked." Mallory rolled her head from side to side, trying to ease the tension from her shoulders and think.

"I know you did. Or at least you think you did."

Mallory whirled around. "What's that supposed to mean?"

"Please don't get upset." Rafe waved his arm over the spreadsheets. "I only meant that clearly your husband—"

Mallory stamped her foot. "Can we stop calling him that? Please."

"All right," he said quietly. "Look at all the work Blake went through to hide his money-laundering scheme. He would have done the same thing with the hard drive."

"But maybe he had the drive on him when the plane went down," Mallory suggested.

"Maybe." Rafe shrugged. "But not likely. From everything you've told me, he's not the type to be careless. From what we know in those spreadsheets, it looks like he was dealing with some pretty scary people who wouldn't think twice about taking Blake out. I've been up close and personal with men like that in prison. The only thing that keeps you alive when you're dealing with scum like that is an insurance policy. And that drive was Blake's insurance policy. If they're still looking for it, then it's got to be hidden somewhere."

"So where does that leave us?" She blew out a breath and

threw her pencil on the table. "I need a break." She put her hands on her hips, leaned back, and stretched her torso.

"If we can think outside the box for a minute and be as devious as Blake, maybe, just maybe, the key isn't a separate disc, or hard drive, or anything but another puzzle already stored in those folders."

Mallory shook her head. "Honestly, I'm having a hard time wrapping my mind around any of it." She stifled a yawn. "I can't think anymore. I need to close my eyes, only for an hour or two." She raised her arms over her head and gave a long stretch. Her T-shirt rose, exposing the smooth skin of her waist.

Rafe knew he should look away but couldn't. There was no denying he'd like nothing more than to curl up in bed with her and make love. But Mallory needed sleep. They were both running on fumes, and it was affecting her ability to think. He could see the fatigue on her face. Rest was what she needed. Not him or his desires. That would make him as selfish as her dead husband.

"You take the bed. I'll sleep on the couch."

Mallory shook her head. "Don't be silly. You barely fit on the couch. I can sleep there."

"No." He took hold of her hands and felt the jolt of desire. "You've been working nonstop." He put his arm around her shoulder and led her to the bedroom. "Get some rest." He gave her a gentle push over the threshold. "See you soon." He closed the door before he had time for second thoughts.

The couch didn't look half as inviting as the bed in the other room. But that ship wasn't going to dock tonight. Flopping down, he found he was wide awake and frustrated with thoughts of Mallory. A warm sensation flooded his groin, and he shifted his position on the couch and groaned.

Rafe opened his eyes and blinked. It took a few moments for his mind to register where he was. Streaks of sunlight slanted across the wood floor, and he bolted upright and frantically searched the room.

The dining table held the laptop and papers, but no Mallory. He rushed to the bedroom and stopped short at the threshold. In the center of the king-size bed, Mallory slept, fully dressed, curled in a ball. Glancing over to the bedside table, he checked the time on the alarm clock—barely seven in the morning.

They'd slept for four hours. Had he given her enough time to rest? The woman lying in the bed looked peaceful, so at odds with their situation. In the last three days, he hadn't seen a relaxed look on her face. As much as he didn't want to wake her, time was not on their side.

Backing out of the room, he left the door open and began loudly rummaging through the kitchen cabinets, prepping breakfast, in the hopes the noise would wake her and she'd have a moment to herself before coming into the kitchen.

He poured coffee beans into the grinder. The rich cocoa aroma gave him something familiar to hold on to. It reminded him of his mother. This was her morning ritual. God, how he missed her.

Rafe spooned the freshly ground beans into the coffee maker basket and pressed the start button. Absently, he stared at the machine and lost his thoughts in the drip, drip, drip, of the rich brown liquid into the glass carafe.

"Wow. I was out."

Rafe turned to find Mallory rubbing the sleep from her eyes. "You didn't sleep that long. Only about four hours."

"No wonder I feel like a truck ran me over. Then backed up and hit me again for good measure."

"Here. Have some of this." He poured coffee into a mug and placed it on the kitchen island "You'll feel better."

"Thanks." Mallory took the steaming mug in her hands.

"You've been hunched over that laptop for hours, poring over numbers. That might have something to do with how you feel."

"Maybe." Mallory shrugged. "But I think it has more to do with not being able to figure out if we're missing a drive, or a key, or a puzzle or whatever it is we need to open those folders and get the evidence." Mallory sighed and focused on the countertop. "Truth is—I'm a bit distracted. I miss my baby girl." She chewed on her lip. "You think I could speak with her?"

The plaintive tone in her voice hit him in the chest. The look on her face told him she was hurting. While he was empathetic, he couldn't risk having her make a call. "Mallory, I'm sorry. But that's a no-go. We can't take the chance."

"But why?" Her tone was a half plead, half whine.

"It's not safe. But more importantly, we don't want anyone to track Justine or my aunts, and making a call for any length of time could put everyone in jeopardy."

Mallory slammed her mug on the counter. "Okay. What you're telling me is, if I don't find this damn drive or whatever it is we need, we could be stuck here? Or worse, running for the rest of our lives?" She put her hands on her hips. "Oh, hell no!" She stomped over to the sliding glass door, pushed it open, and stepped out onto the deck.

Rafe came up behind her and put his arms around her. He could feel her body shaking. She was crying, and it nearly broke him. "Mallory, I know we can get out of this. I believe in you."

She turned to face him, and the pleading look in her eyes was all he needed. He pulled her tighter and pressed his mouth on her lips, taking her in hungrily. He'd wanted her since they kissed two nights ago. He pressed up against her, and she felt as good as he remembered. His tongue greedily entered her mouth. Her moan was all he needed to put his hands under her T-shirt and cup her breasts. He was breathing heavily and wanted to take her right there when she abruptly pushed him away.

"Please, Rafe. We can't do this."

He dropped his arms and took a step back.

"It's not that I don't want you..." She turned away. "The timing is off. I'm sorry if—"

Rafe put his hand up. "Don't. I get it." He let out a breath. "Look, I'll give you some space. Why don't you shower? I'm going to walk a couple of laps around the perimeter of the house. Get some fresh air. I'll be right outside."

She stepped forward. "I didn't mean to—"

"Really. We're all good. We are. I won't be gone long."

Frustration coursed through her, and Mallory wanted to scream, cry, and throw dishes. Instead, she picked up the burner phone, put the battery in, and pressed the number 1, programmed to call Claudia's house. The phone rang twice before Claudia answered.

"Hi. It's Mallory." She held the mobile phone in a tight grip.

"Is everything all right?" Claudia asked.

"Yes. Yes. I can't be on the phone long. Can I please speak with Justine? Please."

Claudia didn't say another word. There was silence, and Mallory checked the screen on the phone to make sure they were still connected. When she put the phone back to her ear, she heard her daughter's voice.

"Mommy. Mommy. Where are you? When are you coming back?"

Justine didn't sound sad, but her questions still pierced Mallory's heart. "Soon, baby. Soon."

"Mommy, where's Teddy? We can't find him anywhere. I can't sleep without him."

There was a rustling in the background, and Mallory heard Claudia telling Justine to say goodbye. The next thing Mallory knew, the phone went dead. She threw the phone on the bed.

Her world was crashing in on her. She'd alienated Rafe, and her daughter was in a strange place without her and the security of her teddy bear. She sat down on the bed and put her head in her hands. Minutes passed before she knew the only solution was to pull it together and get some answers. Maybe Rafe was right, and the key to everything was still in that laptop.

A fresh start was what she needed, and she'd begin by taking a shower and changing her clothes.

The hot water felt luxurious and was doing the trick in reviving her senses. When she was done, she turned off the taps and wrapped herself in a towel. She felt marginally better. The travel bag Rafe packed was sitting in the corner of the room. When she opened the bag, she smiled. Her clothes were folded in neat piles. A pair of jeans sat on top, followed by her white button-down blouse. She dressed, and before leaving the room, she pulled out her jean jacket from the bottom of the bag, and with it came her daughter's teddy bear. "So that's where you got to. How did you get wrapped up in my jacket?" Then Mallory remembered they'd been playing dress-up with the stuffed animal and Justine put him in Mallory's jacket. In his hurry to pack Mallory's things, Rafe must not have realized that Teddy was still wrapped up in her clothes.

She picked up the scraggly bear and hugged it. She froze when she heard the front door open.

"It's me. I'm back," Rafe called.

"Coming." She walked into the living room holding the teddy bear.

"Where'd you get that?" Rafe asked.

"Accidentally packed with my things."

"Oops. Sorry." Rafe pointed toward the bedroom. "You all done in there?"

Mallory nodded and put the bear on the dining table.

"Okay. I'm going to take a quick shower and then make us something to eat. Are you feeling lucky?"

She raised an eyebrow. "Lucky?"

"I mean, lucky that you'll get what we need from that laptop. Looking for the key within the key, so to speak."

"I'm going to give it my best shot."

Rafe smiled, and Mallory appreciated that he was keeping the atmosphere light. If only things were different.

By mid-afternoon, Mallory still hadn't found the answer. Fatigue threatened to take over, and she pushed away from the table. "I need to stretch. Get the kinks out."

Rafe pulled out a stool from the kitchen island and sat while Mallory walked around the dining table several times. She picked up Justine's teddy bear. The feel of the stuffed animal in her arms gave her the odd sensation of being closer to her daughter, which was where she wanted to be right now—with Justine, living a normal life. Not holed up in a remote lake house working out how to stay alive. This entire situation was all too surreal.

"Want some water?"

Mallory shook her head and continued pacing, squeezing the bear to her chest. She stopped. Eyes closed, she tilted her head toward the ceiling, hugging the bear as if it were her daughter. *Stop it. Wake up. The sooner you find a solution to this mess, the sooner you'll see Justine.*

Pulling out the dining chair with her foot, she slumped back down and wiggled the trackpad, waking the screen with the same spreadsheets. Nothing had changed since she took a stroll around the dining room. She placed the teddy bear on the table next to the laptop, facing her, and gave it a weary grin. "Teddy, you and me. We're going to figure this out."

"Are you talking to me?" Rafe asked. The tired smile on his face told her he was suffering the same anxiety and mental fatigue.

"No. Why don't you rest? You didn't get much sleep last night. I'll give this another go. There's got to be a way in. Right, Teddy?" She patted the bear on the head and froze. "Hold on." Patting the bear on the head again, she leaned forward, examining it more closely. "Rafe, hand me a sharp knife," she said, staring at the stuffed animal as though it would get up and walk away if she took her eyes off it.

"What for?" Rafe inched closer to her.

"Please, just get me a knife." She held out a hand, waiting.

His hesitancy had her slapping a hand on the table in frustration. The stuffed animal fell over. "I think there may be something in Teddy."

"Seriously?"

Mallory made a wriggling give-it-here motion with her hand. "Please. The knife."

Rafe opened the kitchen drawer and handed one over.

The paring knife weighed next to nothing in her hand. The steel of the blade was sharp, and she pointed the tip of the knife directly at the top of the teddy bear's head and drove it straight in.

"Whoa. Hang on, what are you doing?" Rafe was by her side in a second. "What are you doing?" he repeated.

Without raising her head, Mallory looked up at Rafe. "I think the key we're looking for has been right here the entire time."

"You mean inside Justine's stuffed animal?"

"That's exactly what I mean." Mallory pulled the knife out and rotated the handle between her forefinger and her thumb. "It's got to be in here somewhere, and I'm going to find it."

"What makes you so sure?"

A sound between a one-syllable laugh and a scoff escaped her mouth. "I've been so stupid. It was right here the entire time." She shook her head in disgust. "This is the only gift Blake personally bought for Justine. All the rest—birthday, Christmas, Easter Bunny surprises, just-because presents, you name it, every single gift my daughter received was because I made all the purchases. It never occurred to him, not even when she was born, to buy her anything. Except for this stuffed animal right here." She placed the tip of the blade at the center of the worn plaid bowtie around the bear's neck.

"Don't." Rafe sat kitty-corner to Mallory and leaned in close. "Think about it. If, and I'm saying *if* the key to Blake's crimes is hidden in the bear, then we need to carefully dismantle the bear so as not to destroy what we're looking for. If it is a drive, we don't want to damage it."

The white-hot rage inside her was bubbling to the surface. "You don't get it." She looked into Rafe's eyes. "He gave her this as a gift, but the way he made her keep track of it was almost maniacal. If he came home and found she wasn't playing with the bear, he'd ask her to stop what she was doing and go get Teddy." Mallory scoffed. "It was strange. Heck, it was even crazy, but so much of him was strange and crazy. He was a cruel man in so many ways. It got to the point that I made up a game for Justine. When I knew Blake would be home, which thankfully, as the years went by, became less frequent, I would tell her to find Teddy because he, too, wanted to say hi to Daddy. How messed up is that?" Mallory put an elbow on the table and rested her forehead in the palm of her hand. She wanted to go back in time and spare Justine from all the madness. She wanted to be stronger for her daughter. At that moment, she made a mental vow if she ever got out of this, she would be a better mother. She would protect her daughter at all costs, and most importantly, she'd never let another man run their lives.

An overwhelming urge surged through her. She wanted to stab the stuffed animal in the chest repeatedly until there was nothing left but shreds. Looking down at her hand, she could see her grip on the knife was tight enough to turn her knuckles white. She dropped it and pushed away from the table. "Okay, Rafe. You do it."

Rafe pushed his chair in closer and turned the bear to face him. Using his right hand, he squeezed each ear and all four paws. "Feels crinkly. Like old stuffing."

Mallory nodded. "Are you prepping for surgery, or are you going to get down to business?"

"Here goes." Laying the bear on its side, Rafe reached for the knife and began ripping the side seams out, one by one. Some stitches were harder to remove than others. But he took his time, forcing himself to be patient, not wanting to take any chances that would damage whatever it was they were meant not to find. Maybe it was the missing key. Maybe it was something else. Maybe it was nothing at all.

"Are you really going to take out one stitch at a time?" In a rhythmic beat, she tapped the pencil on the table.

Rafe stopped and stared at her hand. "What are you doing, beating out Morse code?"

"Oh." She put the pencil down. "Sorry. Nervous."

"In answer to your question. Yes. I'm not deliberately trying to drive you mad by going this slow. We need to do this right. No mistakes."

"Okay." Mallory stood. "I'll go make some coffee. You want some?"

"Uh-uh." He went back to ripping each seam until the furry material could be pushed away, revealing some sort of off-white polyester fiber fill. The stuffing that once made up the shape of a child's teddy bear was now a pile of loose strands and small cotton bags. Rafe first examined the cotton bags located where the paws would have been. "What have we here?" He turned toward the kitchen. "Mallory, there's a flashlight in the top right-hand drawer by the stove. Would you please hand it to me?"

"Sure." Mallory pulled open the drawer and fished out the flashlight, handing it over to Rafe.

With the flashlight in one hand, he separated one of the cotton bags with the knife from the rest of the pile of what was once a teddy bear. Shining the light, he leaned in closer.

"What do you see?" Mallory asked.

He turned to find her looking over his shoulder. "Not sure. Could be nothing. But we're about to find out." He handed Mallory the flashlight. "Shine it on the bag."

Carefully slitting the bag open, dozens of small plastic pellets scattered over the table.

"What in the world are those?" Mallory asked.

"Nothing." Rafe scooped the pellets back into one pile. "Looks like they were used to add weight to the bear's paws. I mean, they aren't anything that will help us."

"Yes, but there are four bags. Try them all."

One by one, he cut through the bags with the same result. Each as innocuous as the last.

Mallory let out a heavy sigh.

"Let's not give up yet. We still have the filling." Cautiously pressing against every single square inch of the fiber filling, Rafe's finger stopped at the center of where the bear's belly had been. He pulled away the individual layers of fibers until he found what he was looking for—a silver nano drive the size of a small child's thumbnail. "And there we have it." His voice was calm yet flooded with expectancy.

"What is that?"

"I think we've found what Blake was hiding. Whoever is after you needs the laptop, but they also need this." Rafe held up the thumb drive. "This, my dear, I believe is the key to the information on the laptop."

Chapter Fifteen

"Give me the drive. I'll put it in." Mallory's fingers nearly trembled with excitement.

"Wait! Don't do that." Rafe closed his hand over the drive. "We don't know what this is. It could be something that wipes out the entire computer." He walked over to his backpack. "Max gave me this laptop, just in case. We'll make a duplicate file of what you've already uncovered. We don't want to lose what we have."

Mallory was hesitant. Her fingers itched to put the drive in now and not wait. "How long do you think it will take?" She watched as Rafe began setting up another laptop and USB transfer cables.

"We can't use the internet, which would be the fastest. So, unfortunately, this is going to take a while." Rafe plugged the cables into a connecting box. "I know you don't want to wait, but better safe than sorry. There's too much on the line."

Mallory knew he was right. They'd come this far, and her gut told her there was information on that drive that would likely save all their lives. She had to tamp down her anxiety.

"Hand me another USB port from my backpack."

Mallory rummaged through his bag and held up a silver square. "You mean this?"

"That's the one." Rafe made the final connections and fired up the second laptop. Within a few keystrokes, the copying process began. "Well, you may not like this, but according to this computer, it says it will take four hours to transfer all the materials."

The scream lodged in the back of her throat nearly choked her. A tantrum was wholly unnecessary, but that's precisely what she felt like doing. Throwing things. She clenched her jaw and balled her fists.

"Mallory, please breathe. Your face is turning an unhealthy shade of red."

She took in a deep breath and relaxed her jaw. "I'm trying not to scream."

"I see that. And I understand your frustration. But this is necessary. We need to take this precaution. Trust me. Let's just be happy that we're close." He looked at the clock over the kitchen cabinets. "I'll tell you what. It's nearly dinnertime. I'll make us something quick and easy. We can eat while the computer cooks away."

It wasn't as if she had any choice. So she agreed.

"You like omelets?"

"Sure. Anything's fine. It's not like I have a big appetite." Mallory sighed. "I'm going to sit out on the deck."

"Turn on the heat lamp," Rafe called out. "It's getting toward dusk, and the chill will move in fast."

Out on the lake a pontoon boat silently slipped across the water. Probably the last ride of the season before they docked the boat. She smiled. People were living their lives, going about their business, unaware that someone living right down the road from them was digging into money laundering and who knew what else. "Ahhhhh." She tilted her head toward the sky and rubbed her hands over her face, wanting to erase the last few days from her mind.

"Mallory. We're about to eat. There's nothing we can do until the computer is ready. Please, difficult as it may be, try to relax." Rafe set down two plates and went back inside.

She hadn't thought she could eat anything. Her stomach was twisted into one big knot. But the beautifully cooked omelet and the aroma of melted brie, basil, and scallions filled the air and made her stomach growl.

"I thought we could use a little wine. We have some time before you have to go back to work." He placed two wine glasses and a cold bottle of Chablis on the table.

"Uh… I don't know."

"Yeah, yeah. I know you need to stay sharp. You don't have to have any if you don't want."

Mallory considered that one glass over a four-hour period wouldn't hurt. And if she needed to take a nap after dinner, she had plenty of time. "Okay. One glass."

Dinner was peaceful except for the worried look on Mallory's face.

"You okay?" Rafe asked.

"How I feel is all relative."

"Relative to what?" Rafe frowned.

"The moment. The minute." Mallory sighed. "Whatever stray thought pops into my head. I'm okay one second, and the next, I remember what's happening, and my heart pumps faster, my body fills up with adrenaline, and I start doing the mental fight-or-flight dance."

Rafe reached for her hand, and this time, she didn't pull away. "I'm so sorry for everything you've been through."

"Thank you." She leaned in closer and kissed him. It nearly took his breath away.

When she kissed him with more intention, he whispered, "Mallory, if you're not ready to take this to the next level, then stop."

When she deepened the kiss, that was all the answer he needed. He scooped her up in his arms, and without taking his eyes off her, carried her to the bedroom.

As he gently lowered her to the bed, her arms wrapped around his neck, and her legs encircled his waist. He hovered over her. Kissing her mouth, her chin, her neck. Her body pressed against his hardness.

"Your jeans?" she whispered.

He didn't need to be asked twice.

She helped him with the buckle and slipped her hand inside and held him. He thought he'd lose it right there. He gently removed her hand. He wanted this to last longer than a minute. He slowly unbuttoned each button on her shirt, and when he saw the lace of her bra, he smiled. His teeth moved the fabric to the side, and his mouth descended onto her breast.

She moaned and arched her back, giving him better access. His hand traveled to the center of her core, gently stroking.

"Condom," she whispered.

Forcing himself to break away, he rolled over to the other side of the bed, reached inside the bedside table, and pulled one out. "My brother keeps a stash. Don't ask."

Mallory giggled, and her eyes softened.

"You're so beautiful," Rafe said, and those were the last words he spoke.

Mallory opened her eyes and turned on her side to find Rafe gone. She must have fallen asleep. She stretched, feeling relaxed, before she remembered about the computer. Making love with Rafe had been blissful. But also dangerous. She'd forgotten how tender and exciting it was to be with a man she cared about. Rafe always had a habit of making her forget where she was. And tonight was no exception. For a time, her mind had been completely wrapped up in him. She smiled, then internally admonished herself for losing her edge or even forgetting why she was here in the first place. She needed to stay sharp and keep focused.

After throwing the covers off, she quickly got dressed and went into the living room.

"There you are." Rafe smiled wide.

Mallory looked at her feet, feeling the blush creeping up her face. "I must have fallen asleep."

"Don't worry. There's another eleven minutes before the transfer is complete." Rafe kissed her on the cheek. "Want something to drink?"

"Water. Please." She walked over to the table and took her place in front of the computer. Tapping her foot on the floor, she kept her gaze glued to the screen while the progress bar inched down second by second until the transfer was complete.

When he set the water glass down beside her, Mallory avoided his gaze, embarrassed she'd let things get so far. She was aware she was withdrawing but was physically and mentally incapable of stopping it. They had no future together. Trusting any man, even Rafe, was asking too much of her emotionally. After years of living with abuse, it was the only way she knew to protect herself. Rafe would never understand. How could he?

The computer chimed, bringing her back. "I think it's done. Do I wait for you to unhook the cables?" Her words were clipped and emotionless. She didn't want him to get the wrong impression that what they'd done was a forever thing.

"Uh, yeah." Rafe reached over her shoulders to get at the cables, leaning his chin on top of her head.

Mallory wiggled out from under him and stood. "I'll get out of your way." She saw the hurt in his eyes. If there was time, she would have explained what she was feeling. But that wasn't a luxury they had. They'd already wasted four hours.

Rafe stepped away from the table. "All yours."

Mallory sat. "Thanks."

It took a few more minutes to unhook the connections, for Rafe to check the backup computer, and for Mallory to confirm that everything had been copied. Once she was satisfied, Rafe shut down the backup laptop and placed it in the backpack.

They'd finally arrived at the moment they'd been waiting for. "Here goes." She held her breath as she pushed the tiny nano drive into a slot at the side of the laptop. A rainbow-colored circle appeared and began spinning. Mallory moved in closer, and Rafe was leaning on her chair, looking over her shoulder.

The swirling ball stopped, and the computer screen went black. Mallory gasped. "No. What happened? No, no, no," Mallory yelled. She was about to hit the enter key when the screen came back to life, and a single document appeared. She put her fingers on the trackpad and began to scroll. There were hundreds and hundreds of sequences of letters and numbers.

"Well, he didn't make it easy," Mallory said.

"What do you mean?" Rafe asked.

"This may, in fact, be the key, but it doesn't spell anything out. I'm going to have to do some digging back in the original folders."

"I don't get it," Rafe said. "I thought this would be the answer."

Mallory held up an index finger and shook her head, her eyes never leaving the screen.

"The bastard." Rafe shoved his hands in his pockets.

"Apparently, the key works if you know what you're looking for," Mallory said.

"Of course," Rafe said and punched his fist against the door-jamb of the bedroom.

"Please, let me think. I need a minute. I have to put myself into Blake's mind and see how this all comes together." Mallory looked up. "Maybe you should wait outside."

Rafe looked surprised, but Mallory didn't have the patience for explanation or civility. "Out. Now. Seriously, I need quiet. I have to concentrate."

Rafe didn't move, but his reluctance was no match for her stare. He finally turned, grabbed his jacket, and left.

Mallory picked up a pencil and the spreadsheets she'd been working on earlier. Moving her gaze from screen to spreadsheet, she had to push away the feeling that this was an impossible task. She went through the same procedure as before—writing down numbers, checking the screen, and then going back to the beginning of the column and checking again. Twenty minutes had passed when Rafe stuck his head in the door.

"Out!" Mallory demanded without looking up.

Forty more minutes crawled by before she finally put the pencil down and pushed her chair away from the table. To the casual observer, it looked as if she were thinking. But Mallory's hands were shaking, her throat was dry, and her heart was racing.

She'd not only cracked the code, but she almost wished she hadn't.

What she had in front of her were account numbers, the location of billions of dollars in various offshore accounts, and where the money had been transferred. Mallory stared at the names on the accounts, barely able to breathe. In her wildest thoughts, she never could have imagined that Blake would be involved in such an enterprise.

In her possession was concrete evidence of dozens and dozens of names of known arms dealers, terrorist organizations, and several government officials who were responsible for the disruption of foreign governments, bombings, drug smuggling, human trafficking, and cybercrime. A ripple of fear crawled up her spine. These were the kinds of people who would have no trouble getting rid of her, and anyone she had ever known, without a moment's hesitation.

Mallory nearly jumped out of her seat when the door opened.

"You okay?" Rafe hung his jacket on the peg and walked toward her. "What did you find?" Rafe knelt in front of her and grabbed her hands. "You're ice cold. Mallory, what's happening?"

Mallory physically shuddered and took in a breath. "I am not okay. None of us is okay. What's on there—" she nodded toward the laptop "—is evidence of money laundering and criminality that goes as high as you can possibly get in government. And right now, I'm in so deep, and I don't think anyone can protect me if they found out what I now know. In fact, I'm not sure who we can trust."

"Mallory, start at the beginning. What did you find?" Rafe said.

"I cracked the code. Once I did that, the documents became accessible. And…well…have a look." Mallory stood and motioned to the laptop.

Rafe leaned over the table and passed his fingers over the trackpad waking the screen. Mallory leaned against the wall, watching his expression as it went from non-comprehension to shock and then to what she was sure was disbelief. Those had been the gamut of emotions she'd experienced when she went through the documents.

"Son of a bitch." Rafe slammed his hand on the table. "This is…this is…this is…"

"*Extraordinary? Unbelievable? Criminal?* Are those the words you're looking for?"

"Actually, there are no words," Rafe said.

"Well, I've had a few more minutes to digest this, and I have a few thoughts." Mallory moved closer to Rafe. "I think we're in more danger now than we were before we broke into that laptop." Mallory raked her hands through her hair and let out a defeated sigh. "The fact that someone from our government is involved… Well, I think we have a situation. And I personally have no idea how to get out of it. None."

"Take it easy, Mallory. It's not the entire government. It's one person." He wrapped his arms around her.

She pushed him away. "Do not tell me to take it easy! And please, do not try and comfort me. Right now, that's an impossible task." Mallory chewed on her thumbnail and paced the length of the room. Everyone in Rafe's family and her daughter were in danger. Any one of the people listed on those spreadsheets could be after her. The thought was terrifying.

"Listen, let's take a moment to think," Rafe said.

"If you have a suggestion that gets these criminals behind bars until they die and keeps us safe, without having to hide in witness protection, I'm all ears. Because I'm thinking that's the only way we get out of this alive." Mallory's voice took on a shrill quality, and Rafe went to her.

"Don't, Rafe. Don't try and comfort me. Please. If anything, this is a time to stay alert and be ready for anything. I don't need your comfort. I need solutions. Last week, this felt like a bad dream, but I know better now. This is a living nightmare. And I feel as if I'm never going to wake up." Mallory rubbed at a burning sensation in her chest. "We are dealing with very, very bad men. Men who will stop at nothing to get at what we have. We've stepped into some deep—"

"Shh." Rafe looked around. "Do you hear that? How could a phone be ringing?"

Chapter Sixteen

Following the sound, Rafe ran into the bedroom. He threw the covers to the floor in search of the muffled ringing. Kneeling, he looked under the bed and spied the phone. Reaching with his fingers, he pulled it toward him and pressed the talk button.

"Get the heck out of there now! You've been tracked." Max's voice came screaming through the receiver. "Don't say anything. Get out. Call me when you get to where you're going." The call went dead.

With quick precision, Rafe dislodged the battery. He'd turned to find Mallory in the doorway, hand over her mouth.

"Did you use the phone?" His voice was steely.

She nodded.

"They've found us. No time to discuss now." He stormed past her and into the dining area.

"I'm sorry," Mallory cried. "I… I…had to speak to Justine. I forgot to take the battery out."

"We need to pack up now!"

"That's all you're going to say?" Mallory asked.

Rafe practically bit his tongue, suppressing his rage. Anything he said now would be cruel. He'd told her not to call her daughter. It wasn't safe. Maybe he could forgive that. But to leave the battery in the phone—that was careless, bordering on reckless. It was the kind of disregard that might lead the criminals directly to them.

"Please. Rafe, say something. It was a mistake."

Rafe remained silent, moving with speed and determination throughout the house, gathering the equipment and spreadsheets, and unplugging the laptop. He grabbed the two backpacks and shoved everything inside. "Don't bother to pack. Just put on your sneakers." Mallory didn't move, seemingly frozen in place. "Mallory, go. Now."

The look on Mallory's face telegraphed her fear. He wasn't sure if she was afraid of him or the situation. Either way, there was no time to dissect feelings. He needed to come up with a plan.

Within minutes, Rafe had the backpacks stuffed and ready, as Mallory walked back in from the bedroom.

"Grab one." Rafe strapped a backpack onto his shoulders. He picked up the phone and reinserted the battery.

"What are you doing?" Mallory asked.

"Insurance," Rafe said, placing the phone on the table. "Whoever traced us will still think we're here. Let's go."

Mallory headed toward the front door.

"We're not taking the car. We're on foot." Without waiting for her response, he opened the sliding doors to the deck. It was nearly two in the morning, the quarter moon providing little light. "Stay close behind me."

Mallory nodded.

They made their way up the path, away from the lake and toward the surrounding woods. The wilderness seemed to swallow them instantly, and Rafe turned on the flashlight. "We need to get to Saranac. It's about nine miles west. We can get help there."

"Help?" Mallory said. "But we don't know who we can trust."

Rafe couldn't read her face in the darkness, but he could hear the tremble in her voice. As angry as he was, the situation called for them to work as a team. At least until they could get some help. He let out a deep breath and, with it, some of his anger. "We can trust my brothers and my cousins. That's who we'll call. They'll help us figure this out. For now, we need to stay two steps ahead of whoever has tracked us."

* * *

Within thirty minutes, they were in the dense forest on a steep rise. Mallory was having difficulty keeping up with Rafe. Given that she'd put them in this mess, she wasn't about to tell him to slow down. Gritting her teeth, she matched him stride for stride as they made their way up the seemingly endless incline. Rafe asked her if she wanted to stop and rest. But she waved him off. "I'm good."

They continued upward, and her breath came in raspy gasps that seemed to echo in the forest. They passed towering pines and birch trees that looked like ghosts in the dull moonlight. The shriek of an owl sounding so much like a human cry made her stumble.

"You okay?" Rafe whispered.

"Yes." She bent over and placed her hands on her thighs. The sweat dripping down her back against the cool night air made her shiver. "I need a minute." Mallory took in a deep breath, telling herself these nocturnal forest sounds were normal. The fact that she happened to be on their turf at this time of night wasn't comforting. But she needed to buck up. It was imperative they get to Saranac no matter what.

"I'm ready. Let's keep going." She took hold of Rafe's hand and continued upward. The thin sneakers she wore were no match for the forest floor. It felt as if she were barefoot, stepping on every rock, pine cone, branch, seed, stone, and nut. Her jaw tightened in determination, and she continued forward. She would not be the reason they didn't make it to Saranac.

They hiked for what seemed like an hour before Rafe abruptly stopped.

"I can keep going. We don't need to stop." Mallory was breathing heavily.

"I think we may have veered off course slightly." Rafe pulled back the sleeve of his jacket and checked the compass on his smartwatch. "Looks like we're going a bit more north than west. We need to double back a few hundred feet."

In the distance, they heard twigs snap, and they both froze. Rafe grabbed Mallory's hand and put a finger over her mouth, signaling they should remain quiet. Another snapping sound and her heart caught in her throat. The forest seemed to be an echo chamber. She couldn't tell what direction the sound came from or its distance. She looked around, but the dense foliage made it impossible to see anything.

Rafe tugged on Mallory's hand. Without warning, he shoved her under some nearby underbrush and huddled beside her. Her heart hammered in her chest, and she put her hand over her mouth to stifle the sound of her ragged breath.

They waited without moving for what seemed like an eternity. More minutes passed, and the silence was all-consuming except for the whooshing sound of blood in her ears.

She wondered if maybe they'd imagined someone was there, or it was an animal in the woods. And then, to prove her wrong, came the unmistakable sound of human feet walking on the forest floor. From a distance, she saw a flashlight beam. She closed her eyes in the childlike hope that no one would see her. Rafe held her hand, and she held her breath.

They waited. Slowly, she opened her eyes. From her vantage point, Mallory couldn't see anyone, but she could feel him—a malevolent shadow inching closer, her heart rate accelerating with each passing second. It took every ounce of willpower not to bolt and run. Rafe's steadying hand was the only thing keeping her grounded.

Sitting on the back of her legs was becoming uncomfortable, and her feet were beginning to fall asleep. She desperately wanted to get the blood circulating, but a movement of any kind might alert whoever was out there.

When she spied the worn hiking boots of the pursuer, about fifty feet away, she held her breath. The flashlight beam seemed to be circling the area, and she prayed they were far enough into the underbrush not to be found. Rafe's hand on hers was a lifeline of sanity because she was sure she was about to go crazy with fear. Squeezing her eyes shut, she thought about Justine. About getting back to her and holding her and smothering her with motherly kisses.

When she opened her eyes, the beam of light seemed to be moving up the mountain, away from them. She could still hear the pursuer's receding footsteps. Rafe's arm went across her chest to hold her in place, sensing she was about to bolt.

Another eternity passed before Rafe whispered in her ear. "Follow me and do what I do."

Mallory nodded and watched as Rafe got on his side and silently rolled out from the underbrush. She followed suit, and when he grabbed her hand to help her up, her legs collapsed. The numbness of pins and needles was the only feeling. She lay there trying to massage some life into her right leg.

Rafe knelt and massaged the other leg. Together, they worked without saying a word. Her gaze darted around, making sure they were alone. When she could feel a sensation in her toes, she gave Rafe a thumbs-up, and he helped her to her feet. This time, she remained standing.

Once again, Rafe checked the direction on his compass. He took hold of Mallory's hand, and they wordlessly traveled west. This portion of the forest was a dense canopy of trees with barely a sliver of moonlight coming through. There were no trails, and they were forced to push the branches out of their way while the undergrowth grabbed at their ankles. Without any real tread on the soles of her sneakers, Mallory slipped several times on the mossy ground.

When they finally reached the top of the hill, they could see the glow of soft lights in the distance.

"That's Saranac." Rafe spoke low. "Another four miles or so, and we're there. It's all downhill now."

It didn't matter what direction they were going, uphill or down. Every one of Mallory's muscles screamed in protest.

For the last mile, the backpack had begun to feel like it was filled with a hundred-pound weight instead of a spare laptop. She could feel a wet ooze in her sneakers. She couldn't see in this light, but she was certain it was blood. Regardless of how battered she felt, she would not give up. She would not slow Rafe down. Not until they were safe. If she could hang on, and make it down the hill, then there would be time to tend to her aching body.

The forest was denser on this side of the hill. As they continued their descent, she found she was battling low-hanging branches that scratched the sides of her face, tangled in her hair, and snagged on her jean jacket. Just as she was getting the hang of the rhythm and pace of the descent, Rafe came to a sudden stop, and she nearly toppled him over. They both stood still and remained quiet until she heard it. Footsteps coming from behind.

Rafe grabbed her hand and pulled her along as they took off running. They ran over roots and ducked under low-hanging branches that ripped at her clothes. Mallory's heart beat like a war drum as they raced down the mountain.

The sound of their assailant's footsteps getting closer, adrenaline spurring her on. She turned her head to see how close he was, and without warning, she tripped over a rock. Letting go of Rafe's hand, she fell and rolled over on her side. The searing pain seemed to travel from her ankle to the top of her head.

"Come on, Mallory," Rafe whisper-shouted.

"I can't. I think it's broken." She cradled her foot, willing herself not to cry, but the intensity of the pain was almost unbearable. She pressed her lips together, forcing herself not to scream.

With no time to waste, Rafe scooped her in his arms and carried her. His heart hammered in his chest as he ran. Before long, he knew he couldn't keep the pace needed to outrun their assailant. Not with Mallory and the two backpacks. He needed to find a place to hide.

Veering off to the left, he charged back up the treacherous slope. He had to lose whoever was chasing them.

"Where are you going?" Mallory asked.

Rafe couldn't speak, so he shook his head. She seemed to understand he could either carry her and run or stop and talk.

He continued for several yards until he came to a small ridge that appeared to be flat ground. The trail was going in the opposite direction from the town, but he needed to find some shelter until he could assess if Mallory could walk. Hopefully, their assailant wouldn't guess they were no longer headed for Saranac.

He traveled the ridge for several more yards until it came to an abrupt end with two enormous boulders sitting in the middle of the path, halting any further progress. They were co-joined at the top, with a cavelike opening at the base. It wasn't passable, but it could serve as a place to hide until he could figure out their next step.

He set Mallory down inside the makeshift cave.

"I'll be right back."

"Where are you going?"

Rafe looked around. "You can't make it down the hill, and we're too exposed out here. I need to find something to conceal us until I can figure out our next move. I won't be long."

He didn't have to go far before he found several large rocks he could roll into place, building a blockade in front of them but leaving a little more than a foot at the top to ensure they didn't suffocate.

Putting the last rock in place, he sat back and turned on his flashlight.

Mallory covered her eyes, and he lowered the beam.

Gingerly, he pushed back the pant leg and saw the swelling and discoloration. "I have no idea if it's broken or if it's a very bad sprain."

"While you were building this fort, I moved my ankle. It's painful. No question. But if I can wrap it, I think I can make it the rest of the way. We have to try."

Rafe raised an eyebrow. "Wrap it with what?"

She pulled the bottom of her blouse out of her jeans. "Does that flashlight come with a Swiss Army knife?"

Rafe shook his head. "No, but I actually have one of those." He reached into the inside of his jacket and pulled out a knife.

"Cut the bottom off. We'll use it as a wrap."

Rafe did as instructed and now held a long strip of material in his hand. "You know if you take your sneaker off, that things going to blow up like a balloon."

"What choice do I have?"

"You'll never get that sneaker back on, and you'll need it to get down the hill." Rafe tried to think. He needed her to be able to walk. There was no way he could carry her the rest of the way. "We'll wrap it with the sneaker on. It will at least give you some support."

The flashlight beam caught the skepticism and fear in Mallory's eyes.

"I promise. We're going to make it to town. We're going to get help. You'll see Justine again. And we are going to get out of this mess."

"That's a lot of promises, Rafe."

"And I intend to live up to them." He lifted her leg onto his lap and began wrapping the material around the sneaker.

Mallory gasped.

"Sorry." Rafe stopped for a moment. "Hang on, I need to get this tight, so it'll support you."

Mallory closed her eyes and took in a deep breath.

Rafe wrapped the material around the sneaker a few more times and gently placed her foot back on the ground. "There. Finished."

"Thanks."

Their hiding place wasn't tall enough for Mallory to stand, so they had no way of knowing if she could walk. Rafe prayed it would hold.

"Now what?" Mallory asked.

"I think we wait until dawn. I have a feeling whoever is pursuing us doesn't want to be seen in the light of day." Rafe pulled back his sleeve and looked at his watch. "It's four o'clock. Sun should be up in another two hours. Why don't you get some rest?"

"Rest?" Mallory scoffed.

The sudden spine-chilling scream startled them into silence. A second primal scream reverberated through the air.

"What is that?" Mallory's gaze darted around.

"Bobcat," Rafe shouted to be heard over another hair-raising scream by the predator right outside their makeshift barricade. "At least, I think so."

Rafe stiffened at the sound of something climbing the rocks toward the small opening at the top. In a moment, two hazel eyes glared back at him, and a claw swiped into the opening several times.

"What do we do?" Mallory backed as far away as she could as the growls grew louder.

"Stay still. Do not look at him. Bow your head and force yourself to slow your breathing. If we play dead, maybe he'll go."

Rafe only hoped that was true. He had zero experience being up close to a bobcat. He only knew what they sounded like, and right now this one was too close for comfort.

At first, the snarls and growls only grew louder and more exasperated. Rafe could almost sense the animal's frustration. In time, the growls became guttural purrs. But Rafe didn't dare look up and barely took a breath. He had no idea how much time had passed, but eventually, there was only silence. "Don't move," Rafe whispered under his breath. There was no telling what was beyond the rocks—was the animal gone, or only playing a cat-and-mouse game, ready to pounce as soon as they poked their heads out?

Streaks of dawn peeked through the opening as Rafe slowly lifted his head. Despite the uncertainty of what awaited them, man or beast, he knew they had to take their chances and leave the cave and make it into town. By removing one of the rocks at the top, he was able to peek through the opening. With no way of knowing if it was safe or not. He opted to trust his gut that, for the moment, they were alone, and all nocturnal creatures had decided to rest, leaving them the opportunity to get down the mountain.

One by one, he removed the rocks forming the barricade until the opening was cleared. The early morning daylight streamed in, magnifying the weariness in Mallory's eyes and the dried blood on the side of her face, evidence of their fight during the night with the naked tree branches as they ran through the woods.

"Are you okay to go on?"

She nodded. "I have to be." Her tired smile didn't reach her eyes.

"Come on. Let's get you out of here." He crawled out, then reached in and helped her slide out of the cave. He helped her stand. "Lean against the rock for support. I'll be right back." Without giving her the opportunity to say anything, he stepped away from their temporary shelter and walked a few feet into a wooded area, searching the forest floor for a branch of some kind that could serve as a crutch. Within minutes, he found a fallen tree, some of its branches scattered around. He selected one that appeared sturdy enough, about four inches in diameter and over five feet tall. Too tall, he thought; she could accidentally poke an eye out with a misstep. Resting his foot on the tree trunk, he placed the branch across his knee and tried to snap off about twelve inches of the branch. The veins in his neck bulged as he asserted more pressure until the piece finally snapped off.

When he returned, he found Mallory leaning against the wall. Her eyes drooped. "Mallory. Wake up. Come on. Use this as a crutch." He placed the branch in her hand. "Here, put your other arm around my shoulder. This will give you the support you need. It's a steep slope."

As they made their way slowly down the mountain, Rafe checked behind him every few yards to see if they were being followed. Something was amiss. There had to be a reason whoever was trailing them had vanished.

"Look, Rafe. The village. Oh, thank goodness."

Early morning smoke rose from several chimneys, and Rafe could see cars traveling on the road. Relief flooded through him. He could almost taste safety. "We'll head straight for the police station and call my brothers from there."

When they finally made it to the police station, Mallory collapsed onto a bench just inside the door. The large clock against the opposite wall indicated it was barely six thirty in the morning. Patches of the gray linoleum floor were still wet with bleach, and the smell permeated the air. The waist-high wooden partition separated the five utilitarian desks from the small waiting area. Only one desk was occupied. The nameplate read Jenna Bower, Receptionist. The look of alarm on the round-faced woman told Mallory everything she needed to know.

Covered in dirt, with visible scrapes and bruises, she and Rafe appeared more like fugitives on the run.

"We need help." Rafe stepped forward, his voice urgent.

Jenna flinched. Her gaze moved from their hands to their backpacks. Without taking her eyes off them, she picked up the phone and pressed a button. "Sheriff, you need to come out here. Right now."

From the back of the room, a frosted glass door opened and

a burly, bald-headed man over six feet tall hurried toward them, his hand resting on the butt of his gun. "What the hell is going on? I'm Sheriff Michael Mitchell. Who the hell are you two?"

The sensation they'd stepped from one bad experience and into another nearly had Mallory in tears. Mentally, she recoiled from the lawman with his finger inches from the trigger. This place felt anything but safe. She would provide only the essential details, enough information so they could quickly get back to Justine and Rafe's family. She relayed the details of their harrowing night in the woods and explained they had no idea who their assailant was but needed to get back to Saratoga Springs so she could pick up her daughter.

The sheriff's wrinkled forehead and pursed lips told her he was skeptical.

Mallory didn't care what he thought or what she had to endure as long as he hurried up and helped get her back to her daughter.

"I'm gonna have to see some ID. And I'm going to have a couple of my deputies take a ride over to that mountain. Take a look around the trails." The side table against the wall held two-way radio equipment. He issued instructions through the handset and when he was finished, replaced it back on the receiver. "Now, why don't you hand over a driver's license or something that tells me who you folks are."

They did as they were told.

"Jenna, please run these." He turned back to Rafe. "Real gentle, take off the backpack, and slide it right over here."

Rafe did as instructed.

The sheriff turned to Mallory. "Now, your turn."

Rafe went toward her to help.

"Nuh-uh. Stay right there," the sheriff said.

Mallory saw the glint of mistrust in his eyes. She hurried to remove the backpack. In too much pain to stand, she kicked it over with her good foot.

"All right now," he said to Rafe, "you sit over there by your girlfriend while I have a look."

The expression on Rafe's face mirrored how she felt—trapped and anxious.

Without ever taking his eyes off them, the sheriff placed both backpacks on one of the empty desks. He pulled out a laptop and opened the cover. Mallory took in a sharp breath. "Hey—"

Rafe put a hand on her forearm and shook his head.

She sat back, pressing her lips firmly against each other. While she understood the need for the sheriff to be cautious and in control, she couldn't afford for him to mistakenly press the wrong button on the laptop and erase anything or damage the information they had.

"Sherriff, I think you want to see this." The receptionist peeked out from behind her desktop computer screen.

"Can it wait?" He pulled the spreadsheets from the backpack.

"It most certainly cannot." Her voice was urgent.

Mallory squeezed Rafe's hand and turned to him.

His furrowed brow communicated he hadn't a clue what was happening.

The sheriff took two quick steps to his receptionist's desk and looked over her shoulder. Mallory watched as his expression turned from annoyed to surprised, his eyebrows raising a considerable inch.

The sheriff cleared his throat. "Uh, Mr. Ramirez. You need to call your brother Max. It's urgent. The FBI's with him. You can use the phone on that desk."

"What the hell is going on?" Mallory stood, and instantly, her leg buckled. The pain shot through her.

Rafe turned to her. "Mallory."

She waved him off. "I'm okay. Call Max now."

"Sheriff, do you have any first aid back there? Her ankle's pretty bad off."

The sheriff nodded and headed to the back. Rafe raced to the phone on the desk but didn't lift the receiver.

"Rafe, what in God's name are you waiting for?" Mallory slammed her palm down on the bench. "Call now."

He scrubbed his face with a hand. "I call up favorites on my phone. I don't know Max's phone number by heart."

Perspiration formed on Rafe's upper lip. What wasn't the sheriff saying? He looked over at the receptionist, whose frown only reinforced that something wasn't right. "What is going on? What's on that computer screen of yours?" He took a step toward her, and Jenna pushed back, the wheels of her chair moving her a foot away.

"Hey, hey. What's going on?" the sheriff said as he approached with what looked like a first-aid kit. "Step away from there, Mr. Ramirez." He put his hand on the butt of his gun.

The sheriff had used that intimidating move before, and Rafe thought it did the job. He backed up. "Listen. I need to know what you saw that has made both you and your receptionist jumpy."

"Call your brother."

"I'd really like to do that, but I don't know his number by heart."

"Oh damn. Smartphones make everyone dumb." Sheriff Mitchell gave his receptionist a weary look. "Give them the number here. Tell them to call." He passed through the swinging Dutch door and settled next to Mallory.

"Why not just tell me," Rafe demanded.

The sheriff didn't answer. Calmly, as if he had all the time in the world, he lifted Mallory's leg and placed it across his lap. After removing the dirty makeshift bandage, he cleaned the area with rubbing alcohol. Then he cracked open an instant ice pack and placed it on her ankle.

The ring of the phone startled Rafe, and the sheriff nodded.

Rafe picked up the receiver. "Max, what's going on? Is everyone okay?" Rafe listened, and the blood drained from his face.

"What? What's he saying?" Mallory yelled.

Rafe held up a hand, then held it over his ear so he could hear Max more clearly. The call lasted only a few minutes. When he hung up the receiver, he turned and went to Mallory. Taking both her hands in his, he looked straight into her eyes. "Blake kidnapped Justine."

Chapter Seventeen

"What are you saying? Blake's dead." Mallory's voice had an eerily calm quality.

"Apparently, he's not. And now he has your daughter. You get her back when you give him the drive."

Her eyes filled with tears, and she covered her mouth with her hand.

Rafe could see she was trying to process what he said.

"How? How did this happen?" Tears streamed down her face.

"At the moment, there are a lot of unknowns. The FBI's still trying to figure it out. But he left a note. He directed Max and Zack to get back to Hollow Lake, and he'd give further instructions once we arrived."

"How did the FBI get involved?"

"This is a kidnapping case, and it involves Blake Stanton. They had to be called in."

The far-off look in her eyes told him she might be in shock. He put his hand on the back of her neck and pressed his cheek to hers. "We're going to get her back. I promise."

They were driven to an empty field ten miles out of town where an FBI helicopter took them back to Hollow Lake.

The moment Mallory and Rafe stepped off the elevator at the RMZ offices, they were greeted by Zack and Max.

"Oh, thank god you're here," Zack said, pulling them both into a hug.

"Never mind about us. Tell me exactly what's happening. Any word on Justine? How long has she been gone?" Mallory's words came out in a rush.

Zack gently put his hand on her forearm. She saw the concern in his eyes and understood the entire family was upset.

"*Tía* Claudia put her to bed at around seven thirty. She checked on her around nine, and that's when she discovered Justine was gone. A note was left with the demands you already know about." Zack shoved his hands in his pockets. "Jack and Andres were there, and they called the FBI."

With a house full of adults, including Rafe's detective cousins, she had a hard time understanding how this had happened. And as quickly as she had that thought, she remembered that her dead husband wasn't dead. He was as devious as ever. If he'd managed to have an entire plane and its black box disappear, then he could get past several adults and take her sleeping daughter in the night.

"So what happens now?" Mallory took in the scene. The low hum of at least a dozen men and women talking on phones, typing on tablets, all stationed around the common office area beyond the reception desk. Some wore badges that hung on chains around their necks, identifying them as agents. Others were dressed in dark blue T-shirts with the unmistakable yellow letters *F-B-I* emblazoned across their chests. Mallory stiffened. "Why so many?"

"This is Blake Stanton we're talking about," Max said, as if his simple explanation were enough to warrant what appeared to be over a dozen agents. "They've been here for hours."

"Let's head back." Zack nodded toward the conference room. "The head of the investigation is going to fill us in. All we know right now is they're setting up wiretaps on the phones."

"Wiretaps?" Mallory asked.

"According to the FBI, this is a hostage situation. The next move is Blake's, and he'll make demands on where to drop off the drive. They're hoping to have the tap on the phones up and running before his next call," Max informed them.

Mallory took a step to follow the brothers but nearly fell. She put a hand on the wall and lowered her head, squeezing her eyes shut, waiting for the pain to dissipate.

"Mallory?" Rafe stepped in front of her and cupped her chin in his hand. "What's the matter?"

"My ankle. It's…"

Rafe lifted the hem of her jeans. "It's still pretty badly swollen." He put his arm around her waist. "Lean on me."

"I'll get some ice." Zack headed toward the kitchen.

"I don't have time for this," Mallory complained.

"I get it. There's a lot going on—" Rafe spoke in a hushed tone "—but take a deep breath. Come on. Let's go in and find out what they know."

They entered the conference room, the smell of stale coffee already filling the air. Two FBI agents were set up at the head of the table. Rafe settled Mallory in a chair.

"This is Agent Robert Byron," Max said, pointing to a tall, thin man wearing an open-collared light blue button-down shirt and jeans.

Agent Byron nodded and turned to a red-headed woman wearing dark-framed glasses. She barely acknowledged them as she continued talking on the phone. "That's Agent Shore. She's the lead on the case and will fill you in." He went back to typing something on his tablet.

Zack came in with a fresh ice pack. "Here you go."

"Thanks." Mallory rested her ankle on the seat of a nearby chair. "Can you please place it right on top?"

"Sure thing." Zack rested the ice pack on the outside of her ankle and took a seat next to Max. The four of them waited.

Mallory settled back in the seat and tapped her other foot on the wood floor, waiting anxiously for the agent to end her call. When it appeared the agent wasn't in a hurry, Mallory began drumming her fingers on the table one after the other. The gentle touch of Rafe's hand on her forearm stilled her.

She followed every movement Agent Shore made as she rose from the chair, turned, and faced the window, continuing her phone conversation in whispered tones. Her trim frame had the physique of an athlete. Mallory thought she couldn't be more than thirty years old. If that. She looked so much younger than Agent Byron or, for that matter, any of the agents Mallory passed in the office common area.

She chewed her thumbnail raw, not sure how much longer she could wait to get answers.

Max checked his phone while Rafe peppered Zack with questions about Justine.

But Mallory had already been told about how Blake managed to take Justine and the ransom note he left. There wasn't any more information that Rafe's family could tell her. Justine had been gone for over twelve hours. She wanted to know what the authorities were doing now, in the present. From where she sat, it looked like a lot of nothing, and no one had given her any information since she arrived. Minute by minute, she was losing hold of her patience until she could no longer wait for answers. "Excuse me." Mallory slammed her hand on the table. "Agent Shore, are you ever going to get off that phone and tell me what the hell is going on with my daughter and how you plan on rescuing her?"

The room fell silent, and within seconds, the red-headed agent ended her call and turned to face Mallory. "I'm Agent Taylor Shore." She placed both hands on the table and leaned forward. "I understand you're very concerned, but we are doing everything we can."

"Concerned?" Mallory scoffed. "How 'bout Out. Of. My. Mind. This is my daughter."

Agent Shore held up a hand. "I get it." She pulled out a chair and sat. "Here's what we know and what, in all probability, will happen next."

"I'm listening." Her lower lip trembled.

"Blake said he knows you have the drive and is demanding it in exchange for your daughter. So, before we go any further, we want you to hand over that drive and tell us what's on it that would make Blake Stanton mysteriously rise from the dead and orchestrate a kidnapping." She leaned back, crossing her arms over her chest. "Please understand we have no intention of giving him what he wants. The bureau, along with several other organizations, has been watching him for years. That is before he quote, unquote died in a plane crash. We know what he's capable of. We just don't have concrete evidence. So, we're aware if he took your daughter, there's some pretty damning evidence on that drive. And we want it."

Mallory's mouth went dry, and she gave Rafe a sideways glance. Should she tell them what was on the drive? Could she trust any of them?

While she thought, a dissonant hum coursed through her body and settled in her bones. It was the hum of rage. Six years with an abusive husband, days on the run, discovering heinous crimes committed by people in power, a treacherous hike through the Adirondacks, and her daughter's kidnapping. She'd had enough. It had to stop now, or she was certain it would never stop.

"No." Mallory shook her head. Her voice was firm. "That's not how we're going to play this." The words were out of her mouth before she knew what she was saying. "First of all, I don't know what's on the drive. I wasn't able to open it," she lied. "Secondly, it's the only bargaining power I have."

Both agents looked astonished.

"How?" Taylor Shore asked.

"As you said, there must be some pretty damning evidence on that drive, and if I turn it over without getting my daughter back, I've lost everything in the world that means anything to me."

"But—"

Mallory raised a finger. "Hear me out, Agent Shore. You plan on giving Blake a fake drive anyway. Correct?"

The agent nodded.

"So. I'll keep the real one until I know that Blake is caught and that you'll protect me and my daughter. Then I'll turn it over." Mallory stared straight ahead, settled back in her chair, and crossed her arms over her chest. "Deal?"

Taylor Shore peered over the top of her glasses and glanced at Rafe.

"Don't look at him," Mallory said. "He doesn't know anything." Avoiding the agent's eyes, Mallory studied her clenched hands in her lap, willing herself to keep a neutral expression.

"Do you honestly believe he would hurt his own daughter?" Agent Byron asked.

"Without a doubt." Mallory's voice was devoid of emotion.

Agent Shore stood. "Seeing as time is of the essence—" she paused "—we have a deal."

Mallory let out a breath. She had to hold on to the hope that the FBI would catch Blake. She had to hope the people listed on the folders on the drive believed she knew nothing. Only then did she have a prayer of living a normal life with her daughter.

A broad-shouldered, dark-haired man stuck his head into the conference room. "We're ready."

Taylor Shore nodded. "Thanks, Agent Cain."

"Ready for what?" Mallory asked.

"Blake's note said he'd call Rafe's cell phone."

"Mine?" Rafe raised his eyebrows. "How does he even know my number?"

Agent Shore waved Agent Cain back in and held out her hand. She took hold of the slim black mobile phone. "This is yours?" she said to Rafe, holding up the case with his initials on the back.

Rafe nodded. "How did you get my phone?"

"Before you took off, you left it with your brother Max so that you wouldn't be tracked. Smart move."

"But why is Blake calling me? How does he even know me?"

"All good questions." She pushed the phone to the center of the table. "In fact, those are questions we were going to ask you."

Rafe frowned. "I haven't a clue." He looked over at Mallory as if she might have an answer.

Mallory shook her head. She was as astonished as Rafe looked.

"Hmm." Taylor Shore turned her attention to Mallory. "Mrs. Stanton. Do you know how your husband got Rafe's number or why he asked to speak to him?"

A brisk knock on the door stopped the questioning. Agent Cain was on the other side of the glass, giving a thumbs-up.

"Okay. We've got the phone taps ready, so at least we'll be able to pinpoint his location when he calls." Agent Taylor sat forward. "If it comes to it, we'll need to show him something."

Mallory nodded.

Agent Byron placed a square canvas case in front of her and

zipped it open. Inside were dozens of drives in all shapes and sizes. "Take a look. See if any in here matches what you have."

Mallory scanned each slot. "This is it." She pointed to an identical silver nano drive.

Rafe's phone buzzed on the table, and the room went still. Both agents put on headsets. The words *Unknown Caller* appeared on the screen. "It's him," Rafe said.

Agent Shore looked at her partner and then nodded for Rafe to answer.

Rafe grabbed the phone and swiped open the call. "Yeah."

"I'm going to assume the FBI has a trace on this call," came Blake's voice over the speaker.

An icy chill spread like branches of a tree across Mallory's back and shoulders. She never thought she'd hear that voice again. Thinking rationally was off the table. The white-hot rage nearly blinded her, and she wanted to leap into the phone and kill him with her bare hands. "Give me back my daughter," she screamed, hurling herself across the table and grabbing the phone.

"Ahhh. Darling. How are you?" Blake's voice, saccharin sweet, was eerily calm. "Have you recovered from your fall? How's your ankle?"

"You son of a bitch. I want my daughter now. She has nothing to do with this."

Rafe pulled her back into her seat and held on to her trembling shoulders.

Blake's cruel laugh echoed in the room. "Much as I'd like to spend time chatting, we have business to discuss. As I was saying, I'm sure you're with the FBI right now, and they're listening in."

Mallory shifted in her seat and looked at Agent Shore, whose expression was unreadable. She hadn't moved a facial muscle since the call began.

"I would expect nothing less," Blake continued. "I know your friends at the bureau are trying to trace this, but I've got this call bouncing off several different satellites, so it's not likely you'll be able to pinpoint my location. I didn't get to where I am by taking stupid chances, so I'll make this fast." A sound between a laugh and a sneer came through the phone.

Mallory cringed. That was the noise he made whenever he was about to "prove" to her he had the power.

"Turns out I have a few things to put into place before I'm ready for the exchange. I'll phone you tomorrow at nine a.m."

The line went dead.

The shocked silence reverberated in the room.

Mallory leaned her head back and let out a cry. Rafe turned her chair to face him and held her in his arms.

"What does this mean?" Zack asked.

Agent Shore took off her glasses and rubbed the bridge of her nose. "He's stalling."

"For what?" Max asked, leaning forward. "What kind of game is he playing?"

Agent Byron stood and paced the length of the table. "If I had to guess, it sounds like what he needs to make his getaway hasn't fallen into place yet."

Agent Cain came back into the room, a sour expression on his face. He shook his head.

"Damn!" Agent Shore said. "We didn't get the trace."

Mallory tried to clear her head. Think the way Blake did. She was married to him for six years. He was always covering his tracks. His ability to lie convincingly was an art form.

"What if he disappears?" Zack said.

Mallory sat up and wiped her eyes. "That's not going to happen."

"How do you know that?" Zack asked.

"Because he doesn't have the drive. That's the whole point here. With that drive, he holds the power." Mallory cleared her throat. "With that drive, I have to assume he has enough ammunition to keep powerful people doing his bidding and keep himself alive." She squeezed Rafe's hand. "He'll call back. He needs us."

Agent Shore smiled. "I appreciate your candor and your confidence. And let's face it. You know him better than anyone."

"Yes. And I wish I didn't."

"So, now what?" Rafe asked.

"You've both had a rough couple of days." Agent Shore stood. "Let us continue to work on tracking him. Maybe we'll get lucky and catch him before he calls tomorrow. In the meantime, you should all go home and get some rest."

"Ha!" Mallory slowly rose from her chair. "I won't be able to rest until I have my daughter back." She looked at Rafe. "But I would like to take a shower. Can you take me back to Ellie's?"

Rafe nodded.

"We'll send some agents with each of you. Station them outside your homes," Agent Byron said. "Although, I don't think Mrs. Stanton should be on her own."

Mallory turned. "It's Ms. Kane."

Agent Byron coughed. "Understood."

"Don't worry. I'll stay with her tonight." Rafe inched closer to Mallory. "And I'll have my phone if you need to reach me."

Zack and Max stood. "We'll drive you."

Mallory and the three Ramirez brothers left the offices and drove the four blocks to Ellie's house.

Rafe held Mallory's hand in the back seat of Zack's car. The eerie silence unnerved him. But he couldn't think of what to say that would allay any of their fears. Mercifully, the ride to Ellie's house was short. When Zack pulled up, Rafe got out of the car and helped Mallory onto the curb. He leaned into the passenger side window. "Thanks, guys."

"Oh, we're coming in with you," Max scoffed.

"Nah, man. I got this." Rafe said. *"No te preocupes."*

"Don't worry?" Max clicked open his seatbelt. "We're way past that. Move out of the way."

Rafe stepped aside, knowing this wasn't the time to argue with his brothers.

Zack turned off the ignition and got out of the car. "We stocked Ellie's refrigerator before you got here. We're going to stay long enough to make sure you eat something and get some rest." He looked over at Mallory. "Well, as much rest as you can get, considering we're waiting on a madman to get back to us with his instructions." Zack marched up the porch steps, took the key from his front pocket, opened the door, and waved Mallory in.

Rafe came up behind Mallory, who stood in the foyer, not moving. He walked around, facing her. Her glazed-over eyes worried him. She looked slightly catatonic. "Mallory. You okay?"

"Hmm."

Her response wasn't encouraging. "I know you're worried." Rafe looked at his brothers. "We all are. I'm not sure there's more we can do until Blake calls back."

"I know." Mallory's voice was barely above a whisper. She dropped her backpack onto the floor.

The concern for Mallory's state of mind was beginning to grow. Rafe never imagined he'd ever see Mallory this defeated. He raised his eyebrow and glanced once more at Max and Zack, silently asking them for help.

"Hey, bro." Max put his hand on Rafe's shoulder. "You both need to eat something. We'll get it ready. But first, why don't you help Mallory upstairs? I'm sure she'd like to get cleaned up."

Max was right. Maybe that's all she needed. They were both a little worse for wear after their flight through the mountains. "Come on, Mallory. Let's get upstairs, and you can take a shower. You'll feel better." He knew the words were wrong the moment they were out. She wasn't going to feel better until her daughter was safely back in her arms. "I mean—"

"I know what you meant." Her tone was lifeless. Dull. "I'm sure I smell. I'll wash up so I don't offend anyone."

"Here." Rafe handed the backpacks to Zack. "Don't let them out of your sight." He turned and climbed the stairs behind Mallory.

She went into the room she'd stayed in at the beginning of this ordeal and sat on the edge of the bed.

Rafe wanted to go to her but stopped himself. He'd been sitting on a question since they left the FBI at his office. Why had Mallory decided to keep the real drive? Why had she lied and said she hadn't opened it and that he didn't know anything about it? Clearly, she had her reasons. But he wasn't sure she was thinking straight. She probably needed a minute to herself—alone with her thoughts. She'd been through so much in the last few days. It was a lot for anyone to take in. The fact that his head hadn't exploded was a miracle. He couldn't imagine what she must be going through. Before this night was over, he was going to find out what she was thinking.

For now, there wasn't much any of them could do but wait for Blake to make his next demand. Rafe let out a heavy sigh and headed into his cousin's old room, where there were several pairs of jeans and some shirts hanging in the closet. Ellie kept clothes for Rafe and his brothers to change into whenever they did work around her house. Of course, they never needed to change. They'd simply perform whatever chore needed doing, then head home to change because they all lived so close to one another. He suspected Ellie liked the clothes hanging in the closet because it made her feel less alone. For whatever reason, he was happy to have something clean to change into. He pulled a pair of black jeans from a hanger and a dark blue shirt. As he was closing the closet, he saw the tip of a boot at the back. "What have we here?" Bending down, he reached into the back of the closet and grabbed the tip of the boot by the laces, knocking over a couple of shoe boxes in the process. "So this is where you got to." In his hands, he held his old work boots. He smiled, remembering he'd done some repairs on the back porch and needed more than sneakers as protection for his feet in case a hammer or heavy board slipped from his hands. What he couldn't remember was leaving them here, but he was glad of it. The sneakers that took him through the mountains and to safety were fairly destroyed.

He grabbed a towel from the linen closet and stepped into the bathroom. He stripped off his belt and emptied his pants pockets, pulling out his phone. One look told him the battery was nearly dead. They needed it in case Blake called. He ran down the stairs to the kitchen.

Max was at the stove and turned. *"Mano, ¿qué pasa?"*

Rafe held up his phone in his hand. "Battery dying."

"Give it here," Zack said. "I'm charging mine. But yours is way more important."

Rafe handed him the phone. "Thanks."

"How's she doing?" Zack lifted his brow toward the ceiling.

"Not great." Rafe dragged his hand over his face. "I mean,

can you blame her? She told me horror stories about him. But I never really got it until that phone call." Rafe shuddered. "His voice sounded like pure evil."

"Totally," Max said. "Even if you never heard his voice, what kind of man kidnaps his own daughter? *Bestia*." Max spat out the last word.

"Hey, man," Zack said, pointing to the ceiling. "I don't hear any water running. You sure she's okay?"

Rafe flew out of the kitchen, taking the steps two at a time. He turned the corner and found Mallory still sitting on the edge of the bed, staring straight ahead, her gaze not following him when he walked into the room. "Mallory? You haven't moved from this spot." He knelt in front of her. "Come on. Let me help you."

Mallory didn't respond.

Rafe felt helpless. But he had to do something. He needed her to be strong. "Listen to me. Now is not the time for you to fall apart. Your daughter needs you." Rafe squeezed her hands. "I need you. Please."

Her eyes filled with unshed tears. Rafe didn't move. A single tear fell down her cheek, and he took her in his arms.

Mallory sobbed into his shoulder. She needed the release. When she backed away, his shirt was wet with her tears. "Sorry." She wiped her nose with the back of her hand. "I needed that." She looked down at her feet. "I don't know what I'll do if he does anything to Justine."

Rafe grabbed her by the shoulders. "Don't even think like that."

"But he's a crazy person." Mallory walked toward the window. She huffed out a breath. "Justine's innocent. She shouldn't be a pawn in his vicious game. And it's all my fault. I married him."

Rafe came up from behind and rested his hands on her shoulders. "Don't think that way. Come on. Dim thoughts won't bring her back."

Mallory stepped out of his arms. Her eyes were no longer dull. There was a fury, an inner rage.

"You and I both know what's on that drive. We know the kind of people that bastard Blake was dealing with and who he was helping. We know what horrific crimes they were and are committing. Do you imagine, for one minute, Blake gives one damn for Justine? To him, she's a pawn." Mallory let out a sob and clasped her hand over her mouth. "Somehow, I will make this right. And I will get my daughter back."

"We're all here to make sure that happens. We will get her back. There are no other options. Now, let's get cleaned up. And something to eat. You need your strength." He turned her by the shoulders and marched her into the bathroom.

Rafe pushed the shower curtain back and turned on the faucets. "You're going in for a nice hot shower. If it doesn't make you feel better, at least you'll be clean."

She let out a small laugh.

"And after that, we'll get you fed and some rest. Tomorrow will be here before you know it, and you'll have your daughter back."

"I'm okay. I don't need any more coddling. I'm over my shock."

"Happy to hear that," Rafe said, noticing the room was beginning to fog up.

"I do, however, need help with taking off this bandage and this sneaker," she said.

Rafe knelt before her. "Put your foot up on my knee." He gently unwrapped the bandage, untied the shoelace, and began to ease off the shoe.

Mallory hissed.

"Does that hurt?"

Mallory's eyes were squeezed shut. "I think this needs to be quick." She gripped the side of the sink. "Yank it off and get it over with."

"Are you sure?"

Mallory's face tilted upward. "Uh-huh. Just do it."

He pulled the sneaker off and heard the gasp that escaped her lips.

"Are you all right?"

"I will be." She lowered her head and faced him.

"Breathe," he said.

She took in a deep breath and slowly blew it out through her mouth.

"Well, it's turning an interesting shade of purple. I'll give you that."

"Thanks." Mallory rolled her eyes. "Listen, Rafe, I need a favor, and I really hate to ask you, but I don't think I can get into that shower by myself. I don't think I can put any weight on my ankle."

Rafe raised an eyebrow.

"That wasn't an invitation," Mallory said.

"No?" He tilted his head.

Mallory paused. "Well, maybe. I don't want to be alone." She swallowed. "Stay with me."

"You don't ever have to be alone." He lifted her up. "Lean against the wall." He pulled her shirt out of her jeans and ran his hands down her waist to her hips. His fingers gently released the top button at the waistband, then slowly slid her pants down.

The fog in the bathroom continued to build as he slid his hand up her legs and unbuttoned each button on her shirt and helped slip it off. Reaching around the back, he unhooked her bra, letting it fall forward. His hands made their way to her waist as he slipped her panties down and helped her step out of them. "Wait right there."

Rafe pulled his shirt over his head and stepped out of his pants and underwear. He was hard. And he wanted her.

In one movement, he scooped her into his arms and lifted her into the shower, placing her gently under the showerhead.

She leaned back, and the warm water cascaded down her face.

Rafe thought she was the most beautiful woman he had ever seen. Old feelings and new ones emerged. They'd been through so much together these last couple of days. He loved her strength, her mind, her determination. If he couldn't take away her anxiety, at least he could make her feel better.

He reached behind her and took hold of the shampoo bottle. Placing a small amount in his hand, he rubbed it into her hair, massaging and caressing her scalp.

"That feels so good," Mallory moaned.

When he was done with her hair, he took the bottle of liquid soap, lathered it in his hand and began to wash her back. With his fingers, he gently kneaded the muscles in her shoulders.

Her arms stretched out, and her hands pressed against the tile wall.

As she held herself upright, Rafe washed her in slow caressing motions. They didn't speak. Her sighs of pleasure mingled with the sound of running water.

Mallory closed her eyes. A deep shiver ran through her as Rafe touched every part of her body. When he was done, she turned, leaned against the wall, and watched him as he washed away the dirt and tension of the last few days. He was as magnificent as she remembered. As teenagers, they'd never been shy around each other. Making love to Rafe had always been sexy and easy. He made every part of her tingle.

When he moved toward her and pressed his lips against hers, she willingly opened her mouth and let his tongue explore hers. His kisses traveled to her breast. She felt the tenderness as he sucked at her nipple. She melted into his arms. She needed him now. Grabbing his face in her hands, she said, "Take me now. Please."

Without another word, he was inside her. As he thrust, she felt as if she would explode.

"Mallory. I love you."

She couldn't speak. Her love for him was strong, but she couldn't get the words out. Without Justine, it wouldn't be right. At this moment, her heart wasn't her own. All she wanted was to ride this feeling until she could no longer take it.

His thrusts were deeper. She grabbed onto his back and wrapped her legs around him until they exploded at the same time.

She lowered her legs, held his face in her hand, and kissed him gently on the mouth. He picked her up and toweled her off.

"You look like you could use some sleep," Rafe said.

Mallory shook her head. "No doubt you relaxed me. But I can't sleep. Not until I know what's happening with my baby."

Rafe nodded. "Okay. Well, let's get dressed and get something to eat."

Once they were changed, Rafe helped Mallory down the stairs to the kitchen.

"Hey. That was a long shower. You two should be extra clean," Max teased.

Mallory felt the flush in her cheeks. She was embarrassed. Not only had she done something so personal in Ellie's house, but her daughter was in danger. Instantly, she wanted to take back the last hour. She lowered her gaze to the floor. "Sorry," she mumbled.

"Oh, shoot. Mallory, I was only kidding." Max stood and went to the stove. "Come on. Sit. I've got some *sancocho*."

"You had time to make that?" Rafe said.

"What is that?" Mallory asked.

"It's a soup with plantains, yuccas, and chicken." Max lifted the lid and stirred the pot. "And no, I didn't make it today. It's leftovers. I cooked up a big batch before I went on vacation and froze it. And you all are the lucky recipients of my efforts."

"Max is the wannabe chef in the family," Rafe said.

"Wow. That's right. We all took a vacation. That seems like a lifetime ago instead of a few days." Zack shook his head. "So much has happened. You couldn't make it up. Or maybe I could."

The sharp look Rafe gave Zack didn't go unnoticed. "Don't mind him, Mallory," Rafe said. "He's the wannabe novelist."

Mallory gave a faint smile, sat, and kept her head down. What she'd put this family through. It was unthinkable. Here she was in Ellie's house, and Ellie couldn't even be here because of Blake and what he'd done. "I'm so sorry. I've caused you all so much trouble."

Rafe grabbed her hand. "Don't think like that."

"I'm sorry I said anything," Zack said. "We're in this now. All together. No regrets. We move forward, get your daughter back, and get to the other side of this."

Max put the spoon down, walked to the table, and touched her shoulder. "We're all here for you, Mallory."

Regardless of what the brothers said, and she knew they meant well, once Justine was safely back, she'd disappear. The information she'd found out from the drive was too dangerous. The wrong kind of people might discover what she knew. She couldn't take a chance and put this family through any more. She would get her daughter back even if she had to kill Blake Stanton with her bare hands. She closed her eyes and took in a small breath. "I'm okay. Really."

Max gave her shoulder a gentle squeeze. "All right then. Let's eat."

After dinner, they washed the dishes and cleaned the kitchen.

When Rafe checked his phone for what seemed like the hundredth time, Mallory said, "Blake isn't going to call. This is exactly how he gains control and holds the power. He keeps you second-guessing. You wonder how a man could hold his daughter for ransom. It seems unthinkable. And maybe it is for most fathers. Not him. He was never a father." She spat the words out like something foul had crawled into her mouth. "This is how he operates. He said he'd call tomorrow. Believe me, he won't call a moment sooner—just to keep us all on edge."

Rafe put down the phone. "He's doing a really good job of it."

The sudden ringing of the house phone startled everyone, and Mallory nearly dropped the plate she was about to place in the cupboard.

The brothers froze.

Max nodded for Rafe to pick it up.

He walked to the green wall phone and lifted it from the receiver. "Yes." Rafe's face was tight, his voice brusque. Within a moment, his expression seemed to relax. *"Aún no. Sabremos más mañana."*

"Who is he talking to?" Mallory gripped the dish towel. "What is he saying?"

"It sounds like he's talking to one of our aunts. He's telling her we don't know anything yet."

She lowered her eyes. The aunts were calling. This wasn't right. The whole family was in this, and she needed to find a way to extricate them from her problems. As much as it pained her to lose Rafe, it was the right thing to do.

After they cleaned the kitchen, Zack insisted they play cards to pass the time and get their minds off the clock. Mallory went through the motions, and by midnight, she was physically weary. Knowing she would face Blake tomorrow made her insides turn, but also made her realize she needed to be strong. Being dead on her feet would not help the situation. So, she'd force herself to sleep.

Stretching her arms overhead, Mallory yawned. "It's time for me to get a little shuteye."

"Good idea." Max turned to Zack. "It's time for us to go and let them get some rest."

Mallory nodded. "Okay then. See you in the morning. And wake me if you hear anything."

"Of course," Max said.

"I'll help you up." Rafe stood.

She held up a hand. "No. I can manage." The hurt look on his face stung but keeping him at a distance was the right thing to do. She had to end this thing between them.

Chapter Eighteen

By six o'clock the next morning, Mallory was dressed and waiting for Rafe on the porch. She knew Blake wouldn't call until nine, but she wanted to be at the RMZ offices anyway. Her formerly dead husband was full of surprises, and she didn't trust that he wouldn't do something crazy before then.

"Zack's on his way," Rafe said, as he closed the front door behind him.

"Thanks."

"You sure you want to leave this early? I mean, there's not much we can do just sitting in the office."

"There's not much we can do sitting here either." Mallory didn't look up. Her focus never strayed from the street.

Zack pulled up with Max in the passenger seat. Mallory stood and limped to the car.

"Good morning," Max said. "Did you get any rest?"

"If you call tossing and turning restful, then I got plenty." Mallory snapped her seat belt in place.

"Same," said Zack, and he pulled away from the curb. The drive to the office was silent and somber.

When they entered the RMZ conference room, they were met by Agent Shore, looking impossibly fresh and rested.

"It's early." Shore checked her watch. "What are you all doing here?"

"We're here in case something happened sooner than expected," Mallory answered.

Agent Shore let out a breath and tilted her head toward the back of the room. "Well, make yourselves comfortable. Coffee's fresh."

After several hours and many more cups of coffee, it was finally time for Blake's call. They were all in the conference room, in the same positions as yesterday.

At nine o'clock exactly, Rafe's cell phone rang, and he swiped it open.

"Write this down," Blake barked. "I'm not going to repeat it. I want the drive delivered to Hampstead Farm, off Route 23. Leave it at the entrance of the old grain elevator. Once I'm sure the drive's in working order, I'll call you with your next instructions."

"No, Blake, that wasn't the deal. The drive for Justine." Rafe's voice was firm.

"You have thirty minutes."

"That wasn't the deal." The words rushed out of Rafe's mouth. "It could take longer than that to get to Hampstead Farm."

"Rafe—" Blake's voice dripped with venom "—you and I both know your motorcycle can make it there in less than that. I expect you, and only you, with the drive. If I see another car, police vehicle, chopper, or even the local traffic cop, I disappear with Justine. You all got that?"

"That's not happening." Rafe shook his head. "No way."

"Come alone, with the drive. You've got thirty minutes, or you never see Justine again." The phone went dead.

"He's bluffing. Right?" Rafe's question was directed to Agent Shore.

Her expression gave nothing away except for the almost imperceptible shake of her head. "It's hard to know," she said. "The guy sounded amped up. Nervous people in his position are capable of pretty much anything. So it's best if we work within his request."

"Work *within* his request? What does that even mean?" Rafe asked.

"It means we do as he says, except for the part where there's no FBI presence and that we give him the actual drive."

"How does this guy know so much about Rafe?" Max asked. Until now, both brothers had remained quiet. "I mean, they've never met, so how does he know my brother owns a motorcycle?"

"And, yesterday, on the call, he mentioned Mallory's fall," Zack said. "How did he know about that?"

"We don't have time to dissect that right now." Agent Shore began typing into her phone. "But it's definitely worth investigating. I'm giving this new information to one of my agents, and they'll start digging into it. In the meantime, we need to move out fast. I take it you know where this Hampstead Farm is?"

"Yeah. It's been abandoned for years."

She handed Rafe the fake nano drive. "Where's your motorcycle parked?"

"Hold on." Mallory put up a hand. "That's your plan? Send Rafe in there with a fake drive?"

"We'll be there providing backup for Rafe. Once Blake has the decoy, he'll be surrounded by agents and we'll take him into custody," Agent Shore said.

Nothing Mallory heard instilled confidence in the FBI's plan. When she first entered the RMZ offices, she felt reassured that so many agents were on the case. Surely, they would find a way out of this and rescue her daughter. In her wildest thoughts, the plan was never this. Rafe could get hurt, and she'd lose her daughter in the process. Neither option was acceptable. Mallory put her face in her hands. "I feel sick."

Rafe was by her side. "You okay?"

"I think I need to splash some water on my face. Where's the bathroom?"

Rafe put his arm around her waist to help her up.

"I got it." Mallory stood on her own, the pain shooting from her ankle to her hip bone. "I won't be long." Gritting her teeth through the pain, she quickly made her way to the ladies' room, her mind racing. She looked in the mirror. Evidence of her harrowing night in the deep woods was revealed by the scratch marks on her face and hands. She splashed water on her face several times and then reached for a paper towel. Holding in a scream, she buried her face in the towel and worked on taking in deep breaths. She had to stop Blake, and she didn't trust the FBI to have her daughter's interest as their priority. The gleam in their eyes at the thought of capturing Blake Stanton told her everything she needed to know.

When she walked out of the bathroom, the common area buzzed with agents packing up and Taylor Shore giving orders. Keeping her head down, Mallory continued unnoticed toward the elevator and pressed the button several times. "Come on. Come on." She punched the button with her finger again. "What's taking so long?"

Finally, the elevator arrived, and she slipped in. She hit the button for the ground floor several times until the doors closed. Mallory closed her eyes in relief as the car descended.

When the elevator doors opened, Rafe stared at Mallory. "Going somewhere?"

"How did you—?"

Ignoring her dazed expression, Rafe pulled her off the elevator and to the side. "Just what do you think *you're* doing?"

"I'm scared Blake will spot the fake drive."

"That doesn't answer the question." Grabbing Mallory by the shoulders, he was inches from her face. "You're not thinking of going up against Blake by yourself—are you?"

"I can't let anything happen to my baby girl." She was breathing hard. "I thought we could give him the fake drive. But I was wrong. I spent the night turning it over and over in my mind. Who was I kidding? I know who Blake is and giving him the fake drive is too dangerous. We can't take the chance. So I'll give him the real one and tell him I never opened it. It's my only chance to get my life back and keep my daughter safe."

Rafe tried to process what she was saying. *Her life back*. A life without him. "And you thought that was a viable plan?"

"You heard Blake. He's insane, but he's smart. And I don't trust him. For that matter, I don't trust the FBI. Everyone wants what they want, leaving Justine as the pawn in all of this." Her voice was harsh. "Knowing Blake, he'll have a way to check if the drive's authentic right on the spot, and I can't take that chance. I know I'm right. The only way to get my daughter back safely is to give him the real drive." She pounded on his chest. "Please. I need to go."

The pleading in her voice nearly broke him. Rafe, too, had doubts that the authorities had the same priority. They wanted that drive and Blake Stanton behind bars. He was beginning to understand Mallory's thinking. "If people think you were never able to open it, then you're free."

"Exactly. Please, Rafe." She held up the key fob to Max's car. "Justine first."

"Where did you get those?"

"I took them off the table when Max was looking at his phone."

Maybe she was right. Maybe she was the only one who knew how to handle Blake. Rafe ran his hand through his hair and looked at the elevator panel. It was still on the ground level. No one had called for it. But there was precious little time before the agents came down. He needed to act fast. "You're right. Blake is insane. We'll give him the real drive." Rafe held out his hand. "Hand it over."

Mallory's confused look didn't stop him from leaning in close. "Give me the drive. He's expecting me to have it, and we don't want to deviate too far from the plan."

She reached into her back pocket and handed it over.

"Okay. That's it then." Rafe turned and ran out of the building.

"Rafe. Wait for me!" Mallory cried.

He didn't turn around. He knew her ankle wouldn't hold, and he could get to Justine faster than anyone. Besides, for whatever reason, Blake wanted him as the messenger. Mallory had been through so much. But it hurt knowing she wanted her life back without him. How could he begrudge her wanting to be free of any man after what she'd been through? If he couldn't have her, at least he'd rescue her daughter from a monster.

Rafe ran the four blocks to *Tía* Ellie's house, where he stored his motorcycle in her shed. By the time he reached her house, his lungs were on fire. Raising the shed door, he jumped on the bike, flipped up the kickstand, jammed on his helmet, and took off.

* * *

Mallory slumped against the wall when the elevator opened and out poured Agents Shore and Byron with Max.

"Where is he?" Max looked around the lobby.

"He took the drive," Mallory said.

"What do you mean *he* took the drive? Who is *he*?" Max asked.

"Rafe. I'm talking about Rafe. He took the real drive," Mallory said.

"Dammit," Agent Shore snarled.

"What the hell is my brother up to?"

"He's going after Blake," Mallory said, and felt as if her heart would break. What if Rafe wasn't successful? What if he got hurt? What if she never saw her daughter or Rafe again?

"*¡Temerario!*" Max followed the agents toward the front door.

"What are you saying? Where are you going?" Mallory cried. "Please, Max, what's happening?"

Max didn't stop but called over his shoulder, "I said, my brother is being reckless. I can't let him go in there alone."

Mallory felt bile rise in the back of her throat. Exactly what Blake didn't want was happening. She only hoped Rafe would get there and grab Justine before this army of law enforcement arrived. The exact thing that would make Blake do something crazy. She hobbled behind Max but came up short when he suddenly stopped outside the steps of the office.

"Where the hell are my car keys?" Max patted his front and back pockets. "Damn it. Damn it. Rafe took my keys."

"No. He didn't. I have them." She held up her hand. "I'm going with you."

He quickly swiped the keys out of her hand. "No, you're not." Max's long strides took him around the car to the driver's side in seconds.

"We're wasting time arguing. I'll ride on the hood if I have to, but I'm going." Mallory's hand was already pulling on the passenger side handle.

Max gave her a stern look and then pressed the door release on the key fob. "Get in," he said.

* * *

Taking a shortcut through the back streets of town, Rafe made his way to Route 9W within a few minutes. The route featured one lane in each direction, winding through the mountains along the broad Hudson River. Heading north, he was going over fifty miles an hour on hairpin turns, passing cars that didn't have his urgency.

Rafe thought of all the possible ways he could trip up Blake. From what he knew about Mallory's husband, he couldn't be trusted to live up to his end of the bargain. His mind went around and around with possible scenarios, and none of them were good. Everything about Blake screamed wild card. He was a madman who had no compunction about faking his own death, terrorizing his wife and child, and then holding his daughter for ransom. What kind of sicko did that? He ached for Mallory and what she must have endured at the hands of that psycho. There was no more time to think. He needed a plan that didn't include walking straight into what could be a trap.

After all, he didn't know Blake, and yet he specifically asked that Rafe bring the drive. That alone meant he had to watch his back. He checked the time on the dashboard. He was perilously close to being late. Ignoring all road signs, Rafe gripped the throttle and twisted it toward him, increasing his speed.

He checked his mirrors and wondered where the Feds were. Surely, they were already on the road. He hoped they had the good sense to stay hidden and out of the way. There was no telling what this maniac was capable of and how far he'd go to get what he wanted.

Ten miles before the exit, Rafe jerked the bike to the right, veering off the road onto the grass and disappearing into a wooded area. He knew this stretch of land well. Growing up, his mother took them on weekly trips to Hampstead Farm for fresh eggs and homemade cheeses. While she made small talk with the owners, he and his brothers played explorer all around the property. His only advantage over Blake would be his familiarity with every square inch of the property, including the nooks and crannies where one could hide.

Instead of coming up the main road alone on his motorcycle,

which Blake would expect, he'd arrive behind the grain elevator. If nothing else, at least he'd have the element of surprise. Maybe even some time to scope out the situation.

Mallory sat in the passenger seat, tugging at the chain around her neck with one hand and biting what was left of her nails on the other. "We should have caught up to Rafe by now."

Max nodded. "I was thinking the same thing."

"Where could he be?"

Max blew out a breath. "I can't believe I didn't think of it."

"Think of what?" Mallory's voice rose.

"He didn't take the interstate. He took the long way around on Route 9W."

"Why would he do that?"

"Because, on a motorcycle, he can cut through the woods and ride around to the back of the farm. It's faster."

"What?"

Max explained the alternate route and that it was only possible with a motorcycle because of the trees. "He'll be there soon."

Mallory turned her head. The agents were following close behind. "What are we going to do when we get there?" Max didn't answer. "Max, are you listening? I said—"

"I heard you. The truth is I don't know."

Mallory felt the car jerk to the right as Max pulled the car onto the shoulder. "What are you doing? Why did you stop?" She turned to find the agents pulling up behind them.

Max got out of the car.

Mallory unbuckled her seat belt and was out of the car seconds later. Clenching her fists, she ignored the pain and limped as fast as she could to catch up to Max.

She reached Agent Shore's car just in time to hear her curse.

Taylor Shore smacked the dashboard. "A shortcut to the farm? Unbelievable."

Max nodded. "Straight through the woods. And impossible for any of our cars to get through."

"Then we'll have to keep going until we get to the farm. Hope we get there in time," Shore said.

"No. Absolutely not. We can't. He'll take Justine," Mallory

pleaded. "Listen to me. I know he will. He said no cops. Let's let Rafe handle this."

"It's too dangerous. This isn't how we're playing this one out," the agent said.

"We're wasting time," Max said. "We could argue all day. The fact is, Rafe is probably already there. The shortcut will take him right through to the back of the grain elevator—" Max stopped. "Wait a minute. Rafe's going to try and end-run Blake. He's going in through the back to try and sneak up on him. At least that's what I would do."

"And...?" Agent Shore said.

"Keep following me," Max said as he ran to his car.

Mallory followed and jumped into the passenger seat. She barely had time to close the door when Max peeled out onto the road.

"How do we know the agents won't call in reinforcements?" Mallory asked.

"They probably already have. Let's hope they have the good sense to stay hidden until we get Justine and Rafe away safely."

Chapter Nineteen

The dense woods began to thin out, and Rafe sensed he was a couple of hundred yards away from the farm. He rolled the throttle back, slowing the bike while squeezing the lever on the right handlebar. He swung his leg over the seat and walked his bike toward a fallen tree, laying it on its side to keep it out of sight.

Crouching low, Rafe made his way toward the back of the grain elevator. He moved as quickly and quietly as he could.

The neglect of a decade of abandonment was evident everywhere. To his left, a rusted threshing machine sat among three feet of weeds. A large hole could be seen in the roof of the elevator that once stored grain. The barn no longer sported the vivid red Rafe remembered as a child. Instead, it looked more like a washed-out brown with a sagging back door. The sounds of a working farm were gone. No chickens clucking, dogs barking, or the mechanical sounds of the milking machine. He moved farther along, stepping over fallen trees and piles of leaves from autumns past.

The piercing scream stopped him where he stood. His heart pushed against his chest as if it wanted out. The roar of blood through his ears made it difficult to discern where the sound came from. A deep male voice yelled, but Rafe was unable to make out the words.

The grain elevator was in sight, and Rafe took several tentative steps in that direction.

"I want my mommy."

He looked at the deserted buildings but couldn't determine where Justine's cries were coming from. Getting on all fours, he crawled to the back of the grain elevator.

Justine's cries grew louder.

"Shut up, or I will give you something to cry about."

Rafe didn't recognize the voice but sensed it was coming from the barn, not more than fifty feet away. He lay flat on his stomach and inched his way around the grain elevator to get a better look. From this vantage point, it was difficult to see beyond the barn door. He was about to stand when he heard the click of a gun at the side of his head.

"Get up, slowly."

Rafe didn't move.

"I said get up!" Blake's voice sounded hoarse but no less insistent.

Slowly, Rafe raised himself up.

"Get your hands up and walk," Blake ordered.

With the gun to his back, Rafe walked into the dark barn. A shaft of light filtered through from a missing board on the side wall, illuminating the ten empty stalls. A decade's worth of dried hay lay all about. A strong smell of rotted wood hung in the air. When his eyes adjusted, he spotted Justine in the corner. His heart kicked up another notch. A tall man with bulging forearms was holding her around the waist, and his hand clamped over her mouth. He caught a glimpse of the man's hiking boots. The same hiking boots that followed him and Mallory in the woods last night.

"Stop walking," Blake commanded. "Now, slowly, and I do mean slowly, get to one knee."

All Rafe could think of was how to get to Justine. The unexpected appearance of an accomplice wasn't helping. The current situation didn't bode well for either of them.

"I said get down, now."

Justine's muffled cries clawed at this soul.

"Keep your hands up," Blake barked.

With his hands over his head, Rafe got to one knee.

"I know you have the drive. So tell me which pocket it's in, and do not even think of trying anything."

Rafe had less than a second to think. With his back to Blake, he lied and said, "Back right pants pocket."

"Don't move a muscle." Blake's tone was low and menacing.

He felt Blake behind him and knew this was his last chance. After this, he'd probably be a dead man. He placed a hand on the ground to push himself up, and instead of standing straight up, he hoisted himself backward and pushed the top of his head into Blake's jaw.

Stunned, Blake dropped the gun to the ground.

Rafe kicked it to an open stall, turned, and punched Blake in the gut.

Blake fell backward but quickly sat up and kicked the legs out from under Rafe, who went down hard. Blake jumped on top of him, pinning him to the ground, and threw a punch.

Reflexively, Rafe turned his head to the side. The punch managed to clip his ear, and the blow stunned him, giving Blake time to land another punch. This time, square on his jaw.

With adrenaline coursing through his body, he blinked, quickly shook his head, and with all his might, managed to push Blake off and straddle him across the chest, punching him in the face once, twice, and a third time before he felt a sharp kick in his back throwing him off balance and giving Blake enough time to roll out from underneath.

Each man now crouched, fists ready, walking around each other in a circle.

"Don't hurt Rafe. No. No. Let me go," Justine screamed.

"Get the gun," Blake yelled to his accomplice.

"Noooooooo!" Justine yelled.

"You stop that fussing," the man in the boots said.

"Let me go."

"Ow. She bit me. You little—"

"Run, Justine! Run!" Rafe yelled.

She ran past him and out of the barn.

"Don't let her go," Blake sneered.

The tall man in the hiking boots ran.

Rafe only hoped his brother and Mallory were somewhere nearby so they could get to Justine before the booted man.

As Rafe and Blake continued to circle, each eyed the gun.

Rafe knew it was too far to reach without turning his back on Blake. A dangerous proposition, but he had no choice. He had to dive for it. Rafe reached it first, closing his finger over the trigger.

Blake dove on top of him and grabbed his wrist, banging his hand on the ground to release the gun. Rafe bit down on Blake's wrist until he screamed in pain, released his hand, and jumped back.

Rafe quickly turned on his back and pointed the gun at Blake. "Don't move. I won't hesitate to shoot you." Slowly, Rafe got to his feet. Never taking his aim off Blake's chest. "Now, this is how it's going to go down. You—"

"Let me go, let me go."

Rafe stiffened. He didn't take his eyes off Blake, but he knew the tall man, and not Mallory, had caught up with Justine.

"Rafe, please help me."

From the corner of his eye, he could make out Justine's tear-stained face. She was being dragged by the hand into the barn.

"Stop crying, you little brat," the tall man said.

"Bring her over here," Blake said.

"No, Daddy. I don't wanna." Justine was trying to pull away from the man, but he continued to drag her across the floor.

"If you don't stop, I'll slap you again," he snarled at Justine.

Rafe wanted to kill them both.

"Come here, Justine. And stop crying. Or I'll have to hurt your friend Rafe." Blake grabbed Justine and held her in front of him. "Cal, get over to the landing strip. Make sure the plane's ready. I'll be there shortly."

Rafe had no idea how Blake thought he would get out of this. He just sent his backup away, and Rafe was the one holding the gun.

"Justine, did you know your mommy used to be in love with this guy? Imagine a nobody like him. A criminal," Blake sneered. "I found his letters to your mommy. She loved him more than me, you see, and I couldn't have that. I knew one day she'd come running to him. So, I had no choice but to destroy him. Set him up for a crime he didn't commit." Blake laughed. "I did a good job."

"I want my mommy." Justine sobbed, tears streaming down her face.

"That's not going to happen unless your friend here gives me the drive and the gun. Otherwise, your mommy will never see you again."

Rafe didn't move. This was the man who tried to destroy his life. Now he understood how Blake knew so much about him. Rich, powerful people could find out anything. "Put her down, and let her come to me, and then I'll put the gun down."

"You think I got as far as I did by acting stupid? Far from it. I sent the threats to Mallory. I needed her scared so she'd leave the house and I could get the laptop and the drive inside that damn teddy bear. I was the one who vandalized the house. It was easy. I had the key, and my fingerprints being everywhere wasn't unusual. Remember, it was my house. But I didn't count on her taking the laptop to a computer store. And I certainly didn't count on Justine taking that stupid bear with her," he sneered. "It doesn't matter anymore. From the beginning, I've been tracking the two of you. So, no. I'm far from stupid, and we're going to do this my way." Blake continued to hold onto Justine, inching his way toward the first stall.

"Stop moving," Rafe shouted.

"Or what? You coward. I'm holding my daughter. You wouldn't take a chance of hurting her. Would you?"

"Stop. We've all been dancing to your tune since you disappeared. You've been pulling the strings. No more."

Blake let out a laugh that sounded more like a bark. "You've watched too many bad movies. I'm holding all the cards. I'm the one who arranged for that plane to go down. Those people knew too much. Now, it's only you, me, and Mallory who know what's on that drive. Isn't that right?" His lips curved into a menacing smile. "Give me the gun, goddamn it, or someone's going to get hurt." Blake moved toward the barn door.

"Owww. Daddy, you're hurting me," Justine said.

"Am I?" Blake said.

Rafe noticed him squeezing harder.

"Daddy, stop." Justine's face turned red.

"I can keep this up for a long time. So long, in fact, there's no telling what could happen to her tiny little organs."

"You are as awful as Mallory said you were. Actually worse. What kind of man hurts his own child?"

"Happens every day. This is not a kind world," Blake said.

"No, Daddy, stop."

"Shut up." Blake turned her around and smacked her across the face.

Something in Rafe snapped. He pulled the trigger and shot Blake in the foot.

Justine screamed.

Blake fell to his knees.

The look of terror on Justine's face let Rafe know she was afraid of both of them. "Let her go."

Blake shook his head and dragged himself to the first stall, holding Justine against his chest like a human shield.

"Stay where you are."

"No. Give me the drive. Give it to me, and I'll leave."

"Not going to happen. Stay where you are. I mean it, Blake. I'll shoot you if I have to."

"Doesn't look like you have a clear shot, does it?"

"Stop right there. Do not move." The strong voice came from Agent Shore. She was standing at the entrance of the barn, Agent Byron a few steps behind. Both took a wide-leg stance with their arms straight out, aiming their guns. "Get up slowly. Now."

The next few seconds seemed to happen in a slow-motion blur. Blake let go of Justine, and Rafe ran for her while Blake rolled toward the first stall, reached in, and pulled out a small revolver. Blake stood and aimed at Rafe, who was holding Justine.

Rafe dived into the next stall—the sound of gunshots ringing throughout the barn. When the gunshots stopped, he looked around the edge of the stall to find Blake lying face down, not moving. He turned back and slumped against the stall. "Justine, are you okay?"

"Uh-huh," she sobbed. "But you're not, Rafe. You're bleeding."

Chapter Twenty

Rafe stared out the rain-splattered window. The dreary day made his hospital room feel depressing. He sensed his father before he heard him clearing his throat. It was that Old Spice cologne he'd never stopped wearing. A dead giveaway. Rafe turned his head toward the doorway.

"Can I come in?" his father asked. The humble look on his face made his six-foot-two frame seem a little smaller. The white hair didn't seem so dashing and the expensive suit and tie weren't intimidating.

"Sure." Rafe waved him in. "Sit down."

The judge sat in the teal blue leatherette chair positioned near Rafe's hospital bed. *"¿Cómo te sientes...hijo?"* The words were slow, soft, and deliberate.

"They say I'm going to get out of here in two days, so I must be doing better, but I don't think my leg got the memo."

His father gave a slow smile. "I bet it hurts. It took guts to do what you did."

Rafe shook his head. "No, anyone would have gone after that little girl. I just happened to be there."

"And you happen to be in love with her mother. Aren't you?"

Rafe ignored the question and instead asked one of his own. "What are you doing here? I hate to bring it up, since you paid for the private room and all—"

His father raised a questioning eyebrow.

"Max told me. But anyway, we're not exactly on speaking terms. What do you want?" Rafe tried to keep the anger and the hurt out of his voice. He'd been through a lot these past ten years, and this last month had made him realize he wanted to live for today. He was in love with Mallory, and while he'd been lying in this hospital bed with not much else to do but think, it was her that his mind focused on. They'd both seen their share of bad times, and now they were both free to create whatever future they wanted. He'd come to the realization that he wasn't going to chase after people for their affection anymore. That included his father. He knew now that he deserved to be loved.

"Rafe, I can't make up for what I did. For the way I treated you. I'll never get that time back. I was wrong. Dead wrong." The judge's voice cracked. He paused and looked at the ceiling.

Rafe knew he was trying to compose himself; his father's facade had never weakened until now, and he could see that this was difficult for him.

"I realize you may not want to forgive me. And if you don't, I understand. I wanted you to know that not only was I wrong, but I love you, and in my way, I never stopped loving you."

Rafe stared at his father as the tears rolled down the side of his face. He said nothing. These were the words he'd waited ten years to hear, but somehow, it wasn't enough. It wasn't nearly enough.

The judge got up, took a handkerchief from his back pocket, and blew his nose. "I'll be going." He started toward the door. "If you need anything, you know where to find me."

Max came in as the judge was heading out. "Hey, Pop." The judge nodded and hurried through the door.

"What happened?" Max asked. "Pop looks pretty upset, and so do you."

"Nothing, just nothing."

"I don't want to pry, but it can't be nothing. I know it took a lot for the old man to come here today."

"Yeah, you're probably right. He had to swallow his pride—admit he was wrong."

"Well, that for sure took something out of him," Max said.

"You don't get it."

"Enlighten me."

"I'm his son. He should have loved me no matter what. He should have believed me. He raised me, and he knew what kind of man I was. I didn't want to hear that he was wrong. I wanted to know that he was sorry he could have ever thought that of me. Mom knew the truth. I've waited years for a reconciliation. I just didn't realize until today how angry I was about the whole thing. And it's going to take a minute for me to get over being pissed off."

"Hi, Rafe." Justine bounded into the room. "We bought you a sub sandwich with lots of mayo 'cause Mom said you were getting sick and tired of hospital food."

Rafe quickly wiped his eyes, plastering on a smile. "Thank goodness, I was about to starve. Did you bring chips with that?"

"Of course, silly." Justine giggled.

Mallory walked in, huffing. "Justine, I've told you not to get too far away from me."

"Soo-rr-yy, Mom," she said in mock exaggeration.

"Hey, Max." Mallory smiled at Max and instantly recognized she'd interrupted. "Punkie, let's wait outside for a minute. Max and Rafe are in the middle of something."

"But, Mommmmmmm…"

"Yeah, yeah, no buts, come on, we'll get a soda from the cafeteria."

With Justine and Mallory gone, the only sound was the ticking of the clock on the wall above the doorway.

"Max, you've always tried to be the peacemaker. And because of you and Mom, I'll tell you what. I'll give it a try. But this is going to have to take a natural progression. If we make it, we make it. Nothing forced. At this point in my life, I'm obliged to nothing and no one."

Max nodded his understanding.

Two weeks after his release from the hospital, Rafe was still on crutches. Most nights were spent with Mallory at Ellie's house. She'd wanted to stay until Rafe was fully recovered.

"Hey," Mallory said, walking into the living room. "Guess who I got a call from?"

"The lottery commission? You won a million dollars."

"Ha-ha. Very funny. No, it was Ellie."

"Is she okay?" A look of concern crossed his face.

"Oh yeah, she's fine. She said after spending so much time with her sister, she realized she didn't want to come back to this big old empty house, so she's decided to stay there indefinitely."

Rafe could sense concern in her voice. "Is that a bad thing?"

"Well…no… She asked me if I wanted to stay here and rent the house. And, well… I hadn't really thought about it. I know my dad is waiting for us, but now that Blake is really dead, I truly have my life back."

"Come here." Rafe held out his arms. "Sit." He patted the sofa cushion.

Mallory sat beside him, and he put his arms around her and pulled her in close. "Let me ask you something. Do you want to live with your dad and his new girlfriend?"

Mallory sighed. "I love my father, and I want to see him. But this place, Hollow Lake, it's become home again. And with the FBI, CIA, and Interpol making all those arrests, and Agent Shore blasting out to all the agencies that we were never able to open the drive, we don't have to run anymore. I'm safe." She looked up at Rafe. "We're safe. And Justine's so happy here. She can even start school in a week. I hate the idea of uprooting her again."

Rafe pulled her in closer. "You know what?"

"What?"

"I love your smile." He kissed her lips.

"And your beautiful green eyes." He kissed her eyelids.

"And, well, there isn't anything I don't love about you."

"I bet you say that to all the women you go through a near-death experience with." Mallory laughed.

"Well, I have to admit, I'm looking forward to taking you back to the lake house just for fun. Next time we'll leave all electronic equipment at home." He lightly kissed her lips again. "But seriously, why not stay here. This is a great house. And you just said, Justine is happy here. And it is home. And you have me, and the entire Ramirez clan."

The idea of Mallory and Justine living in Hollow Lake made him enormously happy. He'd lost her once to the big city, and he wasn't ready for that to happen again. "Listen, I'd love it if you stayed. You can visit your father. Visit him every month if you want."

Rafe kissed her temple. "Mallory, I've spent a lot of time pushing people away. Not getting involved. For the last few years, I've been polite but distant. Never wanted to get too close because I was convinced there was no future for me. But now that I've officially, officially cleared my name, there's nothing in the way."

"Rafe, I still can't believe it was Blake who framed you." Mallory looked down at her hands. "It was my fault."

Rafe leaned his head against hers. "The fact that you kept my love letters—well, I was surprised to hear that."

"I suppose I've never stopped loving you."

He turned her face toward him. "Those eyes of yours, they hypnotize me. You captured my heart a long time ago. You've broken down walls I'd spent a few years building. I love you, Mallory Kane. I want to be with you and share my life with you."

"What are you saying?"

"Marry me. Marry me."

Mallory embraced him. "I will marry you. Yes. Yes. Yes."

Rafe kissed her firmly on the mouth. When she deepened the kiss, he was lost.

Mallory pulled back. "Rafe Ramirez. I love you."

Epilogue

The clock above the mantel at the judge's home struck seven.

"Don't worry, Pop, they'll be here," Max said.

The judge grumbled under his breath. "They're late to their own engagement party."

"Pop, it's only just seven," Zack said, as the doorbell rang. "See, that's them now. I'll get it."

Rafe, Mallory, and Justine were greeted by the entire family. Ellie and Claudia rushed up to Mallory and Justine and hugged them tight.

"You look great. I'm so happy to see you," Ellie said.

"How's my little *chiquita*?" Claudia kissed Justine on the cheek.

"Come on, now. Let them take their coats off and come in," the judge said. "Welcome."

Rafe smiled at the balloons, streamers, and signs announcing their engagement that were strewn across the living room.

"Oh look, Mommy, a dog. A real pretty dog." Justine tugged on the judge's pants. "Hi, I'm Justine. Is that your dog?"

The judge laughed. "That's my dog all right. His name is Elliot, and if it's all right with your mother, you can go over and pet him. He's old and gentle."

"Can I, Mommy?"

Mallory nodded and took off her coat, handing it to the judge. "It's nice to see you after all these years."

"Mallory, the feeling is mutual. The rest of the family is dying to say hello." While Mallory knew Ellie and Claudia's children from high school, she hadn't seen them in years. She was grateful for their help and hugged each one.

When Mallory came to the end of what had become a receiving line, she was surprised to see Zack standing next to Agent Taylor Shore. "Agent Shore, what a nice surprise."

"Please, call me Taylor. I'm not on duty."

"Okay. That's going to take a little getting used to." Mallory thought she looked so different out of her FBI garb. Her red hair fell loose around her shoulders, and her emerald green sheath dress hugged her in all the right places. She thought Taylor was beautiful. "I didn't expect to see you here." Mallory turned and waved Rafe over. "Look who came."

"Wow," Rafe said. "Look at you."

Taylor blushed, and it nearly matched the color of her hair. "Um, Zack invited me."

Mallory did a double take.

"Bro?" Rafe said. "Is this a date?"

Zack grinned sheepishly and put his arm around Taylor's shoulder.

"Let's get this party started," Max said, clapping his hands together.

Rafe held up a hand. "Can you give me a few minutes?" He turned to his father. "Pop, can we talk?"

The judge nodded and tilted his head toward his study. Rafe squeezed Mallory's hand and then followed his father.

Rafe lowered himself into the leather chair opposite the desk and stared at his hands. His mouth was dry, and he didn't exactly know how to say what he was feeling. The time he'd spent recovering gave him a chance to reflect. Something he hadn't done in a long time because he was too busy being angry. Almost losing his life changed everything. It made him realize nothing's guaranteed and that making the most of the time with your family is more important than holding on to hurt feelings. While Mallory and Justine completed a big part of him, he recognized there was a hole that would be there forever unless he made peace with his father.

Rafe blew out a breath and looked up. "Pop, thanks for the party. It means a lot."

"You're welcome, son." His voice filled with emotion. "For a minute, I thought you wouldn't show. I thought maybe you couldn't forgive me. I'm just so terribly sorry—"

In one smooth motion, Rafe was on his feet, embracing his father. "Let's not rehash." He whispered in his father's ear, hugging him tightly and then patting him on the back before straightening.

The judge brushed away a tear.

"No time for crying, Pop—"

"Who's crying? What are you talking about?" He cleared his throat and put his arm around Rafe's shoulder. "Come on, we've got a party to get started."

The judge opened a couple of bottles of champagne and made a Shirley Temple for Justine. "Please, everyone—" he lifted his glass "—I want to toast my son, Rafe, and his beautiful bride-to-be. Mallory, I can see you've made my son a very happy man. And for that, I am grateful."

Mallory blushed.

"May you be happy and healthy and continue to enjoy each other's company for years to come."

"Hear, hear," was the chorus from all present.

The initial awkwardness Rafe felt when walking into his father's home for the first time in years washed away. He was with the woman he loved and surrounded by his family. He was being given a second chance, and he wasn't going to mess this up. For the first time in too long, he felt whole. The last missing piece in his life was falling into place. After all these years, his family was together. They were complete.

Rafe raised his glass. "To the woman I love, to family, to futures."

There wasn't a dry eye as the rest of the family lifted their glasses.

* * * * *